MW01492389

DEN OF SPIES

A TRANSYLVANIAN HISTORICAL FANTASY

RR JONES

APOLODOR PUBLISHING

This book is a work of fiction. Many names, characters, places, and incidents are the product of the author's imagination or are used fictitiously. The historical events, locales, or persons, living or dead, are however accurate.

Copyright © 2023 by Rada Jones

All rights reserved.

No part of this book may be reproduced in any form or by any electronic or mechanical means, including information storage and retrieval systems, without written permission from the author, except for the use of brief quotations in a book review.

APOLODOR PUBLISHING

DEN OF SPIES

The Ottoman Empire, Hungary, and the Romanian Countries in the XV century.

PROLOGUE

TARA MOȚILOR, TRANSYLVANIA, 1440; TWO YEARS EARLIER

For a few heartbeats, the silence is so deep it hurts, then the earth shakes like a muddy dog and the world goes crazy. The pots and pans hanging on hooks above the stove clang against each other, then crash to the ground. Whitewashed walls tremble and crack, spitting out a cloud of plaster dust. The woodpile by the fire bursts apart as if someone kicked it, scattering the logs all over the packed dirt floor. A gust of wind blows the door open and throws it off its hinges.

Ion squeezes out of his bed and steps closer to see.

It's chaos outside. The mountains wail, the wolves howl, and a murder of enraged crows cackles, blown away by the wind. The barn door bursts open and splits apart with a deafening crack. Cows bellow their panic and stampede into the woods, their round eyes wide with fear.

Little Neta wakes up and rubs her eyes.

"What happened, Ma?" she cries.

"Shh, it's OK." Mother picks her up. "It's just an earthquake. Be quiet, baby girl, or you'll wake up your brother."

Laying in his crib with his thumb in his rosy mouth, little Petrica is still asleep. How can that be? Ion shakes his head in wonder and feels under the chair for his leather opinci. He slips them on his feet, then crisscrosses their strings around his legs and ties them right under his knees. He grabs his vest and his tall shearling hat.

"Ma, I'll go look for the cattle," he whispers.

Mother nods. "Just be careful. It's ugly out there."

She's not kidding, Ion thinks, taking the usual way towards the Pietroasa River where he takes the cows every day. But the trail he knows like the back of his hand is no longer a path. It's a tangled mess of broken branches, exposed roots, and fallen trunks hiding the treacherous clefts the earthquake carved. And the forest doesn't want him here. Broken branches claw at his feet, the howling wind tries to rob him of his vest, and the otherworldly cries splintering the darkness whip his heart into a frenzy.

"Just stop it, will you!" he scolds himself when a shrill shriek freezes him in place. "You're almost ten, you're no longer a child! You have a bunch of cows to find and a family to look after. You have no time to be scared!"

He struggles forward until he reaches the river. But the usually placid waters have gone mad. The stream roars and boils around the dozen tree trunks blocking its passage, making it into a thundering hell. There's no way those cows crossed the river, and neither should he.

Ion sighs. He has to turn around. He's cold and tired, but, even more, he's worried about Mother and the kids. *I'll head back to make sure they're OK, then I'll head up towards the mountains*, he thinks.

The journey back isn't any easier, but knowing he's heading home puts an extra spring in his step. It's still dark when he reaches the end of the trail he's the only one to ever take, but the sky glows dark red straight ahead. *The sunrise*, Ion thinks, then realizes that east is not that way. The strange crimson light seems to come from their house, and Ion's heart skips a beat. He rushes forward, squeezing through the bushes until he hears a voice.

"It's good to see you, even though the years haven't been kind to you, Elena. I haven't forgotten how young and pretty you used to be. My blushing bride."

It's a man's voice, gravelly and rusty with disuse.

Mother laughs without joy.

"Like you have room to talk. Have you looked at yourself lately?"

"Not really. The underground cave your human lover trapped me in was dark. And short of mirrors."

"You didn't deserve any better. And let me be clear: Petru was not my lover. He was my beloved husband and the father of my children. But tell me, how did you get out, after all these years?"

"An earthquake split the rock apart and opened the cave. But where's your beloved husband?"

"What's it to you?"

The man laughs. "I owe him a debt. And we, Zmei, always pay our debts. So where is he?"

"He'll be back any moment, and he'll put you back in the hole you belong in. Better run while you can," Mother says.

But that's not true, Ion thinks. Father won't be coming back soon. As a matter of fact, he won't be back at all, since he's been dead for two winters. That's why every Sunday morning Neta gathers a bunch of wild flowers and Mother spends one of their precious few coins on a skinny yellow candle to place on his grave behind the church.

Ion squeezes to the very edge of the forest to see better, and the sight gives him pause.

Mother stands as tall as a five-foot woman can in the open door of their house, pushing the kids behind her. Petrica and Neta hold onto her skirts to peek, and their curious eyes are round with wonder.

The man laughs.

"I don't think so, my pretty princess. Lightning doesn't strike the same place twice. Your human fooled me once, and that was only thanks to you, cheater. You cut my hair and stole my strength as I slept. But that was then and this is now. My hair grew back, and so did my power. I'll fry your man and have him for lunch as soon as he returns. And guess what? You and your kids get to watch."

Ion leans forward to see better, but a thick pine cuts his sight line.

Mother laughs. "Don't you wish? Now, if there's nothing else, I need to put the kids to bed."

"Not so fast, dear. Speaking about kids. I'm here to claim mine."

Mother turns white. "What?"

"Oh, but you know, Elena. What a liar you turned into! You didn't used to be like this, but being amongst humans did you no good. You've gotten ugly, old, and full of lies."

Mother's eyes fill with tears. "That's enough. What do you want, Zmeu?"

"I want my son. You were heavy with my child when you ran away with your lover. Where is he?"

Mother shrinks like the weight of the world fell on her shoulders. Her lovely face darkens with sorrow. "He... he died. The black death took two of my boys."

The man laughs. "It may have, but not my son. He didn't die. He couldn't have. The son of a Zmeu is a Zmeu, and we don't die from the ailments that kill mere humans. Where is my son?"

"He died, I tell you. He... he fell in the river and drowned."

The man laughs again. "You're getting addled in your old age, woman. We, Zmei, don't drown, we don't get sick, and we don't die like humans do. The only way to kill us is... never mind. I guess you'll need some persuading. Which of your kids would you like to keep?"

"What?"

"You'll give me my son, or I'll kill yours. I'll start with the boy."

"You won't touch him!"

"You think? Just watch!"

A gust of strong wind comes out of nowhere. The old oaks bend like pussy willows, and the shingles fly off the house like sparrows. Its power lifts little Petrica off the ground and twists him in midair. He'd fly away if Mother didn't grab him by the tail of his shirt. She tightens her arms around him. "Stop it, you monster! Let him be!"

"Where is my son?"

Her eyes burning with tears of rage, Mother shakes her head. Ion pushes the branches apart to see better.

A big man as tall as a pine tree stands facing Mother. His face is gaunt, his gray hair falls low down his back, and his eyes burn like embers. He shrugs. "It's up to you, woman. I gave you a choice. Just don't say it was my fault."

His long gray hair flies around him as he somersaults high through the air. He lands with a thud, shaking the earth. Only he's no longer a man.

Shiny black scales bigger than cart wheels cover his long, sinuous body from the horn on his snout to the sting on his twenty-foot tail. His massive paws sport curved iron claws longer than daggers, and enormous leathery wings ending in curved spines sprout out of his back. His spiny head alone is bigger than Mother's whole body, and his ember eyes burn with rage.

"Where is my son?" he roars.

The earth cowers. Birds fall from the sky. The clouds split and run. The wind hides.

Mother sobs and shakes her head no.

The black dragon opens an enormous mouth guarded by six-feet-long curved fangs. He turns his head towards the forest and spits out a river of flames that scorches the grass and sets the trees ablaze just feet from where Ion stands. The flames burn, roar and crackle. A thick smoke darkens the air, choking Ion.

The black dragon turns to Mother. "Listen, woman. This is the last time I ask you nicely. Where is my son?"

Mother sobs and holds Petrica tighter. "You have no son, you filthy Zmeu. And you won't have any of mine."

The dragon shakes his massive head. "Woman, you're just too stupid to live. Can't you see that I'll find him anyhow? But by then, you'll be ashes. And so will your children."

He opens his mouth, and the heat inside him blurs the air. Mother steps back, her eyes wide with fear.

The Zmeu opens his mouth even wider, and red tongues of flames escape between his fangs. He rears on his back paws, flaps his enormous wings, and blasts out a roaring river of fire towards Mother.

She steps back and hides Petrica behind her. Sparks fly as a wave of hungry flames surges towards them.

Ion leaps forward, and the dragon's fire hits him in the chest. A heartbeat later, he's ablaze, engulfed in a raging inferno.

Mother screams, Petrica cries, and Neta sobs. Ion hears them like he's under water. The sounds are far away, hard to distinguish above the excruciating pain that hammers his mind and the pyre that consumes him. Devoured by the river of fire, Ion feels his body dissolve as his skin blisters and chars, thickening into a cast-iron hard crust. His veins course fire through his body, melting his bones that lengthen and pull him apart. Nails burn to ashes and harden into steel claws. Ion's hair burns off, leaving behind a crown of charred spikes.

His eyes glaze, and the world as he knew it disappears. The mountains, the forest, even their hut — they're all gone. All that's left is the agony of the blaze that consumes him. Ion breathes in the flames and his chest fills with fire, swells and bursts, splitting him apart. His insides squeeze out and melt into leathery sheets that wrap around him, taking on a life of their own. His mouth tastes like ashes, and the world smells like smoke and destruction.

Ion knows he's landed in Hell.

He opens his mouth to cry his torment, but no word comes out. Nothing but a roaring river of green flames that surround him like a wall, fighting the red flames that scorch him. He tries to speak, but his throat is so parched that his breath comes out as a wave of roaring fire that takes over the world.

The green blaze surrounds the black dragon. His burning eyes wide with surprise, the Zmeu stops spewing fire to watch Ion's green flames engulf him.

He takes a step forward towards Mother, and Ion's rage devours him. He wants to scream: Let her be, you monster! But instead of words, another wave of green flames pours out of his throat into the Zmeu's open mouth, filling him with Ion's hatred.

The Zmeu wavers.

Drunk with rage, Ion pours his whole heart into his fire. The terrible loss of Father's death, two years ago. His loneliness and his guilt when his brothers died and he lived. The burden of being the man of the house when he was too young to shave. The endless days of work from dawn to dark, caring for the cattle that keep them all fed. His worries about Mother, who works so hard to make ends meet and always eats last. His fears about Neta and Petrica growing up without

Father, with only him. His knowing that he's never good enough, strong enough, or hard-working enough. Ion pours all of it into the green blaze torching the Zmeu.

His amber eyes glazed, his spines wilted, the Zmeu smiles. "You don't know it, but you're good enough, my son. And strong enough. You're even stronger than me. You're worthy to carry on my legacy, and you made me die happy."

He takes one last deep breath, and the massive lizard-like black body bursts into an enormous globe of red fire that lightens the sky. For the time of a heartbeat, the world is brighter than in daylight, then it turns dark and the Zmeu crumbles to the ground in a pile of ashes.

Ion freezes. *What the heck happened?*

He looks at his hands, but they're no longer hands. They've turned into paws covered with shiny golden scales as big as wagon wheels, and they end in iron claws like daggers. His whole body feels foreign and strange. From his head to his toes, he's covered in scales, and a twenty-foot tail ending in a scorpion sting twitches around him on the gritty ground.

Ion brings his hands to feel his face. His nose is gone, and so is his mouth. He's got a snout with long curved fangs instead. And a crown of spines instead of hair.

Ion's heart breaks.

I've turned into a Zmeu. And I killed my father.

CHAPTER I

THE PUPPIES

1442, BĂCEL, TRANSYLVANIA

It's not yet September, but up in here the crook of the Carpathians, the air already smells like smoke and winter. Here, summers are short and cool, and winters last forever, with long nights by the fireplace and snow to the eaves of the roof.

Ana slips out of bed and shivers. She pulls her black overskirts and sheepskin vest over the linen chemise, slips her feet in her opinci, the flat leather shoes tied with strings that go all the way to her knees, ties her scarf over her chestnut braid and she's good to go.

She opens the door and glances back. Mother's gone to the market already, and Nicolae and the baby are still asleep. Good. Sneaking out into the grayness before dusk, Ana pulls her vest closer, listening to the eerie silence. Nothing's awake yet, not even the roosters, just the wind rustling the dead leaves still clinging to the apple trees and the crickets complaining about the coming winter.

Ana grabs the wooden water bucket by the door like she's going to the well. The darn thing is heavy even when it's empty, but she's used to it. Bringing water from the well by the church has been one of her chores ever since she was six. She heads to the gate, but as soon as she turns the corner, she drops the bucket like it's hot and runs to the barn.

She knows she shouldn't. If perchance Mother saw her, she'd know that something's going on. Tina's belly has been growing for weeks, so Mother expects those puppies any day. But Ana can't resist.

Last night, she hid Tina and the puppies in the barn. She knew they'll be warm there, and safe, since Mother rarely goes there at night. She'll find them a better place sometime this morning, but for now, she'll just check on them and give Tina the bread she saved from her dinner.

Ana kneels in the dark and spreads the hay with her hands.

"I'm back! How are you guys doing? Everyone OK?"

She finds Tina's soft head. A wet tongue licks her fingers and Ana chuckles, scratches the dog behind the ears, then gropes for the puppies. One... That's it.

"That can't be!"

Ana pulls out Tina and her puppy and squeezes in to search. But there are no others.

Mother found them.

Ana's rage wants to burst out in a scream, but she bites her hands to choke her sobs. Undone by grief, she hugs Tina and cries and cries like she'll never stop.

Her head throbs and her throat is raw, but Ana's still crying as dusk grows into daylight. A hoarse rooster calls the dawn, then another. The heavy carts screech their way to the market, and men head to the fields, coughing out the morning fog. It's just another day for everyone but for the puppies Mother drowned in the water bucket. She pushed them down with the straw broom until they stopped fighting.

Ana didn't see her do it this time, but she knows. That's why she tried to hide them, hoping to save this one litter. But Mother found them and killed them, like she does with everything Ana loves.

No more.

Her throat raw, her eyes burning, Ana kisses Tina once more and steps into the yard.

She's late. She's been crying for so long that the night faded into the morning milky fog that shrouds the ghost-like trees. The village woke up. The women will be lined up at the well, and by the time her turn comes, she'll be late with the water. Nicolae will tell Mother, as he always does, and Mother will take out Father's belt and lash her until she pees herself and begs for mercy. Not that she cares — she couldn't hurt any more than she does.

But she's had it. Ana tiptoes back inside. The boys are still asleep. Good.

She drops her dark skirts on the floor and pulls on Nicolae's woolen breeches instead. Tying them tight around her with his leather belt, she puts on his tall sheepskin hat and stuffs her braid inside it.

She grabs his shoulder bag and slips in Father's bible, the kitchen knife, and what's left of yesterday's bread. She hangs it on her shoulder and touches the silver cross hanging around her neck. The metal feels hot under her fingers, and she glances down to see the stone glowing red, warning her of grave danger.

Oh well. It is what it is.

Ana pulls the door behind her without looking back.

CHAPTER 2

RUNAWAY

Ana peeks through the cracks in the fence, making sure no nosy neighbor will see her before she opens the gate and walks down the road like she means business. She's made up her mind. She's going to Kronstadt, the big city, where Grandma lives.

At least that's what Father said. Sadly, Ana has never met Grandma, since Mother doesn't like her, but now it's time. She'll ask around, and somebody is bound to know and point her in the right direction. She'll go from door to door if she needs to.

But what if she can't find her? Ana doesn't even know her name. Or how she looks. Father said she's beautiful and has a cat, but is that enough? How many beautiful cat-owning grandmas can there be in all of Kronstadt?

So what? She'll go and see them all. And, if she can't find Grandma, maybe someone else will take her in. The nuns maybe — Mother often said she'd send her away to the nunnery, where they'll teach her to behave. Or the gypsies. Mother said they love to steal bad children and put them in a bag and Ana always wondered what they do with them afterwards.

She walks and walks, grateful for the morning sun that warms her back. Up here, the brown fields gave way to orchards of twisted apple trees, their claw-like branches heavy with fruit. She steals a green apple and bites into it. It's not yet ripe, so it's crunchy and tart and makes her mouth water so hard it hurts. But the juices soothe her dry throat, and the chewy flesh makes her belly feel less empty.

By the time her shadow grows short, Ana has gotten to places she's never seen. The narrow dirt road is crammed with heavy hay carts, black-clad women returning from the market carrying empty bags on their shoulders, and impatient riders raising clouds of dust.

Ana keeps walking and takes it all in, wishing she could find some water, hiking up Nicolae's pants every once in a while. He's younger, but his pants are too big for her. Sure they are. He's a boy, so he always eats first.

She walks and walks until her shadow lengthens again. By now, her throat is dry and sore, and her feet hurt worse than her heart does, but she's almost there. The fortified city of Kronstadt rises straight ahead. Ana forgets her thirst as she gapes at the red and yellow flag with the rooted golden crown that flies on top of the mighty tower guarding the six-feet-thick stone walls.

What an amazing place this city is! Here, even the roads are paved with stones. They're narrow and winding and lined with houses in more colors than the flowers in the fields. And they're crammed with people. All tall, well-fed, and dressed in fancy Saxon clothes.

Ana has never seen a busier place, nor so many important-looking people. She can't stop staring as she shuffles towards the tall castle gate, wondering if leaving home was a good idea. But it's too late to worry. Mother would kill her if she went back. Or worse.

Oh well. They may need help in the kitchens. For sure, they'll give her water, and maybe even something to eat. She's a good worker and can build a fire, do the dishes, sweep the floors, and do whatever else they need. And if they beat her, so what? God knows she's used to it.

She ambles to one of the guards. They're so big their halberds alone are twice her size. Ana's about to ask him about the kitchens when he looks down and shakes his head.

"You're late. What took you so long? They've already gathered in the Red Tower. You're the last one. Come on, I'll take you there."

He heads to the drawbridge leading to the tower, and Ana hustles to keep up. The guard crosses it in two steps, then opens a heavy, iron-studded door and walks into the castle. Ana rushes to follow, and she's right behind him as the twisted dark stone corridor opens to a vast room.

"There."

He pushes her in and slams the door shut.

Ana opens her mouth to say something, but it's too late. He's gone.

She turns to the great room to find a hundred eyes staring at her.

CHAPTER 3
THE BOYS

The great room is gray and cold and so enormous that Ana's village church with its whole cemetery could fit in with room left over. The stone floors are smooth with wear, and the walls, shiny with moisture, are so tall they vanish in the ceiling's menacing darkness. But the sizzling torches bring it to life, even though it's empty, but for the kids.

They're all peasants, dressed just like Ana in thick woolen pants held up with leather belts, long-sleeved white tunics, and open sheepskin vests to keep them warm. They all wear tall shearling hats that fall over their ears, just like hers. So then why do they all stare at her like she's weird?

Ana scratches her head and notices that her hat is gone. She must have lost it while chasing the guard. Now, her thick chestnut braid falls over her shoulder, betraying she's a girl.

Oh well.

Ana takes in a deep breath and straightens as tall as a scrawny, five-feet-tall girl can, and pulls her stomach in, hoping the boys won't hear it growl.

And if they do, so what?

She clenches her jaw to stop her teeth from chattering and inspects the room. The boys are many, all bigger than she is. The massive hall dwarfs them all, with its tall ceiling fading in the darkness and its thick cold walls seldom broken by narrow dark windows like so many blind eyes. The place smells like a long-forgotten tomb, and Ana knows in her heart it's evil. These walls crushed women's hopes, drank men's blood, and destroyed children's futures. These stones are imbued with secrets and sorrow. Ana feels the vileness in her bones and shivers.

She wishes she was closer to the roaring fire that lights the short end of the room. The carved fireplace is large enough to roast a whole boar and then some. But there's no boar, not even a piglet. Just a blistering tree trunk, so angry it spits sparks and so hot that it blurs the air.

The two Saxon men sitting in the high-backed chairs by the fire are the only grown-ups in the room. They murmur to each other, keeping an eye on the kids.

Why not?

Ana drifts from the kids towards the fire. A few more steps, and she's close enough to warm her hands and hear them chat in Saxon.

"What do you think?"

The tall man rests his chin in his hand. His face, turned away from the fire, is just a dark shadow, but his restless fingers tap his jaw, setting his massive ruby ring on fire.

The fat man shrugs. He wipes the sweat off his forehead with an embroidered golden sleeve as his hooded eyes slip from one kid to another.

He's too close to the fire, and hasn't missed many meals, Ana thinks, then hushes her mind. She's not here to judge anyone, not even fat Saxons. She's here to eat.

"I don't know what to say, Burgomaster. It's way too early."

His eyes fall on Ana, and he startles.

"That one there! That's a girl. What on earth are you going to do with her?"

The burgomaster turns to stare at her with sharp eyes. His forehead wrinkles, and the thick black brows come together in a threatening frown. He opens his mouth to say something, but doesn't. A wide smile lightens his face, and he chuckles.

"You're right, Karl. That's a girl. Isn't that something? So what? Girl — boy — what does it matter? As long as they're bright, strong, and loyal?"

Karl gets so mad that he stutters.

"But... but... but... look at her! She's smaller than a field mouse and only half that pretty! Look at that pointed chin, those stormy eyes, and that silly mop of chestnut hair. What on earth do you think you can do with her?"

"*Komm schon, mein Freund.* Don't forget that women can sometimes reach places even the best men can't. Even more so at the sultan's court. How many uncut men ever got to see the inside of the Edirne sarayi and lived long enough to tell the tale, you think?"

Karl shakes his head.

"Come on, Burgomaster. Say you got her there — I don't think you can, but let's say you did. Then what? You know as well as I do that no woman leaves the harem alive. None. Not even the sultan's mother, the validé. Once there, she'll stay there till she dies, which won't take long, I bet. As for you, you'll have wasted your time and our money."

The burgomaster shrugs.

"Only if they know she's a girl."

Karl sniggers.

"So if she's not a girl and she's not a boy, what will she be? A peacock?"

"Close. How about a eunuch?"

Karl chokes.

"A eunuch? She doesn't look like a eunuch. She can't be a eunuch."

"I'll bet you a thousand ducats."

"You're out of your mind. I'll bet you a hundred."

"Deal."

Ana warms her hands to the fire, pretending she didn't listen, but her heart is in turmoil. *What's a eunuch?* she wonders.

CHAPTER 4

THE CHANCE OF A LIFETIME

His dark eyes glued to Ana, the burgomaster leaves his chair to work the crowd. He may be six-foot tall, but he's humped and skinny as a rake. And, unlike his flashy companion's gold-embroidered coat, the burgomaster's black cloak melts into the shadows. There's nothing striking about him but the ruby ring. Still, when he stops by the kids, they shrink under his searching gaze.

“Hey kids. You all know why you're here?" he asks them in Romanian.

Most shake their heads. A few shrug. Not Ana. She knows why she's here. She's here to escape Mother and eat.

"You're here to change your lives," the burgomaster thunders, stepping from one kid to the next and challenging them with his sharp, narrow gaze. And, one after the other, they lower their eyes to their opinci.

"You're here to seize an opportunity that few ever get. And even for those, it only comes once in a lifetime. *If* they earn it."

A deep shiver goes down Ana's spine and she hugs herself for warmth.

"You will get tested. We'll check your wits, we'll test your courage, we'll challenge your determination until we find out everything there is to know about you. We'll unearth your fears, uncover your dreams, and measure your worth. Day after day after day, we'll test you again and again until we get to know you inside and out. We'll get to know you better than your mothers and your fathers, and even better than you know yourselves. That's how we'll find the best one. The bravest one. The smartest one. The one who grabs life by the horns. The one who never quits."

The silence is so loud it hurts.

"There'll only be one. Or maybe two of you."

The burgomaster stops by Ana and his eyes meet hers.

“Do you have what it takes? Are you the one? Are you smarter, braver, and stronger than all the others?"

Ana stares back without blinking. She knows she's not; Mother made sure she knows she’s neither smart, nor strong, nor worthy.

But she's got nothing to lose.

The burgomaster hides the shadow of a smile and moves on.

"Because if you are, you'll seize the opportunity that your parents brought you here for. You’ll have a once in a lifetime chance at a better life. But only if you are the Chosen One.

“We’ve asked the priests in every corner of Transylvania to send us their smartest, their strongest and most reliable kids. That's you all. And we paid your parents for you, because some of you won't go back home, though most will. Those of you who don't make the cut will go back to your lives and forget you’ve ever been here."

The burgomaster stops to look at a tall, dark kid with a thick brow growing from one ear to the other, and seems to speak to him alone.

"But if you stay, your life will change forever. You'll have the best teachers that will help you become the most learned kid in the whole of Transylvania. You'll learn a thousand things your parents have never heard about, and you’ll live better than they ever did. It won't be luxury, but you won't freeze, and you'll never go hungry again."

Unibrow's face lights up. The burgomaster nods and moves on.

"But that's just the beginning. After training, you'll be sent on a secret mission on behalf of your country. You'll get to see amazing places and do extraordinary things. You'll have the incredible honor of risking your life for your country, you'll get a stab at changing the course of history, and maybe even make the world a better place."

His eyes rest on a handsome kid with shoulder-length golden hair and eyes like clear water. The kid's just as light as Unibrow is dark, and he glows like he's lit from inside. *That's how young Jesus must have looked*, Ana thinks.

"Your mission will be long and dangerous. It will take years, and years, and you'll have nobody to help you but yourself. When it's finally over, you might come back — or not. There's a good chance that you'll die alone in a foreign land without a friend, without your mother, without even a priest to give you your final rites. You'll die alone like a dog, and your parents will never know what happened to you."

The Jesus kid blanches. For a moment, he looks ready to crumble, but he steadies himself and sighs.

The burgomaster stops to look at Ana. He towers over her, but his gray eyes are warm and kind, and he seems to speak to her alone.

"But if you return, you'll never be poor again. You'll have your own home, and your land, and you'll have horses and oxen and servants. But, more than anything else, you'll have the knowledge that you served our Lord Jesus and you've made our country proud."

His thundering voice reverberates against the thick stone walls like there are four burgomasters talking, not just him. Their mouths hanging open, the kids listen in awe.

"But first you'll have to earn your spot. If you dare. Now, which of you would rather go home?"

The kids stare at each other, wondering who's brave enough to go on, and who's brave enough to quit. The air crackles with tension.

A small kid sobs. "I want to go home."

Another one follows, then another. Soon, a third of the kids are gone. The massive door slams behind them with a thud while the remaining kids measure each other with the narrowed eyes of would-be fighters.

The burgomaster nods. "I take it that the rest of you are here to stay?"

Heads up, fists tight, the boys glare at each other and nod.

"Very good, then. I'll see you all tomorrow."

He nods and leaves with Karl. The boys eye each other like young roosters ready to fight.

Ana shrugs. She leaves them be and follows her nose to look for food.

CHAPTER 5
THE GIFT

With her belly full of crusty warm bread, fresh sweet cheese, honey, and milk, Ana slept like a log. She hasn't eaten like this since Father died. Neither has Mother, or even Nicolae.

She wakes up before dawn as usual and slides out of bed. The fire's out, and the floor is cold as ice under her bare feet. The stone walls, slick with water, glow like silver in the meager light of the torch. The long, narrow slits meant for archers are still dark, and the other kids are still asleep on the straw beds they made for them last night. Two armed guards sleep standing, like horses, leaning against the massive wooden door.

This isn't home.

Ana's heart flickers with a pang of remorse. How will they manage without her? Who'll build the fire? Who'll carry water from the well, sweep the floors, wash the clothes and feed the chickens? Mother's got her hands full with working the fields and going to the market. Nicolae, maybe? Surely not the baby. He's too young, and he's a boy; boys never do women's work.

Ana shrugs and squeezes back between her blankets. Whatever they do is no longer her problem.

She touches her cross to make sure it's still there. The warmth of the stone reminds her of Father's warm breath when he slipped it around Ana's neck.

"Don't lose it! When I'm no longer here to keep you safe, this cross will look after you like it looked after me. My mother gave it to me when I left home, years ago. 'Watch the stone,' she said. 'Beware when it's red. That means great danger. Green is good luck, yellow is jealousy and looming betrayal, and blue is friendship and protection. But if it ever turns black...' Father's voice trailed off. 'Touch it for protection whenever you need it. Knowing it's there will give you strength.'"

"What does it mean when it turns black?"

Father sighed.

"When it's black, it's time to give it away, like I'm doing now. It means that you no longer need it. Just make sure to give it to someone worthy."

Ana caresses the cross like it's Father's cheek, and the stone blinks blue. She wonders if Father would still be alive if he kept the cross. But there's no way of knowing, so she lets herself drift to sleep.

The sun's halfway up when the bell rings to wake them. The massive door opens, and the kids follow the guards to the inner courtyard of the castle, a long patch of grass protected by thick walls. The burgomaster and Karl are already there, sitting in high-backed chairs and drinking from steaming silver cups. The tall man dressed in black who sits with them watches the kids file in the courtyard with sharp blue eyes.

The boys line up in front of the chairs. Ana squeezes between them, but the sharp morning wind cuts through her linen chemise like it's nothing, so she stomps and rubs the goosebumps off her arms to ward off the chill as she waits for her turn.

The blue-eyed man examines one boy after another, then gets to Ana. He pokes and prods her like he wants to buy her, then checks her teeth. He makes her bend, crouch, and jump, then lays his ear on her chest to listen. He finally nods.

"She's good. Next one."

One by one, he checks all the others. They're mostly good, but for two who don't make it: one has a limp, the other a lazy eye. A guard takes them away.

Ana stays. So does the blond kid standing next to her. So do a dozen more.

"What's your name?" he whispers.

"Ana. Yours?"

“I’m Ion."

Ion smiles, and his clear blue eyes make her warm inside. She can't remember the last time someone smiled at her.

The burgomaster glares at them and frowns. They go quiet. "So all of you here are healthy and strong. We're about to start testing you. But first, has any of you changed their mind? Would you rather go home to your mother?"

His sharp eyes focus on Ana, and she shivers. She can't think of anything she’d hate more.

The burgomaster nods. "Good. So for your first test, we have a special prize."

A black-clad woman servant fetches a covered wooden platter. She takes off the cover for them all to see, but Ana doesn't need to. She already knows it by the smell, but she stares anyhow. The mouthwatering aroma of roasted meat raising from the steaming pork chop makes her dizzy. She hasn't seen anything like that in many winters. Sometime before Father died.

The woman covers the platter and takes it away. Every eye in the place is glued to her as she walks the platter to the other end of the courtyard and sets it on the ground by the crenelated stone wall where the grass is white with frost.

"OK, everybody."

The eyes glued to the plate swing to the burgomaster.

"Get ready to dash. When I say *‘go’*, you go. Whoever gets to the pork chop first gets to keep it. Whoever’s last gets to go home."

They line up. Ana's heart pumps like crazy. Meat! She can eat meat if only she gets to it first! She hasn't forgotten how meat tastes. Sometimes in her dreams, she eats a whole roasted chicken by herself. She wakes up even hungrier, but it's worth it.

"Go."

Ana flies like the wind. Her feet pound the grass and her skinny arms slice the air, thrusting her forward. Her feet hurt, her chest burns, and the wind whips her bare legs with a vengeance, but Ana doesn't care. She runs like she's never run before. She hears the other kids heave and pant behind her, but she doesn't look back. The only thing her eyes see is that platter.

Ten more steps. Eight. Five.

Her right foot slips. A searing pain grips her ankle as she rolls over the frozen ground and smacks her head, but that's nothing compared to the pain in her heart and the void in her stomach.

She bites her lip and crawls forward.

Too late. The platter's empty. The pork chop is gone.

Ana digs her nails in her palms to stop her tears. She struggles back to her feet and limps back, trying to ignore her pain. She's the last one back, and she stands behind the others, awaiting her fate.

"You, you, and you." The burgomaster points to a short chunky kid, a red-haired one, and a skinny dark one, barely taller than Ana. "You three were last. You're going home."

The guards take them away.

"How about the girl?" Karl asks in Saxon.

"She wasn't last."

"But she fell!"

"Still, she wasn't last. She crawled forward."

"That's crazy," Karl says, looking at her. "She's a girl. She can't do it."

"Maybe not. But what do you have to lose? Let's get through the day and see what happens."

Karl shrugs. "Your plan, your call. But don't say I didn't warn you."

The burgomaster nods and stands before the nine kids left, speaking Romanian this time.

"Who here can swim?"

Five boys raise their hands. So does Ana.

She shouldn't — good girls don't swim. They stay home to look after the house, wave linen into sheets and towels and embroider them into their dowry. But Father loved fishing and he always took her with him.

Mother didn't like it. "She should stay home to take care of the house. That's what women do."

Father had laughed. "My little girl can do whatever she sets her mind to. Can't you, Ana?"

Ana's heart swelled with pride, but Mother's face darkened. She went into her stormy mood, and Ana knew that bad things were about to come her way.

Father didn't care. He took her with him to his secret fishing spot in the mountains. They rode for hours to reach Bâlea Lake, the glacial lake up in the Făgăraș Mountains. Its midnight-blue waters were ice-cold even in summer, and said to have magic. That's where Father taught her how to swim and showed her how to dive, and how to control her breath, and get deep. It was long ago, but Ana remembers.

Karl glares at her. The boys do too.

The burgomaster smiles. "Those who can't swim: You're done. Your parents are waiting."

Ana shivers. Thank God she can swim, since the one person she doesn't want to see is Mother. But she wouldn't be here anyhow. Mother has better things to do than to worry about her useless daughter. Here, in Transylvania, daughters are worth less than nothing. To get them a husband, you need to give them a dowry, whether it's land, cows or sheep; otherwise, you can't get rid of them. That's why a daughter is nothing but a burden.

A hay cart is waiting for them by the gate. Its muddy black oxen crowned with twisted horns chew their cud and slap the flies with long tails caked in dry mud. The old peasant that drives them pulls his sheepskin cloak closer and gives them a cursory glance.

Ana plants her good foot on one of the wooden wheel's spokes and pulls herself up. She limps to the furthest back corner and nests in the straw to keep herself warm, then closes her eyes. As the cart crawls up the dusty road, she listens to the wheels squeak, the oxen moan, and the man shout orders the beasts are slow to follow.

She thinks about Father. About how they rode up to the secret lake. How she sat behind, holding on to him and listening to him sing. She remembers his voice, the smoky scent of his shirt, the rough touch of his cheek, and her throat swells, choking her.

She looks away to hide her tears. A murder of angry crows circles above, screaming their hate. The fields by the road are brown and dry, spiked with dry husks waiting for the snow shroud. Far away, the mountains frown. They're dark blue, but for the jagged peaks where the snow never melts and winter lasts forever. Nothing but ugly sadness.

Ana sighs. Something warm touches her hand. Ion, sitting next to her, looks away.

She looks at her hand. It's the pork chop.

And just like that, she starts crying like a girl.

CHAPTER 6

THE ARCHERY LESSON

TÂRGOVIȘTE, WALLACHIA, 1442

A hundred miles south of the fortified city of Kronstadt that guards Transylvania's southeast corner sits Târgoviște, Wallachia's capital. It wouldn't be far, but for the mountains. The frozen peaks of the Southern Carpathians, reach for the sky everywhere between them, preventing passage. As they should.

Because even though Transylvanians and Wallachians are brothers — they all speak Romanian, eat the same food and pray to the same smoky Orthodox God — Wallachia is its own country, while Transylvania is just a province of Hungary, subject to the Hungarian king who's often at war with Wallachia. That makes the Romanian brotherhood into treason.

The two countries are not alike. Transylvania, the Land Between the Forests, is wild and always cold. Its dark forests hide Godless shape-shifting creatures with curious powers that you wouldn't want to meet at night. And the women are witches.

Not Wallachia. Barely a hundred miles south, Wallachia enjoys long summers and mild winters. There, the fields are golden wheat, long-horned Grey Steppe cows graze the green meadows, and countless busy bees roam the flowers' corollas cooking their scent into fragrant sweet honey.

And, while the moody Kronstadt Castle grows out of a cliff, challenging the Carpathians' peaks, the New Royal Court of Târgoviște looks over miles and miles of undulating wheat fields to the sleepy Ialomiţa River.

They call it new because it is. Sort of. The New Royal Court is not yet a hundred years old, and Mircea the Elder, the best voivode Wallachia ever had, built it to last. To defend it, he protected it with six-foot-thick stone walls he surrounded with a seventy-foot-wide moat where sharp stakes lurk just below the water's surface, waiting for their prey.

But Mircea died, may God bless his brave soul and keep his memory alive. These days, the court is home to his bastard, Vlad Dracul, and his family: Doamna Cneajna, his wife, and their three young sons: Mircea, Vlad, and Radu, who are meant to become voivodes someday, God willing.

But deep in his heart, Radu hopes that day never comes. The last thing he needs is having Wallachia to look after. That may be fine for Father, who's old and wise and a master of swords and men, but not for Radu. He's better with the quill, the rübap, and the brush.

"That's not what being a voivode is about," Father said. He took away his quill and sent him to join Vlad for his archery practice. And God knows there's nothing Radu loves less, other than maybe sword fighting. And being anywhere near Vlad.

Radu sighs and wipes his brow with the sleeve of his linen chemise, hoping this ordeal will soon be over. The courtyard has no shade, so the merciless June sun roasted him inside his leather armor. And both his hands hurt from pulling the bow string. He'll surely get blisters. But the worst is that he needs to pee.

He should have gone before practice, but he hustled to finish his poem, because archery always ruins his mood. Even more so today, when Vlad's back from his hunt and they practice together.

It's true that Vlad is older — by four years. But even when he was Radu's age, he loved to fight more than anything else. Vlad hates the quill and despises the brush, but he can't get enough of his bow, his sword, and his mace — anything that can draw blood. Because Vlad loves blood.

"Your turn, princess."

Vlad mock curtsies, and his greasy black hair falls over his poison-green eyes shining with glee. He can't wait to laugh at Radu and his mistakes, and Radu knows he's about to oblige.

His leather boots are stiff and heavy as lead as he shuffles to the white spot on the grass that old Gheorghe marked with wheat flour. Radu's shoulders climb up to his ears as he raises the bow and pulls the string to his right cheek.

But he's way too tense. He breathes deep and tries to soften his shoulders, but it's a no go. He can't relax with Vlad staring at him like a hungry wolf at a rabbit. Oh well. Radu prays to Jesus Christ for mercy, closes his eyes and lets the arrow go.

Like a bald chick too young to fly, the arrow plops down over a patch of grass barely halfway to the target.

Radu drops his head as Vlad's shrill laugh echoes from the thick stone walls. It's like the whole courtyard is full of evil laughing Vlads who can't get enough of Radu's humiliation. Vlad laughs until he's out of breath, then straightens and steps forward with the soft, low walk of a cat. His shoulders are relaxed as he pulls his bowstring to his hooked nose and liberates the arrow.

The arrow sings like a strummed chord. It pierces the air and falls upon the target like an angry falcon on a hare, nailing it in the eye.

The left eye that is. The target is Sultan Murad the Second, Vlad said, but the sultan's own mother couldn't recognize him from Vlad's drawing. Vlad prefers human targets, but that does no good to Radu. Just the thought of blood spurting out of the sultan's eye makes him sick.

The old soldier who trains them nods approvingly. "Nice shot, Prince Vlad. A fast one, too."

His eyes turn to Radu and he shakes his grizzled head.

"You need to put your heart into it, prince. You must will your arrow to fly like a bird of prey and bring death. Look at your brother. He's the best archer in three counties, and he's been like this since he was younger than you."

He's right; Radu knows it. He should put his heart into it, but... he hates hurting people. Or animals. He doesn't want to be anything like his brother, even though everyone wants him to. The soldiers training him wish that he was better with the sword, the mace, and the horse. His elder brother, Mircea, wants to take him hunting for boar and teach him to set the goshawks loose on hares. Father wants to teach him history and strategy, and tactics to instigate their enemies against each other. Even Mother wants him to become a fighter.

But fighting isn't his thing. He'd rather read, or sing.

"That's not what a prince does. Nor what a man does," Mother said, and fired his beloved Venetian tutor, who knew all about music and arts. She hired a Serb soldier instead. The man knows nothing but weapons, armor, and horses, and he never stops talking. That's why Radu's ears buzz with lances, swords and trebuchets.

Still, Radu is nothing like Vlad, who loves all his weapons, especially his sword. The soldiers training him learned to keep him at bay. Their arms and swords may be longer, but Vlad is quicker than a falcon and meaner than a snake. You never know when he'll sneak close and get you. That's why they all have weeping wounds reminding them: Don't let Vlad get close. He's the devil.

Father gave Radu a sword last year. The blade is shiny and beautifully crafted, made just for him by the Ottoman swordsmith who makes weapons for the sultan's young sons. Radu's sword is lovely to look at, but way too sharp. To him, the pleasure of a sword fight is in the dance. It's all about the rhythm, the moves, and the pan-pipe wail of the blade slicing the air, not about the blood.

The day Vlad grabbed a bunny rabbit by his hind legs and crushed his head against a rock, Radu threw up, then locked himself into his room and stayed there for three days.

Father got mad. "A voivode has no room for pity. To win, you must be strong and ruthless. The rabbit died. So what? Rabbits die. Whether eaten by wolves or boiled in a pot, they're just as dead. And it's the same with cows and sheep and dogs. Even people. A voivode can't be a crying baby. Learning to handle death is part of a prince's life. Not music, drawing, and dancing. That's for the wimps."

That was last year, but it still holds true.

Radu sighs and eyes the target, wishing he was elsewhere. Out in the fields, or down by the river, playing with Yellow, or in his room, sharpening his quill. Anywhere but here.

He lets go the arrow and misses.

Vlad laughs and readies his bow. The old soldier shakes his head, ready to lecture Radu again, when the tower door opens. Gheorghe, Father's right-man man, limps towards them. He's out of breath as usual, and his stormy eyes move from Vlad to Radu.

"Voivode Vlad Dracul wants to speak to you both."

Radu drops his bow like it's hot, thanking God this ordeal is over.

Vlad stomps away. "I'm not ready."

He puts his last arrow in the bow and eyes the target which is a hundred feet away. He lifts the bow, twists like an angry snake and sets the arrow free.

For a while, the arrow flies high like it's about to reach the sun, but it changes its mind. It coils in the air, then falls like a goshawk on its prey. With a sickening *thunk*, it sinks into old Yellow who's sleeping in the sun by the door.

His surprised eyes popping up, the dog leaps, then falls back to the ground. A river of dark blood spurts out of his mouth, choking him. He struggles to stand, but falls back in a shivering puddle. The dog's chest heaves around the arrow skewering him, and he screams just once like a baby, then falls limp as the thirsty earth drinks his blood.

CHAPTER 7

A REASON TO KILL

Radu stoops, holding back his blond hair to retch. A hot wave runs down his legs. He tries to stop it, but he can't. A river of piss darkens his brown woolen pants before filling his tall boots.

Oh, how he wishes he was dead, like Yellow. But he's not, and he needs to go see Father. Right now.

Vlad throws his bow at the old soldier, striking his eyebrow, then strides towards Father's rooms without sparing a glance back. Radu waits for his stomach to settle before following him. He'd love to go and get changed, but when Father says now, he means now, and Radu's already late. He hustles along the empty hallways sloshing in his boots, the drumming of his heart louder than the clatter of his steps on the stone.

He's huffing by the time he reaches the throne room where the voivode is waiting. Straight and unsmiling, Father sits on his throne with his hand on the hilt of his sword and measures Radu with his piercing green eyes, so much like Vlad's.

"Nice of you to join us."

His voice is soft, and, under the proud dark mustache, the fleshy mouth hints at a smile. But the sword in his hand and the golden dragon pinned to his chest, the effigy of the Order of the Dragon that bought him the name of Vlad Dracul, make it clear that he's the voivode, not just Father.

Radu hangs his head and squeezes into the shadow between two narrow windows up the wall. They're just slits carved high in the six-feet-thick stone wall, made to let in the light but not the arrows whenever the New Royal Court gets attacked, which happens without fail every year. Sometimes more than once. Whenever the sultan decides to change the voivode.

His face scrunched in anger, his brother Vlad stands at the foot of the throne with his hands on his hips and glares at Father. "Your man interrupted my archery practice. I didn't get to finish!"

Father's eyes crinkle at the corners as they rest on Vlad. "How did you do?"

Radu sobs. He'd love to tell Father about Yellow. He was old, Yellow, so old that Radu can't remember a life without him. They always hung out together, swimming, fishing, or lying in the shadow of the old tree to eat pears.

Yellow loved any pear that Radu had started, but a pear was not a pear to Yellow until Radu bit into it. He couldn't care less about the whole ones, but, as soon as Radu took a bite, he stared and begged with his lusty yellow eyes. They shared many pears. Stories too.

Yellow listened to Radu tell him about his troubles with Vlad, about how he missed his Venetian teacher, and about his real mom, who was loving and kind. Radu was going to find her someday.

Some of his stories were true, and some were not. The story about his real mom was made up, of course. There was no other mother but Doamna Cneajna, even though she was Vlad's mom too. But Yellow didn't care about the truth. Just about the pears. He'd listen and ask for more as long as there were any pears left.

Vlad smiles. "I did good. I got the dog through his heart. I killed him dead," he says.

"The dog? What dog?"

Radu sobs. "He killed Yellow," he says, though he knows he shouldn't. Nothing will bring Yellow back; And Father will see him cry and he'll know he's a wimp.

Father's green eyes look at him with pity and something else that

Radu doesn't understand. Is it anger? Fear? He doesn't know, but he can see he disappointed Father again, and he squirms.

Father sighs and watches them quietly from the height of his throne. It's not much of a throne, really. It's more of a high-backed wooden chair. If not for the eagle with the cross in its beak carved in its back, you couldn't tell it from the seats around the dining table. But that throne is the seat of his power. That's where he rules Wallachia from, and his sons squirm under the power of his gaze, like everyone else.

This is where Father sits to hold court with the boyars, and anyone else who comes to ask for justice, whether somebody stole their cow, raped their daughter, or killed their son. Or so they say. Father looks through their eyes into their soul and makes justice. Never revenge. Always justice.

Father can read people's minds like Radu can read letters. He understands people's souls. Radu's soul, too, no matter how Radu tries to hide it. Father knows he's terrified of Vlad, and he's a coward and worthless.

Vlad Dracul's eyes move to Vlad and his brow furrows over the green fire in his eyes. "You killed Yellow?"

"Yes."

"Why?"

Vlad's chin juts forward. He tightens his fists and shrugs. He doesn't know, and he doesn't care.

"Did the dog do anything to you?"

Vlad shakes his head.

"So why did you kill him?"

"I was angry. And I had an arrow left."

He grins at Radu, mocking him.

Radu has nothing to say. Hot tears run down his cheeks to his chin, soaking the breast of his chemise. They'll think he's a wimp, and that's almost as bad as being a woman, but he can't stop crying like he can't stop breathing. Yellow was his only friend.

"Is that a good reason?" Father thunders, staring down at Vlad with hard cold eyes. "Is that a good enough reason to kill?"

Vlad is in trouble. Father's not happy with him. And, as always when he's challenged, he gets even more defiant.

"Yes, it is. Any reason is a good reason to kill."

Father stares at him like he's never seen him before. He sits high in his crown chair and looks down into Vlad's eyes, so much like his own.

"You are mistaken. There are very few reasons good enough to kill."

Vlad shrugs. "So what? He was just an old dog. Who cares he's dead?"

Radu opens his mouth, but nothing he can say will make a difference. He gives up.

Father doesn't. "I care. Radu cares. And the dog cares. *Cared*," Father says, looking Vlad in the eye as if he's trying to shove the idea into his brain. "Useless killing is worse than useless. It's stupid, and it's wrong. This is not what a voivode does. You want to be a voivode someday?"

Vlad's dark eyes shine with tears. Father has never spoken to him like this. "Yes, Father."

"Then you must get hold of yourself and learn to manage your anger. We don't kill because it feels good. We don't kill because we can. We don't kill because we have an arrow left. We kill because it gets us closer to our goal. We kill to protect our land. We kill to harm our enemies. We kill to make people afraid to hurt us. You got that?"

Vlad nods.

"Don't you ever forget it!" Vlad Dracul says. "Killing is not a purpose in itself. It's just the means to something that matters."

He turns to Radu. "And you. What did you do to stop Vlad?"

Radu's mouth falls open. "What did I do?"

"Yes. Vlad killed your dog. What did you do?"

Radu has nothing to say. He did nothing.

"He puked," Vlad says. "In the bushes."

And I peed myself.

CHAPTER 8

SAYING GOOD-BYE

Father looks at them with no joy. They disappointed him.

His steady gaze weighs on Radu, who looks at his soaked boots, wishing he was anywhere but here. He'd take the courtyard with its wretched fighting lessons, Mother's scolding, even Vlad's wrath over Father's silent disappointment.

It feels like forever until Father looks away. He sighs and stands. The golden dragon pin catches a dart of light and snarls, and the scabbard of his long, straight sword clangs against the carved throne.

He looks out the window. His eyes, like deep green fires, take in the land, the miles and miles of wheat fields, the pastures covering the soft rounded hills, and the white-capped Carpathians where Wallachia ends, and Transylvania starts. Those mountains are so far away that they let your eyes rest on the horizon. And think.

Finally, Father's burning eyes return to them. He looks inside them, reading their souls like he always does with people. Radu feels the strength of Father's mind searching his, and he knows he's busted.

Radu has no courage, no pride, and no worth. He's nothing like his father, and nothing he can do will change that. He shrinks into himself, itching to look away, but he knows better.

Father's eyes move to Vlad. He sinks his dark light into Vlad's soul, and Vlad shrinks. And for the first time ever, Radu realizes that Vlad is also just a child. It's just the evil inside him that's big.

Father sighs. He sits back on his throne under the crown carved in the high back. "Come forward."

They step forward to face him. He's taller than them even seated, so they look up into his eyes, which are dark, sad, and kind. "You both are my sons, and I love you both."

Radu startles. He's never heard that before. He knows Father loves Vlad, and he's proud of him. But him? Radu?

"You two are as different as the night is from the day, but you're both my sons, and the future of Wallachia sits with you. One of you."

His eyes turn from one to the other, measuring them from head to toe. "Being Wallachia's voivode is hard. It's hard to balance the needs of the realm, the Hungarian king's expectations, and the sultan's demands. The hell difficult, it's impossible. Nobody can get it right. I know I can't."

Radu's heart skips a beat. He has never heard Father swear. Ever.

"You two are the future of Wallachia, but you're also her servants. God willing, one of you will rule the country and do his best to keep it safe. If you live long enough. In our land of wars and sorrow, few children get to grow into men. Should you die, someone else's sons will run this country and see to her future."

Father sighs. He looks out through the narrow window at the blue sky, and his voice is soft and pained when he speaks again. "I love this country more than I love life. As her voivode, I must keep it safe no matter what it costs and give her all I've got.

"And all I've got to give are you two. I'm sending you away for Wallachia's sake, hoping that one of you will return someday and see her through. Never forget that you are here to serve her, not the other way round. The realm needs our love and sacrifice, and I'm making mine today."

Father's eyes sparkle like never before. Radu sees tears flowing down his cheeks, and can't believe it. Father? Crying? That can't be! He's heard a thousand times that princes don't cry; real men don't cry. And yet, he is.

"You, my sons, will leave for Edirne, the capital of the Ottoman

Empire. You'll grow up at Sultan Murad's court. He asked for you as a token of my loyalty, and I can't say no. It's either you or Wallachia, and she always comes first.

"You may come back someday, or you may not. This may well be the last time I speak to you, so listen carefully and don't forget.

"My blood, the blood of Wallachia, runs through your veins. You are not Ottomans; you are their slaves. You'll be there for their pleasure while our country cries. Whatever they tell you, whatever they teach you, no matter how well they treat you, don't forget that they are not our people. They are the ones who enslaved our people.

"Every other year, they cross the Danube and come to rip our children from their mother's arms. The cursed devşirme, the blood tax, steals thousands of our children every other year. They take them back to the sultan's court and brainwash our boys into leaving their own God for Allah and fighting their wars for them. They force our girls to forget their parents' God and bear them Ottoman children. There's never been a more horrific servitude. Our own children, ripped from their parent's arms, come back as janissaries to kill their brothers."

Father sighs. "Don't let that happen to you! Don't you dare forget who you are! You must study their ways and learn everything they teach you. Learn their language, their habits, their religion, everything there is to know about them. Then do all you can to come home and save Wallachia from the misery they inflict on it. You must do whatever it takes.

"I don't know which of you will make it. You boys are so different, yet you both are strong in different ways. I hope that one of you returns someday to serve our country. I'll no longer be here, but I'll watch you from God's Heaven and beam with pride."

Father walks to Radu and hugs him. Radu knows he'll never forget the horse and leather smell, the rough mustache tickling his cheek, and the warmth of his breath as he whispers: "Radu, you are stronger than you think; you just don't know it yet. I believe in you."

He then walks to Vlad. He kisses his forehead and speaks to him so softly that Radu can't hear him, but he can see tears running down Vlad's cheeks.

Then, for the first time ever, Father bows to them and leaves. Radu glances at Vlad, who glares back. Vlad's eyes are dark, hateful, and murderous like they've always been ever since Radu can remember.

Vlad will kill me someday.

Dread fills his heart like it always does when he's with Vlad.

Then a thought comes out of nowhere.

Unless I kill him first.

CHAPTER 9

MEHMET'S SÜRGÜN

EDIRNE, OTTOMAN EMPIRE, 1442

Three hundred miles south of Târgoviște and yet another hundred south of Kronstadt stands Edirne, the Ottoman Empire's capital. Nestled inside its priceless gardens, the empire's sparkling jewel, Edirne Palace, is the home of Allah's Chosen, Sultan Murad the Second, may Allah bless his soul, his many women, and his son Mehmet.

Not one expense was spared to make the place worthy of Allah's Chosen. From the sultan's bedroom to his hammam, the fragrant gardens, and the many kitchens, everything glows, glitters and shines. But nothing compares to the gilded splendor of the Imperial Room, where the sultan keeps council with his viziers, receives foreign dignitaries, and awards justice to his subjects under Allah's watchful eye.

The Imperial Room is big enough to hold half of Edirne, and it sparkles in a million colors. Still, its light is cobalt-blue, because of the azure tiles that make its ceiling into an inside blue sky.

This place is closer to Heaven than anything else young Mehmet has ever seen. The calligraphed golden letters adorning the walls remind the faithful about Allah's endless mercy and beauty. So do the precious Smyrna incense smoke twirling above the filigreed incense burners and the sussuring fountains chilling the air. Everywhere you look, engraved silver platters bend under the weight of golden quince, purple grapes, and translucent sour cherries, making Mehmet's mouth water. In every corner, whole potted trees drip water from the tips of their fat green leaves. Ten feet above, a lemon-yellow parrot flaps his wings, trying to escape his elaborate gilded cage. From the eye's many pleasures to the mesmerizing sounds and enchanting scents, the Edirne sarayi is as close to Heaven as the money of the mighty Ottoman Empire and its power can get it.

But right now, for Mehmet, this is Hell. He sits cross-legged on a blue brocade pillow amongst the other dignitaries, looking up at his father.

Up on his podium, Sultan Murad sits above them all on his raised throne-sofa. He wears rose-colored shalwars and a golden kaftan, and his right hand rests on the bejeweled hilt of his kilij. Crowned by his snow-white turban, his face is so stormy that the egret feather caught in his egg-sized emerald flutters with fear.

Mehmet stares at the intricate details of the cinnamon-colored floor tiles and bites his tongue, but he knows he can't hold it much longer.

"You'll leave today," Father says. "Your mother will go with you. So will your tutors, Molla Gürani and Akşemseddin.

"You will apply yourself to learning the things that matter. You'll learn how to rule. You'll learn the law, governance, strategy, history, and languages. Above all, you will learn Allah's word. Every day, you'll study the Holy Quran. For that, you'll set aside calligraphy, plants, and hawking. There may be time for those after you've learned everything else. Or not. For now, your job is to learn how to lead."

Mehmet knows he shouldn't speak, but he can't keep it in anymore. "But why? Why do I have to learn all this?"

"So you can be the sultan someday. A good sultan. To lead the Ottoman Empire to higher glory, if that's Allah's wish. To conquer the world in his name, if He wishes it."

"But it won't be me! I'm not going to be the next sultan. Aladdin is. He's older."

"He should be, if Allah wishes it. Aladdin is not only older, but he's also better in every way. Aladdin is a better warrior, a more faithful

Muslim, and a better son. He knows the value of education and the importance of respecting his father. You don't. You spoke without permission. Again. You confront me, question me, and anger me. You made me lose my contemplative mood. Again."

The sultan's voice rises to a roar.

The parrot goes quiet. The two slaves fanning the sultan with peacock feathers fall face-down to the ground. Even the susurrant fountains fall silent.

Mehmet breaks into a cold sweat. His blue shalwars and silk chemise cling to his body. Fear sweat, smelling feral, drips off his chin onto the red tiles.

He crunches deeper and touches his forehead to the floor, wondering if his father has signaled the guards. They only need three steps to cut his throat with their curved kilijes. And he won't be the first. Others, foolish enough to anger the sultan, left the Imperial Room feet first. That's why the floor tiles are rust-colored, the color of dry blood. They're easier to clean.

"Do you understand me?"

"Yes, Father."

"Will you do as I said?"

"Yes, Father."

"I'll let it go this time. You're still young and inexperienced. But you'd better learn fast if you want to stay alive."

"Yes, Father."

"Aladdin will be the next sultan if Allah wants it. He surely deserves it. But Allah's ways are not for men to understand. I was just one of my father's five sons, and not the eldest. Still, Allah chose me out of them all to become sultan and build the Ottoman Empire into what it is today. If you prepare and learn, he may choose you. Or he may not."

"Yes, Father."

"As the governor of Manisa, you will learn to rule your people. You'll take care of their needs, lead them right, and give them justice. Your job is to make sure they live to please Allah, and they make our country proud. You too. Your mother will help you. So will your tutors."

"Yes, Father."

"Good. Go now."

Mehmet bows once more. He takes one last glance to the sarayi, the place he was born, knowing he'll never see it again unless he becomes sultan. The sarayi is the home of the sultan and his women. The sultan is the only man who can step on these tiles and rejoice in the blue air and the freshness of the fountains. He, and his women and children.

Now that Mehmet is almost twelve and therefore no longer a child, he has to go.

Two eunuchs flank him. The one with deep mahogany colored skin must be a Nubian. The other one's a Serb, by his crooked nose and hazel eyes. They wear the eunuchs' uniform — blue shalwars and kaftans — and stony expressions. Their eyes are glued to Mehmet and their right hands to their kilijes, just in case he thinks about attacking his father. But Mehmet has never thought about attacking his father.

Never before.

CHAPTER 10

LEAVING EDIRNE

Mehmet sighs and stops in the gilded doorway that's wide enough for a chariot and tall enough for five of him standing on each other's shoulders. He lets his eyes linger over the only home he's ever known, trying to carve it in his heart forever. His eyes feast over the green hunting grounds around the palace that last as far as the eye can see. He rode his horse over every inch of them with his hawk, looking for deer, boar, and hare. He sated his hunger with the plump, sweet figs he picked fresh from the trees, quenched his thirst with the cold water he drank straight from the streams, and slept in the woods, breathing in the scent of cedar and dreaming about his future. This has always been his home.

No more. He's going far, far away. Beyond the sleepy Tunca River, beyond the vast green fields hugging its edges, and beyond the tidy villages past them. He's going beyond any place he's ever known.

His new governorship is Manisa, all the way in Anatolia, by the shore of the Aegean Sea, and it's a long trip. The moon will shrink, then grow, then shrink again before they get there. IF they get there, Allah willing.

He chokes a sob and kneels to kiss the doorstep.

"I'll be back," he whispers to it lovingly, then takes the wide stone steps to the courtyard where his caravan awaits.

Rüzgar, his beloved black stallion whose name means wind, is dancing on his feet. He's just four years old, and Mehmet has looked after him since the day he was foaled.

Rüzgar catches his scent. He neighs, and rises on his hind hooves, dancing with impatience. Amil, Mehmet's old servant, has to hold on to him with all his strength.

Mehmet smiles. He pats the horse's shoulder, hugs his neck and whispers in his ear, telling him to wait, then walks to the ornate carriage in the middle of the procession. The eunuchs guarding it move aside.

Mehmet lifts the heavy velvet curtain.

His mother, Hüma Hatun, sits in the back. She's all dressed in black, but her pale face is so white it glows, and her red hair seems on fire. She's straight and slim, so she's got plenty of room on her wide seat, but the three women squeezed together in front are too crowded to scratch.

"Mother."

She smiles. Her dozen gold bracelets chime like bells when she touches Mehmet's cheek with a soft white hand smelling like precious rose oil. The green emerald ring Father gave her on the day of Mehmet's birth steals the light.

"I'm so glad to see you. I was worried."

"Why?"

"That you may confront your father. That you may anger him."

Mehmet shrugs. "I'm here."

"Praise Allah."

Her soft voice has almost lost its accent, now that she's been at the Ottoman court for fifteen years. She's nearing thirty, but her skin is still smooth and snow-white, and her hair flame-red, like Mehmet's. Her green eyes smile as they take him in.

"I know you're mad, Mehmet, but you shouldn't be. It's all for the best. You're almost twelve and a şehzade. You'll be a grown man soon, so it's high time for you to spread your wings and learn to govern. We're so lucky that your father is sending you to Manisa, the birthplace of your forefather Murad I, the blessed one who conquered Adrianople from the infidels and made it into Edirne, the Ottoman Empire's capital. That's a great omen, and Manisa is a great place to learn to be the sultan."

"I won't be the sultan. Aladdin will."

Mother smiles. "If Allah wants it. Or maybe not. Allah's ways are complicated and hard to understand. And He sometimes needs a little help. You take care of your training, and I'll take care of the rest."

Mehmet glances at Mother's three women. Their eyes are shut and they're barely breathing, acting like they're asleep, but Mehmet knows better. Here at the sultan's court, everybody is someone's spy, whether the sultan's, the grand vizier's, or one of the other consorts. Every word can mean great danger, should it fall on the wrong ears. Mehmet points his chin to the women and frowns to warn Mother, but she laughs.

"Don't worry about them. I don't need anybody's spies; that's why I only took these three. I know they're mine. The other ones, I'm not so sure."

"So you're saying that..."

Mother shakes her head.

"Me? I'm not saying anything. But I've been told that Aladdin's health is not as good as it used to be. I don't know if that's because of his new wife, or maybe the Bursa air doesn't agree with him. Either way, his new doctor is the friend of a friend of mine. He's sure to help him feel heavenly soon."

Mehmet's jaw falls. "But..."

"Don't you worry. You just take care of yourself, my son. Bad things can happen to good people if they aren't careful. Halime Hatice Hatun, Aladdin's mother, is just as devoted to her son as I am to you. So be careful. Don't eat or drink anything before having your people taste it. Unless you must, don't tell anyone but me where you're going and when. And, most importantly, don't trust anyone but me."

Mehmet nods. "Yes, Mother."

"You're my only son, and I love you dearly. When you become sultan, I'll become validé, and I'll be the most powerful woman in the world. It sure beats being Stella, the Rumelian slave your father's men bought fifteen years ago. They bought me for the price of two oxen and ten sheep, one blind, two with lamb. That's what I was worth to my father, may Allah curse his greedy soul. I hope the old bastard's still alive, because I can't wait to get my revenge someday. But first, you need to become sultan. Let's go."

Mehmet kisses her cheek and lets the curtain fall over the window. They'll be traveling for weeks and months before reaching Manisa, and the women will be closed in their cart all this time. *They won't see the sun for days,* Mehmet thinks, and feels sorry for them. But then Rüzgar neighs with impatience, and he forgets. That horse always makes him smile.

Mehmet jumps in the saddle and hugs the strong black neck. He loves the fire-breathing stallion almost as much as he loves the freedom that riding him brings him. He never feels stronger or more free than when he has a worthy horse between his knees, and there's none worthier than Rüzgar.

Time to go.

He gives the signal and darts ahead. His white-turbaned tutors spur their horses and follow, their rich beards fluttering in the wind. Behind them, the orderly formation of sipahis armed to the teeth spur their proud horses, followed by the blue-clad eunuchs guarding the cart.

When Mehmet glances back, the carriage has fallen behind, and it's enveloped in so much dust it's hard to see. For a moment, Mehmet feels sorry for Mother who has to travel in the dark cart with the women, breathing everyone's dust, while he dances on Rüzgar, spearheading the caravan.

He shrugs. Oh well. That's too bad, but she's only a woman. What can she expect?

CHAPTER II

SINK OR SWIM

BÂLEA LAKE, TRANSYLVANIA

It took the heavy oxen cart hours and hours to crawl up the steep cold mountain. Not to the top, of course — nobody but the Carpathian black goats with their hooked horns or the golden eagles make it that far. But to the end of the dirt road, where the steep road turns into a narrow, twisted footpath that sneaks its way through the forest.

Up here, old pines, shivery spruce, and solemn dark cedars conspire to soften your steps, filter the sunlight and imbue the thin air with the churchy scent of incense. The woods are so quiet you'd think there's no life in them, but Ana knows better. These forests are home to plenty of busy woodpeckers, hopping rabbits, crafty badgers, and majestic deer crowned with antlers so massive that the mighty King of Hungary himself comes here to hunt. The deep shadows hide shrewd red foxes, packs of howling grey wolves and grumpy brown bears that look fat and lazy unless you happen upon them when they're hungry.

Ana hugs herself to curb the wind's chill and breathes in the resin scent that reminds her of Father. She watches the dust cloud that's been following them catch up and turn into the carriage bringing the burgomaster and the doctor.

The two men wrap their fur-trimmed cloaks around themselves and look at the kids.

"From here, we go on foot," the burgomaster says.

The boys' faces darken. It's cold and late, and they're hungry. A chunky boy spits the stick he's been chewing. "You said swim, not walk."

The burgomaster shrugs. "Go wait in the cart, then. You're going home."

The others bite their tongues and head up towards the lake. It's not a short walk, and by the time they catch their first glance of the magic blue water, the shadows lengthened, and the fall sun lost most of its power.

Ana's eyes meet the lake and something stirs inside her. The shimmering water sheltered inside an old crater shaded by the Carpathians' jagged peaks is bluer than anything that Ana has ever seen. The lake is deep and dark, and the milky mist that raises above it shrouds it in mystery and silence. The air is thin and it smells like incense, just like it did the last time she was here, three summers ago.

"See that lake? Nobody has ever seen its bottom," Father said.

"Maybe it doesn't have one," Ana answered.

Father laughed. "How did you know?"

Then, Ana thought he was joking, but now she's not so sure. The water's still, but its surface glitters in the setting sun like it's bewitched. Ana's eyes rest on the mesmerizing shimmer, and out of nowhere, a heaviness falls upon her heart like a bad omen. She shudders and tells herself that it's the cold, but she knows better. That shroud around her heart is the lake warning her to stay away.

Ana's soul grows cold. But she won't let that stop her. She's here to swim, and swim she will, even if it kills her. Anything is better than going back home. She cups her hands around her silver cross that glows red and thinks of Father, and feels the omen slowly fade.

The light clean air is a joy to breathe. The forest's scent fills her lungs, washing away the foulness of the Kronstadt fortress that reeks of refuse, dung, and dirt, and the lake's silence cradles her like a hug. She feels Father's soul watching over her, and her heart overflows with tenderness and sorrow. "You can do anything you set your mind to," Father said. God willing, she'll make him proud. Or die trying.

She follows the others to the tall cliff overlooking the water the burgomaster stands on. There are only five of them left, and Ana is the littlest and the only girl. Her new friend Ion, who's half a head taller than she is, comes next. The other three are all bigger. The boy Ana nicknamed Raven is the largest one. He's dark and unsmiling, with raven-black matted hair and burning eyes darker than a moonless night. He leans towards her and scrunches his nose like she stinks. "What are YOU doing here?"

Ana shrugs and looks away.

"You think you're going to win? You?"

The boy snickers, and his two buddies laugh with him.

Ion steps between them. He touches her shoulder with a hand so hot that it burns Ana's skin. She knows that he's trying to protect her, but he needn't bother. After growing up with Nicolae, Ana knows better than to answer a bully. She shakes him away and takes a deep breath, absorbing the magic of the forest and holding on to her memories.

The dusk is coming fast and the air grows cold.

"Are you ready?" the burgomaster asks.

"Yes," Raven says.

The burgomaster digs in the deep pouches of his fur-trimmed cloak and takes out three reeds, about one foot long, weighted with a metal ring to one side.

"I'll throw them in the lake. They won't sink all the way, so you get a chance to retrieve them. Whoever gets them stays. Whoever comes back empty-handed goes home. Whoever doesn't come back..." He shrugs. "God's wish. One more secret for this lake to keep. Old wives say that Lake Bâlea's fish are the largest in the country, since they fed on the thousands of Hungarians Sultan Murad II and his worthless ally, the two-faced Vlad Dracul, slaughtered three years ago when they invaded Transylvania. They took thirty thousand captives and sold them into slavery, so those who fed the fish were the lucky ones. But enough about that. Let's see how lucky you all are. Ready?"

He looks them in the eye like he wants to find something inside them. One after the other, they look down. All but Ana.

She has nothing to hide, and she doesn't much care if she never comes back. Popa Anghel, the black-clad priest in her village, said that all good people raise up to Heaven to be with Jesus when they die. And wherever He is, it's warm, and there's no pain and no hunger. Father was such a good man that he's got to be there. Ana can't wait to be with him again.

"Go!"

CHAPTER 12

ANA'S DIVE

Like a pack of long-legged waterbirds, the three sticks fly together in a lazy arch until the earth pulls them down and they vanish into the dark water.

The kids hold their breath to watch the liquid darkness swallow them, then jump.

Raven goes first. His two friends follow heartbeats later.

Ion's warm hand touches Ana's shoulder.

"You don't have to do this, you know. The Saxons won't hurt you. They'll just send you back home."

Ana shakes her head. She'd rather drown than go home.

She touches her cross. It's cold, and the stone glows green. She takes a diving breath — deep, but not too deep, just like Father taught her. Then she jumps.

She soars like a heron and dives through the thin air, cherishing the glory of her flight until her body pierces the water's surface like a blade. A heartbeat later, the freezing water closes around her, so cold it makes her gasp.

But Ana knows better. She holds her breath as she cuts though the water like a knife, letting her speed carry her deeper and deeper, all the way down. Her eyes are wide open in the midnight blue, looking for the ringed sticks as she wills her body towards the bottom. This is her best chance to go deep, since her speed helps her down. Soon enough, the air trapped inside her will lift her up, and she won't get that deep again.

The water is dark blue and clear, just like Mary's robe on the stained-glass window at the church, which is made of shards of blue glass that barely let through a hint of light.

Ana is no longer cold as she cuts the water, pulling herself forward. But her breath wants out.

She tells it to wait.

She swims and swims, pushing the water behind her with her arms and slapping it back with her feet as her wide-open eyes search for the reeds. But there's nothing. No sticks, no bottom, no fish. Nothing but the celestial blue light she's flowing through.

And her fierce thirst for air.

She lets out a bit of air to keep her chest from bursting and pushes lower and lower.

It's dark down here, and hard to see, and cold.

Her hand touches something.

She grabs it, choking with hope. But it's not a stick, it's just seaweed, telling her she's close to the bottom.

Good. I can't stay any longer. I need air.

It takes all she's got to stop herself from taking a breath right here, on the bottom of the lake. She lets out more air and allows her body to carry her up. The water grows lighter and lighter as she nears the surface until it's bright blue, like the sky. She can't hold her breath anymore; she really can't. This is it.

She reaches the surface just as something touches her hand.

CHAPTER 13

AN UNLIKELY WINNER

Ana grabs it and goes up for air. She makes it just before her tortured lungs explode. She opens her mouth to suck in a gulp of fresh air, then another, holding the stick in her hand and beating the water with her feet to keep afloat.

When she's finally sated with air, she looks around. The haunting full moon poured quicksilver over the dark waters, softening the darkness with its shimmer. Towards the other end of the lake, the glimmering water ripples around three dark spots. Must be the other kids. But why three? Why not four? And which three?

Ana swims quietly to the shore, clutching her stick. She looks around just in case. For what? She's not sure. Another stick? Another kid?

She's almost ashore when her right foot touches something. She curls and grabs it.

It's another reed. Ana got two out of three. Now what?

She could give them both to the burgomaster to better her chances. She can see him standing with the doctor on the lone cliff bathed by the moonlight up above. They're alone, so the other kids must still be out there, looking. Nobody else will have two sticks, so they'll send home three more kids. There'll be only one left. Maybe Ion.

But maybe not.

Ana walks up on the rocky shore into the deep shade of the trees. She sits, hugging her knees, and watches the water. The other kids can’t see her, but she can see them just fine. They're still swimming, but she can't tell who's who.

She's still shivering and waiting when a terrible howl coming from the lake splits the night. It's a gut-wrenching, soul-crushing cry of sorrow that makes her skin crawl and freezes her breath in her chest.

The wind stops and the birds go silent. The silence is so deep it hurts.

Ana shivers. She melts into the tree trunk she leans against and hugs herself tighter. Her teeth chatter like hail, so she bites her lips to stop them as her worried eyes glide over the lake that mirrors the moon to count heads. There are two left. Two are missing. Did they drown?

Her heart beats like a drum as she sneaks closer to the water’s edge and holds her breath to listen.

But why should she care? They have their fate; she has hers.

But Ion gave her his food. And he smiled.

So what? He's a rival. She needs to win.

But he's a friend. The first friend she's had in forever. She can't lose him already.

But what can she do?

She sighs and sits to wait.

It takes forever.

The moon starts its descent, then the black sky fades to purple, then blushes to pink, and Ana gets restless. She's wasting her chance to be the first one back, and that matters. They don't really want her, since she’s a girl. She must be way better than the boys to make it through.

But she has two sticks. Nobody else will have two.

Still, what is she waiting for? She doesn't know.

Sure she does. She's waiting for Ion to come back.

But what if he doesn't? What if he's on the bottom of the lake? What if he's last?

The moon fades. As the first sunrays peek over the mountains, the water churns to her left. A dark head breaks the water, and a boy steps ashore. Is it Ion? Does he have a stick?

She holds her breath, waiting for him to step into the light. Dark face. Darker hair.

It's Raven with a stick. Ana's heart sinks.

She watches him climb the hill and hand his stick to the burgomaster. The doctor wraps him in blankets and hands him a skin flask, and Ana sighs. He's warm and drinking while she's shivering and hungry, though she has two sticks.

And still she waits. And waits.

Two more shadows come out. Empty-handed, of course. And none of them is Ion.

She waits some more, but nothing happens. He must have drowned.

Her heart aching, Ana gets up to join the others.

The water churns again. A body crawls out of the water.

Ana grabs the back of his shirt to pull him out. He's godawful heavy, and strangely hot for someone who's been swimming freezing water for hours.

He lies on his stomach, panting, right where she dropped him. She rolls him on his back. "Ion."

He opens his eyes, and they're full of darkness. Blood spurts from a gash on his head, so Ana picks a handful of dry leaves and sticks them to the wound.

"Hold here."

She rips off the bottom of his shirt, ties it around the wound and knots it twice, like Father taught her, to stop the bleeding. Some ash would be good to pour in the wound, or maybe forest honey, but she has neither.

"What happened?"

"Someone hit me in the head and took my stick. I'm going home."

"Not yet," Ana says, handing him one of her sticks. "Take this."

Ion's eyes widen. "And you?"

"I have another. I'll go join the others. Come up as soon as you're ready."

She heads up the steep slope, tired and frozen and shaking like a leaf. She clenches her jaw to stop herself from biting her tongue and hands her stick to the burgomaster. He smiles.

The boys don't.

The doctor wraps her in blankets and hands her a leather flask. She drinks deeply and chokes. It's not water. Not even milk. It's sweet and sour and harsh.

The boys laugh.

"Drink it. It will warm you up," the doctor says.

"What is it?"

"Wine."

That's what the grown-ups drink at weddings and funerals. Not the kids, though they get a taste of it for communion at Christmas and Easter. Popa Anghel would give her a sip from his precious silver cup, the one the whole village drank from. He said it was the blood of Jesus Christ but Ana knows better. She'd seen them make it out of grapes. It's thick and red, so it looks like blood, but it doesn't taste the same. Ana knows how blood tastes, since she gets to taste it whenever Mother slaps her.

The wine is cold, but drinking it warms her inside, like they said. She takes another sip, then sits to wait with the others.

CHAPTER 14

AN UGLY FIGHT

The ghostlike moon fades to nothing as a sun without warmth climbs higher and higher in the sky, and they're still waiting. The boys snore, wrapped in their blankets, and Ana wonders what can take Ion so long.

Finally, the burgomaster shrugs. "I guess that's it. The other one didn't make it," he tells the doctor in Saxon.

"We may as well go then, or they'll freeze to death up here."

Ana would like to stop them, but she can't. She doesn't want them to know she speaks Saxon. Not many Romanians do, but she learned it from Frieda, her friend across the street. When Father was still alive and she had time to play, they used to play together every day. Ana told Father that she was learning Saxon, but he told her not to tell anyone.

"Don't brag," he said. "You won't make any friends, and you'll waste your weapon."

"What weapon?"

"Your knowledge. That's your weapon. Everything you know: Hungarian, Saxon, the letters, counting, and everything else I taught you. Don't tell anyone unless you have a good reason. Everything you know makes you stronger. Doubly so if they don't know it."

"Who's they, Father?"

"The others. Those who aren't your friends."

So Ana keeps quiet as they get ready to go. She touches her cross, and it glows blue. She glances back to the lake.

Raven laughs. "Waiting for your friend, are you? Don't bother. He's gone."

Ana can't keep quiet anymore.

"You! You hurt him."

"Prove it."

"You..."

The blow comes out of nowhere. Raven falls back. A fountain of blood spurts from his long nose that now points left.

Ion glares at him and spits on the ground. He drops the rock from his fist and hands the last stick to the burgomaster.

The burgomaster's narrow mouth tightens further.

"You damaged him," he says. "Look at that nose."

"He damaged me," Ion says, pointing to the bleeding cut on his forehead. "I swear he tried to kill me."

The burgomaster shakes his head and turns to the doctor. "Can you fix them?"

The doctor shrugs. He takes out a wine flask and hands it to Ion. "Drink this." He throws a blanket over him and turns to Ana. "You hold him. Make sure he gets warm."

He turns to Raven who's sitting on the ground holding his nose.

"You. Lie down."

He finds a branch as thick as his thumb and sticks it into Raven's mouth. "Bite it. Hard."

He turns to Raven's friends. "You. Hold his arms above his head. You. Hold his legs against the ground. Sit on his knees and don't let him move, no matter what."

He pulls on his leather gloves, kneels by Raven's head, and glances at the boys. "Ready?"

They nod, too frightened to speak.

The doctor grabs Raven's chin in his left hand. He places the heel of his right hand on his nose and puts his whole weight in it to push it back into its place.

Bones cracks. Blood spurts. Raven screams.

Ana’s stomach climbs to her throat, filling her mouth with bile. She's heard that raw scream before. That's how pigs scream when they get slaughtered for Christmas.

Blood gushes everywhere, spurting them all. The boys turn to retch, though they have nothing to throw up but wine.

"There now," the doctor says. He takes off his gloves and, with gentle fingers, he checks that Raven's nose is back in the center of his face, where it belongs. He picks a stick thinner than Ana's pinky and breaks it into two, then wraps the two halves in white cloth and soaks them into wine. He turns back to the boys.

"Hold him again. And you, bite, as I told you. Otherwise, you'll bite your tongue or break your teeth.”

With a swift move, he pushes the wine-soaked sticks deep into Raven's nose as far as they go. A stream of blood pours out of Raven's mouth along with a flood of curses and screams. He struggles to break free, but the two boys hold him down.

"Hold on to him until he stops struggling. Those sticks will help stop the bleeding. If he pulls them out, we’ll have to do it again."

He leaves them be and turns to Ion. He takes off Ana’s makeshift bandage, and examines the wound. "I need more wine."

The burgomaster hands him another flask.

The doctor pours wine over the wound to wash it, scrapes out the leaves and the dirt, then rinses it again.

“That’s odd,” he mumbles in Saxon.

“What is?” the burgomaster asks.

“The wound. It’s a deep puncture, like a bite, but it’s already healing. I’ve never seen one heal so fast.”

He rummages inside his soft leather bag for another white cloth and a small flask, then wipes the wound dry and pours in it something thick and yellow.

"It's honey,” he tells Ion. “It will help with healing, but it will also entice the flies. But then, so does the blood."

He bandages the wound with the white cloth and knots it twice. “God willing, the pressure will stop the bleeding. That's it for now. I'll recheck them when we get back, but they should be OK."

"Thank you," the burgomaster says. "I very much appreciate it."

"You should. I only did it for you. Bone setting is a bloody barber's job, not worthy of a doctor."

The burgomaster changes to Saxon. "You did it for the money, not for me. We pay you well."

"That's true. But why on earth should you care about that kid's nose? It won't stop him from snooping or fighting or doing whatever else you need him to. It will just make him snore. So unless you plan to share his bed..."

The burgomaster laughs. "Not me, thanks. I need them for the Ottomans. They only take the best of the best of the boys. They have to be perfect. Healthy, good-looking, smart."

"But..." The doctor glances at Ana.

"Don't you worry. She's perfect for what I need her for."

Ana shivers.

CHAPTER 15

YOU'RE ALI

It's a long, cold walk back down to the ox cart. By the time they get there, the sun is already on its way down. Ana is tired and frozen, but Ion and Raven are worse.

They find the carriage where they left it. Karl, the burgomaster's friend, rubs his eyes as he comes to meet them.

"Which ones are left?"

"These two. And the girl."

"Those two and the girl? Really? Are you crazy?"

Karl stares at Raven and gasps. The boy's nose is swollen and purple like a ripe eggplant. His bruised eyes have turned into slits, and the two bloody sticks sticking out of his nose like makeshift tusks make him look like a sick boar.

Ion, next to him, is as pale as a corn husk and just as shaky, and the blood-soaked bandage around his forehead is black with flies.

"What on earth did you do to them? Nobody in their right mind will want them now, least of all the Ottomans!"

"I did nothing. They did it to each other. But they're alive, and they made it," the burgomaster says.

Karl sighs. "I always thought that your plan was crazy, but this? You've clearly lost it."

"Nah. You'll see. These kids are tough, smart, and ruthless. They have what it takes, and they'll learn the rest."

"You plan to keep and train all three?"

"Of course."

"But why? We only need one. Training three will be three times more expensive."

"That's OK. The guilds have deep coffers."

"Not bottomless. Why keep three when you only need one?"

"If there's three of them, they'll be more competitive. They'll work harder, learn better, and challenge each other — look at them, they already have. They'll be better off in the end. And I wouldn't even know which one to keep."

"Try them again, then. Give them another task."

"Karl, things happen. People disappear. People fail. People die. How would you like to find yourself empty-handed after spending all the gold and time we need to train them? What if you choose one and he breaks his neck when he falls off a horse, or dies from the Black Death, or changes his mind and goes home? What will we do? Having three is insurance. If one fails, if two die, you still have one left. It's worth it to me. And training three is hardly more expensive than training one. The only thing to triple is the food. The rest is all the same."

"The hell it is. Three horses. Three sets of armor. Three shields. Three swords. Three of whatever you're going to throw their way."

"But only one man to teach all three and the same guards. And the same amount of time."

The fat man shakes his head. "You're nuts. And you shouldn't have started by damaging them. They look half-dead already."

"They're tough, and they'll recover. A little rest and some good food, and they'll be stronger than ever. Won't you, boys?" he asks them in Romanian.

"Won't what?" Raven asks.

"Won't you boys feel better after you get something warm in your belly?"

"Yes," Raven says. Ion nods, too weak to speak.

"How about you?" the burgomaster asks Ana.

"I'm not a boy," Ana says.

The burgomaster laughs. "Oh, but you are, my dear. From now on, you'll be one of the boys. You'll watch them, and you'll learn. You'll start to talk, sit, scratch, and behave like a boy in every respect. You'll be a boy starting today."

"I'm Ana."

"No longer. From now on, you're Ali."

CHAPTER 16

THE POSSE

BERZUNŢI, MOLDOVA, 1443

A hundred miles northeast of the Kronstadt fortress, just beyond the white peaks of the Eastern Carpathians that separate Transylvania from Moldova, the grassy meadows shelter more sheep than the scattered villages shelter people. The rolling hills of Moldova belong to the shepherds, their flocks, and their dogs. Few strangers ever wander so far from everything that matters. But then Ștefan isn't quite a stranger.

He sits on the three-legged milking stool by the door to tie his opinci, then wraps himself in the long shaggy sheepskin mantle he used as night cover and pushes the hut door open. Old Vasile is still snoring gently between his sheep skins, so Ștefan walks out quietly to check on the sheep as the old rooster starts clearing his throat.

It's not yet morning, but the night's black, made darker by the glimmer of a million stars, has thinned into gray. Up west, the jagged mountains are still raven black, but down the hills to the right, the sky blushed into a timid pink.

The dogs rush to greet him: Lucky, the sheepdog, is tall and white, other than the striking black target around his blue left eye. Old Rina is low to the ground and almost black but for her white collar and the graying around her long sharp muzzle. They smile like dogs do, smacking their heavy tails against the frosty grass, then stretch and head to their bowls. The foot-long wooden sticks hanging from their collars to stop the wolves from ripping open their throats clang against the empty bowls like semantrons.

Ștefan scratches them behind their ears and feeds them the glop he boiled for them last night. He made it with chicken bones and the whey left from cheese-making and thickened it with stale bread. This is their one meal of the day, since they don't get fed in the evening. "Fed dogs sleep. Hungry dogs stay awake to guard the sheep and the men," Vasile said. And he knows.

Ștefan leans over the water pail. A thin layer of ice sits on top, so he breaks it with the handle of the ax, then cups his hands to splash his face. The water, colder than water ought to be, freezes his fingers and shocks him awake. Fall is coming, he muses, looking at the white frost that covers the grass as far as the eye can see.

He dries his face and hands on the scarf Lena made for him. It's sturdy white linen, embroidered with a bowl of red apples and yellow pears, and it bears his initials, SM, from Ștefan Muşat, curling around each other like a pair of purple snakes. But for his father's dagger and his grandfather's ring, that scarf is the one thing he brought up the mountain when he came to hide from the fray. He hangs it around his neck to let it dry, then rests his eyes on the fog-shrouded valley.

Something's moving. It's a rider. He's too far away to be sure, but he looks like a small man on a brown horse eating up the distance. Ștefan shivers. Not from the cold, but from the foreboding. He looks for more riders, but can't see any.

They can't be after me. If they were, they'd be a whole posse. It's got to be a messenger, he thinks, but that doesn't give him any joy. The messenger, if that's what he is, is killing that horse to come faster, so he's bringing bad news. He wouldn't burn up a horse for good news.

Ștefan opens the door to the hut. "Someone's coming."

Vasile stands like he's never slept. He wraps his sheepskin mantle around himself, grabs his short ax and steps outside. "Get ready," he says, his voice rusty with disuse.

Ștefan grabs the bag with the handful of coins hidden inside his hay bed. He fills a leather flask with water, then cuts two thick slices from yesterday's bread. He stuffs a chunk of cheese between them, ties them into a cloth, and drops them in his brown shoulder bag with his dagger.

He grabs his tall shearling hat and plops it on his head. It's too big, so it falls over his ears, down to his eyebrows. But it will keep him warm.

By the time he steps out again, the rider's close enough to recognize. It's Lena, riding like a man on old Ilie, the horse they both grew up with. Ilie's breath surrounds them like a cloud, and his round eyes are wide and scared. Lena's blue eyes sparkle against her flushed cheeks, and her thick braid slaps her back like a yellow whip. She's grown in the months he hasn't seen her. She's almost a woman, he ponders, his eyes glued to the budding breasts that rise and fall with the gallop.

She jumps to the ground.

"They're coming. The posse came to the village yesterday. They went from house to house, asking about you. Last night I saw them taking the road up the mountains, so I took the shortcut. They'll be here before sundown."

"Who's they?" Vasile asks.

"The men."

"Whose men?"

Lena shrugs. "The voivode's men, whether it's Ilias or one of his brothers. I don't know which and I didn't stop to ask. The one thing I know is they weren't Bogdan's. They were not our friends."

"What flags did they carry?"

"The gold and blue, like they all do. But what does that matter? Either way, they're after Ștefan."

She stomps her feet impatiently, and old Vasile stares at his daughter as if he wonders how could this comet of a girl come out of her meek mother and a soft-spoken man like him. *I wonder, too*, Ștefan thinks, but there's no time for that. Not now.

"I need to go."

"Go where?"

"I'll go to Wallachia, to the New Royal Court. Doamna Cneajna, the voivode's wife, is Father's sister. She'll take me in."

"How will you get there?"

"I'll head south, then turn west after I clear the mountains."

Vasile shakes his head. "That will take days, maybe weeks. And winter is coming."

"I don't have a choice. If they catch me, they'll kill me."

"You could hide in the woods. They'll look around and leave. You can come back in a day or two."

Lena shakes her head. "They brought dogs, and they took Ștefan's boots and chemise when they came to the house. They'll find him by the scent."

That settles it.

Ștefan hugs Vasile and his unshed tears choke him. Will they kill the old man? They'll want to know where Ștefan went. They'll ask Vasile, and if they don't like his answers, they'll ask again. Louder.

"Why don't you leave too? They'll come and go. You can come back in a few days," he says.

Vasile shrugs. "And the sheep?"

"The dogs will take care of them for a day or two."

"Not against people with swords and bows."

Lena jumps back on old Ilie.

"Let's go."

"Where are you going?" Ștefan asks.

"I'm taking you south. Let's go."

Ștefan stares at her. What a girl. She's no older than him, but she's full of fire. She's been his best friend from birth, since she's his milk sister. They learned to walk and talk together, so she's closer to him than his blood brothers. When Bogdan, his father, threw his hat in the ring and decided to fight his half-brothers for Grandfather's throne, he sent Ștefan to stay with Lena's family, thinking he'd be safe. But now that they found his track, he needs to get moving if he wants to stay alive.

Vasile sighs. "Take the shortcut through the river. The water's low enough to cross now, and it will make it harder for the dogs to follow your scent. When you get to the river, don't cross. Walk down through it a mile or so to make them lose your trail. And take care of Ilie. He's not young anymore, and he's already tired. A dead horse will do you no good."

"Yes, Father."

Ștefan jumps on the horse behind her and grabs the reins. Her blue eyes scorch him.

"What do you think you're doing?"

Ștefan drops the reins and holds on to her waist. Under his left hand, her heart drums like crazy, just like his.

CHAPTER 17

ON THE RUN

The sun's halfway down by the time they reach the river. They stop to splash their faces and drink enough to soften their dry throats, then Ștefan leads the horse downstream, walking through knee-deep ice-cold water. Lena follows, but it's hard going. The rocks are slick with moss, and the bottom is an entangled trap of hidden branches and treacherous patches of slippery mud.

Lena sighs. "I'll miss you."

"I'll miss you, too."

"Will you come back?"

Ștefan stops to stare at her. "Of course. This is my country. This is my home. Where else could I go?"

She glances up at him through long, dark lashes.

"Will you come back to... us?"

Ștefan puts his arm around her shoulders. "Lena, you are..."

A horn splinters the silence, followed by the cries of the dogs. Their followers are close, much closer than they ought to be. They're closing in, but they sound like they're still on the other side of the river.

They gasp and rush downstream as fast as the perilous river bottom allows. Ștefan grabs Lena's hand to help steady her, and holds Ilie's reins with the other.

Massive old trees lean towards each other across the stream like they're trying to hug, throwing dark shadows that blind their eyes burned by the sun. They walk and walk through the water as the sun goes down and the shadows grow longer.

Ștefan's lungs crave air. His legs, shaky with exhaustion, slow him down to a crawl. Lena is even slower. *Those damn dogs will rip us apart if they find us, like they do with foxes,* Ștefan thinks, wishing he'd left Lena behind with her father. Then he shrugs. *Who knows if she'd be safer there? It's too late, anyhow. We are where we are.*

Lena's face is haggard with fatigue, and she drags her feet like she's walking through molasses. Ștefan pulls her forward, but she stumbles and falls. The swift current drags her downriver, but her foot gets trapped in a hidden branch and holds her captive. Under the two inches of rushing water covering her face, her blue eyes stay glued to Ștefan's.

He struggles to break her free, but he can't. He lets go of the horse and lifts her head above the water to let her breathe, then tries to pull her back to her feet, but the hidden branches hold her down. He lets go of her head and tries to free her foot, but his hands are clumsy with cold and shaky with fear.

Lena grabs onto his shirt and twists like an eel towards her trapped foot.

"Knife," she says.

He remembers his dagger. His frozen fingers search inside his bag. He grabs it and tries to cut the branch, but their struggle turned the water into mud, and he can't see a thing.

"Give it to me."

Her cold fingers grab his father's Venetian dagger. She slips its double-edged blade along her shin. One sharp move, and her foot is free. So is she, but the quick waters pull her away before she can regain her footing and drag her downstream.

"Lena!"

Ștefan runs after her, but the current is too fast. They're just above the Maiden's Falls, where the wide lazy river narrows to a thin plume of water that falls twenty feet to crash over the boulders below, and Ștefan's heart freezes. *No way can I catch her before the falls,* he thinks.

The water's twists and turns roll Lena, throwing her into a boulder. She tries to hold on but she can't. She drifts towards the opposite bank, and grabs onto a pussy-willow branch hanging low over the water. The branch straightens and creaks, but it holds.

Ștefan jumps after Lena. He grabs her braid just as the branch breaks and she's about to slip into the roaring falls. He plants his feet and pulls her up, holding her tight to his chest. Her face ashen, she leans against him, breathing hard. "Thank you."

He nods, too weary to speak.

"The knife's gone," she says.

Ștefan sighs. That was their only weapon. It wouldn't do much against a pack of dogs and a posse of soldiers, but having it felt good.

"Ilie?"

They look upriver. Nothing. Downriver, the waterfall's thunder is a death sentence.

"We'll walk," Ștefan says.

Lena shakes her head.

"Not me. Not for a while."

She points at her ankle, and Ștefan sighs again. He helps her limp to the shore, and they stop to listen for the hounds. There's nothing but the roar of the falls.

If we jump in the falls, we may get to the other side alive. Or not. Still better than getting ripped apart by the dogs, Ștefan thinks, helping Lena sit on a fallen trunk.

Something touches his shoulder. He jumps, ready to kill.

It's Ilie.

They hug him. Lena cries. "Thank God, he made it! Now, get on him. Get on him and go."

"I can't."

"Yes, you can. They'll kill you if they catch you."

"I can't leave you here. You take the horse and go."

"And you?"

"I'll hide."

Lena shakes her head and struggles to her feet. She starts taking off her soaked clothes: off comes the shearling vest, then the linen chemise she spent months embroidering and the dark woolen skirts.

Ștefan can't help but stare. He chokes at the sight of her blooming breasts, then catches himself and pretends to be looking for the posse in the bushes.

Now naked, Lena undoes his leather belt and pulls down his heavy woolen pants.

Ștefan gasps. "What on God's earth are you doing?"

"Taking off your clothes. Help me."

"But why?"

"I'll lead them away, so you can hide. The dogs will follow my scent. You'll wear my clothes and hide until they're gone."

"But if they catch you..."

Lena shrugs. "Same if they catch you. Move."

She puts on his pants and his shirt and wraps herself in his heavy sheepskin mantle. She plops his hat on her head and tucks in her braid, then climbs in the saddle and looks at him, her blue eyes smiling.

"Good luck. Make sure you put on the skirts the right way, otherwise nobody will believe you're a girl. And braid your hair."

Ștefan stares at her. His love is too big for his heart.

She takes off just as they hear the dogs cry. They're awfully close.

"Lena!"

She glances back.

"I'll be back."

"You'd better."

She vanishes into the woods. Heartbeats later, the hounds scream as they catch her scent.

CHAPTER 18

PEEING LIKE A BOY

KRONSTADT, TRANSYLVANIA, 1443

A hundred miles southeast of Moldova's green pastures, in the stone-walled Kronstadt Castle, the first rays of sun sneak in through the narrow slits meant for archers, turning the dancing flecks of dust into gold. It's a rare glimmer of beauty here, since the fortress, as grand as it is, is not pretty. It's not even as comfortable as most merchants' homes in the city below. The Kronstadt Castle is just a fortress meant to guard Hungary's borders and prevent any would-be invader from setting foot in Transylvania. Everything about it is practical, sturdy, and cold, from the bare stone floors to the parsimonious windows, which are still too high for Ali to see through, though she's half again bigger than she was when she came.

She glances at the boys. They're still asleep. Ion to her left, nestled in a pile of blankets, his breath slow and even, his golden curls covering his face. Beyond him, the boy she nicknamed Raven. His real name turned out to be Codru, which means Forest. His one thick brow makes him look angry even in his sleep, and he snores like roaring thunder, even though those bloody sticks came out of his nose long ago.

Ali squeezes out of her nest of blankets. She tiptoes to the tall wooden door studded with iron spikes, and knocks gently. Today's guard is Gica, the giant Romanian. Wrapped in his scratched leather armor, he carries a lance that could spear a boar, but his eyes are warm and his smile is gentle as he opens the door to let her out.

"*Buna dimineața*. Good morning."

"*Buna dimineața*, Ali. How are you?"

"Good, thank you. And you?"

He closes the door, and she walks outside to do her business, which is the most challenging task of her day.

Other than that, becoming Ali has been a breeze. She loves the rough woolen breeches that don't confine her like her skirts used to. Dressed in them, she can run, climb and jump without ever worrying that somebody will see her nether parts and laugh at her.

Cutting her hair was another blessing. The same barber who came to check Raven's nose and Ion's wound sat her on a stool, put a wooden bowl on her head, then cut off whatever wasn't covered. Now that she's a boy, she no longer has to braid and cover it like women do. She can just let it fall over her ears and get ravaged by the wind.

The one thing that still gives her trouble is passing water.

"Now that you're a boy, you'll pee like a boy," the burgomaster said, so she's no longer allowed to squat. But sadly, no matter how hard she tries, she always ends up wet and filthy. She tried opening her legs wider, bending backwards and leaning forward, but nothing worked. The one thing she hasn't yet tried is lifting her leg to a bush, like the dogs.

That's why she gets up early. If she's out first, she can deal with her water without having the boys stare at her. Codru laughs and taunts her, but it's Ion who bothers her the most. He looks away, pretending he can't see her struggle, and that embarrasses her even more.

The other thing that gives her trouble is the fighting. No matter how much she eats, the boys are still bigger than her, and their long arms reach further. That's why she's always covered in bruises after they fight with their wooden swords. But she loves archery. The guards made a small bow just for her and they taught her to make her own arrows, so she can practice all she wants once she's done with her other tasks.

She walks behind the guard's post and looks around. There's

nobody watching but the sun that warms the back of her neck like a hug. The birds calling for a partner, the bees looking for the first dandelions, and the wind snaking through the new green leaves — they all enjoy the glorious spring morning and mind their own business.

Ali moves close to the stone wall, like she's seen the boys do, and unties the rope that keeps up her woolen breeches. They drop to her ankles, and she pulls them out of the way of the stream.

She opens her legs and curves her back, pushing her sitting bones forward like she's seen the boys do. She holds her breath and wills out the stream with all her might.

The stream starts bright yellow, steaming in the cold, and hits the stone wall ahead of her. She holds her breath to push it all out, more focused than when she's fighting. This is harder.

The stream stops. Ali pulls up her pants, which, for the first time ever, are almost dry. She ties them around her waist and heads back inside with a big smile on her face.

I did it. I peed like a boy.

CHAPTER 19

NO DINNER FOR YOU!

This morning's first lesson is geography, followed by the Ottoman language. Then comes fighting, followed by lunch, everyone's favorite. Here, they get to eat three times a day. Unless they screw up. Then, they stay hungry.

Ali is lukewarm about the Ottoman language, which sounds like they always have a cold, but she loves geography. Last year, she'd never heard of maps. Now, she can't imagine life without them. She's in awe of every single one of the painted parchments rolled in the map room whose vibrant colors depict the lay of the land. She'd stay in there forever if they'd let her, but they don't. The map room is the most guarded room in the palace. It has no outside doors, and they can't step in without two guards watching their every move. That's why Ali never got to check what's hidden in the locked metal-plated coffers.

More maps, I bet. She yearns to touch the intricate shapes painted in red, black, and gold, but she knows better. The maps are too precious to touch.

"This is a parchment. It's made of sheep skin that got soaked in lime for weeks before being scrubbed clean of flesh and hairs. After that, it was stretched on a frame until the skin fibers aligned to form the smooth sheet you see here. It took the parchment makers many months to make it. After that, the mapmakers spent even more months to turn it into the map you see today. These maps are as delicate as eggshells and more precious than gold, so you will not touch them with your filthy fingers, you hear me?" Professzor Géza thundered.

The three of them nodded and put their hands behind their backs. That was at the beginning of their training, but they already knew better than to ever question Professzor Géza from the University of Pécs. The ghost-like Hungarian with a proud mustache and a sour downturned mouth like he got weaned on vinegar is here to teach them Hungarian, geography, history, and the Ottoman language. He's an expert in just about everything but the fighting skills. And he's never happy. *He's old, but he hasn't yet learned how to smile*, Ali thinks.

He glances at her like he's heard her thoughts, and she lowers her eyes to the map.

The map depicts the world. It has everything there is in the world, only smaller. Ali can't believe that the world is so big. There are three continents: Europe, Asia, and Africa, floating in a big pool of blue water. Believe it or not, between the oceans, the rivers, and the seas, it looks like the world is mostly made of water. *Where does it go when it reaches the end of the earth*, Ali wonders? Maybe there's a dam to keep it in, like the one in her village they built to make a fish pond? But then, who built it?

She finds Kronstadt Castle on the map. To its right, a black dot stands for her village, Băcel, and a curvy blue line for the river that runs through it. Back home, they call it the Black River, but it's not. It's blue in summer and it turns brown after the spring rains. Still, even on the map they made it blue.

"Where's Kronstadt?" the professor asks.

Codru points at it with a dirty finger.

"Where's Belgrade?"

Ion points at a dark spot in a sea of green, which is Serbia's color.

"Where's Edirne?"

Ali points at a scatter of black dots crowding each other in the middle of the giant stretch of red that represents the Ottoman Empire. "It's so big! It's got to be almost as big as Kronstadt," she says.

Codru laughs. "Stupid girl!"

Like a snake uncoiling to strike, Professzor Géza whips around and slaps him hard across the face. The slap booms like thunder in the small windowless room, and they all freeze and stare at each other with frightened eyes, wondering what that's about. Nothing like this has ever happened, no matter how bad their answers were.

"You! You're in detention. No food for you today. You'll go to work with the builders and carry stones for the new tower instead of attending my class. Get out!"

Codru glares at Ali and follows the guard that takes him to his punishment. The heavy door slams behind him and Professzor Géza turns to Ion and Ali. He's so angry that his droopy mustache trembles over his puckered mouth.

"You two. Do you understand what happened?"

Ali shakes her head. She has no clue.

"Was it because he called Ali stupid?" Ion asks.

The professor shakes his head. "No. It was because he called Ali a girl."

CHAPTER 20

THE FIRST KILL

MOLDOVA, 1443

A hundred miles east, in Moldova, Ștefan's heart pounds as he hides in the shadow and holds his breath to listen for the dogs calling their catch.

But they don't. It feels like forever, but their cries finally vanish in the distance, and Ștefan sighs with relief. He lies on his back, listening to the silence, and stares at the million blinking stars, wondering which one is his and which is Lena's. He hopes they're together somewhere. Or at least that her star is still up there, watching over her.

Sick with worry, he tosses and turns for most of the night, then wakes up at the first light stiff and frozen. He scrambles to his feet and tries to limber, only to discover that it's not him who's stiff. It's his clothes. They're frozen, and they aren't his. They're Lena's.

He curses softly and scratches his head. He's never worn women's clothes before, and he doesn't like them one bit. How on earth do they even walk in these narrow skirts that hold their legs together? *What a foolish contraption*, he thinks, hitching his skirts up to his waist to jump over a fallen tree. He's never worn something so stupid.

He shakes his head and gets on his way, with the morning sun on his left side and the river flowing south to his right. He hasn't gotten far when his stomach churns, reminding him he hasn't eaten.

He drinks his fill of cold sweet water from the river, then heads south again. Between climbing over dead trunks and squeezing through the brush, it's awful slow going, but at least he's no longer cold. Even the stupid clothes are almost dry after he's walked in them for hours. Only the thin braid hanging down his neck is still wet and slaps his back with every step like a damp whip. *It sucks to be a woman; I'm glad I'm a man*, he thinks, as he reaches a logging road.

The road is muddy and narrow, but it's still faster than cutting through the brush. And it should take him someplace where there are people, and maybe some food. He's still got his shoulder bag, his flask and the gold coins Father gave him. Sadly, his Venetian dagger is gone, but he still has Grandfather's priceless ring. Before Ștefan was born, his grandfather, Alexandru the Good, was Moldova's voivode for more than thirty years. He was brave and well-loved, and his hard work and wisdom made Moldova prosper, but when he died, his many sons started fighting for the throne. Ștefan's father, Bogdan, was one of them. The fight never stopped. That's why these days alliances last less than the paper they're written on, and nobody sits on the throne for very long.

"Moldova's glory days died with my father, but I plan to resurrect them someday. And if I don't, you will," Father said, watching Ștefan sew the precious ring inside his bag for safekeeping.

"Don't use that ring unless you absolutely must. This is your very last resort. It may get you help if you ask the right people, but, if the wrong people get wind of it, that ring could get you killed."

"But how will I know my friends from my enemies, Father?"

Father shrugged. "I don't know, my son. I'm almost forty, and I still struggle to tell my true friends from my enemies. And they're my brothers. My wonderful father, God rest his soul, had too many sons. Way too many for our small country. Anyhow, the best I know is to follow your heart."

Ștefan hopes that's good enough. He's bone tired, but he can't stop now. He needs to find food and shelter and get as far as he can from the posse that's looking for him. He shuffles down the road tethered by his skirts and tries to act like a girl, whatever that means. *How do girls even act? Lena doesn't behave like any other girl. But the women at the court in*

Suceava take small steps and smile a lot. Ștefan tries to imitate them, keeping his eyes on his feet and crossing his hands over his groin, and he feels like a dunce. Why on earth would anyone walk like this?

"Hey, you!"

Ștefan was so deep in his thoughts that he didn't hear the thickset man riding a small mule catching up with him. He's got to be a merchant, since the poor mule is loaded with a mountain of bags and wicker baskets, besides the man's not inconsequential girth.

The man's small eyes study Ștefan from head to toe, making him feel dirty.

"Where are you going?"

Ștefan mumbles something into his chest, hoping the man will mind his own business and let him be. No such luck.

"Where?"

Ștefan mumbles again, something nobody can understand, not even him.

"Brăila?"

Ștefan nods with relief, even though he knows nothing about Brăila and has no wish to go there.

"Come on. I'll give you a ride."

Between the full bags, the loaded baskets, and the man himself, the tiny mule is overburdened already, but Ștefan can't think of a good reason to say no. And his achy feet could use a break. The man gives him a hand, and Ștefan finds himself sitting sideways on his lap.

It's not much fun. He's never ridden sideways, but he's seen women do it. That's how they ride, all but Lena. How on earth can they do it? They can't use their knees or their heels, let alone the spurs! But fortunately, the mule requires none of that. This ride is all about not falling off, so he takes a deep breath and shifts his weight to balance better.

"What's your name?"

"Lena."

"And where are you going?"

"To Wallachia, to see my aunt."

"That's a long trip," the man says as his fleshy arm wraps around Ștefan's body.

Ștefan sighs. The man smells rancid, like raw onions and bad teeth. And he's way too close. Ștefan has never been that close to a man before. His whole left side is stuck to the man's rotund belly, and the man's right arm wraps around Ștefan's back to hold the reins. Like that wasn't bad enough, the man's left hand wanders to Ștefan's chest, slips inside the sheepskin vest's opening, and crawls towards the open neck of his chemise. Ștefan watches the thick fingers crawl like fat slugs towards his chest and shivers.

"You'll need a friend to help you on your way."

The fat hand descends towards Ștefan's groin, and he gasps. Ștefan may not know much, but he knows that down there, he's not built like a girl. And this man is not his friend. His touch and smell make him sick.

He grabs the errant hand. "No."

"Why not? Are you a virgin?"

Ștefan isn't sure whether he's a virgin, since he doesn't know what that means, but he knows he doesn't want this man's hand inside his pants. Then he remembers he has no pants, and he curses. A heartfelt Moldavian curse listing the man's mother's private parts, the holy saints who supervised her baptism, and every candle she's ever lit for them. This is just one of the many curses he's learned from Nicu, Father's blacksmith, who curses like a drunk sailor every time the horses act up. His wild imagination is something to behold.

But Ștefan doesn't curse aloud, of course, since that would buy him a swift kick and a tumble down the side of that mule. He nods to the virgin question instead. He'll confess to whatever can keep those dirty hands away from him.

"OK, my beautiful, then I'll teach you a thing or two," the man whispers in Ștefan's ear, and his foul breath turns Ștefan's stomach.

"I'll take good care of you."

The man guides the mule off the road. He pushes him to a patch of forest by the river and slides off. He ties the reins around a twisted dwarf birch, then takes Ștefan's hand and leads him deep into the woods, where the shadows are dark and no sound other than the river's rumble breaks the silence.

"Here."

The man hands Ștefan his flask, and the sharp smell of wine makes Ștefan's mouth water. He takes a deep swig as his eyes roam around for an escape, but there's none. He takes another sip and hands back the half-empty flask.

The man's eyes widen, and Ștefan remembers that girls are not supposed to drink wine. But he's not a girl, of course. He's Bogdan's son, Alexandru the Good's grandson, and Moldavia's voivode one day, should God wish it. He's drunk wine since he got weaned. Watered down at first, but for years now, he's partaken of the best wines of Moldova. Drinking wine comes to him as easy as drinking water.

But this man doesn't know that. Nor should he.

"Nice wine. My father's a winemaker," Ștefan says.

"Where?"

"Cotnari."

The man smiles and leans closer. His hands reach for Ștefan again.

Ștefan sighs. He could try to run, but he's walked forever, and his feet hurt. He's wearing these dreadful skirts, and he doesn't even know where to go. He looks around for anything that he could use as a weapon, but there's nothing. Not even a dead branch within reach.

The man leans forward. He cups Ștefan's face in his hands and covers his mouth with his, and Ștefan's stomach turns. He'd rather kiss a toad, but there's none available. The man's tongue slips inside Ștefan's mouth, making him shudder. He's ready to barf when a rough hand grabs his balls.

The assailing mouth withdraws, and the man's hands pull away like he's hot. "What's this?"

"What's what?" Ștefan asks.

The man spits to his side. His face turns purple, and his eyes roll inside his head like he's been cursed.

"You! You are not a girl! You're a demon! You tried to seduce me and anger God. You devil!"

The man screams like a banshee and runs to his mule as if Ștefan was the one who dragged him into the forest patch. He's raging mad and looking for revenge, and Ștefan is in deep trouble. That man's angry enough to kill him. Too bad Lena set herself as bait to veer the hounds off his track and keep him safe. It was all for naught.

Ștefan gets up to run, but it's too late. The man grabs the back of his vest and drags him to the ground. He's so enraged his little eyes pop out like a snail's, and drops of stinky spittle fly out of his mouth.

"You'll tell them it was me, won't you? You'll tell them it was me who picked you up and brought you here, when you know damn well how you tricked me. You filthy demon! I won't let you destroy my reputation and my life," he sputters, lifting a curved dagger above Ștefan's head.

Ștefan rolls away and leaps to his feet, ready to fight, but his odds suck. The man's knife is not forged with gold and encrusted with precious stones like the one Ștefan lost in the river. It's just plain grey iron, but it looks sturdy and sharp, just like those Father taught him to use since he was five.

The man's ready to cut him, and Ștefan is unarmed. He looks around again, but there's nothing. All he's got are his bare hands and the long narrow skirts he can't run in. His heart pummels as he looks for a solution, and Father's words come to mind:

"If your enemy is stronger, faster, or better armed than you, borrow their strength and use it against them. Make their speed your speed, their weight your weight, and their weapon your weapon."

The man charges like a raging bull, and Ștefan drops to his knee just before the knife touches his chest. The man stumbles and flies over him, then crashes to the ground and drops the knife.

Ștefan leaps like a wildcat and grabs the knife. He kneels on the man's chest, touching the dagger's tip to his throat.

The man is stunned. He opens his mouth like a fish out of water, but no words come out as he struggles to breathe. His anger has vanished, and his face is white with fear. Wide-eyed and sweaty, he begs for mercy with a voice almost too soft to hear.

"Please spare my life and let me go. I really didn't know you were a boy. I thought you were just a fuckable wench..."

Ștefan thinks of Lena, whose clothes he's wearing. If she hadn't set herself as bait to save him, she'd be here in his stead. Just a fuckable wench...

His brain turns dark with rage. He slides the shiny blade across the man's throat in one smooth cut, and a fountain of hot blood spurts thick and salty in his face, reminding him of his first kill ever. The rooster Father had him slaughter for Easter.

"You'd better learn how to kill if you want to take men to war. I hope you never get to like it, but it is what it is. Life and death go together, and you must know how to give either if you're a soldier and a leader," Father said.

The rooster was old and cunning. He put up a fight, and they covered the whole yard with blood and feathers. It got so bad that Ștefan got sick to his stomach. He retched, then tried to run inside, but Father stopped him.

"No. He's your responsibility. Finish him off to end his suffering."

Ștefan caught him again. He sliced his throat, then vomited again when the headless body ran away. He didn't touch the chicken soup that Easter, but he learned that if you need to kill, you'd better do it right.

But, unlike that rooster, this man doesn't put up a fight. His eyes pop out with surprise. He gurgles on his blood, then goes quiet. His frozen eyes look into nowhere as Ștefan wipes the knife on his chest and slips it into his pouch.

He's thinking of Lena as he prompts the mule south towards Wallachia.

CHAPTER 21
THE HAY CART

But the mule couldn't care less about Ștefan's prompts. He's old, tired and placid and has only one speed: slow. He's nothing like the stallions Ștefan used to ride at his father's court, and he's so tiny that Ștefan's feet graze the grass. Even so, sitting on him beats walking on his burning swollen feet.

The mule's gentle sway rocks him into daydreaming, and he thinks about the home he left long ago. About Bogdan, his father, one of Alexandru the Good's many bastard sons fighting for the throne. About Doamna Oltea, his faithful mother. He hasn't seen them in many moons and misses them both, but he misses Father more. He was often away, fighting some enemy somewhere, but whenever he came home, Father was there for him. He listened to Ștefan and taught him the things a prince ought to know, from strategy to tactics and from diplomacy to knife fight. He never failed to give him his undivided attention and make him feel loved. Sure, Mother loves him too, but she loves God more. The black-clad monks with scraggly beards begging her to help build some new church or buy some dead saint's toe for a relic always came first. So did praying and running Father's household. Between serving God and the realm, Mother was always busy. That's why Ștefan feels closer to Lena's mother than to his own.

Still, he'd love to join her and Father if he knew where to go. But all he knows is that they're hiding somewhere from whoever sent that posse to get him. Likely Moldova's voivode or another one of Father's brothers. Or their friends.

Blood ties and friendships are fickle in today's Moldova. When Alexandru the Good died, his sons grabbed the throne one after another, slaughtering their rivals and struggling to forge new alliances to cement their rule, but none lasted long. Mistakes, betrayals, and sheer bad luck toppled them one after another, making room for the next one. So Father's waiting in the wings. His time hasn't come yet, but it will. Then, Ștefan will be the son of Moldova's voivode. Maybe even voivode someday. He'll marry Lena and...

A roll of thunder wakes him from his dreams. He lifts his eyes to the sky, but there's nothing but blue, as far as the eye can see. He glances back. A cloud of dust behind him is growing fast, and the earth trembles under the hooves of many horses.

Ștefan's heart skips a beat. Are they looking for him? Is this the posse he escaped from thanks to Lena, or did someone find the merchant's slaughtered body and they're looking for the killer? Either way, it does him no good to be found.

He tightens his knees and pulls on the reins, prompting the mule towards the woods to his right. But the mule, like all mules, resists. Ștefan has to waste seconds he doesn't have to dismount and drag him off the road. He pulls him behind a row of low pines just as a posse of two dozen or so gallops past. They show no regard for their horses, who look wasted, covered in spumes and dust like they've traveled forever. So do the men. They're armed with bows, swords, and maces but no armor, so they're not going to war.

Ștefan waits for them to be gone. He'll continue on foot, though he'd much rather ride. But a lone, bloodied girl riding a traveling merchant's mule? That can't but look fishy, especially after they find the body. How on earth could he explain his bloody clothes and riding the dead man's mule? But he won't need to. They'll hang him first and ask questions later. He'd better do something about it now.

Ștefan unloads the mule, looking for something he can use.

There's flour and sheepskins and dry beans, but no food and no weapons. Still, he finds a pair of brown woolen pants and a chemise that smell like sweat, cheese, and last winter's smoke. They're too big for him, but they're a man's clothes and clean. He takes off Lena's bloody skirt and vest, puts on the fat man's clothes, and ties them around him with a rope. He rolls up the trousers to keep them from dragging on the ground, undoes the stupid braid, and, just like that, he's a man again. Thank God!

He pats the mule, who glances up from the fresh grass. "Good luck, my friend."

He grabs his bag and heads south, keeping close to the edge of the forest, ready to hide at the first sign of danger, and walks. And walks.

He's walked for a day and most of the night without food or drink when he hears the wagon. The oxen stop, and the old peasant driving them looks him up and down.

“You want a ride?"

His throat too dry to speak, Ștefan nods. He climbs and sits next to him on the wooden bench in the front, since the back is loaded with hay, piled high as a house.

"What's your name, kid?"

"Ștefan," he screeches.

The man hands him a flask, and Ștefan drinks and drinks. He's never had better water, he surmises, then remembers to leave some for the man.

"Drink it. I have more. Where are you going?"

"Târgoviște."

"Why?"

"To find my aunt."

The old man looks him up and down, taking in his ill-fitting clothes, his face burned raw by the sun, and his dusty opinci. "You ran away?"

Ștefan nods. He struggles to keep his eyes open, but he's too tired, and his head falls forward. He shakes himself awake, but the old man stops the cart and points to the hay. "Get in there. Get some sleep. It's a long way to wherever you're going."

Ștefan nests deep in the hay, which is prickly but warm, and smells like summer. Rocked by the steady pace of the oxen, he falls asleep.

He’s back with Lena, running from the posse. But they're getting close, really close, and they're about to grab them when the men’s voices break through his sleep.

He's not dreaming. They're here. He holds his breath to hear better.

"What are you carrying, old man?"

"What do you think?"

"Don't get smart with me now! What do you have?"

"Hay, Your Highness. Nothing but hay for the garrison's horses."

"Anything else?"

"No."

"Did you see anyone on the road?"

"No."

"A girl? On a mule?"

"No girl and no mule."

"Anybody else?"

"No."

"Check the hay," somebody says.

Ștefan holds his breath and curls into a ball to make himself smaller, wondering what they mean. Something sharp stabs his hip, and the pain is like nothing he's felt before. He opens his mouth to scream his agony, but remembers that he’s as good as dead if they find him. He pushes his fist into his mouth and bites on it to choke his screams.

A lance grazes his side and another pierces the hay right in front of his nose, just a finger width away from his right eye. He bites his hand even harder.

He feels weak and exhausted, and the pain fades. So do the voices. He feels like he's about to float away.

"Check the other side."

"There's nothing, I told you. You're wasting your time."

"What's it to you?"

"You're wasting mine, too. I look forward to being home by the fireplace with a cup of red. Aren't you?"

The guards laugh. They try a couple of halfhearted stabs to the other side, then the cart moves again. Rocked by the slow pace of the oxen, Ștefan's world goes dark as a deep faintness overcomes him.

CHAPTER 22

MAMA SMARANDA

KRONSTADT, SUMMER 1443

It's summer in Kronstadt, and even the mighty castle throws no shadow at noon. A scorching sun got stuck in the middle of the endless blue sky, and not a wisp of cloud softens its blistering gaze.

Ali rides behind a huge Saxon guard on his cantering gelding. She sees nothing beyond his leather-clad back, and does her best to ignore the pain between her legs, the rancid smell of his body and the sweat burning her eyes as she holds on to him with all her might, wondering where he's taking her.

It feels like forever until he slows down to take a narrow trail through the woods, and Ali sighs with relief. There's no sun here, just deep shade under the thick green canopy of the crooked old trees wrapped in vines. The air is crisp and fresh and smells like a church, and the silence is heavy. Nothing moves as they head deep into the woods, but the milky mist raising up from the ground gets thicker and thicker.

There's something peculiar about this hidden place, and Ali's heart starts pounding. She remembers Mother's stories about parents abandoning their children in the forest. When they couldn't take it anymore, tired parents dropped their disobedient kids in the woods for the gypsies to find, the werewolves to ravage, or the striga to eat. Ana thought they were just that, children's stories meant to scare her into behaving better. But now she starts to wonder if the guard is about to drop her here.

Sure enough, they stop.

"Get off," the guard says, his voice thick with thirst.

"Why?"

The guard shakes his head and pushes her off. Ali stumbles to land on her feet.

"I'll be back to get you at sundown," he says.

"What am I here for?"

The man shrugs.

"The burgomaster told me to bring you here at noon and return to get you at sundown. That's all I know."

He slaps the horse's rump, and he's gone.

Ana rubs the goosebumps on her arms and stares at the dark forest around her. The place is unmoving and silent like a tomb, and she's never felt so alone.

The ghostlike trees shrouded in fog seem to live in three seasons at a time. Bright-green unfurling buds sprout along the twisted branches and red leaves set the ground on fire while the soft tenderness of the air reminds her it's summer.

A few steps to her right, two tree stumps dressed in bright-green moss lean towards each other, joining their branches like two lovers holding hands. Ali smiles and joins her hands with theirs. All of a sudden, the mist vanishes like it never was.

Out of nowhere, there's a little cottage in the forest. It's made of tree trunks loosely fitted together and it stands on four crooked stilts. The old thatched roof is steep enough to shed the snow, and the tiny square windows are covered with stretched pig bladders to let in the light but not the rain. A few lacy ferns shiver on top like feathers in someone's cap, and a profusion of purple petunias hugs the walls, sweetening the air with their fragrance.

The sharp willow palings fencing the house would disinvite visitors if the gate wasn't open. But it is.

Ana heads to the gate, her heart racing. There was this one story about two children who got lost in the woods and got trapped by a witch who wanted to eat them. A cold shiver runs down her spine and she wonders if she'll end in a stew.

But that was just a children's story. Nobody in their right mind would want to eat her. Why bother? She's nothing but skin and bones.

But what if they fatten her first?

Oh well. To gather some courage, she touches her cross, which is warm and glows purple like she's never seen it, and pushes the gate.

The gate screeches open and Ana finds herself eye to eye with a hairy black dog as big as a bear. He wags his tail to greet her.

"What's your name?" she asks.

The dog smiles.

Ali cups his face with her hands to look into his amber eyes and scratches him behind his left ear. The dog pushes back into her hand, wishing her to scratch harder, until he falls on his side. Ali laughs.

"Great guardian you are!"

The dog slaps his thick tail to the ground and rolls to his back, inviting her to scratch his belly.

"Negru likes you."

The woman standing in the door looks like no woman Ali has ever seen. She's tall and slim like a poplar, and the fluttery veils she's wrapped in make her look like a ghost. Her long thin fingers are adorned with rings in every color of the rainbow, and her wrists are heavy with golden bracelets that jingle when she moves. She's achingly beautiful, with her midnight-blue eyes and black hair braided with coins cascading down her back, but the set of her jaw and the crinkle of the soft skin around her eyes tell Ali that she's no longer young.

"I'm Ali."

"Welcome, Ana."

And just like that, Ana starts sobbing like a child. And she shouldn't. She's way too old to cry.

"I'm Ali now."

"I know. Call me Mama Smaranda. I've been waiting for you."

"For me?"

"Of course. Come in."

The cottage is tiny and cool. The single room is bedroom, kitchen, and pantry all in one, with a packed dirt floor, like Ali's old home. There's even a door at the back, like the one that went to the attic. But the resemblance stops here. The tall narrow bed is piled with sheep skins, and the log walls are studded with nails, hooks, and shelves loaded with drying herbs, leather flasks, clay pots sealed with wax and a hundred wicker baskets, large and small, full of seeds, rocks, and strangely shaped things Ali doesn't recognize. And piled in every corner, cloth bags in which unseen things squirm and moan fight each other for the place on top.

The wooden table that takes up most of the room is piled with pails, pots, jars and cooking tools. There's a rusty scale complete with weights, an hourglass full of red sand, a ratty leather-bound book, and an ink pot with a quill.

Standing guard over them all, a black cat stares Ali down with her unblinking yellow eyes.

This place is stranger than strange, Ali thinks. Even the air is thick with odd scents, mystery, and foreboding. She feels deep in her bones that her life will never be the same after today, and she shivers.

CHAPTER 23
THE APPRENTICE

"Take a seat," Mama Smaranda says.

Ali sits on the milking stool by the fireplace, thankful for the heat. She stretches her hands to warm them by the flames, but the fire hisses, cracks, and spits out a wave of orange sparks that fly out the door. Mama Smaranda frowns.

"Leave her alone."

The fire hisses again.

"Leave her alone, or I'll put you out."

Ali looks around the room. There's nobody here but the cat, and she didn't even blink.

"Who are you talking to?"

"The flames."

"Can they hear you?"

"Of course. Can't you?"

"But... I'm alive."

"So are they. So are all things, but most people are too self-centered to notice. Weren't you just speaking to Negru outside?"

"Yes, but he's a dog."

"I couldn't help but notice."

What an odd place, Ali thinks. *I wonder why they sent me here.*

"They sent you here to learn."

"Learn what?"

"About life. How to bring things to life. How to hear them and speak to them. How to see the things that aren't obvious. How to grow the things that need growing. How to heal those who need healing. How to kill those who need to die."

"Why do things need to die?"

"It's nature's law. Nothing lives forever, so everything has to die sooner or later. If you understand and respect Mother Nature, you'll be able to help things along to where they need to be."

"How did you learn?"

"I learned from my mother, who learned from her mother, who learned from her mother."

So why me? Why aren't you teaching your daughter? Ali thinks, but doesn't say it.

"I don't have a daughter. But I have you."

I need to be careful with what I think. This woman can hear my thoughts.

Mama Smaranda laughs, and the room suddenly gets warmer.

"Very good. That was lesson two: Be careful with your thoughts. Those who know how to listen can hear them."

"What was lesson one?"

"Everything is alive, and everything dies. Including you."

"What's lesson three?"

"You'll start to listen. Look at the cat. What does she say?"

Ali looks at the cat. Black and silent, she sits in the middle of the table, her unblinking yellow eyes glued to her.

"I don't know. She's not talking."

"She is, my dear. You just need to listen."

Ali looks again.

"Don't touch me."

"Very good. Also, 'I don't trust you,' and 'I have my eye on you.' See? It's not hard once you put your mind to it. What did the fire say?"

"You're too close. Go away."

"Excellent! You'll be a wonderful student, and we'll have a great time together. Now let's get to work."

"What work?"

"I told you, you'll learn to keep things alive. We'll start with the healing herbs."

Mama Smaranda picks up a cloth bag hanging on the wall.

"Tell me about it without looking inside."

Ali weighs the small bag.

"It's light."

Smaranda nods.

Ali shakes it and listens to the soft rattling.

"Something dried. Not an herb. It's not light enough." She brings it to her nose. It smells of wood.

"Open it."

The brown shriveled pieces fall in her hand.

"Tree bark?"

"Yes. Taste it."

She bites into it, and her mouth puckers. It's sharp, sour, and bitter, all at the same time. She wants to spit it out, but that would be rude, so she swallows it instead.

"It's white willow bark, one of the most useful remedies Mother Nature invented. Its tea will ease headaches, cure back pain, bring down fever, heal zits, and remove dandruff. A poultice made from it, wrapped around a sprained knee, will drive away the pain and lessen the swelling. You'll get slimmer if you drink a cup of tea made of it every day. But if you give your enemies a strong potion of white willow three times a day for a moon or two, they'll die slowly and smoothly. This will take a while, unlike other poisons that kill people overnight. But your enemy will be sick for too long to raise suspicion."

"Who's my enemy?"

"Good question. Who's your enemy?"

"I don't know."

"You'll find out soon enough, little girl."

Ali stands up straight, though she only reaches to Smaranda's chin. "I'm not little. And I'm not a girl."

"What are you then?"

"I'm Ali."

Smaranda smiles.

"You're just like your father."

"You knew my father?"

"I did."

"Tell me about him."

"Not today. Today we learn about plants. In the right hands, they can heal, or they can kill. You'll learn how to find them, harvest them, and how to prepare them to get the results you want. Willows always grow near the water. Any part of the tree is good to use, but the dried bark is the best for tea. But if you need it when you're outside, even chewing on a young branch will help. I'll show you next time. We'll go to the forest to learn and pick herbs. But for now, let's make some willow bark tea."

Ali crushes the bark into powder with a stone mortar and pestle. Smaranda checks it.

"It has to be very fine, otherwise, it won't release its full power into the drink."

She pours the crushed bark into hot water and boils it, then sieves it through a clean cloth as she chants in a language that Ali can't understand. She pours it into a wooden cup and hands it to Ali. The potion is dark yellow and pungent.

“Taste it."

The bitterness takes Ali's breath away. She shivers.

"It's evil!"

Smaranda laughs.

"So what do you do to help it out?"

"Add honey?"

"Very good. You can also dilute it to make it less astringent. But, no matter what you do, it's hard to ignore. This is not something you'll slip in somebody's drink and hope they won't notice. They will. So what do you do to make them drink it?"

"Tell them that it will make them feel better?"

"What if they aren't sick? If you want to poison somebody, you must give them lots of it for a long time. What do you do?"

Ali shrugs.

"Come on, you just said it."

"Add honey?"

"Precisely. You add honey. And what's honey?"

"Honey is made by the bees..."

"Of course. But that's not what we're talking about now. Honey is sweet. Honey is something people love. In this case, adding honey means promising them something they want so badly that they'll drink the poison and ask for more. You understand?"

Ali nods.

"What would you drink it for? What do you want so much that you'd drink more and more of it, provided it gets you what you want?"

"I want to know about Father."

"Very good. So, if I promised you that if you drink enough of it, you'll get to hear about your father, you'd drink it?"

"Yes."

"It's the same with everybody. If you know what people want, you can make them do what you want. You just need the right bait."

"I understand. Like fishing. Father said you have to have the right bait for the fish you want."

"Just so. Let's talk baits. What do women want?"

Ali shrugs. She doesn't know that many women besides her mother.

"Come on. What does your mother want?"

Ali remembers that Smaranda can hear her thoughts.

"What does she do that she doesn't need to do? Just does it because she wants to?"

"She looks in her silver mirror?"

"Why?"

"To see how she looks?"

"Why?"

"Because she's beautiful?"

"So what?"

"Everybody loves beautiful people?"

"Precisely. Your mother looks in her mirror, hoping she's still beautiful, therefore worth loving. Love is what half of the people on earth are looking for. That's one of the best baits there are. Love. If you tell them the bitter potion will make them attractive and that people will fall in love with them by the droves, they'll drink all you've got and ask for more. Love is a powerful bait."

"How about the other half?"

"The other half want power. Power is like love, but not quite. Love is power over somebody. Power is power over everybody. Most men want power. Most women want love. But not always."

"So half of the world wants power, and the other half wants love?"

"Sort of. Most want both. Some are more complicated, and those are hard to bait. Not impossible, but it's hard."

"What do they want?"

"All sorts of things. Money. Knowledge. Revenge. Justice. Pleasure. Equality. Truth. You have to figure out what they want so you can set the right trap."

"What do you want, Mama Smaranda?"

Mama Smaranda laughs and opens the door. The guard's waiting outside.

"I want you to come back so we can talk some more. What do you want, Ana?"

"I want to learn what I want. And how to get it."

"Come back then."

CHAPTER 24

A FRIEND IN NEED

Ali and Ion dine alone this evening. Codru hasn't been back since this morning when Professzor Géza slapped him and threw him out of class for calling Ali a girl. They haven't seen him, but they know he's out there, breaking his back to carry the massive stones for the new tower. He's got to be hungry and pissed.

His absence weighs on them, but they don't talk about it. They sit side by side on the long bench by the heavy wooden table loaded with food for three. Ali slices chunks thicker than her hand from the warm crusty bread which smells so good it makes her dizzy. Ion drools, waiting for his trencher, then they dig into the golden roasted chicken fragrant with cooked onions and wild herbs. There's also yellow butter, dark forest honey, and fresh milk.

They eat like starving wolves until they quell their hunger, then slow down to chat and enjoy.

"What did you do today?" Ali asks, gnawing on a chicken wing.

Ion finishes his chicken leg, then rolls his shoulders and rubs his neck with his left hand.

"Hand-to-hand combat. Since Codru wasn't there, I had to wrestle Grgur, the Serbian guard. There's not an inch of me that doesn't hurt. He's way too strong and too fast. I'm no match for him."

"You're just a kid. He's twice as big as you."

"Well, yeah. But still. And what's the point of wasting your time with bare-handed combat when we have bows, swords, and lances? Why bother?"

"What if you have to fight and have no weapon? You have to be ready."

"If I have to fight and have no weapon, I'm done," Ion says, reaching for the other chicken leg.

Ali slaps his hand away. "That's mine."

"But you don't even like chicken legs!"

"Still, that's mine. Have a wing."

Ion shrugs and grabs a wing. "What did you do?"

"I went to see Mama Smaranda."

"Mama Smaranda? The witch?"

"She's not a witch!" Then she remembers everything she saw and heard. Maybe?

"What did you do?"

"She taught me how to cook a potion."

"What potion?"

"For healing."

"Will you teach me?"

"Maybe. If I learn better."

"I wonder why they teach you one thing and me another."

"Not always."

"No, but often enough. Like they never have you do hand-to-hand combat."

"But we all learn the Ottoman language and writing and geography..."

Ion glances around, then whispers: "You think it's because you're a girl that they teach you different things?"

Ali chokes on her milk. "Are you crazy? Didn't you see what happened to Codru? I'm not a girl."

"What are you then?"

"I'm Ali."

Ion shakes his head.

"I don't think it's that easy. Just calling you something different doesn't change what you are."

"It totally does. Today I peed standing. I'm not a girl."

Ion shakes his head and stares longingly at the other chicken leg sitting on the wooden platter.

"Are you going to eat it or what?"

"That's none of your business." Ali grabs the leg, puts it between two chunks of bread, and slides it under her shirt. "There. You happy now?"

She gets up and heads to her bed. Ion shrugs and follows her.

Their room is dark but for the lonely glow of the flickering torch set in a high iron ring. They wait for their eyes to adjust to the darkness, then Ion squeezes inside his bed of blankets piled on straw.

Ali walks to the farthest corner of the room where Codru's bed is. He's got to be here, since it's too dark to work outside. But he's not snoring.

She touches the dark shape with her foot.

"What do you want?"

"There." She hands him the chicken leg and the bread, then slides under her blankets, hugging her knees to get warm and thinks about Father. It's been years, but in her heart his voice is as warm as ever, and his memory just as sweet.

"You can do everything you set out to do, my girl. Anything."

But he isn't here. And she's no longer a girl.

She drags her blankets over her head and lets her tears run unchecked. For Father, who's been gone for years. For Mother, who never loved her because she's a girl and useless. For her dog Tina, her only friend after Father died. Ali hasn't seen her in many months. *How is she? Does she remember me? I hope Mother isn't mean to her,* she thinks.

She cries herself to sleep like she does every night. As she falls asleep in the silence populated only by her ghosts, Codru says:

"Thank you, Ali."

CHAPTER 25

A TERRIBLE DANCE

MOLDOVA, SUMMER 1443

Lena opens her eyes to a patch of blue sky. It's crisscrossed by tree branches, so she's got to be in a forest, somewhere. But where?

Then she remembers that she was riding Ilie. But now she's lying on the ground, and everything hurts, especially her head. It's like a mud storm rages in her brain, and her senses are hazy and muddled. She has to struggle to think straight.

She didn't make it, and it's only her fault. She should have pushed Ilie even harder, but she wanted to make sure they'd follow her and leave Ștefan alone. So when the dogs jumped and pulled her to the ground, it wasn't anybody's fault but her own.

A bunch of riders stand above her. They stare at her like they've never seen a girl as Lena struggles to get up. She manages to sit, then stands on wobbly feet, but there's no way she can run. The men are everywhere, a dozen, maybe two, and they have bows and swords.

"This isn't him," a young man says. "This isn't a boy. It's a girl."

The old captain leading them shakes his head. His voice is soft, but his weather-beaten face is unsmiling.

"Thanks, Your Brilliance. Where would we be without your guidance?"

The others laugh, but it's not a happy laugh. It's a harsh, nervous sound that gives Lena goosebumps.

"Who are you?" the captain asks.

"I'm Lena."

"Where are you going?"

"What's it to you?" She glances at old Ilie munching on the young grass by the road, and wonders how she could mount him and run. Slim chance. The men are mounted, and their palfreys, every one of them, looks younger and faster than poor Ilie. And then they have the dogs.

The captain frowns. "Where's Ștefan?"

"Who's Ștefan?"

His face darkens. "Listen, girl. I'm not kidding. Your life may depend on your answer. Where is he?"

"Damned if I know."

The men laugh again, and their laugh makes Lena feel dirty. It's neither joyful nor funny. It's a warning that something terrible is coming.

"How about we help her memory?" a foul-smelling man says. He dismounts, and gets so close that she can see the gunk in his eyes.

"Come here, sweetheart."

He pulls her closer with his dirty hands. He brings his filthy mouth to hers, and the stench of garlic turns her stomach. His lips touch hers, then his tongue forces her mouth open.

She bites it hard. Her knee finds his groin, and he screams and folds down to the ground with his knees to his chin.

The others dismount and surround her like a pack of hyenas circling a fresh kill. Their glazed eyes glitter and they drool with excitement as they close around her.

Lena backs up to the tree behind her.

They get closer and closer, and dozens of hands reach toward her. In a mesmerizing dance, they swirl around her, closer and closer, until their fingers touch her shoulders, her arms, her chest, her belly, her groin. She melts into the tree, but there's nowhere to go. They get even closer, their eyes glazed with hunger. They bare their teeth, and the white of their eyes shows all around the iris like they're drunk with something Lena can't understand, but it's scarier than anything she's ever seen.

"Step back and leave her be," their captain shouts, but nobody seems to hear. The men are in a trance nothing can break. They squeeze even closer until one unties the rope holding up her pants. Another one pulls them down, baring her legs. The mob sighs like a roll of thunder. One of them grabs her shoulders and pulls himself between her thighs, and Lena freezes with fear. They're all around her, almost inside her, and there's nowhere to go.

But forward. The man between her legs collapses to the ground with a battle ax sticking out of his head. The others step back, their eyes frightened like they awoke from a nightmare.

"Step back, everybody," the captain shouts, holding his bow ready. "The next one to touch her is dead. Then the next, and the next."

They step back. They stare at her, at him, at the ground as if they don't understand what happened or why they did what they did and they're ashamed.

"You. Get dressed."

Lena pulls up her pants and ties them with shaky hands. She steps back to lean against the tree, looking at the dead man laying at her feet with his pants around his ankles and a battle ax in his head.

She takes a deep breath and tries to pull out the ax, but it's stuck. She wiggles it out like she does when she cuts green wood, then wipes the bloody blade on his clothes and sticks the handle in her makeshift belt.

The captain smiles. "Let's go."

He signals the men, then waits for Lena to get on Ilie and follows her on his short, sturdy horse. They trot along the river until the old soldier gets close enough for her to hear him whisper.

"Listen, girl. I won't let these hoodlums have their way with you, because you look just like my granddaughter Ileana. But I don't know that I can stop them next time. You need to escape, but not now, or they'll catch you. Tonight, after they fall asleep. Get the red horse — he's the fastest — and go south. Don't stop, and don't talk to anyone.

You don't look or sound like a boy. You'll have a better chance if you cut your hair and catch a cold. Be careful, and don't trust anyone ever."

Lena rides on like she hasn't heard him. But she has.

CHAPTER 26

LENA'S ESCAPE

The forest is dark and full of strange noises after nightfall. As the fire dies down, the light circle gets smaller and the shadows grow deeper. The men ate their bread and their cheese and drank from the river. Now, they lay with their feet to the fire and their heads on their saddles, and the cacophony of snores get louder and louder as they fall asleep one after the other.

Curled under Ștefan's sheepskin mantle away from the fire, Lena lies in the shadow, faking sleep.

The old captain has the first watch. He stands, yawns and stretches, then glances at his men and walks into the bushes. Minutes later, he returns tightening his belt. He glances at Lena and points with his chin to the forest.

Lena tiptoes to the bushes and looks for the red horse. He's saddled and ready. She spares a grateful thought for the old man, grabs the reins and leads him away. They make no noise as they walk over thick leaves and soft ground. Minutes later, she jumps in the saddle heading south. Maybe. She wishes she knew where she's going.

South is Wallachia. That's where Ștefan went, since he's got family there, but she has no business going there. She doesn't know a soul. Except for Ștefan, of course, but he won't be there yet. Who knows where he is? But she can't think about anywhere else to go, so she heads south. She'll detour back north towards home once she's sure she lost the men.

She rides and rides until she's tired, hungry, and thirsty, but she still doesn't dare stop. She goes and goes, and it's still dark when she sees a strange light in the sky. It's towards sunset, where there should be no light. Did she misjudge her direction? Is that the dawn? But it can't be. It's too early for sunrise, and that light looks nothing like the morning sky.

She heads towards it, until the horse smells smoke and rears, way before she gets there. This red palfrey is nothing like old placid Ilie, who'll go wherever she takes him. Red's a young gelding with fire in his belly, and he'd rather dance on his feet than go where she leads him.

But Lena has been riding since before she could walk, and she's not about to let a horse tell her where to go. She tightens her knees around his belly and shortens the reins. Red skitters and rears, but Lena won't take it. She pushes him forward towards the light.

It's a village on fire. Every single house is burning, and the straw of the roofs is all gone. It's now down to the wooden walls and the barns. Down in the middle of the village, the old church with the cross on its steep roof burns red, hissing and sputtering sparks as if God himself got angry with his people.

There's not a soul in sight. No people, no horses, no cattle, no cats, no chicken. Nothing but greedy flames devouring the villagers' livelihoods.

Lena has heard about villages burning. Every year, the Ottomans make raids across the Danube to kidnap people and steal their harvest. They take all they can carry, then set fire to the rest, leaving behind nothing but dread and devastation. They kill anybody who stands against them, whether young or old, man or woman. To escape, people run deep into the forest. When they come back, they find their homes destroyed and their belongings gone.

But this doesn't look like that. There are no dead. No life either, not even a chicken or a cat.

Red rears again and neighs. He doesn't like being so close to the fire. Lena dismounts and ties him to a tree branch, then walks into the village. She steers clear of the burning buildings, but she goes close to look at the ones that turned to ashes, hoping to find something looking like food. But there's nothing.

She searches one burned house after another, until she hears something odd. It's hard to make up between the crackles and the hissing of the fires, but it sounds like someone's crying.

It's a small kid. He lays curled on the ground, holding on to a dog behind a burned building. The dog sees her and snarls. The kid lifts his head and stares.

"What's your name?"

"I'm Dan. This is Lupu."

"What are you doing here?"

"We heard that the Ottomans were coming. They raided the village south of us, so the elders said, 'Let's take everything and hide in the mountains, rather than go into slavery.' So they loaded the carts and left."

"So how come you're here?"

"I couldn't find Lupu. We left without him, but then I ran away and came back to look for him. I couldn't leave him here. But now they're all gone."

Lena feels sorry for the kid, but what can she do? She can't take him with her. She doesn't even know where she's going, she has no food or water, and she's running away.

"If you wait till the morning, you'll see where they went. Those loaded carts will leave a track, and the horses and the cattle will leave droppings that will point you in the right direction. But you may not need to. Your folks must have noticed you're missing, and they'll come back to get you."

"But I'm scared. I'm afraid to be alone."

"You're not alone. Lupu is with you."

"But he can't talk."

"Sure he can. He can bark," Lena says.

Then she realizes that, should the Ottomans come, they'll find the kid by the dog's barking. And when they see that he's the only soul left in the entire village, what will they do to him to send a message to the others? She shudders to think.

The boy cries. "Take me with you! Please?"

"I can't. I don't know where I'm going."

"Don't leave me here. Take me with you."

His sobs break her heart. She can't say no. She curses herself as she says: "Let's go then."

He stands up, and he's even smaller than she thought. "How old are you, Dan?"

"I'm five."

Lena shakes her head, wishing she wasn't soft-hearted and stupid. But it's too late. She takes his hand and goes back to get her horse. She looks and looks for the tree she tied him to, but he's gone. Frightened by the fire, he must have broken the branch she tied him to and ran away.

Lena curses her stupidity. Bad enough to be running from a posse on a stolen horse. But now? The horse is gone, the Ottomans are coming, and she's got a kid to look after. *How stupid can I be?*

"Where are we going?" Dan asks.

I'll be damned if I know, Lena thinks, but she answers. "We're going to find your people." They may as well, since there's nothing else she can think about. "Which way did they go when you left?"

"We went by the church towards the mountains. At the river, they turned right."

"Let's go then."

The sky starts blushing towards east. God willing, they'll soon have enough light to see the trail. But they walk and walk, and there's nothing.

"I'm tired," Dan says.

"Sure, you are. I am too, but we can't stop here. We need to get away from the village."

"But I can't go any further. My feet hurt."

Lena sighs and picks him up. He's not big, but she's already spent. She can't carry him far. Her feet hurt, her throat is scorching with thirst, and she hasn't eaten in days. She walks as fast as she can, getting deeper and deeper in the forest to look for the trail, but there's no sign of it.

She starts to worry. Has she gone in the wrong direction? She hopes not. If the kid's right, they should soon find the river. They'll at least have water to drink and soak their raw feet. She keeps going as the sun goes up, but there's no sign of the river. She keeps going with the kid asleep in her arms.

I'd better figure out where we are.

Lena lays the kid down in a thicket where the bushes will keep him shaded and hidden. She tells Lupu to watch him, but there's no need. The dog lays down by the kid, watching her.

She looks around for the tallest tree she can climb. It's an old oak with low branches, and Lena starts climbing. Step by step, she climbs higher and higher, just like she does in the fall when they harvest the apples. Father sends her up the tree with a shoulder bag to pick the apples up on top, that are always the ripest and sweetest. Lena's mouth waters as she remembers the crunch of the freshly picked apple and the sweet-tart juice running down her chin. She swallows her saliva and keeps climbing until she's above the tree line. All of a sudden, the view opens, and she can see the sparkling ribbon of the river shimmering in the sun far to the left.

Dang. They somehow veered away.

Lena finds an oddly bent maple and a group of three pines to use as milestones, then starts climbing back down when she hears a bark. She looks down. It's Lupu, warning her. Of what?

She looks around. The Ottomans are coming. They're already past the burned village, heading their way. Dozens of them, looking like an army.

Lena's heart freezes. What should she do?

Then she realizes she's safe. She's way too high in the canopy for them to see her. She can wait for them to go away, then get down and leave. They'll never even know she was there.

But there's Dan. And Lupu. Even if they miss the kid in the bushes, the dog will give him away.

What can she do? She can't bring him up here, he's too heavy to carry. And there's no way she can bring the dog.

She should stay here and wait. After all, it's not her fault that the kid ran away, that his family didn't notice, and that the dog will bark.

And he's not even her kid. She hadn't even heard about him until a few hours ago. Maybe they'll let him live. They say the Ottomans take kids to Edirne and treat them well. Perhaps it's better to just leave him there. After all, what can she do against an Ottoman army? She's just a girl. A very tired girl.

But she can’t. She just can’t.

She curses herself as she starts climbing down the tree.

CHAPTER 27
KRONSTADT, SUMMER 1443
FINDING GRANDMA

The sun is about to set beyond the Carpathians' jagged peaks when the guard drops off Ali in Smaranda's forest. But she's been coming here for months, so the little cottage feels like home. Still, her heart fills with wonder as she watches the sky turn purple, the crooked trees' shadows chase each other, and the million blinking fireflies.

Smaranda's house knows her too, so she dropped all pretense of being normal. She greets her with a blink of her windows, then lifts one of the stilts ending in powerful claws to scratch an itch under the thatched roof. An indignant red-headed woodpecker flies away, cursing loudly in bird.

Negru jumps as she opens the gate. He puts his paws on her shoulders and licks her face with his long slobbery tongue. Ali laughs and scratches him, then knocks at the open door.

"Come in."

Leaning over the fireplace, Mama Smaranda stirs something thick and green in the black cauldron, murmuring softly. Ali remembers Ion's words: *"She's a witch,"* and she shivers.

"So what? What's wrong with being a witch?" Smaranda asks.

For a moment, Ali forgot that Mama Smaranda can hear her

thoughts, and her cheeks catch fire. She doesn't know much about witches, but she remembers how the people in her village looked askance at Baba Biris.

"Stay away from her. She's a witch," they whispered. "Last year, when the priest refused to give her communion, she cursed his cow into going dry. And she's got to be the one who commanded the hail storm that destroyed the miller's crop last year."

Folks stayed away from her. But at night, when nobody could see them, many jilted women went to Baba's house with newborn lambs and pots of honey, asking her to curse whoever made their husbands stray; old men came looking for something to give them back their strength; and unmarried girls looked for love potions, or herbs to help them lose the fruit of forbidden love.

Smaranda shrugs. "So what's wrong with that? That's just what we're talking about. Having knowledge gives you power. Power to help, and power to hurt. The hard part is knowing how to use it and how to tell apart the good from the bad."

"Isn't that easy? Knowing good from bad?"

"That's the hardest thing in the world, Ana. And many people never learn. Tell me, if the witch curses the woman who stole someone else's husband, is that good or bad?"

"That's good."

"For whom?"

"For the woman who lost her husband."

"How about the husband? What if his wife is lazy and mean? What if she lies to him and beats his children? And the other woman, what if she's got no one else and she loves the man?"

"But he's not her man!"

"He is now. See, Ana, good and bad aren't that easy to tell apart. What's good for one is often bad for another. Or for many others. You shouldn't take power lightly. You need to think long and hard about what's right and what's wrong, and let your soul speak to you. And sometimes even our souls lie to us. They won't let us see the naked truth, because truth often hurts and lies taste sweeter. But enough of this for now. Are you ready?"

"For what?"

“We're going to the forest to harvest herbs. Tonight's full moon is the shortest of the year, and it’s magic. It pours all its power into plants, so now's the best time to pick them.”

Ana shivers. Smaranda’s not looking at her, but she feels it. "What?"

"We'll go out tonight? In the forest, under a full moon?"

"Yes."

"But... what about the Vârcolaci?"

"What about them?"

"What if they catch and bite us? Then we'll become werewolves, just like them?"

"Oh, Ana. What else?”

"The vampire bats. Mother told me they come at night to bite people's neck and drink their blood."

Smaranda laughs. "You speak like a human. Let's go."

Her heart heavy, Ali follows her out. Smaranda releases Negru, who steps ahead to lead the way. His huge dark shadow leaping joyfully under the full moon makes Ali feel a bit better, but not much.

They walk along paths almost too narrow to see as the forest’s darkness envelops them in its embrace. They stop to pick some herb here, some flower there, and head towards the raising silver moon. Ali struggles to focus on the herbs, on how to find them and recognize them, but her heart isn't in it. Her soul shrinks with fear, and, of course, Smaranda knows. "What are you afraid of, little girl?"

Ali lets that go, since she’s more afraid of werewolves than she is of Professzor Géza, and even the burgomaster.

“Werewolves.”

"Why?"

“Because they eat the moon. And the sun."

Smaranda laughs. “So what's it to you? It's not like they're eating your dinner."

Ali knows she’s teasing her, but she doesn’t feel like laughing.

"But if they bite me, I'm going to become one of them."

"So what?"

"Every time there's a full moon, I'll become a hairy wolf, and I'll run around in the darkness to eat the moon and sun."

"That sounds like fun," Smaranda says. "I'd love to take a bite of the moon. Wouldn't you like to see it really close? And taste it?"

Ali shakes her head in outrage. "But I'd be a large hairy beast. I'd run around the fields under the full moon, not able to regain my human shape."

"That sounds awful," Smaranda says. "Negru must hate it."

Far ahead, Negru runs up and down the hills, following his nose on invisible paths he's the only one to know. All puffed up, he looks even bigger. He rushes forward, then runs back to keep an eye on them. He pricks his ears to the song of the nightingales, the whisper of the trees, the gurgling of the hidden streams. Negru is the king of the forest and he knows it. He turns to them for a moment and smiles, then takes off towards something only he can hear. Ali's never seen someone happier, human or dog, and she struggles to wrap her mind around the fact that being a werewolf may feel good.

"But I'd bite people, and they'd become werewolves like me."

"Who would you like to bite first?"

Ali stares at her as if she sees her for the first time. Smaranda takes everything Ali has ever learned, everything she thinks she knows, and turns it on its head. Good and evil, life and death, truth and lies are all relative in Smaranda's world. That puts Ali's understanding of the world upside down, and she no longer knows what to think. She drops her head. "I don't know."

"That's exactly the point. You don't know. Humans taught you a world that doesn't exist. They taught you that the good is good, the bad is bad, and there's nothing in between. The women are meek, the men are strong, and there's no other way. Werewolves are bad and witches are evil and the priests are all blessed by God. That world doesn't exist."

"But I've always lived in it!"

"How long is that?"

Ali shrugs. "Mother said I was ten, a while ago."

"How old is your mother?"

"Almost thirty, I think. She's very old."

Smaranda laughs so hard that her eyes tear up.

"That's the funniest thing I've heard in ages," she says, wiping her eyes with her sleeve. Ali wonders what's so funny, but Smaranda is too choked with laughter to talk. She finally settles down and takes a deep breath.

"OK. How old was your father?"

Ali shrugs again. She doesn't know, but to her, Father will forever be young and handsome.

"Fifteen?" She gives a number that's lower than her hands and toes put together.

“Oh, how I wish it were so," Smaranda says, wiping her tears again, though she no longer looks happy. "Your father would be thirty today."

"That can't be. That's too old. And how would you know?" Ali asks, giving in to her anger and rebelling against this woman who’s turned her world upside down.

Ali’s world was not much fun to live in, but it had rules. In that world, Ali knew right from wrong, and knew her duty, whether she chose to do it or not. Mother was always right, since she was Mother. Whenever Ana disobeyed her, she opened herself to the devil’s temptations, whatever that means, and the eternal damnation of Hell. Even Popa Anghel said so.

But Smaranda took that away. After listening to her, Ali no longer knows right from wrong and good from bad. She doesn't even know if she's Ana or Ali, a girl or a boy. She’s lost in this complicated world she doesn't understand, so she’s confused and frustrated. And touching Father was going one step too far. Father is her one touchstone in this weird world melting around her. She bites her lip to keep her tears in check and glares at Smaranda.

Smaranda sighs and touches her cheek. "I know. I’m his mother," she says.

And just like that, Ali’s world tumbles.

CHAPTER 28

A FRIENDLY WEREWOLF

Ali's world just turned upside down once again. Seconds ago, she was an orphan who ran away from home to escape her mother, and nobody in the world cared about her. Now, she has a grandmother who happens to be the most amazing person she's ever met.

If that's true.

Smaranda has upended her world so many times that Ali no longer knows what to think. Time and time again, she showed her that the things she took as self-evident truths were just lies she got fed from the cradle. And now this?

"I never lied to you, Ana."

Ali blushes.

"But why didn't you tell me?"

"You weren't ready. You needed to learn to rely on yourself."

"Am I ready now?"

"I think you are. For the first time ever, you questioned me and my judgment. You're starting to think on your own."

"Tell me about Father."

"Not now. We have..."

A terrible howl shatters the air. It's the scream of a tortured soul, so heavy with suffering, pain, and loneliness that it gives Ali goosebumps.

"What was that?" she whispers.

"You're about to find out."

Ali's heart races, and she steps closer to Smaranda. Despite the glowing orb of the moon, the woods couldn't be darker, and Ali wishes she was anywhere but here. She'd take Smaranda's place, the Kronstadt fortress, even her old home to flee the terror in her heart. She shivers and looks at Smaranda, who stands waiting, unmoved.

"Where is Negru?"

"He's with his friend."

His friend? But Negru is a dog. He doesn't have friends.

They wait, and wait. Ali tries to ignore the foreboding fouling the air, but she can't. The birds stopped singing, the wind stopped blowing, even the gurgling of the stream went quiet. The silence is solid and heavy like a stone wall.

Ali would love to flee, but she doesn't know her way back. And she can't leave Smaranda behind. So she bites her lips and waits by her side, even though she's shaking like a leaf and her heart pumps like it wants to break through her chest.

"What are you afraid of?"

What is she afraid of? She doesn't know. Death? Not really. She was ready to die when she dove for those reeds. She still is. So, if she's not afraid of dying, what's she afraid of?

"The unknown?"

Maybe. She's afraid of the things she can't understand, though why would they be scarier than death? But, to her, they are.

"That's why you learn, so you can understand more," Smaranda says. "The more you know, the fewer the things you're afraid of."

Ali nods, though right now the last thing she wants to do is to learn. She wants to get out of here, and she wants it bad.

Smaranda nods. "We'll be leaving soon. But in the meantime, try to open your mind and reach beyond your panic. You can't live in fear. And even if you could, it wouldn't be worth it. Grow beyond it. It's not easy, but I think you can."

Ali takes in a deep breath and faces her terror. What is she afraid of? That howl? It's just a sound. If she's not afraid of death, why would she be afraid of a sound? What can be worse than death?

"There are a few things, and they're different for everyone. But there aren't many. For most humans, death is as bad as it gets."

Ali scrutinizes her brain and focuses on her fear. She struggles to push it in the back of her mind like she'd try to move a heavy coffer out of the way, but it's not working. That darn fear is not like a coffer, it's more like a rabid dog that snarls, lunges and tries to rip her apart.

But Ali isn't afraid of dogs. So she puts her heart into it, and persists. It takes a lot of work, but when she's done, she's pushed that sucker out of her way. The dread is still there, but Ali is no longer its hostage.

Smaranda nods. "Well done."

Two dark shadows appear on the horizon. They run side by side, eating up the distance, and Ali's fear tries to return. She tightens her fists and elbows it back.

The massive black shadows grow larger and larger. Ali's heart beats to break out of her chest.

They can't do worse than kill me, she thinks, and the thought is strangely comforting.

Smaranda touches her shoulder. "Good job. I couldn't do better."

Ali nods, making sure that she keeps her fear back where it belongs. It is. She's scared, sure she is. But she's scared like she's cold or tired or hungry. It doesn't feel good, but it doesn't blind her and rob her of her reason.

The two shadows are now upon them. The first one leaps.

Ali takes a deep breath as Negru puts his paws on her shoulders and licks her face, then turns and runs to Smaranda.

The other one would look like Negru's twin, unless you looked closer. He's humongous, twice Negru's size, and his curved fangs are as long as daggers. The thing leaps towards Ali but doesn't jump on her. He wags his tail and sits facing her just six feet away, like a well-trained dog. He looks in her eyes, and his glowing eyes feel familiar, and they're talking to her. She doesn't know what he's saying, but she's no longer afraid. She steps forward and reaches out her hand. The beast puts his paw in her hand and smiles.

Ali smiles back. He's not a beast. He's a friend.

"I'm glad to meet you. I hope to see you again," Ali says.

Sooner than you think, the beast answers, and Ali understands she can read his thoughts. The beast never spoke, but she heard him in her head.

He wags his tail once more and vanishes as they return to Smaranda's cottage.

"Who was that?" Ali asks.

"You tell me."

Ali searches inside herself. She knows those eyes. And she knows that voice, even though she only heard it in her head. "Codru?"

"Very good. Now you know why you shouldn't fear werewolves. Some of them are your friends."

"What happened to him?"

"He got bit."

"And then?"

"Getting bit doesn't change who you are. It just changes what you are. Codru's curse is to turn into a werewolf under every full moon. If he fails to drink his potion."

"What potion?"

"That, my dear, you're about to learn."

The whole way back, Ali struggles to understand how she can have a friend who's a werewolf, and she fails. The idea is mind-boggling.

"If you think that's hard, think about how it must feel to be him," Smaranda says, and Ali understands three things.

First, she'll never be safe around Smaranda, who can hear her thoughts.

Second, she'll always be safe around Smaranda, who will protect her no matter what.

Third, whether mind-boggling or not, one of her friends is a werewolf.

And that gets her thinking. What about the other one?

CHAPTER 29

RADU'S SPOILED BATH

EDIRNE, 1443

It's a glorious morning in Edirne. A cloudless blue sky smiles upon the palace gardens, where flowers in every color of the rainbow soak the sun, and a hundred birds in gilded cages flap their wings and outdo each other with the sweetness of their songs. A soft breeze caresses the branches loaded with luscious fruit and carries the scent of the roses through the intricate grilled windows inside the cool blue rooms of the sarayi.

Radu has been here for months, and he's never been happier. If he was to draw the perfect place on earth, this would be it. It has splendid buildings, exquisite gardens, and an attention to beauty and comfort that nobody in Wallachia even dreamed about.

As soon as Radu wakes up, a servant brings him his morning drink and a wet towel to clean his hands and face. He wipes his eyes with the soft white cloth that smells like oranges, then drinks the fragrant lemon sherbet to cleanse his palate. It's chilled with snow brought on the back of mules all the way from Anatolia, and reminds him of the ice-cold water he used to drink from the springs at home. But they didn't have sherbet.

Life at the sultan's court is nothing like life at the Royal Court of Wallachia. Here, everything is clean, beautiful, and smells delightful.

The court in Târgoviște was always cold, even in the scorching days of summer, since the six-feet-thick walls of gray stone stored the winter's cold throughout the year. The courtyards reeked like refuse, manure, and worse, though nobody noticed. And the people were unsmiling, scruffy, and worried.

In Edirne it's all about beauty, comfort, and serenity. Even the walls are works of art made from thousands of colorful tiles shaped into elaborate designs. Here, he sits on brocade pillows instead of cold stone ledges, listens to the bewitching song of exotic birds instead of the screaming street vendors, and wears smooth silk instead of rough wool and linen. Radu feels like he got to Heaven without even dying. He's never been happier.

"Time for your bath, my prince," Adir says.

His blue shalwars and rose kaftan set off his mahogany skin and brilliant white smile. He's a Nubian, coming from the Nile, like most black eunuchs do, and he's lucky to serve in Sultan Murad's harem.

Radu follows him along the twisted corridors to the hammam, where the air's so thick with scented steam you can hardly see beyond a few feet. Adir helps him out of his shalwars and chemise, and Radu lays to rest on the washing ledge, where the bath eunuchs will scrub him cleaner than he's ever been. He looks forward to being scoured from head to toe with the rough loofah pads and the olive soap that smells like jasmine.

He can't remember having a bath back home, though he must have. At least when they baptized him. They didn't wash that much in Wallachia. Like all good Christians, the Wallachians believed that a man only has to bathe twice in his life: when he's born, and when he dies. Baths are bad for the body, they said, but Radu can't understand why.

The masseur's steel fingers dig into the knots of his shoulders to soften them, then slide down his back and below, and Radu sighs with pleasure. He loves the bath like he loves everything about this Ottoman palace. Everything but his brother. If he could never see Vlad again, his life would be perfect.

But, alas, Vlad's right there as he dips in the cool pool after being thoroughly scrubbed and rinsed. Even worse, Vlad wants to talk to him.

"How are you, princess?" Vlad asks.

Radu would love to crush his grin with his fist, but he knows better. Vlad's not only four years older, but he's bigger, stronger, and mean as a snake. And he hates being here. He hates everything about this place. Everything but the food.

Vlad loves harassing Radu. He taunts him, teases him, and hurts him whenever he can. And there's no better place than the bath, since the guards and the teachers aren't here to stop him. Here in the bath, they're on their own. And Radu hates wasting the pleasure of the bath almost as much as he hates listening to his brother. He sinks deeper into the clear water trying to hide his white, hairless body.

"I'm a prince, not a princess, thank you."

They couldn't be more different. Vlad is short and wiry, Radu is lanky and lean. Vlad is dark and hairy and he's already got a shadow above his upper lip. Radu is rose-petal pink, without a single hair other than the golden curls that fall over his shoulders. Vlad is angry and loud, while Radu is contemplative and soft. Vlad looks forward to his fighting classes, while Radu loves poetry and languages.

Sultan Murad knows them both and treats them kindly. Even more so now, since his son Mehmet is away. Like all the şehzades, sultans-in-waiting, he went to one of the Ottoman provinces to learn how to govern. *The sultan must miss him*, Radu thinks. That's why he spends so much time with Radu and Vlad. He talks to them about the world, the challenges of a ruling a country, and about how, when Vlad and Radu will sit the throne of Wallachia, they'll strengthen the friendship between the Wallachians and the Ottomans.

Vlad's face darkened when he heard that, but he was smart enough to bite his tongue. But now he's got a chance to vent his anger. "Friendship! What a load of crap! Wallachians and Ottomans hate each-other. We'd stop at nothing to destroy each-other if we could."

Radu sighs. "That can't be true, brother. Father wouldn't have sent us here if he didn't want us to be friends."

"Are you out of your mind? Did you forget what Father told us?" Vlad sputters.

As a matter of fact, Radu did. He forgot most of it, but the part about the love for Wallachia and how it was their job to keep her safe. He also remembers that he thought about killing Vlad. But that was long ago. He was just a child, angry that Vlad had killed his dog.

"I didn't," he lies, hoping that Vlad will let him be.

No such luck.

"Have you forgotten that the Ottomans impose devşirme, the blood tax, on Wallachia? Not only do our people have to pay the tribute of wheat and wine and money every year, but they even take our children, some as young as eight. They rip them from the arms of their mothers and bring them here to become Ottomans."

"But isn't being here better? We're warm, and the food is good, and the baths... "

"Are you goddamn stupid? Are you even listening? Our Wallachian children lose their home, their language and their faith. They get converted to Islam and trained into becoming janissaries and sipahis, the spine of the Ottoman army. Then they go back to Wallachia to fight against their own fathers and brothers, pillage the country and bring back even more children."

Radu sighs. He can't understand what's so bad about growing up here. It can't be worse than Wallachia! As for being ripped from the arms of their mothers, he can't remember the last time he was in the arms of his mother. And he doesn't want to.

"But Father sent us here to..."

"Father sent us here because he had to! That was the only way to get the sultan off his back while he works on building his army and forging alliances. He sent us here to learn about the Ottomans, their language, and their fighting. We're to go back and help him overcome them when the time comes. We are not to become them!"

"I'm not one of them," Radu says, wishing he was. Wishing Vlad would go away and leave him alone.

He leaves the bath, allowing the servant to wrap him into a blue silk kaftan embroidered with golden birds of paradise, a gift from the sultan. He wishes Vlad wouldn't follow, but of course, he does. He sits next to him on the resting bench.

He whispers in his ear in Wallachian, which he knows he

shouldn't. They're only supposed to speak Ottoman, unless they're in Greek, Hungarian, or Latin class. Speaking Wallachian is forbidden for a good reason: None of the sultan's spies in the harem speaks it. They're all black, from the Nile, so they can't report what they hear.

"I have a plan," Vlad says.

"What plan?"

"A plan to recover our freedom and help our country. A plan to get us back home."

Radu shivers. He can't think of anything he'd hate more.

"What's your plan?"

"The day after the day after tomorrow, after the third prayer. When we have archery lessons."

"Yes."

"The sultan often comes to see us."

Radu nods.

"We get ready, take our best horses, and pack some supplies. Dried fruit, water, and wine."

"And run away?"

"Yes. After we kill the sultan."

CHAPTER 30

YOU WANT A CAT?

It's been a rough two days for Radu. Vlad's words wiped away the joy from his soul like it never existed. He's been so sick with worry that he couldn't eat or sleep. Unable to settle, he's been pacing back and forth in his small room, wondering what his crazy brother will do. And what he should do about it.

The servants told the validé, of course, since Emine Hatun, the sultan's mother, is the one who rules the harem and everybody inside it. She called him to her personal chambers in the sarayi.

Radu's never been there before, and the display of beauty astounds him. The white marble floors are covered with splendid Isfahan carpets woven from glimmering silk and wool-stuffed brocade pillows in jewel tones that invite you to rest. Bright-colored birds with suspicious round eyes sing their heart out in gilded cages. And the flowers! They're everywhere: red roses, white lilies, armfuls of white jasmine — all filling the air with their intoxicating scents.

The sultan's mother has the best rooms, the best clothes and the best food. And she gets to tell everyone what to do. The eunuchs shiver when she calls their names, and the women, whether servants, concubines, even the sultan's wives, all respect and worship her like she hung the moon.

Sure they do. She's got the power of life and death over them, so they wouldn't dream of crossing her. Even her son, Sultan Murad, fears her, and often asks for her counsel.

Kneeling in front of the validé, Radu touches his forehead to the marble, feeling faint. He hides a secret larger than life that he can't share: a secret that could kill him and Vlad.

"Sit up and tell me. What's going on with you, little one?"

He sits cross-legged on a brocade pillow at her feet, but he doesn't dare look in her eyes. The two black eunuchs who brought him over stand behind him, and Radu can almost hear his head rolling on the floor, severed from his body by their kilijes, if he tells her about Vlad's treason. And it's even worse if he doesn't, and she finds out. Vlad's head would roll too, of course, but that's not much consolation. The urge to tell her stirs Radu's insides.

"Are you ill?"

He shakes his head.

"You miss your mother?"

Truth be told, there are few things Radu misses less. But that's the one thing he can admit to without getting in trouble. He nods, and his tears flow like a river, darkening the red brocade pillow into purple. They're tears of relief, but she doesn't know it. Thank God.

"I'm sorry, little one. Sadly, the lives of princes are not their own. They belong to their country. You and your brother need to do what your country demands of you, and right now, that means being away from your mother. That's not much consolation for a child, but as you grow, you'll understand. It will get easier as you grow and make other friends. I wish I could do more."

Radu looks up to thank her for her kindness and sees her for the first time. She's not young, the validé, but she's beautiful, and her blue eyes are kind. Radu is both grateful and happy that he managed to keep his mouth shut.

"I have an idea." The validé turns to one of the eunuchs. "Fetch Star."

The eunuch fetches a round wicker basket. Inside it, on a red velvet pillow, a sleepy orange cat is suckled by seven wriggling kittens.

"That's Star. The kittens have no names yet. Would you like one?"

His face still wet with tears, Radu smiles. He hasn't had a pet since Yellow died, and his empty heart looks for love.

"Which one?"

Radu points out to a rambunctious yellow kitten smaller than an apple.

"What will you call her?"

"*Sari*. Yellow," he says.

The validé smiles.

"That's a good name. But she needs a little more time with her mother. You can come back to get her in a week."

By the time the eunuch takes him back, he's late for his history lesson. The turbaned professor frowns, but doesn't interrupt his lecture on how the Ottoman Empire's many conquests have made the world a better place, thank Allah.

As soon as he turns to get another map, Vlad leans over.

"Where were you?"

"With the validé."

Vlad's eyes narrow. He shoots him a look of sheer poison and hisses:

“Don't even dream about telling them, or I'll kill you. Unless they kill you first."

He turns back to the map like nothing happened while Radu's heart twists in a muddy turmoil. If he's still alive in a week, he may get a cat. But a week is an awful long time, and Vlad plans to kill the sultan tomorrow.

CHAPTER 31
TORN

What a terrible night, Radu thinks, after tossing and turning in his bed forever. Oh, how he wishes he had it all clear in his head, like Vlad does. And Father. But he doesn't, and he doesn't know what to do.

Radu is a prince of Wallachia. Father sent him here to help protect his people, and he shouldn't care one iota about the sultan or the validé. Not even about the cat. Vlad is right. His plan might get them back to Wallachia, and killing the sultan might help Father and the country. If they pull it off.

But Radu hates Vlad, who's an evil, blood-thirsty killer and loves nothing more than causing pain. Vlad enjoys hurting people, dogs, squirrels, or any other living creature known to God. The others' tears give him joy. Radu would rather be dead than be like his brother.

Still, Vlad is a Prince of Wallachia. He's Father's heir after Mircea and before him, Radu. And he's trying to do right by his country and his people.

Maybe. Truth be told, Vlad would kill anyone just for fun.

Moreover, Radu has few good memories of Wallachia, which is always cold, often dirty, and seldom fun. And there they all look down upon him like he's wanting. Unlike here, where he feels happy, pampered, and loved.

What should he do? Say Vlad manages to kill the sultan. Then what? They'll run away, and they may make it back to Wallachia, or they may not. Probably not.

But the sultan's a good man, and he's been kinder to Radu than his own mother. And the baths are great. So are the gardens, the clothes and the food. Why on earth would he go back to Wallachia?

Because I have to. I'm part of this. Vlad has a plan, and he's raring to go, and I can't pretend I don't know it. Not for long. Soon enough, whether Vlad manages to kill the sultan or not, our fate is sealed. Our heads will roll, and we'll deserve it, Radu thinks, dragging himself down the meandering hallways to the courtyard where they have their archery lesson. He shrinks under the weight of his leather armor that's almost as heavy as his heart, wondering what will happen to the yellow kitten.

Vlad's there already. Sure he is. He loves nothing more than killing. Pigeons, chicken, puppies — whatever. It's all the same in Vlad's world. Radu's stomach churns, and he wants to puke.

But that's because he's defective and weak. Real men are not like that.

But he's not a real man, his brother says. Radu sighs and looks for the sultan, but he's not here yet.

Vlad winks.

Radu nods, wishing he was anywhere but there. He mounts his horse, since they shoot from horseback, like they would in a real battle, into moving targets. Which happen to be pigeons.

The soldiers release the first pigeon. He's brown and fast. But Vlad releases his arrow and the pigeon falls as if God wants him out of His sky.

The second pigeon is Radu's. He pulls the bow taut, and the string sings. The small white pigeon flies off, and Radu lets off a lame arrow that plops back on the grass, way too close. Vlad's shrill laughter fills the courtyard, but Radu ignores him, happy to see the white bird fly away toward freedom.

But she turns around and flies back. Vlad laughs again.

"Watch. This's how you do it, princess."

He readies his bow and aims at her as the stupid bird gets closer and closer.

Radu screams: "Let it be! It's my bird, not yours."

Too late. The bird freezes in mid-air as the arrow skewers it from front to back, then tumbles to the ground.

"You should have gotten her when you could," Vlad says, getting his next arrow ready.

Radu's heart is ablaze with anger, and he'd love to kill his brother. He wonders if he could take him out with an arrow, but he doesn't think so. He's gotten pretty good with his bow, but he's so angry he shakes like a leaf. And Vlad wears his leather armor, so his only vulnerable spots are his neck and his eyes.

As they get ready for the next bird, the guards shout: "Stand for the sultan."

It's now or never, Radu thinks. Vlad only needs a moment to turn around and shoot, then gallop home through the forests and the fields. Radu can go with him, or he can try to do something to stop him.

Like what? Shoot him? Warn the sultan? Drop dead?

Radu puts an arrow in his bow and takes aim at his brother. Mounted on his black palfrey in the middle of the yard, Vlad exudes darkness like the sun emits light. He's ready to kill, and the horse dancing under him absorbs his energy. He's on fire, and he rears and neighs like he's itching to fight. They're ready.

Radu isn't. He glances at the sculpted open door, wide enough for five riders abreast, but it's still empty. The sultan isn't here yet.

He turns to his brother. His eyes lock on the soft spot between the top of his armor and his chin. An arrow right there would pierce through the large veins of his neck and kill him in less time than it takes to say the Lord's Prayer. If Radu's aim is good enough.

But what would the sultan think? Would he believe that Radu killed his brother to save his life? After all, he's had plenty of opportunities to tell someone — the validé, the teachers, the guards — and he didn't. Telling them now that he only killed his brother to save the sultan's life will sound like he's lying to save his hide. Everyone knows that they hate each other.

And what would Father think? And Mother? And Mircea?

Radu doesn't know what to do. He should, since he's almost a man, for God's sake. But he's not a real man. And, in his heart of hearts, he knows he'll never be. There's something wrong with him, like Vlad said. That's why he hates killing, loathes fighting, and loves the Ottoman lifestyle better than his own Wallachian traditions.

Driven mad by the sharp spurs, Vlad's horse dances across the field like he's on fire. His bow ready, Vlad controls him with his knees and spurs alone. He pretends to be looking for the bird to be released, but he glances at the carved door opened for the sultan.

Radu hugs his white mare between his legs and readies his bow. He needs to put his heart in the arrow he's about to launch. But towards who? The dove? The sultan? His brother?

He doesn't know. He hopes the arrow does.

Drums roll. The sultan is at the door.

No armor for him. He's straight and tall and dressed in gold all over but for the snow-white turban that covers his head. He nods at the boys, the guards, and the servants bowing in front of him.

Vlad lifts his bow and fits an arrow in.

Radu's heart beats louder than the drums. He watches Vlad pull the string, and it's like time slows down.

He takes a deep breath, sinks his spurs into his placid mare's belly and drives her forward. They crash into Vlad and his horse just as he releases the arrow.

CHAPTER 32

THE CHRISTMAS EVE FIGHT

TRANSYLVANIA

The short Transylvanian summer vanished like a dream. The fall came like a thief, robbing the sun of its warmth, the trees of their leaves, and the dreary days of any joy, then left the Kronstadt fortress prey to winter.

Winters are long and harsh up here. In the high plateau between the mountains, the snows of November are still there in March. But it's only December, so the days are short, the nights dark, and the long slow evenings are for sitting by the fire telling stories.

Ali, Ion and Codru have been together for more than a year now. They're like brothers, with the good and the bad of it. They eat together, sleep together, and train together every day, but they never talk about themselves. They talk about the weather, the food, their training and the many quirks of their teachers. But tonight is something else. It's Christmas Night, and they're having a feast.

They're already full, but they're still picking from their Christmas dinner. The Saxons have been generous: They had sarmale — tangy pickled cabbage stuffed with meat and rice and baked in a clay-pot. Also fried garlicky sausages, and roasted pork with garlic and herbs, and crusty warm bread with soft yellow butter. They even had cozonac, the celebratory sourdough sweet bread stuffed with ground walnuts, poppy seeds and raisins they only make for Christmas and Easter. And they had plenty of wine.

Now they're sitting at the table, sipping on the last of the wine and watching the flames, remembering past Christmases and those they shared them with.

Ion picks at a yellow slice of cozonac.

"It's good, but not as good as my mother's. She always woke up way before dawn to knead the dough. She covered it with a clean cloth and set it by the stove to raise until it doubled in size. Then she stuffed it with walnuts and raisins and shaped it into long narrow trays. Oh, that aroma! I wish I could show it to you! I got dizzy from the scent of vanilla, lemon peel, and caramelized sugar. The house smelled like that for days. My little sister Neta used to steal a piece of dough and eat it raw. Then she'd get sick and couldn't eat any when it was ready. I wonder how she's doing."

Ion stares into the flames, but he only sees his memories. His eyes shine with tears.

"How old was she?" Ali asks.

"Five. Petrica, the baby, was two."

"Were you the oldest?" Ali asks.

"Yes. I was twelve. I had two more brothers; one was two years younger; the other one three, but they didn't make it. Neither did Father."

"Why? The Black Death?"

"Yes. Half the people in our village died. Then Father died too. Mother did her best, but we just didn't have enough to eat. So, when the priest came to ask if she'll be willing to let me go, she said yes. She had to find a way to feed the kids. The Saxons gave them enough money to make it through last winter. This winter, too, maybe."

"How about you, Codru?"

"We were too many mouths to feed. They sent me away."

"Why you?"

"I... ate more."

"You miss them?"

"Not really. I miss the horses."

Ali sighs. "I miss my dog. I hope she's well. And the cow."

"Do you think we'll ever get to see our families again?" Ion asks.

Codru shrugs and takes another sip of wine. "Probably not. They're probably all be dead by now. We may be dead soon too."

Ion glares at him. "Speak for yourself. My people aren't dead. Not my little sister."

"How do you know?"

"I just do."

"You're being stupid. For all that you know, she's been dead and buried for a year. She's rotten by now."

"You are stupid. And mean."

"Unless they didn't bury her. If she died the Black Death with your brother and your mother, nobody buried them. They let them to the crows and stray dogs."

Ion jumps to his feet so fast that his heavy chair falls backward, and punches Codru in the face. Blood spurts everywhere and splashes them both. Codru curses. He grabs Ion by the shoulders and throws him across the room.

Ion's head hits the stone wall with a thud. He struggles to stand on shaky feet, then grabs the fire poker and aims it at Codru's head. Codru leaps to the side, then throws a high kick that flings the fire poker against the wall. He grabs Ion's arm and twists it behind his back, pushing him down to the ground.

Ion hooks his leg around Codru's knee and jerks it, pulling his legs from under him. They fall to the ground and Codru's head hits the floor with a bang.

"That's enough! Stop it, both of you," Ali shouts, but she may as well be talking to the wall.

Ion struggles back to his feet, but he's not fast enough. Codru punches him in the face and something cracks. Ion grabs the iron candlestick sitting on the table and crushes it onto Codru's skull. Codru drops to the ground dragging Ion with him, then rolls on top of him. His massive hands tighten around Ion's throat and squeeze, choking him.

Ion's knee finds Codru's groin. Codru gasps, and lets go of his throat. Ion squeezes out from under him and grabs the knife that's still sitting on the table. He aims for Codru's throat, but Codru grabs his wrist and twists it. Ion screams and the knife clangs as it hits the floor. Codru reaches for it.

Ali kicks it to the other end of the room and grabs the water bucket in the corner. "That's enough."

She pours the bucket of cold water over them, and they gasp and let go, shaking like a pair of wet dogs.

Ion glares at her. "What's wrong with you? What did you do that for?"

"Yeah. What the hell?" Codru wipes the water from his eyes.

Ali's blood boils. "With me? What's wrong with me? Are you out of your darn minds? What was that all about? What did you almost kill each other for?"

They glare at her, then look away.

"Codru, you started it. What was that all about?"

Codru shrugs. His dark face stormy, his fists tight, he leaves and slams the door without looking back.

Ali follows him.

Codru walks down the dark corridor to the main door of the fortress. The guard lets him out, and Ali watches him walk further and further over through the glittering white field of fresh snow. His track is deep and dark as he walks towards the full moon. Behind him, his shadow grows large, black, and not human.

"It's the full moon," Ion says.

"Yes. That potion keeps him from turning into a beast, but the anger and pain are still there."

"I hope he doesn't kill us one of these days. Tonight was close. What if you made the potion stronger?"

"I don't know. I'll ask Smaranda."

They watch and wait, but he doesn't look back.

As they return to their room, Ali wonders what to do about Codru, who's always quiet, lonely, and full of anger. What can hide in the soul of someone whose shadow is a wolf's?

Ali searches her heart, like Smaranda taught her, trying to read him. But she can't, and she's scared. Not of him, but of the force that hijacks him and that he can't tame.

Will Codru's curse destroy them all someday?

CHAPTER 33

THE GRIMOIRE

Codru came back late that night. The following morning, they went about their business like nothing happened. If anyone wondered what had happened to the room, if the guards even noticed that the boys looked like they'd been to war and didn't talk to each other, nobody said a thing. But the silence was so heavy and the air so thick with tension that Ali couldn't wait to leave and go to Mama Smaranda's.

Half-hidden by a blanket of fresh snow that glittered like a field of diamonds in the sun, the old forest is more charming than ever. Snoring gently in its midst, Mama Smaranda's little house wakes up with a chuckle when Ali pushes open the old creaky gate. The skinny chimney puffs ring after ring of scented smoke that raises to the sky, forming letters.

"Merry Christmas, Ana," they read, and Ali's heart fills with joy.

"Thank you," she says.

"You're welcome," the house puffs, then goes back to sleep.

Ali shakes her head in wonder. She knew the house could talk, since she's heard her squabble with Gigi, the cat, when she was chasing mice in the attic, but she can write, too? That's more than many humans can do.

Negru jumps to greet her, so happy that he tumbles in the snow. Ali laughs, and throws him a snowball. Negru leaps to catch it, crushes it in his iron jaws and asks for more.

Ali obliges, and for a moment, all's right with the world. There's a happy dog and untouched snow and a glorious winter sun, and Ali laughs like she doesn't have a worry in the world until she remembers she's here for a reason. She sighs and walks inside, where it's dark, warm and cozy, and the air smells like cozonac.

Mama Smaranda sits by the fire stirring something in the big black cauldron, as usual. She glances at Ali and smiles, but she can tell that something is wrong.

"Welcome, little girl. What's wrong?"

"Codru. He's not doing well. What if we made the potion stronger? Or gave him more of it?"

Mama Smaranda shakes her head. "That could kill him. What happened?"

"He fought with Ion last night. They almost killed each other."

"Why? What set them off?"

"Nothing. We had dinner then sat and talked, and Codru went crazy."

"What did you talk about?"

"Ion's family."

"Tell me about them."

"He has a mother, a younger sister and a baby brother that he misses terribly. His father died."

"Did he say how?"

"The Black Death. It took half of his village, and his two younger brothers."

"I see. How about Codru?"

"He didn't want to talk."

"You want to know?"

"I do."

"Did you know that Codru is a Roma? Most people call them gypsies."

Ali's jaw drops. She's heard about gypsies. Mother called them the scourge of the earth. They're too lazy to work, so they lie and steal, she said. They have no land and no home, so they live in horse-drawn caravans, wander from one village to the next and steal people's chicken and their sheep. Even their children, she said, when she threatened to give her to the gypsies. In Mother's book, being a gypsy is worse than being a werewolf. And Codru is both.

Ali doesn't say a word, but Smaranda hears her troubled thoughts and shrugs.

"I wouldn't put much credence in anything your mother said. You know how many times she led you astray. Better ask Codru about it. But just imagine how it must feel to be a gypsy in a world that hates you because you are who you are. And then turn into a werewolf through no fault of you own."

Ali sighs. She'd thought she'd had it hard, but this is worse. At least she's human.

Smaranda laughs. "I wouldn't be so sure. And, speaking about that, I have a gift for you."

"A gift? For me?"

Ali's face lights with joy. She never gets gifts, ever. Other than that pork chop Ion gave her last year, the last gift she ever got was her beloved silver cross that Father hung around her neck just before he died. She glances at it, and the stone glows blue.

"That wasn't quite a gift," Smaranda says. "That's part of your inheritance. It was your father's duty to pass it on to you, like I passed it on to him when I could no longer give him help and guidance."

"Where did you get it from?"

"I got it from my mother, who got it from her mother, who got it from her mother. This cross has been in our family for almost a thousand years. Someday I'll tell you its story, but not today. Today I have a gift for you. There!"

She hands Ali a bag barely bigger than her hands held together. The sack is made of bright red silk embroidered with golden dragons and purple flowers, and it's the prettiest thing Ali has ever seen. And it's heavy.

"Merry Christmas."

Ali caresses the silk, loving its smoothness. She shakes it and smells it to guess what's inside, but the bag won't give any clues.

She opens it. It's an old book, as ratty as the bag is beautiful. The brown leather cover is scratched deep, and the edges of the yellow pages are curled and torn with use. And it smells like mold.

"How nice," Ali lies.

Smaranda laughs. "Open it."

Ali turns page after page, all yellow with age and marred with spots and blotches, but they're empty.

She lifts her eyes at Smaranda. "There's nothing written in it."

"Sure there is. Press your palm on the page."

As soon as she does, a steady stream of words flow onto the page, faster than she can read them. They're beautifully calligraphed in black ink, with flourishes and tiny drawings here and there.

March 15. Today was the first time I managed to disappear a rabbit. It was old Mudpie, and it took me forever, but it was worth it. It was the first time I could disappear anything bigger than a sparrow, and I was overjoyed. But when I recalled her, she came back covered in spider webs and dust. I asked her where she'd been, but she was so mad she wouldn't talk to me. Mother laughed and said that I need to work on my incantations. Like I didn't have enough trouble with the potions!

I used a shrinking potion from three golden dragon scales, a teaspoon of rotten bat blood and half a cup of black shrivelfigs. I crushed the dragon scales then boiled them all, stirring left-wise until the potion thickened, then I sprinkled it over Mudpie's tail and whispered Resilio Lagomorphus.

Nothing happened, so I went back to the recipe to make sure I got it right, but when I looked again, Mudpie was gone. But seeing how she thumped her feet at the cat like she's mad, I wonder if she really disappeared. Maybe she just turned into a mouse and had to run into a hole to escape Gigi? That may be why she got so mad?

If I can catch her tomorrow, I'll try the Disparere or the Invisible Oryctolagus instead of Resilio. And the moonstone leech potion rather than the shrivelfigs.

The end of the page shows an angry rabbit thumping his hind feet in the nose of a grumpy black cat looking just like Gigi, and Ali can't help but smile. She lifts her eyes to Smaranda. "Was this Father's book?"

Smaranda nods. "Yes. His first grimoire-journal when he started his apprenticeship. Boy, did he do a lot of blunders! Like that time he..."

"Apprenticeship? For what?"

"What do you think?"

Ali knows what she thinks, but she can't bear to believe it, let alone say it out loud.

"Was Father a wizard?" she whispers.

Smaranda nods.

"Then... you really are a witch?"

Smaranda smiles. "What do you think?"

"But then... if you're a witch and he was a wizard, I..."

"Yes?"

"What am I?"

"What do you think?"

"Am I a witch, too?"

"Not just yet. But we'll work on it."

CHAPTER 34

THE FOUND FAMILY

Ali's heart is in heavy turmoil as she heads back to the fortress. She knows she's not good at anything — Mother made sure to beat that knowledge into her — but being a witch? That's as bad as it gets!

Just about every Sunday, Popa Anghel preaches that witchery and magic come from the devil. He tells the faithful that God's curse will fall upon those who consort with the demons to avail themselves of the powers of the darkness. They'll fall in the river of fire and burn in Hell forever, unless the devils boil them in tar and rip them apart with iron pincers, like they do on the Monastery painted walls.

But that's only after they die. Still, before burning in Hell forever, she might burn right here, on earth. She's heard folks speak about how they burn the witches alive at the stake in Nuremberg and Buda and many other places. They say that God's men hunt for them and test them with water. They throw them in a river to see if they drown. If they do, that means they were innocent. If they don't, they're witches, so they burn them alive. And Ali can swim.

If she had her druthers, she'd rather drown than burn. But the worst part about burning in Hell is that she won't go to Heaven to join Father. She always hoped to meet him there, but now...

Another thought gives her pause. If Popa Anghel is right, and if Father was a wizard, he can't be in Heaven. If God cursed him, he's got to be in Hell, bathing in the river of fire.

But that can't be! Wizard or not, Father was a good man! He deserves to be in Heaven!

Ali is so tormented by her thoughts that she forgets to push her mare forward. The horse stops to dig for grass under the snow, and by the time Ali notices, the sun's almost down. It's dark already when she gets back, and the boys finished their dinner. Their eyes worried, their faces tense, they're waiting for her by the dying fire.

"Where on earth have you been? We were sick with worry," Ion says.

Ali squeezes next to him on the long bench by the table and looks at what's left. Not much. Stale bread, a little milk, and a ball of white cheese. And an apple.

She sighs and cuts herself some bread, then looks at him sideways. "So worried you forgot to leave me any meat?"

Ion blushes.

"There was no meat, only sausage," Codru says. "Still, what happened? Why are you so late?"

Ali chews on the crust pondering what to say. How does one go about telling her best friends: "And by the way, guess what? I just found out that I'm a witch and I'll burn in Hell forever."

She takes another sip of milk.

But it's not that they have room to talk. One's a werewolf and a gypsy, and the other... who knows?

Ali sinks her eyes in Codru's.

"How did you turn into a werewolf?"

Ion chokes. Codru looks down.

"I was a... I'm a..."

"Gypsy," Ali says.

Codru nods.

"Tell us about it."

He sighs. "First, I want to say I'm sorry for last night. I was jealous. See Ion, I never had a family like yours. We didn't even have a home with an oven so my mother could bake cozonac. We only had our wagon that we called a vardo, and our horses. Our family and five others formed a caravan, and we traveled from one village to the next, struggling to make a living. But the gorgers, the settled people, treated us like dirt. They looked down upon us and wondered what we came to steal."

His voice is angry and bitter, and for the first time ever, Ali feels grateful for her mother, who gave her a home, and her community that didn't despise her.

"But we didn't steal. Not often. Father was a blacksmith. He shod horses, mended pots and pans, and fixed whatever else needed fixing. Mother told people's fortunes in the palm and the cards, and we kids gathered berries and nuts and sold them for pennies. It wasn't an easy life, but we were free to come and go as we chose. We never stayed long in one place because the unknown places always beckoned.

"But then one night there was nothing to eat. It had been weeks since Father had found any work. And with the Black Death and all, nobody wanted their fortunes told. Mother made soup out of tree bark and roots, but that didn't quell our hunger. The kids cried themselves to sleep every night, and we were starving with no end in sight. So, one night Father sent me to find food, since I was the eldest.

"The full moon poured silver over the frosty fields as I snuck towards the village, following my nose toward the chicken coops, ready to run if anyone heard me, but they didn't.

I was almost there when a massive black shadow crossed the fields, heading towards me so fast it was eating up the distance. A dog, I thought, and readied my stick to fight it.

"But that was no dog. That feral-smelling snarling thing was twice as big as me, and faster than a venomous snake. Before I could touch it, he'd bitten me in the back

The pain was nothing like I'd ever felt before. It started at the bite, at the root of my back bone, and spread to every inch of my body, from my head to my toes. My skin tightened and cracked, and my blood turned so hot I couldn't stand it. I couldn't help but shout my pain, but my scream came out as a howl.

"I watched my clothes rip into shreds and my hands mutate into hairy paws. Piercing with terrible pain, my nails grew into claws and my teeth sprouted out into fangs. Blind with pain and crazy with fear, I ran back to our wagon. I called Mother, but my call came out as a howl. Mother saw me and crossed herself. Father grabbed his pitchfork. 'Go away, monster, or I'll kill you!' he shouted.

"'It's me, Codru. I'm not a monster!'" I tried to tell them. But they wouldn't listen.

"The kids woke up screaming. The other wagons woke up too. The men grabbed their axes and pitchforks. The women pelleted me with burning coals. See, this one's from Mother," Codru said, pointing to the scar on his left cheek. "I ran away, or they would have killed me."

"But didn't you turn human the next morning?" Ali asks.

"I did. I went back, naked and bruised and burned. But they didn't let me come near the caravan. Mother cursed me. Father spat at me, and told me to never get near the kids. So I left."

"To where?"

"I lived in the woods for a while. Thankfully, winter was over, so I didn't freeze to death. I stole some clothes off a line, and stole food whenever I could. I did odd jobs for pennies and struggled to stay alive until the day I got to Kronstadt and found out they were looking for conscripts. The rest you know."

He hangs his head and turns away to rearrange the fire. His shoulders slump, and the heaviness in his heart weighs on Ali's soul.

He doesn't dare look us in the eye. He's afraid of what he'll see, she thinks.

She hugs his back. "I'm so sorry about all this, Codru."

He stiffens, but Ali hugs him tighter.

"Codru, I'm your friend. No, not your friend. I'm your sister. I have no one closer than you and Ion. I care about you, I trust you, and I love you."

Codru sobs. He turns and hugs her back.

Ion joins them. "I'm your brother. You're my family, my friend, and my backup, and I'll always be there for you."

Codru wipes his tears, and, for the first time ever, he smiles. "OK, then. We are family. But for one thing. Ali, you're not my sister. You're my brother."

CHAPTER 35

THE LONG WAY TO PATIENCE

MANISA, 1443

Three hundred scorching miles south of Edirne, nestled in Anatolia's hot heart, the city of Manisa can't decide if it belongs to the blue Aegean or to the arid Spil Mountain that raises almost five thousand feet above it.

In this Asian province of the Ottoman Empire, summers are sizzling, winters short, and water is hard to come by. The sun is harsh and plentiful, but the rain is rare, thus precious.

Manisa is Mehmet's new governorship, though he's governor in name only. His father, Sultan Murad the Second, may Allah keep him in his favor, sent him here to get taught, tamed, and molded into a worthy şehzade. Just like the red-hot iron shapeless blobs his father's sword-makers pound with their hammers to mold into worthy blades. And he likes it just as much.

Like today. Mehmet had planned to spend the day riding through the woods and hunting with his falcon. Instead of that, here he is, crawling up this goddamn Spil Mountain heading to its goddamn weeping rock.

He stops to wipe the sweat off his brow and take another sip of warm water out of his leather flask to soften his throat. They've been climbing since before sunrise, and it's almost noon. Mehmet is hot and tired, and his temper's running short.

But there's nobody here to vent to. Not even Akşemseddin, his mentor, who didn't stop to wait for him. He's way ahead, almost at the top, and Mehmet curses. *What's wrong with the man? It's like he doesn't feel the heat, doesn't tire, and doesn't hurt, even though he's older than dirt. He's got to be almost fifty.*

Mehmet sighs, puts his flask away, and follows. His chest heaves like bellows as he crawls on his hands and knees up the slope covered with treacherous rocks that roll under his feet. He'd like to stop and rest, but he can't. He can't let an old man best him like that, so he bites his lip and pushes forward until his heart beats so hard it wants to burst out of his chest. But when he finally gets to the top, Akşemseddin is already sitting cross-legged on the highest rock, meditating.

Mehmet drops to the ground, struggling to quench his air hunger. When his ragged breath finally slows down, he finds the shade of an old pine, not too close to his mentor, and waits to be addressed.

Akşemseddin is the most famous doctor and religious scholar in the Ottoman Empire, and Mehmet knows he's lucky to have him as his teacher. Still, he wishes they could have had today's lesson down at the palace, sitting in the shade on brocade pillows with the slaves fanning them with fans made of fluttery peacock feathers and serving them frosty sweet drinks chilled with snow. Instead of that, they crawled on top on this godforsaken mountain where nobody but the goats ever ventures. And, sooner or later, they'll have to crawl back down. What on earth is there to learn here?

Mehmet's eyes fall on the scrawny brown bushes shriveled by the sun, then move to the carved shapes of the ancient Gods some faithless people carved in the face of the mountain hundreds of years ago, before the Ottomans took the city and brought it into the true Faith. He glances at the green valley far below, where the peasants grow grapes and apples and sheep, and the Aegean, glittering far away, catches his eye. Oh, how he'd love to be there, swimming in the clear water instead of melting in this merciless heat.

Why the heck are we here? he wonders again. Akşemseddin will tell him. Maybe.

To escape his misery, he thinks about his hawk, Ok. Her name means arrow, because she's just that fast. He got her the day she was hatched, fed her and taught her how to fly, and he's been training her for a year. She only eats off his leather hawking glove, and she loves to eat brain. After she kills her prey, she waits for him to open the skull with his dagger and let her feast. But, even as she sits on his fist, her round merciless eyes scour the forest for something else to kill. She's always ready for another hunt.

Oh, how he'd love to be with her in the forest instead of baking here with his mentor; but, even though he's the şehzade, he doesn't really have a choice. Father told him to listen to his tutors, and he's not about to disappoint his father. Not here, not now, not ever.

When he's finally done meditating, Akşemseddin turns to him. Mehmet feels his sharp dark eyes search inside his soul.

"Why are we here, Mehmet?"

"That's just what I wondered," Mehmet blurts.

His mentor laughs.

"Believe it or not, your impatience is one of your better qualities," Akşemseddin says. "Especially if you learn to control it. Impatience is purposeless energy waiting to go somewhere, anywhere. You need to learn to direct it and use it."

Mehmet knows he's impatient, though few people ever dare to tell him that he's anything but perfect. His father, his mother, and his tutors. That's about it. And his brother, Aladdin. His half-brother, in fact, but in the harem, that doesn't matter. All the sultan's children are brothers and sisters, no matter who their mother happens to be.

Mehmet and Aladdin's mothers couldn't be more different. Before joining the harem, Mehmet's mother, Hüma Hatun, was a fiery red-headed slave from Rumelia, whereas Halime Hatice Hatun, Aladdin's mother, was a blue-blooded Turkoman princess. But in the harem, that doesn't matter. What matters is that Aladdin is six years older and Father's favorite.

Mehmet nods and waits for his mentor's words of wisdom, but they're slow to come.

"So, why are we here?"

Mehmet digs deep. "To learn?"

"Good. To learn what?"

"Patience?"

"Not bad. Coming up all the way to the top of this mountain in the heat took patience. Did you feel patient when we got at the top?"

Mehmet shakes his head.

"How did you feel?"

"Tired and hot."

Akşemseddin laughs again. "Tell me, how many years have you been training your horse?"

Mehmet started when he was seven. He's eleven now. "Four years."

"And how did you train him?"

"I fed him, brushed him and petted him. I spent time with him every day. I saw to his needs and taught him to trust me."

"And?"

"Then, I started teaching him."

"What do you do before you train him?"

"I take him out his stable and let him run."

"Why?"

"So he can pay attention."

"Exactly. To learn, horses need to pay attention. It's the same with people. To pay attention, they need to get rid of their extra energy, their impatience. To focus, they must be tired but not too tired."

Mehmet nods.

"As the sultan of the Ottoman Empire, you'll be the leader of your people, and their teacher. You'll need to show them how to fulfill your vision for the empire. To learn, they need to pay attention. You need them tired, but not too tired. Like you, after climbing this mountain. Like your horse."

"But I won't be sultan. Aladdin will."

"Maybe. Maybe not. *İnşallah*. But, if Allah wishes it to be you, you must be ready."

Mehmet nodded.

"So, if you were to be sultan someday, what's your vision of the Ottoman Empire? Where will you lead your people?"

Mehmet pushes aside the thoughts of hawks and cold drinks and horses. He struggles to opens his soul to the light of Allah, looking for his mission. Why did Allah choose him to be born Ottoman and the sultan's son, instead of a Greek fisherman or an Albanian farrier or a Wallachian peasant? Or even a woman, Allah help him? What is he here for?

With the sudden force of lightning, Allah's light strikes his heart. He shows him what to do, leaving him dazed and drunk with wonder.

His eyes stare at his mentor, but they don't see him. All he sees is an impossible dream that's way too big for a boy to fulfill. But fulfill it he must. He speaks soft words that come right out of his heart.

"When I'm sultan, there's one thing I must do."

"What's that?"

"Take Constantinople."

CHAPTER 36

THE OLD POISONER

Back in the castle that evening, Mehmet is still drunk with wonder. He's exhausted, but he's too exhilarated to notice.

He found a sense of purpose he didn't know he was missing. He used to spend his days dragging through the drudgery of school, prayer, and training, and looking forward to the best part of his day: Riding and falconry. But now, Allah gave him a mission: Take Constantinople.

He lays on his stomach, looking at the intricate blue and gold mosaics of the bath, and his soul soars. He luxuriates in the soothing touch of the bath eunuch that scrubs his back with a Turkish sponge, which, as he just learned, is older than his mother, since it takes forty years to grow as big as his hand. He breathes in the fragrance of rose petals and lavender, and feels his pain fade under the iron fingers squeezing the knots the hike built in his shoulders. The skilled hands slide down to his tense lower back, and Mehmet's body melts like wax into a puddle of happy flesh.

Once he's done, an old servant dries him with a soft towel made of the finest silk. She helps him lie on the cool marble to rest and hands him a cup of blood-red sour-cherry sherbet flavored with their own crushed pits to purify his breath.

He takes a sip, but the sherbet tastes bitter. He sets it down and goes to see Mother, who has summoned him to her quarters. Mother is more passionate about Mehmet's education than he is, and she checks on his progress daily. She speaks to his tutors and learns what to ask him, and he'd better know his answers.

Her rooms, the best in the palace, are shaded by sculpted wooden grills that cover the windows to block out the sun. Even more importantly, they thwart prying eyes. Though she's hundreds of miles away from the Edirne sarayi, Mother, Hüma Hatun, is still Father's third wife, with everything that entails. No other man but the sultan has seen her face since his men bought her, fifteen years ago. Only women can see her, and the sarayi guards. But they're eunuchs, not men, so they don't count.

Mehmet bows before Mother, touching his forehead to the white marble floor, then kisses her soft hand that flickers green from the massive emerald Father gave her to thank her for birthing Mehmet.

Mother's flame red hair lights the room. She smiles and pats the sofa next to her, inviting him to sit.

"What did you do today, my son?"

"I climbed Spil Mountain with Akşemseddin. Then we talked."

"About what?"

"About patience. About how people have to be tired to learn."

"What else?"

Mehmet feels a strange stirring in his stomach, then a cramp. He takes a deep breath, and the pain goes away.

"He asked me what I'd do if I became sultan."

"Not if. When. What did you say?"

"I'll take Constantinople."

Mother laughs. He's never heard her laugh like this. It's a young girl's laugh. A happy sound, like that time they let a singing bird out of her cage to fly free. That doesn't often happen, since singing birds are precious. They only do it when there's a healthy son born in the sarayi, or they celebrate a prince's circumcision. And sometimes when a well-arranged marriage brings the Ottoman Empire a favored alliance. That's how Mother laughs today.

"Why Constantinople?"

Mehmet tries to explain, but he has trouble focusing.

"*İnşallah*," he says, then his stomach knots and climbs to his throat. A wave of cold sweat bursts out of his skin, making him shiver.

"Are you OK?"

Mehmet can't speak, so he nods.

"Constantinople, eh? Your grandfather, Bayezid Yıldırım, tried to take it and failed. Your father tried to take it and failed. If that's your destiny and Allah's wish, you'll be the greatest sultan the Ottoman Empire has ever known. They won't call you Mehmet, they'll call you..."

Mehmet's heart pounds, and the buzz in his ears covers her voice. His stomach wants to burst out of his belly. He knows he'll be sick, so he tries to run out, but he can't. His knees grow weak, and the marble tiles grow closer and closer. He opens his mouth to speak, but he falls to his knees and vomits instead. The white marble floor turns red with sour cherry sherbet.

"The sherbet," he mumbles, then falls to his side and sees that it's not sherbet. It's blood. Lots of it.

Hüma Hatun jumps to hold him, as he falls into a sleep-like torpor. But it's not sleep. It's weakness, a terrible powerlessness that chains him to the floor. He's awake, but he can neither talk nor move. He can still see and hear, but he struggles to breathe.

"Get Akşemseddin!" Hüma screams.

The guards run to fetch him. Mehmet's tutor, who's the most famous doctor in the land, rushes in. He kneels by Mehmet and takes his wrist to check his pulse, then pulls down his lower eyelids to look inside his eyes. He shakes his head, then lays his hands on Mehmet's stomach and pushes with enough strength to make him vomit again, then again.

The guards bring ice-cold water and Akşemseddin's medical kit. It's a locked wooden coffer big enough to hold a grown man, and it's stuffed with tools, powders, and potions he's the only one to know.

Akşemseddin drops five dark-blue drops in a cup of cold water and holds it to Mehmet's lips. Mehmet tries to resist, but he can't. He swallows the cold medicine, then vomits again minutes later. The blue cup comes back to his lips, and Mehmet drinks and vomits again and again until he's spent and empty. He's no longer vomiting blood, just blue water.

Akşemseddin checks Mehmet's pulse again, then his eyes and his belly. He turns to his mother. She has covered her face with her yashmak, since she can't be seen by a man, even if he's a doctor, and even if her son, her only son, is dying. These are the rules of the sarayi, and they're more important than life and death.

"He'll be OK," Akşemseddin says.

Hüma Hatun's yashmak is so wet with tears it clings to her face, but her voice is unchanged. "Poison?"

"Probably."

Hüma turns to the eunuchs. "What did he last eat, and who fed it to him?"

They bring in Akira. The old woman has been in Hüma Hatun's service since before Mehmet was born. She sobs so hard that her whole body shakes as the guards hold her up. They let go, and she crumbles to the ground.

"Why?" Hüma asks.

The woman cries harder. She tries to say something, but Hüma can't understand her, since she sobs so hard that she's choking.

"Quiet!" Hüma Hatun says, and the room goes quiet like a tomb.

"Listen to me, Akira. You are about to die, and you know it."

The woman gasps and tries to talk, but the eunuch behind her covers her mouth with his gloved hand.

"You're as good as dead. But you've served me for thirteen years. That ought to count for something. You can die fast, or you can die slow. Your choice. If you tell me what you gave Mehmet, and who gave it to you, you'll die before you know it happened. Your head will fall off like a pear too ripe to hang on its branch, and you'll feel no pain. Or you can take many days and die slowly. Piece by piece. First, your toes. Then your fingers. After that, your ears. Then your nose. A foot, then the other. Your breasts. The hands. Not your eyes. Not yet. You need them to see what happens. What you become. You'll watch every moment of it. You'll see the crows eating your spare parts. Our torturer, Kamil Paşa, has studied at Tokat, the academy of pain. He can have you dying for two whole weeks, they say. I'm curious to find out. Aren't you?"

The woman moans.

"Who was it? And what?"

The woman takes out a green vial from her dress and puts it on the marble floor. She sobs.

"They said to put in the whole bottle, to be sure. I only put in half."

"Who gave it to you?"

"My daughter. She's been in Halime's service since she was nine."

"Why did you do it?"

"I'm an old woman, and I didn't have much to lose. But she's so young. Halime Hatice Halime told her it's either this, or her life. I chose her life."

Hüma Hatun nods to the eunuch. He takes her away.

Akşemseddin picks up the vial and opens its seal. He waves his hand over it to bring the fumes closer. He seals it back.

"It's bad poison. He was lucky."

Hüma Hatun nods. "My fault. I shouldn't have waited. I was too slow. It won't happen again."

Brought back to his bed by the slaves, Mehmet falls asleep, wondering what she meant. How was Mother too slow? And how can she stop it from happening again?

CHAPTER 37

THE MISSION

KRONSTADT, TRANSYLVANIA, 1444

Another long winter is finally over, and the smell of spring has reached even up here in Transylvania's mountains. Green shoots of grass and timid snowdrops push through the patches of snow, looking for the sun. A soft breeze carries scents of moist earth and new beginnings, putting joy in the birds' songs, the horses' steps and in people's hearts.

The boys are giddy. They joke and laugh, fighting over the last crust of buttered bread.

But Ali doesn't feel the joy. She's been cold in her heart even since she woke up at dawn and her cross glowed red, spelling danger. Though, thus far in her apprenticeship, she rarely needs the cross to spell things out for her. Deep in her bones, she feels her luck change, and she knows that this day won't be like the others. Something will happen that will change her life forever, and that knowledge sends a chill down her spine.

Oh well. Maybe it's just some bad dream. I'll ask Mama Smaranda.

But the day goes on and she forgets. She gets busy with the geography lesson, where they learn about Anatolia, the Asian half of the Ottoman Empire, then they have their bow and arrow training in the back yard. Today, they're shooting while riding bare-back, and it's a wonder they don't shoot each other.

They're still laughing at each other's antics when a guard comes to fetch her to the burgomaster. The boys drop their bows to join her, but the man shakes his head.

"Not all of you. Only Ali."

The boys' eyes burn Ali's back as she follows the guard, wondering if she's in trouble. This never happened before. Other than her lessons with Mama Smaranda, they do everything else together. They eat together, sleep together, learn together and fight each other like cats. But they're like brothers, and they always have each other's back. No matter who messes up, they all get punished, so they learned that they fare better when they get along. They even decide together. Whenever they disagree, majority rules, for the good or for the bad. The three of them are a team: Ion, always smiling and seeing the glass half-full, Codru, dark and moody but always there when you need him, and Ali. She's still smaller than them, and not as strong, but she can read minds and tell the future.

"How do you know?" Codru asked when she told them that a bad storm was coming.

"I feel it inside. It's like a smell. I just know it's coming."

He shrugged and ignored her, even when the mother of all storms came out of the blue, pelleting the castle with hail as big as chicken's eggs. Stubborn as he is, he still thought it was a fluke, until the day she told him not to climb the apple tree.

"Why?"

"You're going to get hurt."

Codru laughed and climbed it anyhow, then fell from the top and broke his wrist. He couldn't use a bow for weeks, but he finally learned to trust her insights.

Ion didn't need proof. He never doubted her anyhow.

But now that the burgomaster wants to see her alone, Ali wonders if he'll send her back home. She hasn't thought about her old home in ages, since this feels like home now, but she didn't forget about Mother. No matter what, she's not going back. *I'm stronger and smarter than I was when I came. I can run away, and Mama Smaranda will help me.*

The guard opens a massive sculpted door to a room Ali has never seen and steps aside. Her heart racing, Ali steps in.

The room is quiet and dreary. The long table is empty, and so are the gray stone walls, but for the one tapestry hanging on the opposite wall. It's Kronstadt's coat of arms, the golden crown growing from a root, weaved in silk thread over a faded red background. The tapestry hangs there to soften the chill of the walls, but it's failing. Its corners flap in the sharp draft that cuts right through Ali's clothes, giving her goosebumps. She gathers her shearling vest closer. The winter may be over, but the cold is not.

Sitting silently by the table, the burgomaster and the doctor watch her.

The silence is thick enough to cut with a knife. Their backs straight, their faces dark, the men look anywhere but at each other. *What did they fight about,* Ali wonders? It has to do with her, for sure. But what?

The burgomaster clears his voice. "Sit."

Ali sits in the one empty chair and hugs herself for warmth.

The burgomaster's searching eyes peek inside her, and Ali wonders if he too can read people's thoughts. "Your training is almost over, Ali. The time for your mission is coming soon."

"What is my mission?"

"Your mission is to serve your country with honor. Transylvania's voivode, John Hunyadi, the Kingdom of Hungary, and even the whole of Christianity rely on you. This is your chance to make your mother proud."

Making her mother proud leaves Ali cold. As for Transylvania's voivode, she'd never met him, so she's not that keen about him either. But she has a duty to her country. And, like all Christians, she knows she must uphold Christianity against the Muslim threat.

"How?"

"You'll go to Sultan Murad's sarayi in Edirne. Once there, you'll work hard, make friends, and make yourself useful. You'll keep your eyes and ears open, and you'll send us word of anything that can be useful to the voivode and to Transylvania."

"How?"

"We'll let you know. But do you understand what you need to do?"

"I need to make friends, listen, and send you word about everything that can be useful to the voivode and Transylvania."

"Very good." The burgomaster nods.

Ali sighs with relief. She was right that morning when she felt that her life was about to change, but it's all for the good. She's going to the heart of the Ottoman Empire to live in the sarayi, and she can't wait. She already knows a lot about the Ottoman Empire — after all, they'd been pounding knowledge into her head for more than a year: Ottoman language, Ottoman history, Ottoman geography, Ottoman customs. She's looking forward to the new adventure. Except...

"Will the boys go with me?"

"They will, but their mission is slightly different."

"How so?"

"The boys will go with you to help you and protect you, but you won't be together all the time like you are here. You'll meet, but not that often."

Ali's heart aches. The boys are not only her team, they are her family. She loves them and she'll miss them. But they all have a mission to accomplish, so she'll see them from time to time. And at least she's not going home.

"Two more things. You have to be very careful, Ali. If they discover what you're there for, they'll kill you. Without a doubt."

Ali shivers. Ever since the day she found out she's a witch, she avoided thinking about death. She pushed the thought of dying and burning in Hell to the back of her mind and got it out of the way, like she did with her fear of werewolves. And she's not going to start worrying about that now.

"What's the second thing?"

"You'll have an operation."

CHAPTER 38
THE OPERATION

Ali's eyes reach inside the burgomaster's, trying to read his thoughts, but she can't see through them like she can't see through murky water. There's something chilling inside him. Something that terrifies him, and she knows she should be scared too. If only she knew what it was.

"Why?"

"So you can blend in with the others. To keep you safe."

"What's an operation?"

The burgomaster turns his eyes to the doctor, who hasn't yet spoken. The man's face is darker than the sky in a storm, and his eyes avoid Ali's.

"You shouldn't do this," he mumbles in Saxon.

"I'm not doing it. You are," the burgomaster answers.

"You shouldn't have me do this, then," the doctor says, his voice almost too low to hear.

Ali's eyes slip from one to the other, and she bites her tongue to keep quiet. They still don't know that she speaks Saxon, and this would be a bad time to let that cat out of the bag. She'll learn more if they think she can't understand them than if they know that she does.

The burgomaster shrugs.

"You said that it was no big deal. Just a little superficial wound, you said. People get worse things done to them all the time."

"But not by me."

"How about when you cut down a vein to draw blood? Or burn a wound? Or amputate a leg?"

"First, I never amputate. That's for the filthy barbers, God curse their greedy souls. Those leeches have the gall to ask their patients to pay *before* the surgery, since they know that most of them die anyhow. And whenever I treat a wound or bleed someone, that's always for a medical reason. I do it to heal the sick and help the wounded."

"Well, you're doing it to help her not get sick or wounded. You're doing it to keep her safe."

"But think about the risks! She could die from a simple procedure she doesn't even need!"

"She could die anyhow. Life is cheap here in Transylvania, and it's even cheaper in the Ottoman Empire. And just remember that your procedure may save her life. If anyone suspects her and checks..."

The doctor sighs and turns to Ali, who sits quietly, staring at the red tapestry like she's counting the roots, but her mind is in a murky turmoil. What will they do to her? Should she run away? Or should she wait and see?

She takes a deep breath, fighting the nausea that knotted her stomach. She shouldn't have taken that last piece of warm bread the boys fought over. Her stomach wants to turn itself inside out, and she's about to run outside to throw up, when the doctor turns to her.

"An operation is when we cut something out of people with a sharp knife," he says to her in Romanian.

That's it. Ali's stomach has had it. She wants to run out, but it's too late. She bends over and retches, then averts her eyes from the pile of half-chewed bread on the floor. The men look away, pretending not to notice.

Ali clears her throat, which is sharp with acid from her stomach. The doctor hands her his cup, and she takes a deep swig. It's watered-down wine, and it's awful, but it washes away some of the acidity.

"So, what will you cut out of me?"

The doctor sighs.

"Nothing. You know how boys are different than girls and have that stuff hanging between their legs? To make them into eunuchs, they cut that away. It's called castration."

Ali shivers.

"Sometimes they only cut away the nuts. Sometimes they cut everything. But you don't have any of that, so there's nothing to cut out. I'll just make a wound between your legs and sew it together. We'll let it heal, then pull out the thread. After that, your nether parts will look just like a eunuch's, even though nothing will be missing. It's just a flesh wound. It should heal in a week."

"Will it hurt?"

The doctor shrugs, and Ali knows that it will. But doesn't everything in life? And thinking about it won't make it any better.

They take her to a small room in the tower. Up here, the windows are wider, to let the watchers scout the mountains, so the light is better. There isn't much inside other than a table for twenty made of a whole tree trunk that fills the room.

Ali leans out the window to watch a dragon-shaped cloud sail across the blue sky and bites her lip to stop her tears. She hears the boys training for combat outside, and she wishes she got to say good-bye. Then she hears them laugh, and she feels even more alone.

The doctor hands her a cup. It's poison-green, pungent, and so bitter that she wants to puke again, but she resists.

"What is this for?"

"It will put you to sleep, so you don't feel anything."

The doctor turns to rummage through his brown leather bag. It's old and worn and full of tools that Ali doesn't recognize, but they all look rusty and evil. He takes out a knife, its thin blade curved from much sharpening, and a long iron needle.

Ali's stomach flips again, but, by now, the evil drink has started to work. She's so dizzy and weak she needs to lean against the wall.

The doctor claps, and two old women dressed in black, like widows, come in and help her to the table. Ali tries to sit on a chair, but no. They want her up on the table, so they pull her up and lay her on her back.

Ali's heart starts racing. She wants to get off, but she's too weak. A rush of hot blood floods her brain and blurs her vision like she's angry, but she's not. She's just exhausted and scared.

Ali's eyes close by themselves. She feels the women's hands undo her belt and pull down her pants, and she wants to scream, "No!" but she can't utter a sound. She grabs on to them to pull them up, but firm hands unclench her fingers and pull down her breeches.

She struggles to sit up, but an overwhelming weakness holds her down. She's too weak to even open her eyes.

"Don't do this," she tries to say, but she can't hear herself, so she knows they can't either.

"Ready?" the doctor asks.

"Soon now," a women's voice answers. Someone pulls up Ali's eyelids, and she sees the old ceiling covered in cracked white plaster getting darker and darker until it's all black. But it's not the ceiling. The darkness is all in her brain.

"Now," she hears, then she hears no more.

CHAPTER 39

LENA'S NIGHTMARE

EDIRNE 1444

The fire. The fire's coming. Run! Faster! Faster!

The air's so hot that my chest is about to blow up. The kid gets heavier and heavier, but I struggle to hold him, and push myself to run even faster. I trip and stumble, and I drop him, but I don't even notice as I race to escape the flames chasing me. But no matter how fast I am, they're even faster. My hair catches fire, and a black cloud of smoke surrounds me, so thick I can barely breathe. I choke and stumble, then I fall...

Lena sits up and gasps. She's drenched in sweat, and her heart pumps like crazy. But it was just a dream, thank God. Then she remembers that God is no longer in her life. It's Allah now.

Gone is Saint Mary's wooden icon on the wall, the one with the chubby baby Jesus and the golden aura clinging precariously to her head. That used to be the first thing she saw every morning when she woke up ever since she can remember.

No more. Now, her eyes open to the blue and white mosaics that decorate the women's quarters in the Edirne sarayi. Since Islamic faith discourages human figures, it's all intricate geometric shapes, stylized vines, and flowing Ottoman calligraphy that turns writing into art. The creaky wooden floors are gone too. She now steps on cool marble instead. Even the old oil lamp is gone, replaced by thick wax candles. Lena's home is no longer her home.

She's been here for months, but it still doesn't feel like home. And every single night in her sleep she relives the night she failed to save the kid.

God knows she tried. As soon as she saw the Ottomans, she rushed down the old oak tree, picked up the kid, and ran for her life.

To outsmart the Ottomans, she didn't run to the river. She took a wide detour, and ran back to the burning village instead. She ignored her pain, her fatigue, and her thirst, and she ran with the kid on her shoulders and the dog following her, like the devil was after them.

The kid cried: "Put me down," and the dog whimpered and growled, but Lena didn't stop until she got back to the village. There, they had to be safe. The Ottomans wouldn't come back here. Why should they? There was nothing left but ashes.

She dropped to the ground next to the church and laid there, struggling to breathe. She'd almost caught her breath when something sharp stabbed her shoulder blade. She opened her eyes.

A janissary dressed in red poked her with his long lance. His kilij clanged against the ground as he leaned over her, and his tall headgear covered the moon. Lena's heart sank. *I ran all this way for nothing.*

The kid whimpered. The dog snarled. She tried to pull him back, but he snapped at her, so she let him go.

The dog leaped.

The kilij was too fast to see. The curved blade arched, and the dog's head flew like a bird. A rain of hot, thick blood showered them, then the dog's head fell to the ground, his mouth open, as his paws still tried to grasp the dirt and run.

Lena retched.

Dan's wide eyes glazed. He dropped to the ground and curled on his side.

The janissary growled and signaled them to walk. Lena touched Dan's shoulder, but he didn't move. She called him, but he didn't hear. It was like he'd gone somewhere else.

Lena wanted to run, but she couldn't. She was way too tired, and she couldn't leave the kid. She looked for the ax she'd stuck in her belt, a lifetime ago, but it was gone. She'd lost it somewhere along the way.

More janissaries came. They stared at them and laughed, speaking a language she couldn't understand. Lena touched Dan to comfort him, but the kid's glazed eyes stared into space.

Someone handed her a flask of water. It tasted the best she could remember, and she had to fight herself not to drain it. She put it at Dan's lips, but he didn't seem to notice. She tried again. No go. So she drank it all to soothe her parched throat. They gave her another, and she drained that one too.

She fell asleep holding Dan. She woke up still holding him, but he was so quiet he seemed dead.

The janissaries brought them bread, grapes and honey. Lena's mouth watered at the sight of the food. She tried to feed Dan, but he wanted none of it. She ate it all, every delicious bite bitter with guilt.

When the sun went down, the janissary captain came. He was tall and good-looking, and he smiled. "What's your name?" he asked in Romanian.

"Ștefan."

He laughed. "You're not a boy. What's your name, girl?"

"I'm Lena. Who are you?"

"I'm Omar Agha. How old are you?"

"Sixteen."

He looked her up and down. "Really?"

She was lying, of course. She hoped to fare better if they didn't think she was a child. She sat straight, acting grown-up, and nodded.

"Who's he?"

"He's my little brother."

"What are you two doing here?"

"We're running from the voivode's posse. Our father, Bogdan, is the voivode's brother."

"So why is the posse chasing you?"

"We're Alexandru the Great's grandchildren, so they think we're a threat to the throne."

"Him, maybe. But you? You're just a girl."

Lena considered punching him, but that looked like a lousy idea.

The Ottomans were too many, and she had no weapon, no way to escape, and a kid to look after.

"How come you speak Romanian?" she asked.

"I was born here, but I grew up at the sultan's court where they opened my eyes to the true faith and I became a janissary, then an agha. I was barely older than him," he said, glancing at Dan with pity in his eyes. "But enough talk. We have to go."

A dozen janissaries surrounded them. Lena tried to wake up the kid, but he was frozen like he couldn't either see or hear. Omar Agha sighed.

"I'm sorry about the kid, even though we both know he's not your brother. We can't take him with us, and I can't leave him behind. But remember he's going to a better world."

The janissaries surrounded Lena and pushed her forward. She struggled to break free, but there was no escaping the dozen hands holding her. She glanced back to see the agha swing the kilij.

Dan fell.

Lena screamed. Choking with sobs, she tried to rush back, but a dozen hands pushed her forward. She sobbed and stumbled forward between the men dragging her, wishing she could kill them all.

They walked and walked. When Omar Agha came to her side, Lena was too exhausted to care.

He looked her up and down. "Are you a virgin?" he asked.

Lena blushed. Of course she was a virgin. What else could she be? She was just a kid. Then she remembered that she had lied about her age.

"Yes."

He studied her chest and narrow hips. "Are you sure you're sixteen?"

Lena nodded, too choked to speak.

"Have you ever bled?"

She didn't know what he was talking about, so she shrugged.

"We'd better give you a bath then. See what hides under all that dirt."

They crossed the Danube on a ferry, and they stopped in a village across the border where Omar Agha handed her to a veiled woman.

"See what you can do with her, and get her something to wear. Not expensive, mind you, but do your best to make her look marketable."

That was Lena's first bath. She had swam in rivers and got wet under the rain, but what those women did to her, she never had happen. They undressed her, laid her on a bench, and scrubbed the living Jesus out of her with something rough. They did it again and again until her skin got hot and raw, and her hair hurt. Then they took her to a wooden tub of rose-scented cool water. She sunk in and felt her skin shrink and tighten and her blood rush back to her heart, making her feel weightless and alive. She would have liked to stay there forever, but they pulled her out, dried her, and dressed her in a white chemise and a pair of soft blue wide breeches.

Omar Agha ignored her until the woman pushed her in front of him. He stared, then choked and his eyes popped out of his head.

"Wow!"

He handed two coins to the bath attendant.

"We take her to the market?" a janissary asked.

Omar Agha shook his head.

"Not this one. This one is worthy of a sultan. We're taking her to the palace."

CHAPTER 40
THE SULTAN'S SARAYI

That happened months ago, but Lena's memories are just as vivid as if it all happened yesterday. Thankfully, between learning the Ottoman language, taking Quran lessons and her many chores, her days are too busy to think. But the nights are her own to relive her nightmare over and over.

Sitting up on her mattress, Lena leans against the wall, hugging herself. She glances at the dark shapes laying around her. The other women are still asleep, but she's too shaken to go back to bed. She may as well get up.

She grabs the embroidered chemise she's working on and moves under the candle for more light, knowing she doesn't have much time. Any moment now, the muezzins perched in the many mosques' minarets will start the call to prayer to remind the whole Muslim world that Allah is great. Like they need reminding. Then the eunuchs will open the doors, and everyone will get up and get going.

Sure enough, she doesn't get more than a dozen stitches in, and it starts.

"Allah u Akbar. Allah u Akbar. Allah u Akbar. Allah U Akbar." God is the greatest, calls the slow, intricate lament flowing in through the windows from Edirne's many mosques.

The two dozen women jump up like one. They purify their faces, hands, and feet in the water basin in the corner, then bow deeply towards the sunrise and kneel on the white marble floor to pray. They're all beautiful, with firm flesh, glowing skin, bright eyes and lustrous hair in every color, but they're all slaves, like Lena.

They aren't the sultan's wives, not even his concubines. They're just slaves in training, who hope to catch the sultan's eye and get called to his bed. Should they manage to gain his favor and become one of his favorites, they'd be given their own rooms and servants. And if they're lucky enough to give the sultan a son, they'll become one of his wives and they'll get to live a life of luxury and leisure. And one of them will become validé, the next sultan's mother. That's the queen of the harem, and the most powerful woman in the world.

But Lena doesn't want that kind of luck. All she wants is to get out of here. She can't wait to go back home to Berzunți and roam the woods to gather wood, fish, swim in the rivers, and be free. But that's unlikely to happen. Once in the sarayi, the women stay here until the day they die, unless the sultan marries them off to one of his men, and then they move to another harem.

The call to prayer draws on and on. Lena pretends to be praying like the others, but she's not. She's thinking of home, where they put on their best clothes to go to church every Sunday. And for Easter and Christmas, of course. But nobody ever stops working to pray. The most they do is cross themselves, spit in their bosom and say "Doamne ferește," heaven forbid, when something bad happens.

How much longer? Lena's belly growls, telling her it's time for breakfast. And, sure enough, as soon as the prayer is over, the eunuchs bring in large wooden platters loaded with grapes, apples and figs. There's also flat bread sprinkled with white sesame seeds, soft cheeses, yellow and white, shiny olives, black and green, golden honey, and the thick morning soup.

As soon as the tray is set on top of the red Isfahan carpet in the middle of the floor, the women sit cross-legged around it and eat off the same plate until they're full. Lena gets her fill of olives, cheese and bread, which remind her of home, and stays clear of the morning soup which is thick and hot and smells like mutton.

As soon as breakfast is over, the old woman assigned to teach her the Ottoman language and customs takes her aside. Her name is Geveze, which means chatty, and the name fits her well. She's happy and chatty, and Lena likes her, even though she can't understand how she can love life inside the walls. But maybe she's never known anything else.

They sit on wool-stuffed pillows under the window covered with wooden grills that let in the wind, but keep out the sun and the curious eyes.

"How do you say tea?" Geveze asks.

"*Cay.*"

"Delicious?"

"*Lezzetli.*"

"Dog?"

"*Kopek.*"

And just like that, Lena remembers Lupu's head flying through the air, and she chokes. She tries to stop her tears from streaming down her cheeks, but she can't, so she covers her face and takes in a deep breath to keep herself in check then wipes her tears with the sleeve of her chemise.

"*Üzgünüm*. I'm sorry."

Geveze eyes are worried. She can that see that Lena is hurting, even if she doesn't know why. She leans forward and whispers.

"I have a big surprise for you today."

What can it be? Lena wonders. Here, there are no surprises. Every day is just like the last: Prayer, language learning, Quran verses, sewing, bath, repeat. Nobody ever comes. No-one ever leaves. Nothing ever happens.

"Today, after your bath, you are going to see the validé."

"Me? Why?"

"I told her about you. 'We have a new beautiful girl. She's sharp as a tack and she has a wonderful disposition,' I said. So she asked to see you."

Lena sighs. She's not so sure about beautiful. She's grown a lot since they brought her here, since here they do nothing but sit around and eat the whole day. There are no cows to milk, no water to carry from the well, no working the hay in the fields. There's none of the work she used to do at home, and food abounds. Sweets and fruit lay on trays for those with a sweet tooth, since they're hell-bent on fattening them. Here, curvy is beautiful, so she's no longer the stick she used to be. But beautiful?

As for her disposition, thank God Geveze doesn't know what she really thinks. Every day, every night, and anytime in between, Lena thinks about nothing but running away. She's just trying to figure out how.

"And why is that good news?"

Geveze frowns. "You know why. If the validé likes you, she may order the kapi agha, the chief eunuch, to present you to the sultan. You might even become one of his favorites, and you know that every one of these girls would give their right eye to be Sultan Murad's favorite. Though, of course, if they were missing their right eye, they'd never get to be his favorite. But that's a whole different matter. You, my girl, have an opportunity that they all covet."

Lena thanks her, wishing she could decline. If there's something she wants even less than being here, it's sharing the sultan's bed. She hasn't heard from Ștefan since the day she rode away to get the posse off his trail, but she still thinks about him. She hopes he made it to Târgoviște, and he's safe and happy in Wallachia. Well, safe, but not too happy. She hopes he misses her too and they get to meet again someday. That's why sharing the sultan's bed doesn't fit in her plans.

Sure enough, a black eunuch comes for her after her bath, and Lena feels the girls' eyes burn holes in her back as she leaves. They all know where she's going — here, everyone knows everything about everybody — and they're sick with envy. She knows they'll make her pay when she returns.

But it's not like she has a choice. She follows the eunuch along the bright corridors that lead to the validé's rooms, then drops to her knees at her feet and kisses her hand like Geveze taught her.

"Look up, my child."

Lena looks into the kind old eyes of a woman who's seen a lot. Her bright silk chemise is whiter than fresh snow, and her deep green velvet kaftan reminds Lena of pine trees. She looks like the forest in winter, the validé, and Lena's heart aches for her home.

"Geveze was right. You are beautiful. Also very young. How old are you?"

"Fourteen, my lady."

The validé laughs. "Weren't you sixteen when you came to us? How did you manage to get younger? I want to know the secret. So does every other woman in the harem, I bet."

Lena looks down. "I lied."

The validé's laugh is heartwarming and young.

"Good for you. They don't have a right to know your age. No need, either. Tell me, where are you from?"

"Moldova, my lady."

"I've never been there. You miss it?"

"Terribly."

"What do you miss the most?"

"The grass fields sprinkled with red poppies, forget-me-nots, and daisies. The buzz of the bees and the whisper of the river. The smell of grass, and the wind blowing in my hair. The summer rains soaking me."

"I see. You miss your freedom."

Lena's jaw drops.

"Unfortunately, that I can't give you. But I can give you hope. You'll learn to love the walls, the shadows, and the safety of the castle. You'll learn to love the call to prayer and Allah's words in the Quran. You'll learn to love so many things you never knew, and your life will be richer because of it."

"But they aren't my freedom."

"Freedom lives in your soul, my dear. No one can take it from you unless you let them. Your soul is forever free. Now go, little girl. Come back to see me in six months and tell me what you learned."

CHAPTER 41

FATHER'S STORY

KRONSTADT, 1444

Three hundred miles north of the Edirne sarayi, in Kronstadt, Ali wakes up with a terrible pain between her legs. It hurts so bad it's like a dragon spat fire inside her. She tries to reach down there, but she can't. Her hands are tied.

She tries to sit up, but the pain gets even worse. She drops back and looks around, but it's too dark to see. And the silence is deafening. She should be scared, but she's not. She wonders why.

It's the smell. Verbena, chamomile, and mint. She's in Mama Smaranda's magic cottage. Ali doesn't know how she got here, but she knows that nothing bad will happen to her while she's here.

The door bursts open, letting the moonlight flow in. A huge black shadow darkens the door, and Negru leaps in. He puts his paws on her shoulders and dries her tears with his soft tongue, then lays his big head on her chest.

Mama Smaranda follows, carrying a torch and a basket overflowing with plants, roots, and flowers. She sets it on the floor and takes her hand.

"You're up! Good. How are you feeling, baby girl?"

"I hurt."

"I'm sorry. But you'll feel better soon. Here, drink this."

Mama Smaranda unties Ali's hands and offers her a cup. It's sweetened with honey, but it's still so sharp and bitter that it makes her pucker, so she knows it's white willow tea. But soon enough, the pain dulls and she sits up.

"What did they do to me?"

Smaranda sits on the edge of the bed.

"Ana, you know you're not a boy."

"I'm Ali."

"Sure. But that in itself doesn't make you a boy just like calling Negru Mitzi won't make him a cat. Names are just words, and they don't change the essence of things or people. You are who you always were. Nothing changed."

"Why did they say I was a boy, then?"

"To keep you safe. Where you're going, being a girl is not much fun. There, women and girls belong to their masters."

"And boys don't?"

"They do too, but they have more freedom and better chances. They can come and go. They can own money and can carry weapons. They can hold jobs and do many things that women can't. Especially the eunuchs."

"So I'm a eunuch now?"

"You're not. You'll just pretend to be."

"Why?"

"Because eunuchs have amazing powers and lots of freedom. Since they had their boy parts removed, they can no longer marry or have children, so their lives are dedicated to the sultan. That's why he trusts them with his women, his affairs, and his castle. Eunuchs run everything in the palace, and you'll be one of them."

"So, they removed my girl parts, so I look like a eunuch?"

"No, Ana. They removed nothing. They only made a skin-deep cut near your female parts. When it heals, you'll look like a eunuch down there. But that won't make you a eunuch, and won't make you a boy."

Ali struggles to wrap her mind around all this, but she fails. She's a girl who pretends to be a boy who's a eunuch, but she's really neither a eunuch nor a boy.

"Nothing changed, Ana. You are the same you've always been. You just have a secret that nobody should know, because if they do, you're no longer safe. The pain will fade soon, and everything will be just like before."

"Can I still pee standing?"

"You'd better."

Smaranda hugs her, and her eyes shine with tears.

"Oh, my girl, how I wish I could go with you, but I can't. But I know you'll do great. Never forget what your father said: You can do everything you set your mind to do."

"Tell me about Father."

"Your father was a good boy. And a good man, until he met your mother."

"Father was always a good man."

"He sure was. He was smart and kind and strong. He wanted to find his place in the world, so he left home when he was just a young boy, looking for a place to grow. He stopped in Suceava and met Moldova's voivode, Alexandru cel Bun.

"The voivode liked him so much that he took him in his service. He made him a captain, and your father became one of his trusted men. But then one day he fell in love with one of his daughters. And she fell in love with him. That's your mother."

"My mother? She's a princess?"

Smaranda nodded.

"Yes. Alexandru the Good had a lot of children, you see. Your mother was just one of his daughters born out of wedlock, but she was still of royal bone, thus valuable. He'd promised her hand to a Serbian prince, hoping to cement a worthwhile alliance. But she got heavy with child."

"With child?"

"Yes."

Ali knows that getting heavy with child is the worst thing that can happen to an unmarried girl. That's the end of her and her family's honor. She may as well die. That's why Baba Biris, the village witch, lived so well. One way or another, a fresh chicken always made its way to her pot from some girl grateful for her help.

“So what did Mother do?”

“The voivode went mad, and rightly so, that your father broke his trust. He went after him, but your father fled Moldova and took your mother with him. They came to Transylvania, got married, and your father did his best to look after his wife and their children. But no way could he offer her the kind of life she was used to. Your mother grew up like a princess, and she'd never washed a dish or lit a fire in her life before she left Moldova.

“She did her best to learn, but it was hard. Living without servants, without comfort, and sometimes even without food took a lot out of her. She loved your father, but she didn’t love living in a hut and being poor. And she didn’t care about witchcraft either, so she had him swear to never brew a potion or cast a spell again.”

“And did he?”

“Not to my knowledge. But I didn’t see him much the last few years. He did his best to live like a human to please your mother. And she didn’t like him seeing me.”

“Why not?”

“Because of who I am. And she didn’t like to share him. She wanted him all to herself. That’s why she didn’t love you much either. She felt that you were the reason she had to leave her gilded life. Moreover, you were the only person you father loved more than he loved her.”

"So that's why Mother never liked me."

"That's one reason. There are others. You’re just not like her."

"How so?"

“Your mother needs a man in her life. She wants someone to love her, care for her and make decisions for her. Someone to cherish her and tell her what to do."

"That's stupid."

“Your mother doesn't think so. But that's what we’re talking about. You’re not like that and never will be. You're born a fighter. You may be too young to understand, but you're not too young to fight. We live through horrible times when we send our children to fight our wars, God forgive us."

Smaranda wipes her eyes and hugs Ali. She looks in her eyes, and Ali can see her heart.

"Ana, you're not like your mother. You're like no one else. You, my dear, were brought on this earth for one reason: you're here to make this world a better place."

"How?"

"I don't know how. But I know you will."

CHAPTER 42

THE ŞEHZADE

EDIRNE, THE PALACE SCHOOL, JUNE 1444

A joyful sun smiles over Edirne Palace today. The magnificent gardens are in full bloom, the birds sing, and the soft summer wind carries the fragrance of jasmine and roses. This is the kind of day Radu loves to spend laying in the grass, watching the clouds sail across the sky like white ships, and composing a poem. But not today.

Today, he tiptoes quietly out the door, careful not to wake up Sari. Curled on his bed with her nose under her crooked tail, the cat sleeps the day away as usual, since she's out and about, mousing, the whole night. But if she sees Radu leave, she'll follow him, and he doesn't want her out today. Sari is just a tiny cat, and the ruckus out there would scare her to death. Even worse, one of the loaded carts rushing to-and-fro could run her over, or the busy servants could kick her in their haste to get the celebration ready. Because today is a very special day at the palace: Edirne, and the whole Ottoman Empire will celebrate Mehmet, the şehzade.

Radu has been in Edirne for two years, but he has yet to meet the şehzade, and he quivers with excitement. He slips out quietly and sprints to the place on the wall that has the best view of the road, since he wants to be the first to see the caravan. But the wall is already packed.

"They say he rides a horse made of fire," a small kid says. "And he'll come down from the sky."

The tall boy next to him looking like his older brother laughs.

"There isn't such a thing as a fire horse, you silly. Horses are made of flesh and blood like we are. And even if there were, riding a horse made of fire would surely char your privates. The şehzade must be smarter than that."

Radu can't but agree. The future sultan has spent the last two years in Manisa, learning how to govern. People say he's more handsome than the sun in spring, braver than a lion, and wiser than a snake. He also speaks seven languages, paints, and writes poems. That's why Radu can't wait to see him.

He climbs to a spot where he can see down the road through the crenels of the wall, and sets to wait. But he doesn't wait long. He's still looking down the road for the caravan when someone grabs him by the back of his kaftan and pulls him down.

He rolls to the ground, sputtering with anger and fixing for a fight as he gets back on his feet. It's Vlad, of course. Who else could it be? Nobody else here is ever mean to him, or treats him with disrespect.

Since the day Radu crashed his mare into Vlad's mount, thwarting his plans to kill the sultan, Vlad has stopped sharing his plans with him. He first bloodied him with a beating, and might have killed him if the janissaries hadn't intervened. But a few days later, Radu was as good as new. He was starting to think it had all been worth it, beating and all, to have Vlad off his back, until the sultan called him to his chambers and asked:

"What was that scuffle with your brother about, Radu?"

"I... I got mad that he shot my target. So I wanted to ruin his next shot."

The sultan didn't seem convinced.

"Be careful, Radu. Your brother is an angry young man. You don't want to get on his wrong side, especially not when the janissaries aren't there to protect you. You never know what he might do."

The sultan was right.

Radu sighs and looks up in his brother's poison-green eyes, wishing he was the eldest. He'd love to punch Vlad in the face and stomp him into the ground. But he's four years younger and only reaches to Vlad's shoulder.

"What are you doing here?" Vlad asks.

"Watching for the şehzade. He's supposed to arrive soon."

"So what's it to you? Just another Ottoman, looking to suck our country's blood. Like there aren't enough of them already."

"But aren't you curious to see him? They say he's amazing! Only months ago, he was just a prince, then his brother Aladdin died and he became the şehzade and someday, he'll rule the world!"

"Not if I have anything to say about it. But I have to agree, having this thirteen-year old nitwit lead the Ottoman troops in battle is great news. Father and our brother Mircea with their allies will eat them alive."

Radu's heart skips a beat. "But we're not at war. We can't be! Father sent us here as a guarantee of peace and submission. He can't fight against the Ottomans. If he does, our heads are gone!"

Vlad laughs. "Good job. You're not quite as stupid as I thought. But almost. Why did Father send us here?"

"To prove his faith to the sultan."

"So, what's going to happen next?"

"He's going to be faithful, and the sultan will let us go home."

Vlad rolls his eyes and laughs, holding his belly, like he'll never stop. Radu would love to club him with something, but he's got nothing handy.

"Have you heard about the latest crusade, princess?"

"No."

"Well, it's about to happen soon, and the Christians will obliterate the Ottomans. Right now, they're gathering their armies and deciding who's going to lead the fight."

"Who is?"

"John Hunyadi, King Władysław, the pope, and just about every other Christian prince."

"But not Father. He'd never do that. He wouldn't risk our lives."

His brother looks at him with pity, and that worries Radu no end, since Vlad doesn't do pity. That's for the weak.

"You're right. Father won't do that. He won't go against the Ottomans while we're captive here."

Radu breathes a big sigh of relief.

"So, we're OK."

Vlad laughs the worst laugh Radu has ever heard.

"You, kid, are too stupid to live. You want to know what Father will do?"

His heart frozen with fear, Radu shakes his head. He doesn't know what Father will do, and he'd rather never find out. But it's too late. Vlad is on a roll.

"He'll send our brother instead. Mircea will lead the Wallachian army into battle, while Father sits at the Royal Court of Târgoviște, planning his next move against the Ottomans. Or the Hungarians. Or whoever else. As always, Father will hedge his bets. Father has other sons, and he can make more, if need be. You and I, dear brother, we're nothing but bait in the fight of the nations."

Radu bites his lip to stop his tears. He's heartbroken that the world is not a good place. Not a nice place. It's a place where the weak get crushed, the righteous get killed, and the honest get fried. *This isn't what the world should be,* he thinks, but nobody cares what he thinks. He wipes his tears with his sleeve, hoping Vlad won't see him. And, for once, Vlad doesn't. He's up on the wall, staring at the procession.

"What do you see?" Radu asks. He's too short to see above the crowds gathered to catch a sight of the şehzade's caravan.

"I see a kid coming to die," Vlad says. "If there's anything I can do about it."

Too exhausted to join the crowd in greeting the new şehzade, Radu goes back to his room. He hugs Sari and cries, wishing he was a cat, rather than a prince. He'd chase mice the whole night, sleep the whole day, and wouldn't have to deal with the dirty intricacies of politics.

CHAPTER 43

KRONSTADT, JUNE 1444

It was hot as it ever got up in the mountains in June, but that didn't bother Ion one bit. Unlike Ali and Codru, who love snow, he loves to bask in the sun and thrives on the heat. But there was no time for that today.

When the burgomaster told them that their training was almost over and they'd be heading south soon, he asked for a day off. To see his family, he said, but he lied. He was going to see the witch.

He followed Ali's usual path to the charmed forest, half-hopeful and half-scared of finding her. He steeled his heart to gather enough courage to ask for her help.

It was a long trip. By the time he reached the all-season forest hidden in deep fog with the two mossy tree stumps holding hands Ali had told him about, he was almost too tired to care. But he joined his hand with theirs, and seconds later, the fog vanished. The little cottage standing on its scaly bird-legs stared back at him with narrow window eyes.

Ion sighed and pushed the gate open.

The rusty hinges screeched in protest, but the gate led him to the small yard where a huge black dog lay on the doorstep. The dog opened one eye, then the other, then wagged a long thick tail that thumped the floor like a drum, raising a cloud of dust. He looked friendly enough, other than being as big as a bear, but Ion wasn't going to jump over him to go inside.

He didn't need to. A willowy woman with long black hair braided with golden coins jingling like a Christmas sleigh smiled at him. "Welcome, Ion. I expected you sooner."

"You did?" Ion mumbled. "How come?"

He only just decided to come. And how did she know his name?

The woman laughed. "It's not hard, you know. I'm friends with your friends, and they told me about you. Come in."

Ion followed her, wondering what Ali and Codru had told her. But whatever it was, the worst was yet to come.

The cottage was cool and dark, and it smelled like hay, honey, and every kind of tree in the forest. The large table took half the room, and was piled with jars, bags and cooking tools. So were the walls, all covered with bags that moved like they were alive. *That's spooky*, Ion thought.

"Just the first time, then you get used to it. Sit. You want some tea?"

He did. His long journey through the heat had made him thirsty, but truth be told he was afraid to drink the witch's tea. Who knows what she could give him?

On the other hand, he'd come all this way to tell her his secret and ask for her help. What was the point in not trusting her?

"Yes, please," he said. He sat on the low milking stool by the dark fireplace, staring at a green-eyed cat with floppy rabbit ears who landed at his feet out of nowhere. She sniffed him and hissed, then turned tail and disappeared with all the dignity she could muster.

Ion chuckled. "What happened to your cat?"

"Gigi? That's Ana's work. She tried her potions on her, and that's the result. That girl has a lot to learn."

Smaranda gave Ion a cup of tea, then sat by the table and smiled. "Tell me."

Ion sighed and took a sip of tea. It was cold mint with honey, and it helped soothe his throat. He took another.

"I... have a problem. I wondered if you could help me like you helped Codru. Maybe with a potion, or a spell..."

"Tell me about your problem."

"I am... I can be... I can become..."

"You are a dragon."

She said it like it was no big deal, but Ion's heart froze.

"Yes. How did you know?"

"It's my job to know things. So why don't you want to be a dragon? I know many who would kill to have this power."

"I'm embarrassed. And scared."

"Of what?"

"Of myself. Of what that evil power can do to me. I don't want it. I want to be just an ordinary boy. Can you make it go away?"

Smaranda shook her head. "I'm sorry, I can't."

"Why not? You helped Codru to not be a werewolf. Why can't you help me not to be a dragon?"

"It's not the same thing, Ion. Codru is not a werewolf at heart. He's just an unlucky boy who got bitten and cursed. My potions can only suppress his curse during the nights with a full moon. But you are not like that. You are a dragon at heart. That is your nature, and nothing I can do can change who you are. Nobody but you can do that."

"Me?"

"Yes. You. How many times have you changed into a dragon?"

"Once. A few years ago."

"So if it's been years, why do you fear it will happen again?"

"I know it will. Every time I get mad, I get this heat wave inside. It's the fire, wanting to come out, and it takes all I've got to keep it in. Like that night I fought with Codru. I wanted to burn him alive, and I was this close to doing it."

"So how come you didn't?"

"I remembered... I remembered how it felt last time. I killed someone, and it was terrible. I swore to never do it again."

"But you had no choice, did you? That Zmeu would have killed your mother and your brother. What if you had to do it again? Wouldn't you kill to defend them?"

Ion looked inside his soul. He saw the flames roaring out of the dragon's angry mouth. He heard Petrica and Neta scream, and remembered Mother trying to protect them with her body.

"I would. For them, I would. Still, I killed my father."

"That Zmeu was not your real father. He was an evil creature who had kidnapped your mother and was going to kill her and her children. Your real father is the one who brought you up. I know he sees you, from wherever he is, and he's proud of you."

Ion sighed. This was not what he hoped for. He picked his cup and drained it, then stood to go.

"So, there's really nothing you can do for me?"

"Ion, there's nothing you need from me. You have an awesome power that you're wise enough not to use. But one day, when you really, really need it, you'll be glad you have it. One day, you'll use it to save somebody that matters more to you than your oath, your secret and even your life. When the time comes, you'll be glad you're a dragon."

Ion sighed.

"Thank you. I'll try to think of it like you said, but it still feels like a curse."

"It's not a curse, but it's a burden. All power is. It forces you to make uncomfortable choices, but that's how you grow."

The journey home was long and hot. By the time Ion got back to the castle, Ali and Codru had almost finished dinner. Ion sat with them, glancing at the leftovers.

"There's bread. And milk and cheese," Codru said.

"I'm sorry that's it. We were hungry, and we thought you weren't coming for dinner. Where have you been?" Ali asked.

"He went to see his family," Codru said, with just a tad of bitterness in his voice.

Ali shook her head. "No, he didn't."

"How do you know?"

"And you call yourself a werewolf? Can't you smell him? He smells like honey and herbs. He's come from Mama Smaranda."

CHAPTER 44
THE SLAVE MARKET

When she finally sets eyes on the Edirne Palace's crenelated walls, Ali remembers Mama Smaranda's words: "You're here to make the world a better place." But she's got no inkling of her upcoming greatness. Just the opposite.

The trip from Kronstadt to Edirne took weeks. First, they crossed the forbidding Carpathians, then they headed south to Târgoviște, Wallachia's capital. They stopped for a few days before heading south to the Danube, which forms the border with the Ottoman Empire. They ferried across, since the river was half a mile wide, then headed further south to Edirne.

Ali shifts her weight from one side to the other and shrugs to get rid of the stiffness in her shoulders. She's lost count of the days, and she's sick and tired of sitting in the slow-moving ox cart with nothing to do but watch the brown hills go by, the shriveled grass burned by the draught, and the empty fields black with crows.

But the cart's full now, and there's no more stopping to pick up new children. They're thirty, all boys. Some younger than her, some as big as grown men. But they aren't. The dark shadow above their upper lip shows them to be not much older than twelve or thirteen. They want them young for the devşirme caravan.

"Devşirme? What's that?" Codru had asked.

The burgomaster shrugged.

"That's the blood tax. The Christian kids that the Ottomans take to fuel their army, their workforce, and their harems. Thousands of them each year."

Ali, Ion and Codru stared at each other with wide eyes.

"I've never heard of this." Codru pretended he didn't care, but his jaw twitched with anger.

The burgomaster shrugged.

"Here, in Transylvania, we don't have it. That's because we aren't the Ottoman's vassals, thank God, Hungary's Emperor, and John Hunyadi. But that's what they do in every one of their vassal states. In Wallachia, Serbia, Bulgaria, and everywhere else in Rumelia. Anatolia too. Every year, they take their tax in money. Every few years, they come and take kids."

"Why do their parents let them go? Don't they want them?" Ion asked.

"They don't have a choice. If they fight, they get killed, and the Ottomans still take the kid. And they have other children they need to care for."

"Why are we traveling with them?" Ali asked.

"Because it's the safest way to get you to Edirne, in the sultan's palace."

"What if he doesn't want us?"

"He will."

But now, Ali looks at the kids around her, and she's not so sure. They're all dressed in red, so they're easier to spot if they run away. And they're all perfect. Healthy, good looking, smart. Not one of them looks sick or maimed or damaged, like many of the kids in her village. Why should the sultan want her, out of all these kids? Maybe Codru and Ion. They're both big and strong, but her? She's grown a lot, but she's still scrawny compared to the others. She knows she's not pretty either, with her mop of chestnut hair falling in her eyes, her foxlike face and her freckles. She's still wondering when she falls asleep. She only wakes up when the cart stops in Edirne's market, and it's a market like Ali has never seen.

The markets she knows sell onions, wheat, beans, and chickens. Sometimes wool, sheepskins and honey. And butter, and fragrant hot bread. Sometimes even ducks or a goat. But here, there's no food. And no stalls. Just a cover stretched over tall wooden poles keeping the sun at bay, and people. Naked people. Standing around for all to see.

The guards surround the cart, and Selim Paşa, who brought them all the way from Kronstadt, tells them all to get off. He aligns them by height, the short ones in front, the tall ones in the back, in three rows of ten.

"Get naked," he says.

Ali stares at him, wondering if she's heard him right.

"Get naked," he says again, then grabs Ali's arm and drags her to the front row. By height, that's where she belongs, but she tried to hide behind Ion. That didn't work.

She's still wondering what to do when Ion elbows her.

"You heard him. Get naked."

She's still fumbling with the ties of her chemise when she hears the whip. The scream follows. One of the boys refused to get naked, and he got persuaded. He didn't need a second whip.

Nor did Ali. She stands naked, like the others, clasping her hands to cover her groin. Ion stands behind her, and Codru behind him, and Ali can hear their heartbeats. They're as crazed as hers.

A gray-bearded man dressed in green shalwars and a brown kaftan dragging a loaded mule stares at one boy after another, until he gets to her. He looks her up and down, then pushes her hands away to see her privates.

"What's this?"

"That's Ali. He's a eunuch," Selim Paşa says.

"How old?"

"Ten."

"Where's he from?"

"Circassia. His father sold him to the Doge of Venice two years ago, but he can't sing worth a damn. He decided to sell him while he's still young and... trainable."

"How much?"

"Ten thousand."

"Ten thousand? Are you out of your mind? That's more than the sultan's stallion. More than a red-haired virgin, for Allah's sake. Who do you think will pay that?"

The paşa shrugs. "The sultan, maybe. Or someone else who can afford him. Look at him. He's beautiful. He's perfect. Rose petal skin, soft red hair, green eyes — green eyes! And he's fixed already. Like, fixed all the way. He's got nothing left there. Smooth as a girl. You know as well as I do that only one in ten boys survives this kind of castration. Nine out of ten die. Not like when you just cut off their nuts. Those have a fifty-fifty chance to make it, so they're cheap. This one is the whole package. And he's white! How many white complete eunuchs have you seen?"

The man shrugs. "None."

"Of course. Neither have I. Don't you think that's worth something?"

"It's worth something, but not what you're asking. You must be out of your minds. How about one thousand?"

Selim Paşa laughs so hard he chokes. "I don't think you understand me, my good man. Ten thousand, I said."

"You want ten thousand for him, and he doesn't even sing?"

"We both know it's not his singing you're after. At that price, he's a bargain. Furthermore, he comes with those other two. They're a package," he says, nodding at Ion and Codru. "They go together."

"Who says?"

"I do."

"Why?"

Selim Paşa shrugs and dismisses him with a flick of his hand.

"Listen, man. You can't afford him. Stop wasting my time. Check out one of the others. The small one there is only five hundred. More likely for someone like you," he says, pointing to a tiny fair-haired boy, then moves on to another customer.

But the man isn't convinced. He gets closer to Ali to inspect her. He pulls her hair to make sure it's real, then lifts her jaw to look into her eyes. He opens her mouth to check her teeth, runs a heavy hand down the muscles of her back, then squats to look at her groin. He puts down his bag and reaches with both hands to spread her legs.

Ali's heart beats like a drum. Ion's, behind her, is even louder. She feels him stepping forward, ready to jump on the man. Behind him, Codru growls.

"Don't touch him," Selim Paşa says, the steel in his voice as hard as the one in his hand. His eyes throw daggers, and his kilij is ready.

The customer steps back. "Why not? He's for sale, isn't he?"

"Not to you. I told you his price. You can't get that money if you sell your house, your wives, your children, your horses, or if you cut your dick off to sell it to the highest bidder. You can't afford him, you can't touch him. Don't you dare damage my merchandise."

The crowd gathered around screams, and laughs. They place bets on what's going to happen, but nothing does. Besides his kilij, Selim Paşa has ten armed guards and a parchment with the sultan's seal saying he's a faithful subject allowed to do business in the Edirne market. The man disappears like he's never been there. Others come and stare, but nobody touches.

By the end of the day, the kids are all sold. All but one. Bearded men who handled them like they were chattel checked them and bought them one by one. Now they're all gone but for Ali, Ion and Codru, and the little blond kid. Nobody wanted him at five hundred. Not even at two.

They're tired and thirsty. They stood naked for so long they almost forgot how it felt to wear clothes.

"Get dressed and let's go," Selim Paşa says.

"Where are we going?" the little kid asks, and the paşa slaps him across his mouth.

"You don't speak without permission, you understand?"

The kid nods, his teary eyes wide with fear. Ali feels sorry for him, but she's glad she wasn't the one to ask.

The four of them get back in the cart and head to the palace. The moon is up by the time they reach the palace gate, which is taller than any Ali has ever seen, even taller than Kronstadt's. Selim Paşa calls some words she doesn't understand, and the gate opens to let them in.

What's beyond the gates is also like nothing Ali has seen before. It's night, but the windows glow golden with flickering torches, every single one of them, and there must be hundreds. The wind smells like roses, incense, and myrrh.

A side door opens, and a tall black woman covered in veils looks them up and down, then nods to Selim Paşa. He signals them to follow.

They walk down a narrow hallway into a simple room with tall ceilings that smells like a kitchen. And it looks like it too, by the pots, pans, and jars that hang from every hook and pile in every corner, if it wasn't bigger than Ali's whole village church.

The round platter sitting in the middle of the tiled floor is bigger than a cart wheel and loaded with food. There's flat bread sprinkled with seeds, and warm milk and honey. A whole leg of lamb steams aromas of rosemary, mint and garlic. A jug of water perfumed with lemons. It's a feast like they haven't yet seen.

"Welcome to the palace," the woman says.

They reach for the food like a pack of hungry wolves, but she stops them.

"You need to learn some manners. Here, you wash your hands before you eat."

She points at a large bowl full of water sitting in the corner. They stare at it, wondering what to do. She laughs and points to a small yellow brick.

"That's soap. You use it like this." She dips it in the water, then rubs her hands with it until it starts making snow that melts when she sinks her hands in the water. "See? Now you're clean."

They nod and try to do it, but the soap is sneaky. It slips in the water. They try to fish it out, but like a slippery fish, it escapes. They reach for it and catch each other's hands instead, and they laugh like children for the first time in many moons.

Finally clean, they sit to enjoy the feast.

"What's your name?" Ali asks the small kid.

He smiles a toothless smile. He's got to be even younger than eight, Ali thinks.

"Mirko."

"How come you're here, Mirko?"

"I'm here to belong to the sultan and serve him and Allah. Mother said that if I'm lucky, I'll be one of the sultan's slaves, praise him. I'll make her and Father proud, and, God willing, one day I'll be the sultan's grand vizier."

CHAPTER 45

THE FAILED POTION

When they're sated, the woman takes them to the room they'll spend the night in. It's empty, but for the straw mats covered with wool blankets sitting on a raised platform. The boys fall asleep as soon as their heads hit the pillows, but Ali can't. She's bone tired, but her heart is heavy and her head full of worries, so sleep fails her. She listens to the regular breaths of the boys and wishes she could sleep like them. But she can't.

This is likely the last night they'll spend together. Tomorrow morning, they'll be each assigned to their jobs, whatever they are. The boys will go their way, and she'll go hers. All alone.

That shouldn't scare her since she's used to being alone, but it does. She's never been without the boys since she ran away to Kronstadt; they are her family now.

But even worse, she's not ready. Ali knows that she's a lousy witch.

Her mind reading isn't too bad, and she can usually foretell the weather. But, try as she might, she can't gather storm clouds and summon rain to save her life, let alone target lightning. And, despite her efforts, her potions leave a lot to be desired. As for her incantations, they're a joke.

"I haven't laughed so hard in ages," Smaranda said, wiping her eyes, looking at an indignant Gigi. The cat's angry eyes threatened a terrible death, but her ears flopped to her chin, and her tail was all but gone. "What on earth did you do to her?"

"I tried to turn her into a rabbit."

"What did you use?"

"Father's potion. And the *Transformatio Cunniculum* incantation."

"Which potion is that?" Smaranda asked.

"This one," Ali said, showing her Father's grimoire.

- *Three sprigs of wilted lavender*
- *Two tablespoons of dried mandrake root*
- *A cup of fresh carrot juice*
- *One black rabbit foot from the back*
- *One cat hair from the tail of the cat you want to transform*
- *One small piece of moonstone*

Process the thyme and lavender with a mortar and pestle until finely ground. Pour over the carrot juice in a cauldron and stir clockwise three times.

Drop in the cat tail hair while reciting the following incantation: "With this hair, and this potion, set transformation in motion."

Drop in the black rabbit's foot and recite: "From feline to lagomorph, set this metamorphosis on course."

Add the moonstone and simmer until thickened, then pour it over the cat you wish to transform. Within a few minutes, the cat will fully transform into a rabbit.

Smaranda set the grimoire on the table. Gigi hissed.

"Where did you get the rabbit foot?"

"I... I didn't. I used some hair. And I drew a rabbit foot with black ink and threw it in the pot."

Smaranda shook her head and laughed.

"It doesn't work that way, little girl. You must follow the recipe to a T; otherwise, you get this."

She pointed at Gigi, who glared at Ali under her floppy ears.

"So what do we do?" Ali asked.

"About what?"

"About Gigi."

"Nothing. She'll get back to normal in a day or two. Even if you did it correctly, that would only be a temporary transformation."

"But can't you do something to change her back now?"

"Sure, I can, but should I? Witchcraft and magic can be dangerous even in the best of hands. You should never take them lightly. What if something goes wrong, and I make her into a lynx? Or kill her? She's fine the way she is until your potion wears off."

Gigi returned to her cat form before long but never forgot to hold a grudge, like cats always do. But Ali learned her lesson. She never again used magic without a good reason and never substituted items in her potions again.

Still, when she asked to take Father's grimoire with her, Smaranda said no.

"I'm sorry, Ana. You can't take that with you. If anyone finds it, they'll know you're a witch, and that will cost you your life. Everywhere in Christianity, the zealots burn women at the stake for less of a sin than owning a grimoire. As for the Ottomans, I don't know what they do, but I bet it's not any good. The grimoire stays here."

"But I don't know any of the potion recipes. Or the incantations. Without it, I can't to do any magic!"

"Sure you can. Magic is not in the books; it's in your blood and your soul. You just need to nurture it and grow it."

"But I don't know how to do that!"

"You will learn."

Ali tried again, but Smaranda said no, and she took away Ali's book, so she had to manage without it. And she did. Poorly.

But at least she was home. Here, she's a fish out of water. She knows nothing and nobody, and she won't even have the boys to watch her back. A shiver runs down her back, and a deep cold seeps into her bones. She's in trouble.

She glances at her cross, and sure enough, it glows red.

CHAPTER 46

THE GAME OF WAR

EDIRNE, THE PALACE SCHOOL, JULY 1444

It's early morning, and the grassy courtyard of the Edirne Palace is still shady and cool. Not for long, though. The sky is blue as far as the eye can see, with barely a whisper of a cloud, promising another scorching day. That's why the *acemi,* the new recruits, woke up early to train while it's still cool. They come in one by one, rubbing the sleep out of their eyes and tightening their leather armors. The janissary agha aligns them by height, and, as usual, Radu comes last.

There are few things Radu hates more than mock fights like this. They'll divide into two armies and fight with pretend swords made of polished wood that can't cut through their leather armor, so he knows he won't get killed, just bruised. And humiliated. Still, he drags his feet and stares at the sky, hoping for a storm to cancel the fight. But he's got no such luck.

He stands in line and waits, but he knows he's going to be the last one to get picked, as usual. The other kids know that he's soft and slow, so they don't want him. But that's OK. He doesn't want to be on their team either. On any team.

He just wishes they'd leave him alone with his manuscripts, his brushes, and his rübap, but that won't happen. Training new recruits at the palace school is not about pleasure or choice. It's about discipline and duty. They get told when to sleep, when to eat, when to pray, and what to learn and when. For the new trainees, military training is just as important as learning Persian, Greek, philosophy, and poetry. Even more so. After all, Persian poetry isn't going to defeat the Ottoman Empire's enemies and help expand its borders. But their military, the sipahis and the janissaries with their kilijes, bows, and lances will.

The agha hands the two captains the blue and red ribbons that mark the two armies. He steps back.

"Choose your armies!"

Vlad and Şehzade Mehmet turn around to choose their teams. They are the captains for good reasons: Vlad is the strongest and fiercest fighter who always prevails in the war games, so he won the right to command. The şehzade is born with it.

Vlad's armor bears the wounds of many fights. The shiny oiled leather is wrinkled with wear and marked with the scratches and tears of old victories. The blue peacock feather of his helmet is broken, and half of it is missing, but his green eyes sparkle with evil joy. Radu recognizes the vicious look in his eyes and he shivers. He hopes that Vlad won't get them in trouble, but, as always, there's no telling to what his mercurial brother will do.

Mehmet, the şehzade, looks handsome and dauntless in his brand-new shiny armor with the crescent moon embroidered in gold thread on his chest. An errant red curl escaped from his helmet sets off his white skin, and his amber eyes sparkle with excitement.

The two boys glare at each other like a pair of young stallions ready to rip each other's throat. Vlad tightens his fists like he's ready to fight, but Mehmet turns his back on him and grabs the blue ribbons to mark his team.

The janissary guards' eyes are glued to them. They hold their hands on their weapons, ready to intervene if needed. *What would they do*, Radu wonders? Kill Vlad, of course. They're here to protect the future sultan.

"Who goes first?"

"The guest, of course," Mehmet says, inviting Vlad to pick first.

Vlad points to a tall, dark boy who's good with the bow and arrow, and better with the halberd and the lance.

Mehmet laughs.

"Really? You won't pick your own brother first? I thought you Christians made a big fuss over brotherly love. Not all that's cracked up to be? OK, then I'll be happy to have him. Come here, Radu."

Radu freezes. He didn't think Mehmet knew his name, let alone pick him first. His head down, his cheeks burning, he shuffles to Mehmet's side.

"So good to have you on my team, *arkadaş*, my friend." Mehmet touches his shoulder and ties the blue ribbon around his left arm.

If looks could kill, I'd be dead, Radu thinks, catching Vlad's venomous glare. Still, he's grateful to Mehmet for picking him. He's spared him the humiliation of standing there, pretending he doesn't care as he watches everyone else get chosen. But of course, Mehmet doesn't know what a lousy fighter he is.

When the picking is done, the teams of fifteen each go to opposite ends of the courtyard to strategize. His excitement vanished, Radu is sick with fear that he'll disappoint Mehmet and he'll cover himself in shame. He hangs his head and drags his feet behind all the others. But Mehmet waits for him.

"What do you think we should do?" he asks.

Radu looks right and left to make sure the şehzade talks to him. Nobody ever asks his opinion about anything, let alone fighting and battles. But Mehmet just did, so he answers.

"You should take four of the boys and go forward to taunt them. Vlad can't resist showing off, so he'll only take four of his own to respond. Then you should pretend to fight, then retreat. When he follows you, the rest of our team should cut their retreat. We'll disarm and disable them. Without a leader, the other ten won't put up much of a fight."

Mehmet smiles. "Good thinking! I'm so lucky to have your counsel. This is exactly what we'll do. I'll lead the four into battle. After they follow us, you lead the others and cut their retreat."

He turns to the others. "From now on, Radu is my lieutenant."

A few boys chuckle. The others smirk.

Mehmet frowns. “If you want to keep your heads on your shoulders, this won’t happen again. You understand?"

His voice thunders over them, and the boys, deflated, look down. Radu's heart soars.

"You, you, you and you." Mehmet points to the smallest boys in his team. "You're my avantgarde. We'll take them on together. The others: you're under Radu's orders. Got it?"

"Yes."

"Let's go."

Mehmed and his four head to the center, where Vlad and his army are waiting.

Vlad's eyes narrow.

"Where's the rest of your army?"

“They’re chilling. We don't need fifteen to annihilate you and your horde.”

Vlad's cheeks burn like he got slapped.

"You think you're hot shit, don't you?"

He turns to his team, his voice breaking with rage.

"Four of you stay here. The others go back and wait."

The boys stare at each other, wondering what to do. Who should go? Who should stay? They mumble and fumble, then ten of them walk back to the end of their field and sit down to watch.

"Go!"

Vlad and his four fighters burst into Mehmet and his boys. Wooden swords seek chests and soft limbs, but they find each other instead. Rounded ash lances strike leather-wrapped ribs. Bruises bloom, knees twist, and noses bleed. Angry curses cross with screams of pain. The wind smells like sweat, dust and rage.

Vlad curses and leaps at Mehmet like a rabid wolf. His teeth glimmer and his eyes burn with fury as his wooden sword reaches for Mehmet's neck, but it meets his sword instead and gets deflected. Vlad tries again, but Mehmet's wooden sword found the soft spot in Vlad's armpit, where there's no armor. Vlad drops his sword and falls to his knees.

Mehmet lifts his sword to crash it over Vlad's head.

"If this were a real fight, with real weapons, you'd be dead."

Vlad rolls into Mehmed's knees and tackles him. Mehmed falls, but holds on to his sword. But he's too close to stab him, so he smashes the handle in his face. Vlad's piercing scream splinters the air as blood spurting from his nose paints the grass red.

Mehmet stands to tackle another opponent, but his four companions are in disarray. He's got all four of Vlad's boys surrounding him. He feints and swings his sword, but he can't fight four at a time so he runs back.

"Retreat!"

The others follow with their attackers in close pursuit, leaving Vlad behind.

Holding his bloody nose with his hand, Vlad sits up.

Radu waits.

Mehmed gets surrounded. Three swords threaten him, and he's got nowhere to go. He lunges and knocks down one. The other two close in.

His heart pounding, Radu waits.

Mehmed feints and lunges. He knocks down another opponent and glances at Radu.

Radu waits.

Covered in blood and rabid with anger, Vlad picks up his sword to chase Mehmet. One of his boys kicks the şehzade's sword with his lance, and the blade flies through the air like a bird, leaving Mehmet to face Vlad's fury unarmed.

"Now," Radu says.

The blue team leaps like a pack of wolves towards their leader. Radu's first, since he took off before he gave the signal. He gets between Vlad and Mehmet just as Vlad lifts his sword to crash it on Mehmet's head. Radu's sword stops it, but his arm cracks and falls to his side.

Vlad lifts his sword again.

With the hilt of his sword, he smashes Mehmet's neck in the soft spot with no armor where the large shallow veins carry blood to the brain, and Mehmed falls to the ground.

"If this were a real weapon, you'd be dead. But you'll be anyhow."

Vlad grabs Mehmet's helmet and pulls, breaking the tie around his neck. He throws down the helmet and raises his sword.

The blade whistles as it slices the air to sink in the mop of red hair. Vlad's out to kill Mehmet, and the evil joy in his smile reminds Radu of the arrow he shot into his dog, many years ago. His heart burning with rage, Radu kicks Vlad's knee with all his might.

Vlad falls just as the rest of Mehmet's team surrounds him. They disarm Vlad and the rest of his team before those who sat at the other end of the field to watch the war game get ready to fight.

"It's over," the janissary agha says. "The blue team won. The red team lost."

The boys drop their weapons to the ground, too tired to rejoice. Now that the blood rush of the fight is over, Radu's pain engulfs him like a fire. He tries to lift his arm but he can't.

Mehmet stands. His red hair burns like a flame around his bruised white face, but he smiles as he puts his arm around Radu's shoulders.

"Good work, lieutenant. I'll have the best doctor in the world care for you. You deserve it."

Radu smiles, but his smile fades when he sees four guards take Vlad away.

"Where are you taking him? Where is my brother going?"

"He's going to the sultan."

"Why?"

"He tried to kill the şehzade. He will be subject to the sultan's justice."

That's true. Radu saw Vlad rip off Mehmet's helmet and try to kill him. They all did.

Killing a şehzade is a horrendous crime and Vlad's life hangs from a thread. And, even though he hates his brother, Radu feels guilty. What will he tell Mother? What will Father say when he finds out that he, Radu, was there, helping the sultan's son?

He sobs. Mehmet's arm tightens around him.

"Don't worry. I'll put in a good word for your brother. He won't get executed. Not this time."

"You will? Really? But why would you? He tried to kill you."

"My tutors taught me that a wise man knows his enemies. Better an enemy you know than one you don't. And because he's your brother, and you are my friend. Don't worry, it's going to be all right," Mehmet whispers in his ear, and Radu's heart melts.

CHAPTER 47
ALI'S NEW FRIEND

It's been more than a week since Ali and the boys have arrived to Edirne, but she's still in awe of its wonders. She used to think that the Kronstadt fortress, with its six-feet-thick stone walls, watchtowers that scratched the moody sky and fireplaces big enough to roast a whole boar, was amazing. But the Edirne Palace? This is something else.

The palace kitchens alone are bigger than her whole village. Hundreds of cooks and their helpers fuss around ovens, spits, pots, and pans, most of them bigger than the baptismal vessel at Ali's church. The air is thick with the smoke of roasting mutton, the fumes of cooking onions, and the sweet aromas of rose water, pistachios and honey from the fresh baklava. The smells are so potent that her stomach wavers between nausea and hunger, and her mouth waters so hard it hurts. She swallows her saliva, wishing she could spit it instead; but here, that's not allowed.

She knows she won't be eating for a while. First, she must take the breakfast platter to the harem women. That's one of her main jobs, as a junior eunuch in training. She'll get to eat after they do.

She crosses the paved courtyard behind the women's rooms, wavering under the weight of the massive platter loaded with food for a dozen hungry women, when an arm catches her waist. She gasps and steadies herself, struggling to hold on to the tray, and curses, ready to kick the intruder.

But it's Mirko. He must be the only person in the palace who has nothing to do. By the time they discovered how young he really was, it was too late to send him back to wherever he came from. So now, he wanders around the palace without a clear assignment, getting in everyone's way, and that suits Ali just fine.

Sadly, she doesn't enjoy the same freedom, so she needs to find a way to get in touch with the boys. She hasn't seen them since the day after they arrived. That morning, a fat bearded man with eyebrows thicker than his mustache came to get them. He saw Mirko and frowned.

"How old are you?"

"Six, paşa."

"Six!" His stormy eyes turned to the woman who'd fed them.

"Six! Seriously? Who's the idiot who brought him? Everyone knows we don't want them any younger than eight."

"Selim Paşa," the woman said.

The man sighed and turned to Codru. He studied him from his head to his toes.

"Now that's a good-looking janissary-to-be. What's your name, boy?"

"Codru."

"No more. That's not an Ottoman name. Starting today, you're Kemal." He turned to Ion. "And yours?"

"Ion."

"You'll be Isa. You'll both go to the palace school. If you turn out to be worthy, you'll be allowed to join the janissary corps. That's an honor like no other. The janissaries are the most elite army in history, and the only standing army in the world. While those faithless Christians only gather their peasants, shepherds and blacksmiths to arm them and send them to fight when they go to war, the Ottoman Empire, may Allah smile over it forever, has a well-equipped standing army of trained men whose only job is to fight for the sultan. As a janissary, you'll always have a cover above your head, food in your belly, and the most loving family there ever was: your janissary brothers. If you prove yourself worthy."

They all waited for the woman to finish translating the paşa's words like they hadn't been learning the Ottoman language for more than a year, then nodded.

The paşa turned to Ali and his face lit up.

"And what do we have here? Is this what I think it is?"

The woman nodded.

"That's good. Sultan Murad will be pleased. Just the other day, he told the kapi agha that our eunuchs are getting old and fat. We need some young ones to keep up with the sarayi women, he said. Truth be told, the young sarayi women are getting out of control."

He turned to Ali.

"You'll answer to the kapi agha. He'll take care of your training. Come, you three. I'll drop you off."

The woman pointed to Mirko. "How about him?"

The paşa shrugged. "I don't know. Ask me again in two years."

That's how Mirko got to wander around, sticking his pointed dirty nose into everything and getting in everyone's way.

"Have you seen Codru and Ion?" Ali asks.

"They're Kemal and Isa now."

Ali nods, wishing she had a free hand to smack him.

"Of course."

"They're training at the palace school. They got uniforms and weapons and everything."

"Can you find them?"

"What for?"

"To give them something from me."

"What?"

"Some pastries."

Mirko's eyes light up.

"I'll get you one too. Come find me later."

Mirko nods and saunters away and Ali takes the food to the women's room in the sarayi. She kneels to set the platter on the floor, then steps back to make room.

The dozen women, all young and ravishing in their long flowing tunics and brightly colored shalwars, gather and sit cross-legged to eat. Ali's stomach growls as she watches the fragrant cheeses, the creamy yoghurt, the mountain of green and black olives, and the buttered bread dripping with honey vanish like they never were.

She takes the empty platter to the kitchen and manages to steal three pastries. She makes sure nobody's watching, then makes a hole in the dry one that she knows Mirko doesn't like, and stuffs it with the message she wrote for the boys. She hides them in her kaftan, then heads back to the women's room like she's supposed to, waiting for the kapi agha to get busy so she can slip out unnoticed.

She sits in a corner, ready for her next errand, and watches the women preen, chat and sew like they do every morning, sitting cross-legged on their pillows. The older woman supervising them walks from one to another to check their work. She stops by a dark-haired girl and frowns.

"What's this? Where's the embroidery you were working on yesterday?"

"I... I couldn't find it."

"What do you mean you couldn't find it? Where can it be?"

"Somebody stole it," she says, glaring at the smiling blonde by the door. "It was you, wasn't it, bitch?"

The blonde shrugs. "It wasn't me, nor anyone else. I saw you throw it away."

The brunette curses and jumps to her feet. She grabs the blonde's braid and drags her to the ground, then tries to scratch her eyes out. The blonde knees her in the groin and rolls over, then grabs her by the throat and squeezes hard.

The other women scream and scatter like a flock of frightened chickens. The brunette slams the blonde's head against the marble floor. The blonde's knuckles whiten as she squeezes tighter.

Kapi agha wakes up from his torpor. "Stop it, you two!"

Nobody listens.

He grabs the brunette by her hair and pulls her away. The blonde jumps up and punches her in the nose. Something cracks. Blood spurts, splashing everyone in the room. The brunette screams.

This may be a good time to escape, Ali thinks, since they're busy. But they're fighting right by the door, so there's no way to leave unnoticed. She grabs the blonde girl by the waist and pulls her away before she can do any more damage.

"*Lasă-mă in pace.* Let me be," the girl says in Romanian, trying to shake Ali off.

"*Potolește-te, fata.* Chill, now, girl," Ali answers. "You don't want to get into any more trouble. You already gave her what she deserved."

The blonde is so shocked she forgets to fight. She stares at Ali's wide shalwars, her blue kaftan and turban — her new eunuch uniform.

"Who are you?"

"I'm Ali. You?"

"I'm Lena."

"Bring her over, Ali," kapi agha shouts. He's still holding on to the beautiful brunette who's still brunette but no longer beautiful with her broken nose and bloody face.

"Güzel says you stole the chemise she was embroidering and destroyed it. Is that true?"

"No."

"Who did, then?"

"She did. She's too lazy to do her work, so she chose to blame me instead. I never touched her work."

"Can you prove it?"

"Me? Prove it? Can she prove that I did?"

Güzel explodes into a sputtering tirade peppered with tears. Kapi agha shrugs.

"That's enough. You'll have to talk to the validé. Both of you. She'll decide who's lying and who's not, and what happens to them. Let's go."

Ali takes Lena's hand, and they follow kapi agha who drags Güzel along the empty corridors leading to the Validé's quarters. And with every step they get closer, the mosaics become richer, the carpets thicker, the singing birds louder.

When they finally get to her quarters, they drop to their knees. Kapi agha explains what happened, and the validé stays quiet for the longest time. When she speaks, her voice is soft but firm.

"Lena. Look at me."

Lena looks up.

"Did you steal her work?"

"I didn't."

"Who did?"

"Nobody. She destroyed it herself."

"How do you know?"

"I saw her when she thought nobody was watching. Last night as I woke up from a nightmare, I saw her hiding it in the chimney."

"You'll check that, kapi agha. Lena, why did she accuse you?"

"Because she hates me. They all do."

"Why?"

"Because you showed me favor, my lady."

"I did not show you any favor."

"You called me here. That was favor enough."

The validé looks at Güzel, bloody and disheveled, then at Ali, kneeling by Lena, still holding her hand. "And who are you?"

"I'm Ali."

"The new eunuch, my lady. He arrived only a few days ago, and just started training."

"OK. Güzel, if what Lena said proves true, you'll get ten lashes. Next time you lie, you'll get twenty. Kapi agha, make sure the others know it too. Here, we don't do lies.

"Lena. Sultan Murad's third wife, Hüma Hatun, has just returned from Manisa with the şehzade, may Allah look upon him with favor. You will be transferred to her service starting now. Ali, you'll go with her. You'll both serve her and obey her like you serve and obey me. Understood?"

They bow and touch their foreheads to the precious Persian carpet before following the kapi agha to their new assignment.

CHAPTER 48
THE JUDGEMENT DAY
EDIRNE

The sun isn't up yet, but cooped in his small bedroom in the palace school, Radu can't stand his bed anymore. The whole night, he's tossed and turned, waiting for this morning. The day of judgment has come. Today, the sultan will decide Vlad's fate, and Radu's heart is torn with guilt.

He hopes Mehmet will put in a good word for Vlad, but he's anything but sure, since he hasn't seen Mehmet since the day of the battle. He hasn't seen anyone, in fact, but the doctor. And the boy who brings his meals, since he's not allowed out. He's confined to his room, under arrest.

“But why?" he asked the janissary guarding his door the first morning.

“Because Sultan Murad said so."

"But I didn't do anything!"

The janissary shrugged and turned away, and Radu decided that there was no point in pushing it. The janissaries have orders they obey — that's all there is to it. The guard may not know any better than Radu why he's been posted to watch him, and he doesn't care.

So Radu spent the last week in his room, sleeping, drawing, talking to Sari, and working on a Wallachian poem about the gardens. That's his small act of rebellion. He should be writing in Greek or Persian, if not in the Ottoman language. Still, his heart isn't in it; he tried again and again, but couldn't find anything to rhyme with *trandafir,* which in Wallachian language means rose.

The janissary steps aside to let in a young boy dressed in blue shalwars and a yellow kaftan carrying a silver platter loaded with fresh bread, cheese, and fruit. The boy glances at Radu's poem as he kneels to set down Radu's breakfast.

"*Zefir*," he says. Breeze.

He turns to leave, but Radu grabs his arm, choking with excitement. "Are you Wallachian?"

"No. I'm Transylvanian."

"But you speak Wallachian?"

The boy smiles. "The language is the same, my prince. It's just a different dialect. Same with Moldova."

"I know about Moldova. My cousin Ștefan lives there. But I thought Transylvanians spoke Hungarian. Or Saxon."

"Some do. But most speak Romanian."

Radu is befuddled. His teachers taught him all about the Ancient Greeks, the Ottoman Empire, the Venetians, and King Władysław's Poles, but never about Transylvanians, let alone that they speak the same language. How could that be? And is that true?

He takes a closer look at the boy. He's slight, about his age, and quite ordinary. A few strands of chestnut hair escaped his turban to frame a freckled foxlike face too narrow to be pretty. But his luminous eyes change color like the moody sea, unlike any Radu has ever seen. "What's your name?"

"Ali."

"I'm Radu."

Ali laughs. "I know."

"What are you doing here?"

"I'm training to be a eunuch in Sultan Murad's sarayi."

"You? Become a eunuch?"

Radu hopes he's got it wrong. Depriving a man of his family jewels and manly pride is the worst thing he can think of. Most men would rather die - and many do, since the surgery kills them.

Ali shrugs. "I am a eunuch already. I'm just not trained yet."

Radu's heart sinks. *Who would do that to a kid? And why?*

But he knows. In the two years he's been here, he's seen plenty of eunuchs. The old ones guard the women, serve the sultan and are entrusted to look after the Palace business. Some whisper that they're also in charge of the discrete sarayi executions the sultan doesn't want to make public.

He's also seen the pretty young ones who dress in silk women's clothes and wear perfume, jewels, and kohl. They sing and dance at parties to delight the old paşas, then accompany them to places nobody talks about. But they aren't children, like this one.

Ali nods and turns to the door where the janissary shuffles back and forth, getting antsy.

"I have to go. I have work to do in the kitchens."

"Come back, will you? Please?"

Ali smiles. "Of course. I'll bring your food tomorrow."

Radu sighs. "If I'm still here tomorrow."

The sultan's judgment is about to take place, and God only knows what it will bring. Radu hasn't been locked in a cell like his brother, but he's still confined, awaiting judgment.

What will they do? Kill me? Send me to jail? Maybe they'll send me home? Then he remembers he's a hostage, and they won't send him back, not even as a punishment. *But maybe they won't kill me, even if they kill Vlad. It wouldn't do to lose both their hostages.*

Ali's eyes catch his. "You'll be here tomorrow."

"How do you know?"

"I just do."

Ali leaves. Radu's eyes follow him till he's gone, then he turns to his tray, but the janissary shakes his head and nods to the door.

The time for the judgement has come.

CHAPTER 49

THE SULTAN'S JUSTICE

Sitting cross-legged in front of the sultan's podium on his red brocade pillow flanked by two janissaries, Radu cranks his neck to see better. He's so awestruck that he forgets his fear, and he's thinking that the Edirne Palace must be the most beautiful place on earth. Compared to the cold gray throne room in Târgoviște, which is dusty and empty but for his father's wooden seat, this place is like a brilliant bird of paradise next to a humble gray sparrow.

The walls sparkle in blue, white, and gold geometrical patterns that chase each other like waves across the sea. The cinnamon-colored floor tiles are mostly hidden by thick, hand-woven Isfahan carpets where entangled leaves and flowers glow in lively colors. Sussuring fountains chill the air and soothe the senses with the song of water.

But the cross-legged dignitaries dressed in rich brocade sitting around Radu don't have time for the beauty. They examine the sultan with weary eyes, like they expect bad things to happen.

Sultan Murad sits above them all on his podium. His narrow eyes are glued to a window like he can't hear the ruckus inside. *He must be praying to Allah for guidance*, Radu thinks, looking for the şehzade.

He's there too, sitting next to the podium with the other

dignitaries, but his eyes don't meet Radu's, and Radu's heart grows cold.

They wait.

Heavy boots clatter on the stone pavement outside. Four janissaries come in, all dressed in red, with tall felt hats and curved kilijes, bringing Vlad. Their heavy hands push him down to his knees next to Radu.

Vlad has had it rough. He's still in his blood-covered leather armor, and his bruised face is drawn and haggard, but his eyes burn with hate, as usual. Radu feels sorry for him, until he remembers what Vlad did to deserves his punishment. And how he got him in trouble too.

His pity turns to anger. If Vlad goes to jail, or even worse, it's nobody's fault but his own.

The sultan's eyes leave the window to rest on the two brothers, and there's no kindness in them.

"Tell me what happened," he says.

Radu bites his lip to stop his tears. Vlad shrugs.

"I'm talking to you, Vlad. What happened?"

"We fought. That's what we were there for. Then your janissaries grabbed me and put me in a cell."

"Why?"

"Because I'm a better fighter than your son. They didn't want me to win."

"Is that true, Radu?"

Radu shakes his head no.

"Talk."

"They took him after the fight was over. He'd already lost."

"Why did they take him?"

"They said he tried to kill the şehzade."

"Is that true, Vlad?"

"We were learning battle skills. He was the opposing army. What was I supposed to do? Help him? I was supposed to fight. That's what I did."

"You weren't supposed to remove his helmet. That's not something a warrior does. Not something a leader does. That's dirty fighting, and this wasn't even a fight. Just a lesson."

"When you fight, you fight to win. No matter what. I fought to win."

"But you lost. You fought dirty, and you still lost."

There's no end to the hate in Vlad's eyes when they meet Radu's. And Radu knows exactly what he's thinking. If it wasn't for him, Vlad could have killed Mehmet. But Radu betrayed him and stood with the Ottomans against his own brother. There's no bigger sin in Vlad's book.

"Did your brother help you?"

Vlad's face lights in evil joy. He couldn't have hoped revenge was so close.

"Of course."

"How so?"

"He kept his men waiting until it was too late to save the şehzade. He waited for me to kill Mehmet first."

The sultan's face darkens.

"Did you two plan this together?"

"Of course."

"Radu?"

Crushed with shame, Radu crumbles to the floor. He's devastated, because he thinks that Vlad is right. Not about planning this — of course they didn't. But because he's afraid that Vlad is correct. Radu waited until the very last moment. He waited until he knew they could capture Vlad too; otherwise, he'd have retreated and brought in the rest of his team. He waited for too long.

"Radu?"

"Father, can I speak?" Mehmet spoke without permission.

The sultan's eyes turn to him, telling him he'll be sorry, but his voice stays soft. "Yes."

"Radu did everything he could to protect me. If it wasn't for him, I'd be dead now. He got hurt while preventing his brother from killing me. Vlad is lying."

The sultan turns to Vlad. "So. You're not only a dirty fighter, you're a liar, too. Even worse, you lied to hurt your brother. You want him to share your fate. That's low."

"You, Ottomans, practice fratricide. You killed your brothers when you got the throne, didn't you?"

"Fratricide is not petty vengeance, it's politics and leadership. We do that to protect the Ottoman Empire. The *Interregnum*, the last war for the throne, lasted for eight years. Eight whole years when the empire bled and almost died, torn apart by its own sons. That can never happen again. It is our duty to keep the empire whole, in peace, under one rule, no matter what. We owe it to our country."

Vlad shrugs.

"I did what I did for my country. You take our land, kill our people, and steal our harvests, letting my people starve. You enslave our children and take them from their mothers. You steal their faith and convert them to your religion to turn them against their brothers. You send them back to a country they no longer recognize as theirs to kill their families and steal more children. To fight for my country, I will do whatever it takes. I'll lie, I'll steal, and I'll kill for her. Gladly."

Sultan Murad looks at Vlad with new respect.

"I see your point. It is unfortunate that throughout your time with us, you failed to see the superiority of our civilization. We offer your children a better life. We educate them, train them, and we offer them the highest positions, up to the grand vizier, if they deserve it. The Albanians, the Slovenians, and even the Serbs beg us to take their children and give them a chance. But you, Wallachians, would rather live in dirty huts and pray to wooden idols than get educated and have the chance of a lifetime."

"My people love their country more than they want your opportunities."

"Fair enough. I'm glad we understand each other. Unfortunately, we won't get to talk about this again." He turns to the janissaries. "Take him."

"Father!"

Murad's eyes turn to his son, and the love in them is not easy to see.

"Please spare him."

"Why?"

"Because of his brother. Radu saved my life."

"You and Radu may not be that lucky next time. There's no reasoning with Vlad. He's your enemy, the Ottoman Empire's enemy, even Radu's enemy. Our enemies belong dead."

"But he's a valuable hostage. He's a guarantee of his father's faith to you."

Murad laughs. "His father's faith is like a dead leaf blowing in the wind. I bet you right now he's trying to decide who to cheat first. Vlad Dracul plays on too many fronts to be trusted."

"That's what makes Vlad valuable. His father will do whatever he can to keep him safe. If you kill him, he's even more likely to betray you."

The sultan sighs. "Mehmet, you'll soon be the sultan. You need to make hard decisions in uncertain circumstances. You'll make mistakes, and you'll have to learn how to fix them. That's what leaders do. But this is a big mistake. You will eventually wish Vlad had died today."

"Please, Father."

Murad shakes his head, and the egret feather caught in the emerald on his white turban flutters in the wind.

"So be it. I'll let Vlad live. But he will learn that actions have consequences. Betrayal, arrogance, and ignorance get punished. He'll learn things he'll wish he'd never learned, he'll see things he'll wish he could unsee, and hear things he'll wish he never heard. He will never again be who he is today."

Mehmet shivers. Radu chokes. Vlad pales.

"Take him."

"Where... where is he going?" Radu asks.

The sultan looks at him with eyes colder than snow.

"To Tokat."

CHAPTER 50

FATHER'S PLAN

The golden hour around dusk is magical in the palace gardens. As the shadows lengthen, the air grows heavy with the scent of jasmine, cedars and petunias, and the birds, drunk with the mellow evening's charm, sing like it's spring. Mehmet wishes he could enjoy it too, but he can't. Walking between the four janissaries sent to fetch him, he wonders why the sultan invited him to his quarters.

They didn't tell him why he was summoned, but he has no reason to expect good news. Mehmet never defied Sultan Murad in public, like he did today, and his father can't be pleased. He's sure to talk to him about that, but Mehmet worries that the words will be just the beginning. What punishment will his father give him? Mehmet's heart races; he sweats, struggling to swallow the knot in his throat.

They get to the door, and the janissaries step aside. He alone enters his father's studio. Unlike the throne room, this one is small and modest: White walls, a well-worn prayer rug, books, and rolls of parchment scattered on low shelves. A silver tray piled with cherries, strawberries, and apricots, father's favorite fruits. A jug of water. This is Murad's study where he spends most of his time. Sometimes alone, sometimes with the greatest scholars and philosophers in the world. Here, he prays, meditates, and ponders the empire's fate.

Mehmed has never been here before. This is Father's place, and nobody comes here uninvited. Unlike his bedroom, where servants roam day and night and his women visit when he asks for them, or even his bath, where eager hammam servants await to scrub, massage and soothe the shoulders holding the weight of the Ottoman Empire, this study is his alone.

Dressed in a simple white kaftan, Sultan Murad sits on a pillow under an arched window letting in the evening breeze. He's reading, but he sets down the parchment when he hears Mehmet. He points to a pillow and dismisses the janissaries with a flick of his hand. They step back, far enough to be out of hearing, but not out of sight.

Mehmet kisses his father's hand, crosses his legs, and sits.

"How did you do today?" Father asks.

"I... I'm sorry I spoke without being invited, Father."

Murad nods. "Besides that. How did you do?"

"I did what I had to do. I had to protect my friend. I promised him I would talk to you about his brother, and I did. I didn't have a choice."

"You did. You could just sit there and let things happen. Vlad would be dead, and you'd never have to worry about him again."

"But... I promised."

"Don't you wish you hadn't?"

Mehmet looks inside his soul and has to admit he wants Vlad dead. He wishes he never promised Radu to save him. But Radu saved his life, and he felt grateful.

"Yes."

"And you wish that I didn't listen to you and killed him anyhow. That way, you would have kept your promise, but still got rid of Vlad."

Mehmet blushes. His father understands him better than he understands himself.

"Promises can be broken, you know. That's pretty much the norm in politics. People make promises they don't keep. All the time. Sometimes they can't. Sometimes they never meant to. The promise was good enough for their purpose."

"But if you don't keep your promises..."

"Yes?"

"People won't trust you anymore."

"I'm glad you understand that. Trust is essential to leadership. If a leader can't be trusted, he won't be followed. Your people must trust you if you want them to follow you and die for you in battle. Your friends must trust you to be faithful and true. Trust is the glue that binds men together."

"And women?"

"Women are different. They don't have a soul. Not like men do. They lie, they cheat, and they tempt men. That's why we keep them locked up and guarded. Men can't trust women."

"Never?"

"With one exception. A man can always trust his mother. I trust the validé, Emine Hatun, more than anyone else on earth."

"Do you trust my mother?"

"I trust Hüma Hatun to do whatever she thinks is best for you. I know she will never betray you. That brings me to the reason you are here."

Mehmet sits straight, wondering what's coming. He glances to the janissaries. They're watching from the hallway, their hands on their swords, ready to move at his father's sign.

"I was devastated when your brother Aladdin died. He was a good son, a great soldier, and a God-fearing man. And he was my heir. I was heartbroken that Allah decided to take him from us. The empire and I needed him here, and he was almost ready to become sultan. But, sadly, he's no longer with us."

Murad's voice breaks and Mehmet wonders if he's about to cry. But that can't be. Sultans don't cry. Still, Mehmet lowers his gaze to give his father a moment of privacy.

What a terrible loss, Mehmet thinks. Nobody seems to know what happened to Aladdin. He was just eighteen, and he was healthy, strong, and handsome. Then he died.

Mehmet was in Manisa with his mother, training in the intricacies of government, when a messenger came from Bursa to tell them that Aladdin had died. It was hard to believe. Some said he fell off his horse. Some said he got sick after Kara Hizir Paşa gave a banquet in his honor. Some said that he got strangled in his sleep. Still, nobody knew for sure, and no one could explain how his two sons, one barely a toddler, the other one a baby, had died that same night.

But whatever the truth, Aladdin's death had left Mehmet to be the şehzade and the heir to the throne, even though he was not his father's favorite son. But he's the only son he's got left.

As if he heard his thoughts, Murad says:

"Aladdin's death leaves you the şehzade, soon to be sultan. Very soon."

Mehmet's head whips up, and he stares at his father.

"Are you ill, Father?"

Murad laughs.

"No. I'm just tired of governing. I'm tired of fights and intrigues and unfaithful allies that I have to sweet-talk, threaten, or kill for the good of the empire. I'm tired of politics, crowds, and faithless people. I need to rest. I need time to meditate, pray, and think. That's why I decided to retire and spend my days in solitude, reading the Quran."

Mehmed's jaw falls, and he stares at his father like he's never seen him. Sultans don't retire! They get killed or die from old age, but they don't retire.

"But... what will happen to the empire? Who will govern if you retire?"

"You."

"Me! But I'm not even thirteen!"

"I know. You're very young, indeed. But you're smart, brave, and you're a fighter. And I cleared the decks for you. I crushed the Varna crusade, so the Christian coalition is no longer a threat. I won the war in Anatolia, so our enemies in Asia will need time to recover. The Ottoman Empire should have a few good years of peace that will allow you to learn. The grand vizier, Çandarlı Halil Paşa, is faithful and wise. He will advise you and teach you well. And you have your mentors and your mother. Hüma Hatun is cunning, ambitious, and she will do everything she can to promote your interests. I was only seventeen when I became sultan, and I didn't have the support and wise advisors you have. You are well equipped to take over. I know you'll do well."

Mehmet's mouth gapes as he stares at his father. Is he joking? Is he trying him? But he's not laughing. If anything, he looks serene and happy, like he looks forward to a life of peace and contemplation, following the Sunnah, Prophet Mohammad's teaching.

Mehmet is at a loss for words. He's always hoped to become sultan someday, when he was old enough and Father died. Not now! But it looks like the day has come. He's about to become sultan even though he's far from being ready. He thought he had years to learn, but he doesn't. What on earth will he do?

Then he remembers hiking the Split Mountain in Manisa, many moons ago, and he knows exactly what he has to do.

He has to take Constantinople.

CHAPTER 51
HÜMA'S DREAM

The dusk has long gone, and the whole palace went to sleep, but Mehmet can't rest. He's walked the pebbled alleys of the gardens until his feet got numb, but his heart is still racing and his brain is still buzzing with excitement. He needs to tell someone, or his head will explode. He needs someone to talk to, and the only person he can speak to is Mother.

Father warned him: "Don't say a word to anyone until I break the news. You don't know who to trust, and we don't want our enemies to know about this until we're ready. Just a few weeks."

But Mehmet can't wait a few weeks. He can't even wait till the morning, though he knows it's late, and Mother must be asleep. He has to talk to her. Right now.

He walks to the women's quarters of the harem, where his mother's chambers are, and knocks at the door.

Nothing.

He knocks again. A sleepy young eunuch with messy hair opens the door, holding a candle. He must be the one who sleeps on the threshold to make sure nobody comes or goes, Mehmet thinks. He can barely see him in the flickering light, but the boy recognizes him and bows deeply.

"I need to speak to my mother."

"But... but she's asleep."

"Wake her up."

The eunuch nods and closes the door. Mehmet is almost a sultan, but he can't step inside the women's quarters, not even to see his mother. This is his father's harem, so Mehmet has no rights here. Not yet.

He wonders what will happen to the women when Father leaves. Will he take them with him? Leave them here? Give them away?

Who cares? Soon enough, he'll have his own harem. Beautiful young women with milk-white skin living to please him. Blue-eyed blondes with thin eyebrows and delicate features who blush easily, like Radu. Sure he's not a girl, but he's prettier than any girl Mehmet has ever seen — not that he's seen that many. He can't imagine how a lovely boy like Radu can have a brother like Vlad.

The door opens. Mother steps out, covered in dark veils from her head to her toes. He only knows it's her by her warm, earthy scent of rose water and musk, and the massive emerald ring that touches his face when he kisses her hand.

"What happened?" she asks.

He looks around for a safe place to talk. There's no privacy here, standing in the doorway of the women's quarters. Anybody passing by can see and hear them.

Mother understands.

"Ali."

The eunuch appears from the darkness.

"Follow us."

They walk to the gardens. There's nobody here to see or hear them in the middle of the night. Nobody but a million stars shining brighter than ever, the trees rustling softly, and the thousands of roses pouring their scent in the tender night air.

Mother leads Mehmet behind the rose bushes to a stone bench so well hidden that nobody would find it unless they knew it's there.

Mehmet looks back for Ali.

"The eunuch?"

"He's brand new and can't yet speak our language. Don't worry. What's going on?"

"Father."

"What about him?"

"He decided to resign. He'll make me sultan soon."

Mother gurgles, and Mehmet can't tell if she's laughing or crying. Then she puts her arms around him to hug him, and her soft cheeks are wet with tears. She's happy.

"But I don't know how to rule. I'm just a boy."

"Never mind. You will learn. We'll get help. Praised be Allah. I thought this day would never come. You've made me very happy."

Mehmet is pleased. And surprised.

"Aren't you worried, though? What if I don't know enough to be a good sultan? What if I make mistakes and hurt the empire?"

"I'm not worried about that in the least. We'll manage. The only thing I worry about is that whore, Halime Hatice Hatun. I worried she'd get another son in her belly after I killed her first one. But Allah be praised, that didn't happen."

Mehmet's heart freezes.

"What are you saying, Mother?"

"I'm glad you'll be the sultan. From now on, there's no stopping us. You'll be the sultan and I'll be the validé. You'll rule the palace, I'll rule the harem. Together, we'll rule the empire. I've never had better news, ever since that day, twelve years ago, they told me you're a boy, praise Allah."

"Are you saying you killed Aladdin?"

"Of course. Who else?"

"But he was the şehzade. Father's son. The next sultan."

"No more. And that's exactly why I had to kill him. Remember old Amira? The one who poisoned you, and you almost died?"

"Yes."

"That was Halime Hatice's work. She tried to kill you to secure her son's succession. But she failed. I didn't."

"What did you do?"

"I spoke to my friends, who spoke to their friends. Friends are vital for a sultan. The faith of your people will keep you alive — or will sink you. You need to build up faith and love."

Mehmet is stricken. He didn't love Aladdin — he barely knew him, since he was so much older — but he was a soldier, a scholar, and his brother. And Father's favorite son.

No more. He's dead now, thanks to Mother. He, and his babies. One was two years old, one just six months.

Mehmet shudders.

"How did you kill him?"

His mother glares at him, and even in the dark, her anger burns. She speaks slowly, every word cutting like a knife.

"I didn't kill him. He died. By the grace of Allah. That made you şehzade, and sultan, soon. That's all you need to know."

"Yes, Mother." Suddenly, Mehmet discovers that he's afraid of his mother. He's never feared her before.

"We'll need to get ready. How long did he say?"

"A few weeks."

"That should give us time to cement our friendships and set traps for our enemies. They won't know what hit them when the news breaks. I'll do my part, you'll do yours."

"Me? What do I do?"

"You make friends. Your friend Radu will be a valuable pawn against his brother. Same with the Serbian boys. They're both pining for a crown that's out of their reach. You could promise it to one of them. Or the other. Befriend both of them, but not together. Apart. You'll use one or the other, depending on the circumstances. In the meantime, I'll look for a suitable wife."

"A suitable wife?"

"Yes. Sultans marry to forge useful connections. That's how you get power. I'll find someone who will bring us a valuable alliance. Do you care what color she is?"

"What color?"

"Yes. White, yellow, brown, or black. They don't make them in blue. Not yet."

Mehmet's head is spinning. He thought he'd talk to Mother to share his excitement, then cool down. But she just took it to a whole new level. She's about to get him a bride, even though he's not yet thirteen and still a virgin, and he has no desire to get married.

"But Mother..." His cheeks catch fire, and he's glad she can't see him. "I've never..."

Mother laughs. "Of course not. But you will. We'll make sure of that. You'll learn to share your bed, and you'll plant your seed, the seed of the Ottoman Empire's next sultan. But that's for later. For now, you'll just have fun."

Mehmet wishes he never spoke to Mother. He came with one problem — he was too young to be the Ottoman Empire's sultan. Now he's got more.

Mother had Aladdin and his babies killed. He needs to befriend a bunch of people he doesn't like. And get a wife. And impregnate her. All that just because he couldn't keep his big mouth shut.

"Anything else?" he asks, hoping Mother would go to bed and leave him be.

"One more thing. How do you feel about the grand vizier?"

Mehmet feels nothing about the grand vizier. Çandarli Paşa has been Sultan Murad's prime minister forever, but he's never much talked to Mehmet. There was no point to it, really, since Mehmet wasn't the şehzade. But now, he'll become his advisor.

Mehmet shrugs. "I don't know."

"That son of a bitch, he's been rooting for Aladdin for as long as I can remember. He's Halime's man, so we'll have to get rid of him before he gets rid of us."

Mehmet stands up. He's had it.

He helps his mother up and walks with her back to the women's quarters. The eunuch catches up with them and opens the door.

His mother hugs him one last time, and Mehmet shrinks.

"I'm so proud of you, my son."

She steps inside, and the eunuch closes the door.

CHAPTER 52
THE ANATOLIAN HELL
TOKAT CASTLE, SUMMER 1444

It hasn't rained for weeks in the burning heart of Anatolia. The earth, hard and cracked with dryness, shrinks under the ruthless embrace of a brutal sun. After weeks of traveling from sunrise to sunset every day in the harsh, dry lands, Vlad's caravan is finally within sight of their target.

Up ahead, bathed in the sunset's red light, the mountain is on fire. And forbidding. Nobody could ever climb it and build a castle on those evil sharp peaks. And still, they did. The Tokat Castle, their final destination, sits scary and foreboding right where the jagged peaks scratch the sky. Yet, after weeks and weeks of riding every single damn day, it's a welcome sight.

Vlad loves to ride, but not like this. He loves to canter over fields and meadows with the wind in his face, drunk with power and speed, not under someone's command, surrounded by weary janissaries. They're so jumpy that Vlad can't even dream of getting away. And the horse they gave him should be long dead, had God been merciful.

Vlad tightens his fists. He's worn out and so angry he'd love to kill, but there's nothing he can kill, even if he had a weapon.

The caravan stops at the foot of the mountain. They dismount and start up on foot, leaving the horses behind. It's an arduous hike, and the castle looks further away each time Vlad looks up. The abrupt trail soon turns into steep steps, but Vlad keeps going. He looks forward to a drink and a meal that's anything but dried mutton, stale bread, and fruit, like he's had every night for weeks. But, more than anything, he needs a bath. He can't wait for the hot water and the bath attendants to scrub his filthy skin into raw cleanliness and soften the kinks the weeks of riding have built in his back.

Suddenly, the janissaries stop, though they're nowhere near the castle. The steps end at a landing leading to a guarded dark tunnel closed by iron gates. That's where the paşa awaits.

He's dark and unsmiling, and he studies Vlad like he's a piece of yesterday's mutton he paid too much for. "You're Vlad Dracula — Son of the Dragon."

It's not a question. Not an endorsement, either. Vlad stands straight and looks him in the eye, trying not to blink. He knows that first encounters are crucial, and he's intent on impressing the man.

"Welcome to Tokat Castle. This is a castle like no other. Up here, we're very proud of our castle, our mountain, and our mission. Do you know about our mission?"

Vlad shakes his head. He's never heard about this godforsaken place, but by the fact they sent him here, it must be a dirty dungeon where they keep their enemies until they crush them. But they won't crush him. He's too smart and too steadfast for that.

"Our mission is to turn the empire's enemies into friends. We're here to show them the wisdom of obeying the Quran and listening to the sultan. Most people come here thinking they know everything they need to know about the empire, and they hate it. But they're mistaken. So, we open their minds. We help them see the beauty of the Ottoman Empire, and show them how much better their lives will be in Allah's light.

"I know you're not a Muslim. Yet. But I am confident that we'll be able to teach you the beauty of our ways and guide you to see the light of Allah. Before long, you'll become Sultan Murad's friend."

He smiles, and Vlad wishes he could smack the grin off his face into oblivion. He'd love to stomp all over his self-sufficient smugness, but he knows better. He's unarmed and surrounded by janissaries, so he bites his tongue and tries to stare him down.

The paşa smiles again. "I can see that the light hasn't reached you yet, but it will. I'll make sure of that. And you'll be grateful, even if you don't think so now. Tell the guards to call me when you see the light."

He nods to the janissaries, who grab Vlad and drag him into the tunnel carved inside the belly of the mountain, a long dark hole too low to stand up straight and too narrow to walk more than two abreast.

Terrible screams come out of the cells carved into the rock on both sides as they push him through. It's hard to see beyond the flickering light of the torch, but the screaming shadows are people, all old, wild-looking, and despondent.

"Let me out! Let me out, I tell you! I'm a Venetian merchant. I have the right to be free."

"Please! Oh, please! It wasn't my fault! I never knew those thugs were against my beloved sultan! I would have crushed them if I knew!"

"You filthy goat lovers! I've been here since I was a young boy, and now I'm gray and almost blind, but I'll still fight you, mutton eating Allah worshipers, until the day I die, God help me. My king will get me out of your filthy grasp!"

Vlad shudders. These prisoners have all been here forever, and he's about to become one of them. This is the scariest thing he's ever seen, and, as they push him into an empty cell and lock the metal door behind him, he wonders if this was a good plan. Not that it really matters. All that matter is that he's here, and he needs to get out before he grows old and broken like the others.

He's still thinking about a way out when the real screaming starts. The sound rebounds and echoes against the tunnel walls like it's a chorus, but this is no music. It's pain. A hair-rising scream of agony that gets louder and louder, until it breaks, then starts again. Then another, and another. It's a heart-wrenching cry of unbearable suffering, like somebody's being flayed alive. And it doesn't stop, it doesn't fade, it doesn't change. It keeps going on and on and on

A terrible chill goes down Vlad's spine.

This place is Hell on earth. He'd better get out soon.

CHAPTER 53

ȘTEFAN'S NEW FAMILY

TÂRGOVIȘTE, WALLACHIA

It's July. They call it *Luna Cuptorului,* the Month of the Oven, here in Wallachia, and the month lives up to its name. There's little shadow at noon, and no wind. The sun scorched the grass to a dead brown, and up above, a screaming murder of crows chase each other, praying for rain.

Ștefan lays on his elbow under an apple tree, watching them. He bites into an unripe apple, and the green sour-bomb makes him pucker and reminds him of last year when he and Lena sat under the old apple tree in Berzunți, laughing at each other's puckers and throwing the cores as far as they could.

He misses home and misses Father. But most of all, he misses Lena. It's been almost a year since he's seen her. A long year.

He still can't remember what happened after the soldiers' lances skewered him in the cart. When the blackness inside his brain finally faded, he found himself in someone else's bed, in a room he'd never seen. He'd looked around and saw an old woman dressed in black.

She met his gaze and smiled a toothless smile.

"He's awake," she shouted.

The old man who'd given him a ride in his cart shuffled over and crossed himself.

"Thank the good Lord! I was starting to think you'll never wake up! You've been like the dead for days!"

Too weak to talk, Ștefan nodded and fell asleep.

Day after day, they nursed him to health. It took weeks until he walked again, and even then, only with the heavy stick the old man made for him.

When he was finally good to go, the old man took him to the Court of Târgoviște. The armed guards stopped him at the castle gate and wanted to know his business. He asked for Doamna Cneajna, and they laughed.

"Doamna Cneajna? Why would the voivode's wife want to speak to a dirty peasant like you?"

He had to show them Grandfather's ring. They took him to see his aunt, but the rumor that Bogdan Muşat's son was sheltered at the Royal Court of Târgoviște spread like wildfire.

Vlad Dracul didn't like it.

"I wish you didn't do it. It does you no good for your enemies to know your whereabouts. And it does me no good for your uncle Ștefan, the second of his name, who sits on Moldova's throne, to know that I'm sheltering his enemies."

"But he's my nephew. He's blood of my blood," Doamna Cneajna said.

Vlad Dracul shrugged.

"So is Ștefan the second, Moldova's voivode and your half-brother. Boy, I wish your father took more care whose bed he left his boots under."

Still, they took him in and treated him like he was their own.

"I'm so glad you're here. You're just about Vlad's age, and I miss him so. I haven't seen him in years. I wonder if I'd even recognize him," Doamna Cneajna said.

Mircea shrugged. "Sure you would. He'd be the one with blood on his hands."

Mircea, Vlad Dracul's eldest son, is a grown man at almost seventeen. He's dark and strong and full of fire, and the shadow above his upper lip is thick enough to hide his smile, should he ever smile.

Doamna Cneajna gasped. "Mircea! How can you talk like that about your younger brother?"

“Mother, you know that's true, even if he's your favorite son. As for me, I miss Radu. He’s such a nice kid."

"You've always had a thing for Radu. You and most people. Just because he's handsome and soft spoken. But Vlad is brave and determined and..."

"And a bloody asshole. But that's neither here nor there,” Mircea said, and he touched Ștefan’s shoulder.

“I’m glad you’re here, Ștefan. It's been lonely without the boys, and it will be fun to have someone to ride and hunt with."

That’s how Ștefan found himself a new family. Even Vlad Dracul relented. He took him under his wing, started teaching him how to be a voivode, should God wish it so and trained him in the intricacies of politics and strategy. So, these days, Ștefan is pretty much one of the Drăculești. But he misses his father and his mother. And Lena.

At Ștefan’s request, Vlad Dracul sent some men to Berzunți to look for her, but she was gone. Her father said he’d never heard from her after the day they flew from the posse. Even her mother thinks she's dead, but Ștefan knows better. She's there, somewhere, even if he doesn't know where. And some day he'll find her.

"Ștefan!"

He opens his eyes. Mircea called him from the tower.

"Come here!" He signals, and Ștefan takes off.

He takes the worn steps two at a time, so he’s gasping for air by the time he reaches the top. He takes in the 360 degree views over miles and miles of fields, forests, and hills, but nothing seems amiss.

Mircea points to a dark shape growing fast. Down there, there's a horse about to die. He canters through the horrid heat like the Devil himself chases him.

He's coming from the north, and that's good, since the Ottomans, Wallachia’s greatest threat, are in the south. Up north are the Carpathians, then Transylvania and Hungary, and they’re allies. For now. Even so, it can't be good news. That messenger is riding that horse into its grave, and good news is seldom that urgent.

“What do you think?” Ștefan asks.

Mircea shrugs. “I don’t know, but I’m worried. Let's go tell Father. I bet we'll find out soon."

CHAPTER 54
HUNYADI'S MESSENGER

The six-feet-thick stone walls of the Royal Court in Târgoviște keep in the winter's cold even in July. No matter how hot it gets outside, the sun can't get in other than through the slim darts of light coming through the tall archers' slits. That's why the stone under the leaky roof is sleek with water, and the air smells like mold and secrets.

Ștefan sits next to Mircea at the massive banquet table, waiting for Vlad Dracul to finish reading the message. Other than the table and its high-backed chairs, the room is bare but for the stuffed animal heads on the walls. They're all hunting trophies: A red deer with antlers that split eleven times; a grinning black boar with five-inch-long yellow teeth; a fierce-looking brown bear. They all stare at Ștefan with their painted-on dead eyes, and he shivers.

"This can't be true," Vlad Dracul says. He shakes the parchment he's already read thrice and hands it to Mircea.

The Transylvanian messenger shrugs. "The news is coming from inside Sultan Murad's sarayi. There's no one closer to the very heart of the Ottoman Empire."

"Maybe, but that doesn't make it true. Your spy must have gotten uncovered and flipped. It wouldn't be the first time."

"That's not what Transylvania's voivode thinks. John Hunyadi is convinced that the message is genuine, and the news is true. That man was planted there by the Kronstadt Saxons, and they are sneakier and more cunning than the Byzantine. If they don't know intrigue, nobody does."

Mircea looks up from the parchment he's been reading.

"But why? Why would Murad do something like this? And why now?"

The messenger sighs.

"The 'why now' is easy. Murad thinks he's got peace. He just signed a ten-year truce treaty with Hungary. In Anatolia, he pummeled the Karamanids until they asked for peace. That's why he thinks the Ottoman Empire is safe, and there's never been a better time."

"But still, why would he resign? He's still young and healthy, at the peak of his power. And that kid Mehmet is not even thirteen, for God's sake. It's like you'd resign to Vlad!"

Vlad Dracul shrugs.

"Maybe he's tired. He sure has reasons. He's been fighting both in the east, and in the west, for more than twenty years. Maybe he thinks he's done enough, and he deserves to rest. And let's not forget that you were only fifteen when I let you take the throne."

"Still, I was fifteen, not twelve! And it's not like you had a choice. Murad called you there, and you didn't know if you'd ever be coming back, so you had to do it!"

Vlad Dracul shrugs once more. "Whatever. The question is: what do we do now?"

The Transylvanian is ready.

"Transylvania's voivode says we should get ready for war. He also sent messengers to Pope Eugene IV and the Venetians. He thinks it's time we finished what we started with the Varna Crusade."

"Really? But didn't you say he just signed a ten year truce?"

"Pope Eugene says it's not binding. He thinks that the words in the treaty could be interpreted in any number of ways, so he's ready to release Hunyadi from his pledge."

"Still, why go to war? We're so tired of war! We've had nothing but war after war for so many years. Why not enjoy the peace, and let our folks recover and harvest their fields?"

"The voivode of Transylvania thinks we have no choice. He doesn't think that young Mehmet will abide by his father's truce. The boy is untamed and hungry for glory, and he doesn't have enough judgment to stay put. So if we'll have war anyhow, we'd better do it in our own terms than in theirs."

Vlad Dracul sighs and rubs his temples. He looks majestic, with his mink-trimmed velvet mantle and the gold trinkets he donned to impress Hunyadi's messenger, but his shoulders are hunched, and his eyes tired.

"What do you think, Mircea?"

Mircea sits up straight as an arrow. His dark eyes sparkle, and his cheeks flush with excitement. He can't wait to go to war.

"I think it's time. We can defeat the Ottomans, Father. Mehmet is not Murad. He has neither the experience nor the patience. And he doesn't have the janissaries' trust. Plus, they don't expect us to go to war; otherwise, Murad wouldn't have resigned. We have the element of surprise on our side, and we must seize the moment. Just think: If we win this crusade, we'll raise the Holy Cross above the infidel's lands."

Vlad Dracul shakes his head.

"Isn't it wonderful to be so young and full of hope? But don't forget that the Ottomans have the janissaries, the greatest standing army in the world. They're disciplined, well trained, and well-armed. And Çandarlı Paşa, the grand vizier, has seen more fights than you and me put together. And what do we have? We have the boyars who change their allegiance more often than the summer wind changes direction. We have our hard-working peasants who should stay home to work the fields instead of leaving to another war. As for the pope, he changes his mind more often than he changes his clothes. He's ready to rip off Hungary's truce treaty before the ink dries."

Mircea frowns.

"But Father, the janissaries don't trust Mehmet. He's just a kid who never saw a battle. And the boyars are on our side. As for the peasants, they can't wait to take revenge on the Ottomans who steal their children, burn their houses and take their crops. Just think! If we win, we get rid of devşirme! We'll no longer have to send them our children!"

Vlad Dracul sighs. "Speaking about children. Remember your brothers, Vlad and Radu, who are hostages at the Ottoman court? What do you think will happen if we go to war against Mehmet? What will he do to them?"

Mircea blushes. He looks stricken, and Ștefan wonders if that's because he forgot about them, or just the opposite — because his succession is safer without them.

Brotherhood is not for the faint of heart these days.

CHAPTER 55

SULTAN MURAD'S OTHER WIFE

EDIRNE. JULY 1444

The news that Murad is about to resign, leaving Mehmet to lead the Ottoman Empire, spread through the empire like wildfire. Everyone smiled and offered congratulations, pretending to be delighted, but underneath, there's nothing but fear. In Sultan Murad's sarayi, in the janissary quarters, the palace school, even the kitchens. Everywhere she goes, Ali hears people whispering to each other when they think nobody else can hear them. Like now. She's bringing drinks to the hammam, and she hears a voice.

"Young Mehmet is untried and impulsive. Who knows what he'll do when Murad gives him the reins," a woman says. Another one laughs.

“Don't worry. Mehmet is a good boy. And Çandarlı Paşa, the grand vizier, who's seen more wars than anyone should, will keep him on track."

The throaty laugh and heavy accent are easy to recognize. Mara Branković is Sultan Murad's fourth wife and a Serbian princess. And she's beautiful. Her body, resting on the white marble bench, is a wonder of glowing olive skin and eye-popping curves, and Ali averts her eyes.

She's been here for weeks, but she still hasn't got used to the naked women. They aren't ashamed of their bodies. They don't even seem to notice they're naked as they chat, laying on the marble benches, or laugh, splashing one another in the cooling bath. The harem is the kingdom of the women, and men don't belong. None but the sultan, and he's never here. *He's got to be afraid they'd tear him apart,* Ali thinks, then sets the tray with cool sherbets on the marble bench.

Mara smiles.

"How lovely! What's your name?"

"Ali, Your Highness."

"Where are you from, Ali?"

"Transylvania, Your Highness."

"Really! Is it true that you have vampire bats that suck people's blood and werewolves that swallow the moon?"

"The sun, too, Your Highness. Our werewolves are ravenous."

Mara's laughter is low and thick, and it stirs something inside Ali. Out of all the sultan's women, there's something very special about Mara. She's been married to the sultan for years, but she's never been with child. Even so, he didn't get rid of her. Maybe because she's related to all the important people in the world, in the east and the west. Or perhaps because she's warm, beautiful, and self-assured like no woman Ali has ever seen before. Or maybe just because she's kind and funny.

Even the sultan's other wives like her. Hüma Hatun, the şehzade's mother, and Halime Hatice Hatun, the late Aladdin's mother, would gladly rip each other's throats open with their bare teeth. But they're both Mara's friends. Even Emine Validé, who's about to be ousted, looks kindly upon Mara.

"That's funny. How old are you, Ali?"

"Twelve, Your Honor."

"Twelve! Really? How did you get here so young?"

Ali shrugs. "My family didn't need me, so they sent me to serve the empire. They thought that was the best use I could get."

Mara sighs. "I get you. That's pretty much what happened in my family. They sent me here to serve. My father thought that was the best use that I could get."

Ali has heard rumors about Mara having trouble. People whisper that her father, Đurađ Branković, Serbia's despot, had joined an alliance with other Christian leaders against the sultan. Even worse, her brother Grgur was said to have plotted against Sultan Murad. The sultan caught him and threw him in jail, then blinded him as punishment. He only spared his life because Mara begged him to. *It looks like being a blood princess and the sultan's wife is not all that it's cracked up to be,* Ali thinks, and she feels sorry for Mara, who must feel torn between her family and her husband.

But Ali is here on a mission, and these people are her enemies. She's not supposed to like them or care about any of them. Not even about Mara.

Ali picks the empty cups and loads them on her tray.

"I'm sure you'll fulfill the hopes that your family set in you, Your Honor. They're lucky to have somebody like you to help their plight. I can only wish I'll do something remotely worthy."

"Who are you working for, Ali?"

"The validé, in her wisdom, sent me to work for Hüma Hatun. I'm luckier than I deserve."

"She's a strong woman, Hüma. She'll do the best she can do for her son, our future sultan. You're very fortunate."

"Yes, Your Honor. I know I am."

"Ali."

"Yes, princess?"

"If things get rough and you need help, come see me. It may be hard to believe, but I know how it feels to have it rough. Good luck."

Ali nods and drags herself to her next task, but her mind is stuck on Mara.

If such a beautiful, strong, high-born woman has to struggle, what hope is there for me?

CHAPTER 56
ALI'S NEW MISTRESS

The Edirne sarayi must be like no other place on earth, Ali thinks, looking around in wonder. It's as if Allah had to practice before he built His Heaven, so he tried his ideas on the Edirne sarayi first. Everything glows, soothes, and charms the senses. From the sussuring fountains to the intricate incense burners, from the smooth marble cooling the feet to the sculpted window grills that trace delicate shadows on the walls, everything is meant to delight, soothe and enchant.

And, more than any others, Hüma Hatun's quarters in the sarayi are a thing of beauty. There's no more splendid place, not even the validé's. That's because Hüma is about to become the new validé, and she's making sure that her rooms look the part. Exotic birds sing inside their gilded cages. Precious Isfahan carpets, glowing in every color of the rainbow, cover the veined Venetian marble floor. Intricate sandalwood coffers, pillows in glorious brocade the color of the sunset, graceful silver vessels adorned with garnets and emeralds, they all wait to find their place.

Hüma herself buzzes about like a bee, so fast that her flame-red hair flutters behind her. Flushed with excitement, she looks twenty years old as she gives orders as to where everything should go.

"Not there. There, under the window. No, I don't like it there, it blocks the light. Put it back."

Ali and Lena drag the massive Chinese vase, big enough for them both to hide inside it, back to where they first had it. They stop to catch their breath and wait for Hüma's directions.

These are precious gifts coming from all over the world to congratulate Sultan Mehmet for his coronation. There are precious weapons from Damascus, silk tapestries from Bayeux, elegant blown glass vases from Venice — the most beautiful things the world ever created. Ali studies them one by one, curious to know where they came from and wondering what they are for. She's never seen anything like it before, and she's in awe. She shows Lena the workmanship of a silver tray, but Lena turns away, her lovely face drawn and worried.

"What happened?" Ali whispers. "Are you OK?"

Lena shakes her head no.

Ali glances at Hüma who's busy digging in a coffer full of precious silks.

"What's going on?"

"I'm dying," Lena says.

"Why?"

"I don't know. I'm bleeding."

"From where?"

Lena gives her a look, and Ali understands. Before she left Kronstadt, Mama Smaranda told her about the women's curse.

"It will happen to you, too, Ana. Before too long, when you've grown, it will come to you every month for a few days. Bad enough that your belly will hurt, but even worse is the bleeding. First, once you start bleeding, you can become heavy with child if you lay with a man. But, more importantly, nobody can know that this is happening to you. Ever. They don't call in a woman's curse for nothing. It only happens to women. Not to men, not to eunuchs. If they find out you're bleeding, they'll know you're not a eunuch, but a girl. And it's game over."

"How do I hide it?" Ali asked.

"You don't hide it. You stop it. See these herbs?"

"Yes."

"The first time you bleed, you make a tea from them and drink it every day. It will stop you from bleeding — or growing heavy with child. It will also slow down your growing into a woman's shape."

Ali spent countless hours in the palace gardens, looking for every sprig of pennyroyal, silphium and tansy she could find, collecting them and drying them. Her curse hasn't come yet, but she's ready for it.

Should she make the tea for Lena? But why? After all, Lena isn't pretending to be a boy; and here, in the harem, there's no way she'll get heavy with child.

"Don't worry, you're not dying. It's just the women's curse," Ali whispers.

"The women's curse?"

"Yes. When a girl becomes a woman, and her body is ready to have children..."

"What's going on? What are you two whispering about?" Hüma asks.

They look down. They didn't hear her coming.

"I... I'm sorry, my lady," Lena mumbles.

"Sorry for what?"

"I'm bleeding."

Hüma's eyes widen. "You're bleeding? For the first time?"

Lena nods.

"Come here."

Hüma studies Lena like she's seeing her for the first time. She examines her face, her hips, her breasts. She even opens her mouth to check her teeth, like the slave market buyers.

"How old are you?"

"Fourteen, my lady."

Hüma's smile makes Ali shiver. It's like she just opened a surprise gift, and she's got an idea. An evil idea.

"Why don't you go to bed, Lena. I can see you're not feeling well. Get some rest, and come back to see me after your bleeding stops."

"Yes, my lady."

Hüma waits for her to be gone before turning to Ali.

"Ali? How come you know about the women's curse?"

Ali tries to think on her feet. "My grandmother."

"What about her?"

"She... was the village healer. People came to her for potions and ointments. Sometimes men, but often women and girls who got in trouble."

“What sort of trouble?”

"Like unmarried women who got heavy with child. Or married women who wanted children and couldn't have them."

"What did your grandmother do?"

"She gave them a potion and a prayer to set things right."

"Did they work?"

"Yes."

"Did she teach you how to do it?"

"She taught me some things. Not everything."

"Can you make me a potion to put someone to sleep?"

"If I have the ingredients."

"How about putting somebody to sleep for good?"

Ali nods.

Hüma Hatun smiles again. "Very well. I'll have to thank Emine Validé for giving you and Lena to me. I didn't realize what a gift that really was until now. I'm very pleased with you, Ali."

"I'm delighted, my lady."

"I need the list of ingredients for a potion that would put someone to sleep for good. Have it ready by tomorrow."

"But, my lady..."

"Yes?"

"Who are you going to put to sleep?"

Hüma Hatun’s mouth thins to a line. She straightens and glares down at Ali, who barely reaches to her shoulder.

"And this is your business, how?"

"To make the right potion, I need to know who it's for. Is it a human or a dog? A child or an old person? A man or a woman? The recipes are not the same.”

"I see. Let me decide where to start. I'll tell you tomorrow."

CHAPTER 57
VLAD'S MISERY
TOKAT, 1444

Six hundred miles east of Edirne, nestled in Anatolia's burning heart, the Tokat Castle sits on top of a jagged mountain that nobody dares to climb. The castle's towers spear the sky, but, inside the mountain's stone belly, the dungeons twist like bowels choking with human filth and misery.

There in the dungeons, curled inside a cell too small to straighten in, Vlad wakes up. He's sore from sleeping on the stone floor, and he feels like he's been here forever. His head slams the ceiling as he stands, and he rubs the sore spot, feeling his greasy hair, and crushes some fast-moving critter inside it.

He'd give his left arm for a bath, but nobody made him that offer. He's sore, filthy, and weak, and lost count of the time he's been here. Was it days? Weeks? Months? It feels like years, but he doesn't know. There's no window to tell day from night. The only light, ever, comes from the torches, when the guards bring their food. Is that daily? Twice a day? He doesn't know that, either. The one thing he knows is that he'd rather die than spend one more cursed day down here. So when the guard brings his stinky bowl of foul soup, he says:

"I'd like to see the paşa."

The guard stares at him like he's lost it.

"The who?"

"The Paşa of Tokat. Tell him I changed my mind."

The guard laughs and goes about his business, leaving Vlad in the dark.

But for Vlad, the dark isn't the problem. The bugs are. The rats, too. Vlad never liked rats. He's good with spiders and snakes, but rats turn his stomach. Not because of the death stench — unlike anybody else he knows, Vlad loves it. He's wary about their sharp teeth, their hungry beaks with dirty whiskers and their ugly, hairless tails. He hates them, and he'd gladly destroy every single one of them.

He's been dreaming about setting the place on fire. The stone wouldn't burn, of course, but the straw on the floors would. And he could pour some oil to help it out. Then he could set the fire and block the opening. The rats would fry. He smiles, thinking about the dying rats looking for a way out with their tails on fire. The prisoners would die too, of course, but that's nothing but mercy. It can't be worse than spending a lifetime here. And, in one clean swoop, it would kill all the bugs and the lice and the vermin. A clean kill.

He sighs, wishing he'd spent more time in the hammam when he could, and enjoyed it more. But he was so consumed by his hate for the Ottomans that he couldn't give in to their pleasures.

He slaps whatever's biting his ear and remembers swimming in the fast-moving rivers at home. The water was clear and so cold that it hurt. But it felt delightful on his sweaty skin in summer. Oh, how he misses it! He misses riding his horse across the endless green fields, and his sword, and the wine. And his parents, especially Mother. Father too, but Doamna Cneajna is the one person Vlad really loves, or whatever it is that people call love. He dreams about being back home inside her hug.

He waits and waits, but nothing happens other than the other prisoners' screams. They're the same as yesterday, the day before, and the day before that.

He wonders if the paşa decided to let him rot here forever, despite what he said.

He waits, and nothing breaks the darkness and depth of despair.

He curls on the floor, gluing his ear to the rock to hear the steps sooner.

Nothing.

He wakes up to a flicker of light.

"The paşa will see you now."

His head bent, Vlad shuffles back through the tunnel. Crazed with despair, the prisoners swear, plead and curse, begging to be released. But the guards don't seem to even hear them. Vlad does, and he wishes he didn't. But he knows he'll be back soon, unless the paşa decides otherwise.

The paşa responds to the sultan, of course, but the Tokat Castle is under his command. They're weeks away from Edirne, so he's got to have the power to give Vlad a break. And Vlad needs it like he never needed anything before. He'll stop at nothing to buy his favor.

The paşa sits on a red pillow, drinking wine, as Vlad gets dragged in and dropped at the door. The man smiles, but his smile fades as he brings his perfumed handkerchief to his nose to offset Vlad's stench.

"What can I do for you?"

"I've seen the light," Vlad says.

"What light?"

"The light of the sultan. I'm sorry it took me so long, but I finally understood how the sultan is trying to make my country better. I'm glad I finally got that. I will support the sultan's efforts to make Wallachia a better place."

"Are you sure?"

"I've never been more sure of anything. I will respect and uphold Sultan Murad's authority over Wallachia. I will fight his enemies and subject myself to his wisdom."

The paşa smiles.

"You, prince, are a very bright young man. We'll get along well."

He signals, and the janissaries take Vlad away.

CHAPTER 58
THE KIRKPINAR
EDIRNE

It's noon in mid-August, and the sun scorched the earth in Edirne. No matter where you look, there's not a whisper of shadow in sight. Still, the whole back yard of the palace is jam-packed with people baking in the heat. *They're everywhere — standing, sitting, or lying on the ground, so many that you can't scratch your behind without elbowing someone,* Radu thinks. And they're all here to celebrate Mehmet's coronation.

For weeks now, day after day there's been nothing but countless ceremonies, feasts and celebrations. And today is the greatest one — the Kırkpınar. Radu has been looking for a place he could see the fights from, but there's none, of course. The best spots have been taken for hours. But today is Radu's lucky day.

Mehmet sent a servant to fetch him to the podium built especially for the sultan, where he and his highest dignitaries sit above the crowds on golden brocade pillows to watch the show.

Radu bows in front of the sultan, but Mehmet grabs his hand and pulls him up on the podium. He tells him to sit, but there's no room, since the grand vizier, Çandarlı Halil Paşa, sits right next to the sultan. Radu steps behind them, but Mehmet pulls him down and Radu crumbles into the grand vizier's lap. Seeing Çandarlı Paşa's frown,

Radu wishes he was anywhere but there, but he doesn't have a choice. The sultan spoke, and he sits. The grand vizier pulls away to make room.

"This is so much fun," Mehmet says, holding on to Radu's hand. "The Kırkpınar is the best show ever. They've been doing it every year for almost a hundred years, and they always bring in the best fighters. See that red-haired guy to the left? He was last year's winner, and he's my favorite."

The red-haired guy is almost naked, like the others, but for his leather pants that are so tight they leave nothing to imagination. His white skin glows in the sun as he pours something from a copper vessel onto his shoulders and spreads it over his chiseled chest.

"What's that?" Radu asks.

"Olive oil. So that he's slippery, and his opponent can't hold on to him."

"Who is he?"

"I forgot his name, but I know he's a Circassian from the north. He's training with the janissaries, like they all are. They pair them by height, but it's not the height that matters. It's their strength and determination. To win, you have to pin down your opponent. Or lift him above your shoulders, but that hardly ever happens. They're way too slippery."

The Circassian's opponent is dark, sturdy and covered in a thick mat of black hair. He's unsmiling and grim, with a brow that goes from one ear to the other, but the hundreds of oil droplets caught in his curly hair sparkle like diamonds in the sun, lending him magic.

They bow to the sultan, and the smiling Circassian waves to the crowd. The dark boy frowns.

"Red! Red! Red!" the crowd erupts, in love with his good looks and easy manner. He smiles and nods, and they go nuts.

Radu wishes he knew the dark boy's name to shout it. As a perpetual underdog, he always roots for those nobody else cares about.

The referee, wrapped in a long leather apron to protect him from the oil, gives the signal.

Red grabs the dark boy by the shoulders and trips him with a well-placed leg. Dark boy stumbles, but catches himself halfway to the ground and twists back to his feet. He grabs Red's shoulders and pushes his weight into him, but Red pushes back and they entwine in a violent embrace. They stand against each other, neck touching neck, cheek pushing against cheek, their veins popping out with the effort, their eyes closed to focus on each other's touch. Their limbs entangled, their hearts beating next to each other, they barely move in a slow, breathtaking dance, punctuated by the heavy drum beats that stir something deep inside Radu's loins. Mesmerized by the struggling bodies glowing in the sun, he's breathing hard.

The fighters grasp each other's hands and lean into each other, forming a glistening, vibrating human arch. Suddenly, Dark breaks the arc and squats low, pulling Red over his knee. Red twists left, throwing off Dark's balance. Dark crashes to the ground, and Red leaps to pin him down, but Dark twists and rolls in a blink. He gets to his knees, grabs Red's feet and pulls them to unbalance him. Red wavers like he's about to fall but drops to his knees instead. Now both on their knees, they grasp onto each other's glistening body, trying to force each other to the ground, but their fingers slide onto the smooth oiled skin too slippery to hold. Muscles bulge, chests heave, and the drums beat the rhythm like a heart.

Red bites his lip and puts all his weight into the struggle. He pushes Dark so hard that the boy falls to the ground. But he pulls Red with him, and they both fall on their side, face to face, chest to chest, each one trying to push the other down.

Dark weakens. Red leans above him and shoves him down with all his weight. Dark fights with all he's got, but Red is too strong. The muscles of his back quiver with effort as he presses his weight on Dark's chest. Just one more inch until Dark gets pinned to the ground with both shoulders. Red pushes even harder, and the strain of his heart pops out the veins in his temples. Another half an inch, and... Dark twists like an eel and pins Red down before anyone can understand what happened.

The fight is over.

The crowd gasps, then falls silent. They're disappointed, but Dark won fair and square.

"Come here," Mehmet says.

The winner bows deep in front of the podium.

"What's your name?"

"Kemal, my sultan."

"Where are you from?"

"Transylvania."

"You did very well. Congratulations. This is for you," Mehmet says, handing him a golden coin.

Kemal takes it and bows again. Radu stares at his glowing dark body and the unsmiling face with the long thick brow, trying to find something in common with Ali, the only other Transylvanian he knows. But there's nothing.

"You happen to know a young boy named Ali?" Radu asks.

Kemal's face lights up like a Christmas tree.

"I do. How is Ali?"

"He's good. I'll tell him that you won. He will be pleased."

"Thank you, my prince. Please tell him that I'd love to see him someday."

"That can be arranged," Mehmet says. He stands up to leave and grabs Radu's hand.

"Let's go get something to eat."

The grand vizier frowns.

"But, my sultan..."

"Yes, Çandarlı Paşa?"

"The games aren't over yet. Every one of these young fighters trained long and hard for the honor of fighting in front of you. They'll be disappointed if you leave."

Mehmet shrugs.

"Don't worry, Çandarlı Paşa. I promise you they'll have plenty of opportunities to fight in front of me in war. Very soon. Until then, why don't you stay and watch them. I have more important things to do."

Radu isn't sure whether the grand vizier's hateful glare is for Mehmet or for him, but, either way, it's scary.

CHAPTER 59
OSMAN'S SWORD

Radu's eyes grow wide with wonder as he steps inside Mehmet's dazzling quarters. His own bedroom would fit in them ten times with room to spare. But no matter how ornate and spacious, the place is a mess. Precious rugs, piles of books and rare weapons are scattered everywhere. The servants are packing to move everything to the sultan's quarters tomorrow, after the ceremony of the Sword of Osman.

The Sword of Osman has passed from one sultan to the next for more than a hundred years. It's the symbol of the Ottoman power, and receiving it is the equivalent of the western kings' coronation. But it's sacred and secret, and no infidel has ever seen it, since Sword of Osman is too precious to be tainted by infidel eyes.

"I can't wait to hold it," Mehmet says, sitting cross-legged on a blue pillow embroidered with golden birds of paradise and chewing on a sugar-powdered pistachio-flavored lokum. He wipes his fingers on his blue shalwars and picks another, this one yellow, flavored with lemon.

"They say that the blade is made of gold, and so's the handle. Did you know that's how the empire started? Osman Gazi, the founder of the Ottoman Empire, had a dream. In his dream, he watched the moon arise from the breast of a holy man and sink into his own. Then a tall tree grew out of his navel, so big that it shaded the whole world. Then mountains grew tall beneath it, and clear streams of fresh water flowed forth from the foot of each mountain, heading to every end of the world. And happy people came to drink the water and used it to water their gardens.

"When Osman woke up and told the holy man about his dream, the holy man saw Allah's light. He understood that Osman and his descendants were meant to build an empire that would conquer the world in Allah's name. So he gave Osman the sword, and his daughter in marriage. I don't know what happened to the daughter, but the sword is still here."

"What a story! I can't wait for you to tell me about the sword, my sultan," Radu says.

"I will. But you know what? I'll show it to you."

"But, you can't!"

"Why not?"

"The sword can't be tainted by infidel eyes! That's why no foreign ambassadors, no princes or even kings have ever been allowed to participate in the ceremony."

"That was then, and this is now. If I'm the sultan, I can do whatever I want. And if I want you there for the ceremony, who's going to say no?"

"Çandarlı Paşa, the grand vizier. And the dignitaries."

Mehmet laughs. "It's high time the grand vizier understood that I am the sultan, and I will do whatever I want. He's there to obey and serve. And if he doesn't like it, I'll just get myself another grand vizier. How would you like to be grand vizier, Radu?"

Radu chokes. He doesn't want to be grand vizier. Not at all. He doesn't want to be anything, anything at all, other than Mehmet's friend. Mehmet is like the brother he always wished he had. He never laughs at him, never mocks him, and he's never cruel to him, not even when Radu acts silly. That's why Radu couldn't be happier, or more grateful. But grand vizier? No.

"No, thank you, my sultan. I'm happy to be your friend, I need nothing more."

They sit side by side drinking sherbet, eating sticky lokum studded with pistachios, and dreaming about the future.

"How do you see your future, Radu?"

"I see my future like this. Here, with you. I can't wait to witness the grand things you'll accomplish."

"Don't you want to go home?"

"This is my home now."

"But don't you want to be voivode of Wallachia, like your father?"

"I don't know, but I don't think that's something to worry about. The odds are low. Father's strong and healthy, and my oldest brother Mircea is a great soldier and Father's favorite. And then there's Vlad."

Mehmet shrugs.

"That doesn't mean anything. My father's healthy too. My brother Aladdin was a good soldier and my father's favorite. But he's dead now, and I'm about to be sultan."

"We're all fortunate it is so. I know you'll be the best sultan ever, and you'll bring new glory to the Ottoman Empire."

Mehmet smiles. "I surely plan to."

"What are you going to do?"

"The first thing I'll do is take Constantinople. I'll crush the infidels and make Constantinople into the greatest city in the world. I'll lock Emperor Constantine and his filthy clique of Greek thieves in dirty cages and show them to the world. I'll move my palace from Edirne to Constantinople, and I'll make the last bastion of Ancient Rome into the Ottoman Empire's capital. That way I'll be the Qayser-i Rûm, the Last Caesar of the Roman Empire. And you know what?"

"What?"

"For Allah's eternal glory, I'll rip out Hagia Sofia's cross and replace it with the crescent moon. I'll make the world's greatest cathedral into my mosque. From that day until forever, my Constantinople will wake up to the muezzins' calls to prayer."

His brain on fire, his heart frozen, Radu stares at him without a word.

Constantinople is to Radu what Rome is to Catholics and what Mecca is to Muslims. Like all Wallachians, he's an Orthodox Christian, and the priest who baptized him and listened to his confession every

Sunday was a black-clad Orthodox priest. To him, the cross is sacred. And so is Hagia Sophia, the great cathedral that Mehmet covets and wants to make into a mosque. That cathedral is the Orthodox Christians' mother church.

Radu is stunned.

But Mehmet is too excited to notice. He paces back and forth, staring into the future Muslim city of his dreams that he'll build from the ruins of the Byzantine Empire.

"You know, Radu, the greatest problem with taking Constantinople is its Theodosian Walls. They're a five tier defense: an external wall, then a deep moat, then the internal wall. They're so strong that nobody was able to break through them, though Allah knows they tried. Sultan Bayezid Yıldırım tried and failed. Others tried, and they failed. Father himself tried and failed. They all failed, but me. I know I'll take the Red Apple. I can already feel its taste in my mouth."

Radu's brain spins, looking for something to say. But what is there to say? Maybe this is nothing but words. If Constantinople withstood so many attacks and it's still standing, it will withstand one more, God willing. Radu doesn't have to figure that out right now. He'll think about it and, hopefully find a way to reconcile his faith with his friendship with Mehmet.

But he remembers Vlad's words.

"Father sent us here because he had to! That was the only way to get the sultan off his back. He sent us here to learn about the Ottomans, their language, their habits, their fighting. We're to go back and help overcome them when the time comes. We are not to become them!"

CHAPTER 60

PREPARING FOR WAR

TÂRGOVIȘTE. AUGUST 1444

Further north, in Wallachia, the days have shortened, and the sun has lost some of its fire. But the wheat fields are heavy with gold, the trees bend under the weight of sweet fruit, and the pigs are fat and content. Just another month to bring in the harvest, and the church bells can start calling the weddings.

But the country isn't getting ready for weddings. They're getting ready for war. *And what a war this will be,* Ștefan thinks, giddy with excitement.

He's up in the watch tower with Vlad Dracul and Mircea, watching the Wallachian army gather.

Up in the meadows and low in the fields, men harvest the crops, mend their weapons, kiss their wives, and gather for battle. From every corner of the country, long lines of wild-looking men with tall sheepskin hats head towards the Royal Court of Târgoviște mounted on their nimble mountain ponies.

"What a beautiful army they'll make!" Mircea says, choking with pride.

Vlad Dracul shakes his head and looks at them with worried eyes.

"I don't know, Mircea. I'm weary. Look at them. These are not soldiers. They're peasants. Shepherds. Blacksmiths. Instead of letting them stay home to grow our bread, we drag them away from their fields and their families to set them against the largest, best prepared, and most disciplined army in the world. The sultan's janissaries don't spend their lives growing crops, tilling the fields, or mending fences. They do nothing but war. They don't even marry, so they can dedicate their whole life to fighting for the sultan. And that's who we're going against. Again. Unprovoked. Instead of letting our men take care of the land."

"But Father, you heard the last messenger. The war is coming. The sultan's army is preparing for it. They're making swords and armors day and night. They're training like never before."

Vlad Dracul shrugs. "That's what they always do. The janissaries always prepare for war. That doesn't mean they're about to start a war, and especially it doesn't mean they're about to start it with us. They may be going to Anatolia. Or Constantinople. IF they're getting ready for war."

"But Father, Hunyadi said it's the same messenger that sent him the news about Murad's resignation. The man's tested and true. If he was right then, he's probably right now."

Vlad Dracul sighs. His face is weary, his eyes tired, and his shoulders hunched like they carry the weight of the country, and Ștefan feels sorry for him. He doesn't know if Mircea is right or wrong, but he knows Mircea's burning to fight. He's thirsty for battle and glory, while Vlad is old, tired, and weary.

"Youth! It has all the energy, but none of the wisdom. Whereas old age has no energy left. And often, no wisdom either."

"Father, let me do it. Let me lead the men in battle. You don't have to come."

Vlad laughs, but it's not a happy laugh.

"Really? And what am I going to do?"

"You'll stay here to lead the country and build reinforcements. That way, if the sultan hears anything before the fight, you can say you never meant to fight. I took off without your permission. That way, he'll spare Vlad and Radu."

Vlad looks at his son with narrowed eyes. "I hadn't thought of that."

"You gave him your word that you won't go to war against him. If you don't leave Târgoviște, you kept your word, so he can't kill the boys."

"Sure, he can. But maybe he won't. Who knows what an impetuous thirteen-year-old will do? But hopefully, Çandarlı Paşa will keep him in check. So what would you do if I let you lead our army?"

"I'll take ten thousand men..."

"You won't. I don't have ten thousand men to give you. If we're lucky, we can get eight thousand altogether."

"I'll take eight thousand then..."

"I need to protect the castle and the border. You can have six thousand. No more."

"I'll take six thousand then. I'll lead them south towards the Danube. I'll meet Hunyadi's army at Nikopol, and we'll advance together towards Varna. The papal ships will sail up through the Dardanelles. We'll rendezvous in Varna, board the ships and sail to Constantinople. From there, we'll push the Ottomans out of Europe."

"If only it was that easy! You see these men? You see their horses? And their weapons?"

"We have a couple of months to get them trained and equipped. They should be ready by October."

"I still think it's a bad idea, Mircea. The Ottomans will kick our arses, and we'll end up worse off than we are now."

"That's impossible. We have Hunyadi with the Hungarian army on our side. We have the Teutonic knights. We have the Venetian and the Genoese ships, blessed by the pope. God Himself is on our side. We can't lose. Not to an untested thirteen-year-old infidel!"

"That's what they say too. To them, we are the infidels."

"Father! You can't speak this way! What if somebody hears you? We're fighting for Christianity! This will be the last crusade. In the name of God, we'll chase these pagans away from Europe, and we'll have a thousand years of peace."

"If only faith was enough to win wars."

"But it is. It's faith that wins wars."

"Yes, when it comes with healthy, well trained, well-armed soldiers, good horses, faithful allies, and lots of money."

"What are you saying, Father?"

"I'm saying that faith is not enough. But never mind. You're determined, our allies are determined, and the pope is determined, and that's that. I'm afraid that the die is already cast. And you may be right, there might never be a better time to throw the Ottomans out of Europe. I'm just afraid this isn't good enough. Ștefan!"

"Yes, uncle?"

"What are you going to do? Are you going to stay here or go with Mircea?"

"May I go, please? I've never been in a fight."

"You're not going to be in this one, either. You're too young. You won't be fighting, but you can watch. I hope you both make it back."

CHAPTER 61
WITH OR AGAINST ME?
EDIRNE, SEPTEMBER 1444

Summer's brutal heat is finally over in Edirne. The sun's still strong at noon, but the fall poured gold in the leaves and brought new freshness to the mornings and sweetened the tenderness of the dusk that Radu loves.

He also loves everything about the sultan's apartments: the scent of rosewater and frankincense, the softness of the thick Isfahan carpet under his feet, the soothing sussuring of the fountains, and the graceful sway of the peacock feathers the black eunuchs fan them with. But even more, Radu loves the sultan himself, who smiles, lying with his head in his palm to listen to Radu.

This, of course, isn't Sultan Murad. Sultan Murad has resigned and left. He went hundreds of miles away, to Anatolia, to live a life of prayer, quietude, and contemplation.

This is young Sultan Mehmet who's now the most powerful man in the world and the head of the Ottoman Empire. But he's not worried about the empire right now. He's happily listening to Radu playing the rübap, but his unrelenting gaze makes Radu uncomfortable. Still, he does his best to carry on, holding his eyes on the curvy instrument and plucking syncopated note after note.

"Have you ever been with a girl, Radu?"

The delicate music breaks into a cacophony as Radu fumbles to hold on to his rübap.

"A girl? Never."

"How about a man?"

Radu's heart skips a beat. He shakes his head no, without meeting the sultan's eyes.

"My mother wants to give me a girl," Mehmet says.

"A girl? Why?"

"You know why."

Radu blushes.

"What do you want, my sultan?"

Mehmet sighs.

"I don't want a girl, but Mother insists. She says that I'll soon need to get married. This is how we, Ottomans, build alliances. One wife at a time. She's already started looking. But in the meantime, she wants me to... become proficient. So she wants me to have this girl."

"What's her name?"

"Lena. She's from Moldova."

"Is she beautiful?"

"Mother says so. She's a virgin, too. That's important."

"Why?"

Mehmet shrugs. "Good question. I can't imagine why. You'd think..."

The clatter of heavy boots interrupts them, and the janissary opens the door.

"His Highness, Çandarlı Halil Paşa."

The grand vizier bursts into the room, all flushed and winded, so fast that the skirts of his purple kaftan flutter behind him. He falls on his knees to kiss the sultan's hand, then stands and stares at Radu.

"My sultan, I need to speak to you."

"Go ahead."

"I need to speak to you alone."

Radu stands to leave, but Mehmet signals him to stay put.

"No need to worry about my friend Radu, paşa. He's faithful to me. I would trust him with my life."

"Please, my sultan. It's a matter of state..."

"Paşa. I already told you. What is it?"

"My sultan..."

"If you don't like it, paşa, come back sometime when he's not here."

Radu wishes a hole would open to swallow him. But none does, so he makes himself small, pretending he's not there and he's not listening. But of course, he is.

"The crusaders are back at it."

"The crusaders?"

"Yes. The Hungarians, the Bohemians, and the Poles, all under Hunyadi. The Genoese and the Venetian ships with the pope's blessing and his money. And..."

"And?"

"The Wallachians under Vlad Dracul."

"What?"

The sultan jumps up from his pillows, his cheeks dark red like he's been slapped.

"That can't be. His sons are here. He knows what will happen to them if he breaks his oath."

The grand vizier shrugs, looking contrite, but his eyes shine with glee.

"It is true, my sultan. Our best spy at Hunyadi's court confirmed they are all in, and she's never failed us."

"Did you hear that, Radu?"

Radu nods without looking up.

"Look at me."

Radu looks into the black holes that are the sultan's eyes.

"Did you know about this?"

"No. Never."

Mehmet's eyes try to suck the truth out of him, but there's nothing. Radu didn't know about this, and he wishes he wouldn't know now. He had thought that Mehmet's plan to attack Constantinople was terrible, but this is a thousand times worse. If the grand vizier is right, this means war. A war between his father and his best friend; between his country and his adoptive country. Radu wishes he could do or say something, but nothing comes to mind.

He squirms under Mehmet's searching eyes.

"This can't be true, my sultan. My father wouldn't do something like this. He wouldn't leave us..."

He suddenly remembers Vlad's words. *"Father won't go against the Ottomans while we're captives. He'll send our brother instead. Mircea will lead the Wallachian army into battle, while Father sits at home thinking his next move against the Ottomans. Or Hungarians. Or somebody else. As always, he'll hedge his bets. Don't forget that our father has other sons. He can make even more, if need be. We are nothing but bait in the fight of nations."*

So Vlad was right. He may be evil and cruel, but he's the brightest mind Radu has ever seen. Months ago, Vlad knew that this would happen.

"I'm so sorry, my sultan."

"Me too, Radu. Me too. We were going to take Constantinople, and you were going to be by my side as we conquered the greatest city in the world. Instead of that, I have to deal with another bloody crusade. Yet another battle with those filthy Christians and their damn cross that I can't get rid of. That means that I'll have to go to war in the west, instead of going to take Constantinople. I don't like that. I had a plan. I was going to take the Red Apple. Instead of that, I'm back to square one."

Dark with fury, the sultan paces back and forth.

Crushed by Mehmet's rage, Radu tries to melt into the wall behind him. He wishes he could find something to say that won't be yet another provocation, but nothing comes to mind. He digs his nails in the flesh of his palms to stop his tears, and looks down, waiting for this to be over.

The sultan glares at him.

"So I'm going to fight in the west. How about you?"

"Me?"

"Yes. What are you going to do?"

"Whatever you tell me to, my sultan."

"Will you come with me to wage war against your father?"

Radu gasps.

"Or should I just send him your head, like my father, Sultan Murad, promised. He promised to send him your heads. Yours, and Vlad's if your father breaks his oath. And he broke his oath. But I won't break mine. I always keep my promises."

CHAPTER 62

TRANSYLVANIAN EUNUCH

After three days of solitary confinement in his room at the palace school, Radu has worn out the thin carpet from pacing back and forth from the window to the door. It's eight steps. Six if he makes them really big. He must have done it a thousand times, then his feet started hurting. Now he sits on his bed, practicing the rübap to kill time, but his heart isn't in is. Not like he's got anyone to play it to! He hasn't eaten or slept since the sultan sent him to his room with a janissary to guard his door. It's just like when Vlad tried to kill Mehmet, only worse. This time, there's nobody to expect help from. His best friend himself had Radu locked up, and he has no idea when it's going to be over. Thank God he's got Sari to keep him company. And Ali's daily visits. He stops by to chat whenever he brings food.

Just as if he'd summoned him, Ali comes in carrying a tray with fresh bread, roasted lamb, and fruit. He kneels and sets it on the floor. The aromas of rosemary and mint fill the room, but Radu is more excited about seeing Ali than he is about the food.

"The bread is still warm, my prince. And the pastry chef gave me some baklava, soaked in rose water and dripping with honey. You've got to try it."

"I'm way more lonely than I am hungry, Ali. Come sit with me. Talk to me. Tell me about you, your country and your family."

Ali glances at the janissary pacing in front of the door. He doesn't seem to care. And he's unlikely to speak Romanian, but you never know.

"There isn't much to tell, my prince. I was born in Transylvania, near the fortress of Kronstadt. We lived on a small farm, the four of us. I have two younger brothers that my mother loves better."

"Same with me, except that we lived in the Târgoviște Castle. And my two brothers are older. Still, my mother loves them better too. How about your father?"

"Father died a few winters ago. He was always kind to me, and I miss him terribly. Do you miss your father, my prince?"

"I thought I did, but I no longer know, to tell you the truth. Father sent us here as hostages to his oath of faith to Sultan Murad. Now..." Radu glances at the guard and lowers his voice. "Now it looks like he broke his oath, and he's going to war against the sultan."

"What will that mean for you, my prince?"

"I don't know. I hope the sultan won't cut off my head and send it to my father, as he promised. But I'm not so sure."

"But how did the sultan find out about your father's betrayal?"

"That Çandarlı Paşa has spies everywhere. Even at Hunyadi's court. He got word that Hunyadi, the pope, and a bunch of Genoese and Venetian ships are getting ready for war. Father, too."

"Just because Çandarlı Halil Paşa said so, it doesn't make it true. It may be just a rumor."

"Maybe, but he said he's got the news from his best spy, trustworthy, and really close to Hunyadi."

"Did he say who he is?"

"She. No, he didn't."

Ali sighs. "I still hope it's a mistake. But even if it's not, the sultan wouldn't hurt you. You're his best friend. He trusts you, and he relies on you."

"How do you know?"

"I heard him say it to his mother, the validé. I'm lucky enough to be in her service."

"I hope you're right. How is she? I met the old validé once. She was nice."

"The validé is a wise woman, and she's fully dedicated to the wellbeing and success of her son."

"I heard. You know a girl named Lena? From Moldova?"

"I do."

"Is she pretty?"

"Very pretty. Why?"

"The validé offered her to the sultan."

"What did the sultan say?"

"He's not interested, but his mother insists."

"Well, he's the sultan. He's got the last word."

"Not if the validé is anything like my mother."

Ali laughs and stands to leave before the guard throws her out.

"I wish you'd eat something, my prince. There's no point in getting sick. The sultan will send for you as soon as he gets over his anger. And that should be..." Ali stares into space like she's looking inside her head, then smiles at Radu. "Very soon."

"How do you know?"

"I do. Remember last time I told you everything was going to be all right? I was right then, and I'm right now. You will see."

"I hope so. If he does, what should I do?"

"About what?"

"What should I do if the sultan calls me back and asks me to go alongside him to fight my father and my brother? If he asks me to take the weapons against my country?"

Ali shakes her head. "I don't know, my prince. But I don't think he'll do that. I don't think you're old enough to fight."

"What would you do?"

"I don't know what I'd do, my prince. I've never had to make such a choice, and I hope I never do. You should ask your heart what the right thing is and do it, the best that you can."

Radu watches him leave, pondering what the right thing is. Would he betray his country if he went to fight alongside Mehmet? Would he betray Mehmet if he didn't? Should he worry about his father who left him here as a hostage, then broke his oath, knowing that he'll put his life in danger? Should he refuse Mehmet, who's been the best brother he could hope for, and showed him nothing but love, kindness, and generosity?

Curled in his bed, holding Sari close to his heart, Radu's so torn that he almost hopes the sultan will chop off his head and be done with it. At least he wouldn't have to choose who to betray.

CHAPTER 63

NO SULTAN FOR ME!

It's dark and quiet in the sarayi at night. The women's room is hidden in blackness, but for the one flickering torch in the ring by the door, above Ali's bed. Her mattress lays across the doorstep, since her job is to make sure nobody goes in or out unseen.

She lays under her blankets and waits until the torch is half gone, and the women all asleep. When their slow, equal breaths tell her she's safe, she digs inside her mattress for the precious things she stole: a piece of paper, a sharpened goose quill, and a small pot of dark ink made from soot and gum. She stole them separately, in different offices, so nobody'd worry about something missing. Now the time has come to put them to good use.

She lays the paper on the marble floor, dips the quill in ink and writes:

A woman spy at Hunyadi's court informed Çandarlı Paşa about the upcoming crusade. The sultan started preparing for war and threatened to kill the Wallachian hostages.

She's blows dry the paper when a touch on her shoulder makes her jump. She bites her tongue to stop from screaming and turns to see Lena. With her golden hair falling down her back and her eyes still heavy, she looks half asleep.

"What are you doing?" she asks.

Ali takes a deep breath. "I'm writing."

"What?"

"I'm writing a letter to my folks at home to tell them I'm OK."

"Wow! You can do that?" Lena touches the parchment with her finger. Fortunately, the writing is dry.

"Do what?"

"Write? In Romanian?"

"Yes."

Ali rolls the parchment and hides it inside her kaftan. "But please don't tell anyone. I stole the paper. If they catch me, they'll give me the lashes."

"But how will you send it if you don't want anyone to know?"

Good question. She doesn't know either. She'll have to get hold of the boys somehow, and that's not easy. She'll have to bribe Mirko to arrange for a signal and a meeting point. But that's not Lena's business. Bad enough that she saw her writing. Ali remembers something to distract her.

"Hey, I heard something about you today."

"What?"

"Hüma wants to give you to the sultan."

Lena's eyes grow so big they swallow her face, and her cheeks turn white like she's ready to faint. "Who told you?"

"Radu."

"How does he know?"

"The sultan told him."

Lena wrings her hands like she's trying to break them and sobs. "Oh, God, what can I do?"

"You don't want the sultan?"

"Of course not."

"But he's young and handsome. And he's single. Way better match than some fat old paşa with a whole harem of wives and consorts!"

"I don't want to be anybody's wife or consort! I'd rather die."

Ali stares at her. "But Lena, what did you expect? This is the harem. That's what these girls all aim for. Hüma honors you by giving you to the sultan. And if you're lucky enough to have a boy, you'll become one of his wives. Maybe even validé, if your boy becomes the next sultan."

"I don't want to be validé."

"What do you want then?"

"I want to go home."

"But you can't go anywhere. You're in the harem."

"I'll run away."

"But you can't. Nobody runs away from the harem. They all die here."

Lena's sobs get so loud that Ali worries she'll wake the other women. She hides the quill and ink back in the mattress, then hugs Lena to console her.

"Shh! Quiet now. You don't want to wake up the others, and you especially don't want to wake up the validé."

"I don't care. I want to go away."

"But..."

"No 'but'. Being locked in here drives me crazy! I can't stand it! I need to go home!"

Ali sighs. "OK. Let me think about it."

Lena stares at her with her forget-me-not eyes full of wonder. "You will?"

"Yes," Ali says, cursing herself. She doesn't know what to do. She doesn't even know how to hand the parchment to the boys, for God's sake, and she's going to help Lena escape the harem? That's rich.

But it's too late now. She promised she'll try. What on earth can she do?

Then she remembers Hüma's potion. There may be a way.

CHAPTER 64
LOYAL SERVANT

The evening after she asked Ali about death potions, the validé called her back to her rooms. She sat on her bed and signaled her women and eunuchs to leave. They did, glancing back with worried eyes, since they're supposed to always guard the validé. Always.

Not tonight.

Hüma waited for them to be gone, then turned to Ali. "I've decided. I need a potion for a grown woman."

"Yes, my lady. I'll need a strand of her hair."

"What for?"

"To make the potion. I also need ten drops of her blood."

Hüma's eyes narrowed. "What else?"

"Three black candles, the heart of a black newt, the brain of a black chicken and the bladder of a black sheep. And the tongues of three ravens. I also need wormwood, black willow root, and a bunch of other herbs that I'll pick myself, at the right time. It has to be a full moon."

Hüma frowned. "Are you quite sure about this?"

"Absolutely sure." Ali looked her straight in the eye. "Fall asleep for good, you said?"

Hüma nodded.

"I'll start looking for the herbs. Some of them I'll pick in the morning before the dew is gone. Some at night. Whatever I don't find in the gardens, I'll need your permission to leave the castle. I'll look for them in the forest."

"Will this really work?"

"Of course. But there's another decision you need to make. You want her to die overnight? That's fast, but it will get people talking. They'll wonder what happened to her. And they may guess someone wanted her harmed. Or do you want her to dwindle and fade slowly? It would take weeks, maybe months, but nobody would suspect a thing."

"Do you need to know now?"

"No. Only when I start brewing the potion, so I make it the right strength and choose the correct incantation. And I need to get everything first. But remember that the woman will have to drink the potion every day, for weeks, if you choose the slow death."

Hüma smiled and sent her away.

It's been a few weeks now, but Ali's still waiting for the raven tongues. And the blood. She's got the herbs, but Hüma doesn't know it, so she has an excuse to leave the castle. She'll ask for permission to go to the forest and pick herbs. But how will she get Lena out?

Then it comes to her. That morning when she brings the breakfast tray to Hüma's room, she kneels and sets it on the floor, as usual, but doesn't leave. She waits until Hüma's gaze meets hers, then nods.

With a flick of her hand, Hüma empties the room. She sits up in her bed, and in her midnight blue kaftan, with her dark green eyes and her snow-white face surrounded by the flames of red hair, she's the most arresting woman Ali has ever seen. And the scariest.

"What is it, Ali?"

"The potion."

"Yes."

"I need to leave the castle to collect herbs."

"When?"

"Three days from now. At night, under the full moon."

"I'll talk to Kapi Paşa. He'll give you an escort."

"I need a girl to take with me."

"A girl?"

"Yes. The herbs are strongest when gathered by a virgin under the full moon."

Hüma shrugs.

"OK. Take Lena."

Ali bows so deep her forehead touches the golden arabesque weaved in the red carpet. She gets ready to leave.

"Ali?"

"Yes, my lady?"

"I'll get the raven tongues, but how do you expect me to get ten drops of her blood without her noticing?"

Ali smiles. "You can have someone cut her by mistake, then steal the dressing. There should be enough blood on it."

"Not a bad plan. Any others?"

"A grown woman, you said."

"Yes."

"Unless they're with child, they bleed. Every month."

Hüma nods. "They do, indeed."

Her eyes study Ali from head to toe like she's seeing her for the first time.

"You said your grandmother was a healer?"

"She is, my lady. Her magic has the power to heal people."

"What else can her magic do, Ali?"

"Anything you could ever want, my lady. I wish I was half as learned as she is."

"You seem to be doing OK for an untrained young eunuch. Except..."

"Yes, my lady?"

"Your... healing potions smack of black magic. And Allah doesn't like that. If anyone, anyone ever finds out about your potions and your powers, I might not be able to save you. Many eunuchs have died for less."

A great chill washes down Ali's back.

"And I don't know that I'd want to. Nobody likes disloyal servants."

"I'm loyal, my lady."

"I hope so. I really hope you're loyal. And you can keep a secret. If you are, good things will come to you. Many good things. But if you're not..."

Hüma smiles like Smaranda's cat Gigi used to, whenever she saw a particularly fat mouse. She liked the food, but she loved the chase even more.

The mouse didn't.

"I'm loyal, my lady. And I can keep a secret."

Hüma nods and points to the door.

Ali feels Hüma's eyes follow her, and she shivers. She's playing a dangerous game.

Then she remembers that every second of every day, she's just one step away from being exposed and executed. So what does this change? Nothing.

They can only kill her once.

CHAPTER 65

ESCAPE FROM HELL

TOKAT CASTLE, SEPTEMBER 1444

Thank God, Allah, and anybody else who had anything to do with it. The guards didn't take Vlad back to his cell, they took him to a bath, and a much-needed scrubbing. And for the first time ever, Vlad thanked God for the Ottomans. He rejoiced in his bath, ate real food, and slept in a clean bed. Every night since.

Still, the Tokat Castle isn't about comfort. Not the terrible dungeons, not Vlad's simple room with its bed and prayer carpet, not even Sevlet Paşa's quarters. Unlike the sultan's ornate palace, where everything is about beauty, comfort and pleasure, here it's all about function and business. And the business, here, is the security of the Ottoman Empire.

The walls are bare gray stone, but for the rusty iron rings that hold the torches. The carpets are few and thin, further enhancing the austerity of the cold stone floors. Even the cups. There's no silver or gold. Just copper, like the one Sevlet Paşa sips from, as he talks to Vlad.

"The empire's enemies live in our dungeons. Not for long, though. Most of them are quick to become the empire's friends when they realize how much better it is to be the sultan's friend rather than his enemy."

Vlad understood that. It wasn't hard, mind you, but he looks at the fat paşa like he's the fountain of wisdom.

"But not all. Some are stubborn. And stupid. Persuading them of what's good for them takes lots of work."

"But why bother? Why not just kill them?"

The paşa shakes his head. "Killing them would remove one enemy, but won't make you a friend. And it won't dissuade any of the others who are misguided enough to hate our empire. And there are many out there. But persuading them to change their mind earns us a friend, and discourages the empire's enemies."

"How about those who won't be persuaded?"

"They die, of course, but they will be an example to the others. Those others will think twice before they risk suffering the same fate."

Vlad is unconvinced. The paşa sees it and smiles. "You wish to see?"

Vlad nods. The paşa claps his hands, and a servant comes out of nowhere. Vlad startles, even though he's learned that in this castle, which is nothing but a labyrinth of dark corridors, eyes and ears are everywhere.

"We're going to the dungeons."

The servant grabs a torch and leads them through a dark hallway, then down a steep set of stairs, then another, taking them deeper and deeper inside the mountain's stone belly. There's another corridor, this one too low for Vlad to stand, so he bends to follow the paşa. The passage opens to a round room carved inside the rock, ending in a guarded iron gate.

Sevlet Paşa nods. With a noisy clatter, the guard unlocks the door. The prisoners behind it hear it and start screaming. Vlad remembers his time in his cell and he shivers, but nobody else seems to hear them.

"Let me out! Let me out, I tell you! I'm a Venetian merchant. I have the right to be free."

"Please! Oh, please! It wasn't my fault! I never knew those thugs were against my beloved sultan! I would have crushed them if I knew!"

"You filthy pagans! I've grown old and blind in this cell, but I'll fight you all, you mutton eating Allah worshipers, until the day I die. God will help me, and my king will get me out of your grasp, you goat lovers!"

Vlad's heart knows every inch of this long, narrow corridor of misery, though he's only walked it twice. A cold shiver goes down his spine as they pass his former cell. At the other end, the tunnel opens into a round room carved in stone. The many tools scattered inside make it look like a blacksmith's shop or a farmer's tool barn, but these are tools like Vlad has never seen before.

The long wooden table in the middle is a whole tree trunk sewn in half. It's big enough for a large man to lay comfortably on, but by the shackles affixed into each corner, comfort is not what this is about. The veined wood is scratched and marred by countless dark stains.

"That's where you lay the empire's future friends," Sevlet Paşa says. "You secure them with the shackles before you start working. The reason that table is so high is to make sure that your workers are comfortable, since it may take them hours and days to break through. Sometimes even weeks. You've got to protect your workers, since well trained, talented torturers are rare. It takes years to train a good one."

Vlad's throat is too dry to talk. Paşa's worried about the wellbeing of torturers? That never crossed Vlad's mind. Sure they have people doing these dirty jobs in Wallachia too, executioners and torturers, but that's not a profession. They'll use whichever guard is available to deal with the job. Here, they take it to a whole different level.

"You see, Prince Vlad, persuading people is an art. A torturer's job is not to break their bones. That's just a means to an end. Their job is to break their spirit. Some prisoners are easy. You just tell them what you're about to do, and they break. Some take a lot of work. Your job is to know which is which. And, of course, you need to use the right tools for the job. Have you ever seen these before?"

He points to a pair of rusty long-nosed pliers hanging on the wall.

Vlad shakes his head no.

"They're just a starter tool. They're for removing nails. And fingers. How about this?" He points to half a helmet attached by a long screw to a broad iron base.

"No."

"That's a head crusher. You screw it, and it squashes their skull like an egg. But they seldom talk after that one. Quite brutal, I'm afraid. Quickly destructive and unspectacular. See this?"

He points to a sharp iron hook hanging from the ceiling.

"That's for when you need the prisoner to hang. You can hang them by their hands or their feet, depending on what you're trying to do. It also works for stretching them. You tie their hands with a rope passed through a hook on the ceiling and their feet to a hook on the floor, then pull them apart with the rope. You can also just hook them like you'd hook a fish, but that should only be towards the end. They don't last long after that. Much better if you can get someone they care about — a wife, mother, or son — whoever you can find — and hook them instead. That never fails to get them to cooperate. How about this? Have you seen this?"

He hands Vlad a metal device the size of his palm. It's shaped like a pear, slit in four along its length and operated by a long screw.

Vlad grabs it with shaky hands. He doesn't know if it's fear or excitement, but he feels that he's on the verge of an extraordinary discovery like he's never seen before.

"I've never seen it."

"That's the Pear of Anguish. You grease it first, so it slides easier, then you slide it inside the prisoner. It can be either their mouth or their private parts. Then, as you twist the screw, it expands. See? It opens further and further, like a bud blooming into a flower. It will of course expand whatever you placed it in, opening it wider and wider until it can't open any more. Then it rips it apart. They usually talk way before that — unless you put it in their mouth, of course. If you do, they have a hard time talking. But they can still scream."

Vlad's heart pumps so hard he can hardly hear the paşa above the blood humming in his ears. He returns the Pear of Anguish, wishing he could keep it.

"Then there's the wheel, of course. And the fire tools. The teeth and tongue pullers. The crocodile tube. You pull them through it and they come out shredded. The boiler, to simmer them. We have more tools than I can count. But none of them is my favorite. You wish to see my favorite?"

Vlad nods, too choked to speak.

"It's the simplest, but it's the best. Nothing works better."

CHAPTER 66

THE MAGIC OF FEAR

"This is it," the paşa says, gazing lovingly at a nine-foot stake standing on a broad base, the only thing in the last empty room. The stake is about as thick as Vlad's arm, bare and smooth, and rounded at the top.

"This is it?" Vlad asks.

"Yes," the paşa says, caressing it like a lover would. "Isn't she a beauty?"

Vlad doesn't really think so, but he doesn't want to hurt the paşa's feelings. The paşa laughs.

"Do you know what this is?"

"A stake?"

"Do you know what it's for?"

"No."

"This is the one tool that will allow you to control the masses. You destroy one man, but you put the fear of God into every single one of those who see it. This, my friend, is the most important political tool of our times."

Vlad wonders if he's kidding. But he's not.

"Let me tell you how it works. You see the end? It's tapered, but not sharp. See how nicely it's rounded? That's very important, since you don't want to stab people with it. It needs to be smooth, tapered, and well-greased. You part the prisoner's legs, and, with a dagger, you open his butt hole. Only enough to make room for the stake. Then you grease it well, to help it slide. You push it in gently, very gently, since you don't want to rip apart their insides. You want to allow the flesh to stretch and make room for the stake. Some pull it inside with horses. That's barbaric. You have to finesse it in, inch by inch, slowly, and that's not a job for horses. You push it up to about their navel — you can check where you are by pressing on their belly. Even better, measure it first, before you put it in, and make a mark on the stake so that you know how far to push it in. Once you're deep enough, you raise up the stake on its base, and allow them to impale themselves, deeper and deeper, by their own weight. And by their struggle. The more they fight, the deeper it gets."

Vlad's mouth drops open. Paşa's story gives him a flush of deep pleasure like he's never felt before. His shalwars tent around his engorged penis. He swallows, hoping the story will never end.

"You place the stake in a public place, for everyone to see. And you want to be gentle with them. They need to look human, and recognizable. You don't want just a chunk of bloody flesh stuck on that stake. Make sure they're nice and clean, so their families and friends and neighbors can recognize them as they watch them die, little by little, without anybody touching them. Except for the crows, of course. They love the eyes. But that's a nice extra touch.

"Some say the stake should be sharp. Others even say that you should impale them sideways, with the stake entering through their back and coming out through the chest. Some even say you should impale them upside down, pushing the stake through their mouth and having it come out through their behind. Don't listen to those amateurs. If you put the stake through their mouth, you'll choke them right then and there, and then you're left with nothing but a dead body upside down on a stake. And it's pretty much the same if you do them sideways. They bleed to death in minutes, and the show is over. If you really want to make them suffer, so that the others get to see and learn, you do it the way I told you. Gently, slowly, lovingly."

Vlad is about to erupt. He's aching to touch the burning flesh in his pants, but he's got just enough reason left to refrain. He licks his dry lips and sighs.

"Wow. You, paşa, are the master."

"Of course. That's why I'm here. I can make somebody die for days. Weeks, even."

"How long will they live on the stake?"

"It depends. A skilled torturer can keep them alive for a couple of days. That's a long time to die. It's also a long time to watch the death of someone you love. There's no better way to bring a crowd to your side. There's love, of course, but that's hard to get. And it's fickle. People will turn on you for a coin unless they're afraid of you. Fear is stronger than love. It's even stronger than hate. There is nothing stronger than fear."

As they walk back through the narrow tunnels and up the steep stairs, Vlad knows he just learned the lesson of his life. The paşa taught him something that neither his father nor his teachers ever told him. To them, it's all about duty, love, and responsibility.

But Vlad knows in his bones that the paşa is right. Fear is the most important thing on earth. And the most beautiful. Alongside pain. Fear and pain.

Lying in the darkness in his bed in Tokat Castle, Vlad strokes the burning flesh between his legs until it bursts. And as the pleasure overcomes him, he's not thinking about any woman. He sees Mehmet's body struggling on a stake.

CHAPTER 67

SECRET INFORMANT

EDIRNE SEPTEMBER 1444

Sitting on his wide throne in the Edirne Palace, Mehmet plays with his new dagger. It's a gift from Zaganos Paşa, and it's beautiful. The steel ripples with waves, marking the flow of the hot forged metal. The handle is silver, studded with nubby precious stones polished into smoothness that comfort the hand and improve the grip. The weapon is so perfect that it won't slip out of his hand even when he's sweaty or covered in blood. His fingers caress the smooth shape of a garnet as big as half a grape, but all he thinks about is how he'd love to stick the blade into Çandarlı Paşa's wrinkled throat.

The paşa sits on a blue brocade pillow to his left, while Mehmet's mentor, Akşemseddin, sits to the one at his right. And they've been bickering for ages.

"If we don't do it, the janissaries will revolt," Çandarlı Paşa says. His hooded eyes are dark, and the muscle behind his right jaw twitches with anger. "They haven't yet received their due. We need to make them whole, and we must do it before they revolt and refuse to fight."

Akşemseddin chuckles. "Come on, Çandarlı Paşa, don't get so excited. There's nothing to worry about. The janissaries are our elite troops, and they're faithful to the sultan. They'd give their last drop of blood for him, like they have for his father, and his father's father."

"Not so, Akşemseddin. Sultan Murad is a warrior. He fought for two decades, war after war, in the east and in the west. Sultan Murad curtailed the crusades, tamed the Karamanids, and brought peace to the empire. He slept on the ground with his soldiers and shared their horse meat, or went hungry when there was none left. Fight after fight, victory after victory, Sultan Murad earned their trust and respect. But Sultan Mehmet is not Sultan Murad. He's... young. And untested. He was planning a campaign against Constantinople, and that fell apart now that he's got the crusaders coming at the northern border. Sultan Mehmet is not Sultan Murad."

"Nor should he be. Sultan Murad has left to live the life of a thinker and philosopher. He trusts Sultan Mehmet. That's why he left him to see to the future success of the empire."

"Maybe he does. But the janissaries don't. And without their trust and their complete loyalty, we don't have a prayer of beating Hunyadi, the Venetians, the Genoese, the pope, and all the other filthy Christians. Including Vlad Dracul, the sultan's best friend's father."

"That's enough!"

Mehmet can't take it anymore. He gathers all his strength to refrain from cutting Çandarlı Halil Paşa's throat. He's had it with the vizier, who's done nothing but stand in his way at every step. He wanted to stop him from taking Constantinople. He doesn't like Radu, his friend. He opposes everything Mehmet wants or does, and nags him to do all the things he doesn't care for. Like giving those darn janissaries a bonus. What's the point of being sultan if you can't do what you want?

A sudden thought strikes Mehmet. What if the vizier is lying? What if there's no crusade, and it's all just a ploy to stop him from going after Constantinople? Other than his word, there's no proof that the vizier has heard anything from any spy. There's no proof that that spy even exists. What if it's all nothing but a lie?

"Çandarlı Paşa, who is your informant?"

Çandarlı Paşa's jaw falls. He stares at Mehmet in horror.

"My informant?"

"Yes. Your spy at Hunyadi's court. The one who told you the crusade is coming. Who's that?"

"I'm sorry, I can't tell you, Sultan."

"Why not?"

"Sultan, it's my duty to protect the identity of my men. This person has served us and the empire for many years, and they have access to information nobody else has. We need to protect them at all costs."

"Of course. There's nobody here but you, me, and Akşemseddin. You're not saying one of us would out your spy, are you?"

"But Your Highness, there's not only us. There's..." Çandarlı Paşa points to the four guards surrounding the sultan, as usual, and the two gold-clad eunuchs fanning him, the open doors and many windows. "Remember that walls have ears, Your Highness. Just like we have spies in their court, they have spies in our court. It makes no sense to expose our best asset to incalculable risks for no good reason."

"So you won't tell me."

"I can't."

"Sure, you can. But you won't. You choose to defy me, your sultan. I've had enough. I won't hear anything else from you. Anything, but the name and the exact position of your spy at Hunyadi's court. Come back when you're ready to tell me. In the meantime, get lost."

Çandarlı Paşa's face turns ashen. He prostrates himself, then walks out, leaving behind a heavy silence.

Mehmet looks at Akşemseddin. His mentor sits on his pillow looking out the window and his face gives nothing away.

"So? What do you think?"

"I think Çandarlı Paşa is a pain in the backside. He's an old curmudgeon with lousy manners. But he's also a great warrior and an experienced vizier who served your father loyally for most of his life. And I don't think he's lying to you."

Mehmet stares at his tutor. "Really? I thought you two hated each other!"

"And you were right. We do. We have, for ages, and we'll continue to do so. But the truth is the truth, whether one likes it or not. And speaking about truth, you haven't made a friend today. You forced him into an untenable position, and humiliated him. He'll never forget that. And he's not a good enemy to have."

Mehmet shrugs. "So what? What can he do? I'm the sultan."

"I don't know what he'll do, but I bet we'll find out."

CHAPTER 68
THE ESCAPE

A misty dusk falls over the palace as Ali and Lena walk towards the gate surrounded by four guards. Ali wonders if they'll make it back. It's the night she planned to help Lena escape, and Ali had asked Codru and Ion for their help.

Codru stared at her like she'd lost her mind.

"Are you crazy? We can barely send a message outside, and you want us to help one of the sultan's women disappear? You've lost it."

Ali sighed. Codru's right, of course. This is insane. She's putting them all at risk and endangering their mission. But she promised Lena she'd try to help her.

"Well, she'll do her best. She'll either manage to get out, or she won't. But either way, she doesn't know you. Even if they catch her, it's not going to affect you. You'll continue to be with the janissaries, and send back your messengers. You're in good shape."

Ion shook his head, and his blue eyes burn with anger.

"How about you? If she tells on you, you're done. And so are we. Have you ever heard about Tokat? If not, you're about to. The folks there will extract things from you that you didn't even know you knew. They'll get you, then they'll get us, and it's all over. Just because you choose to help this stupid girl we don't even know."

"She isn't stupid. And I didn't choose to. I had to. And we'll be all right."

"Sure."

They nodded, but their faces are dark and worried.

And they're right. What she's doing, Ali knows is stupid. But it's too late.

"Look, boys. Lena is just like us. She's just a girl trapped in a bad spot. This is not her fault."

"It's not ours, either," Codru said. "And she's Moldavian. We have no business risking our lives and our mission for her."

"But Moldavians are just like us. They speak the same language, worship the same god, and eat the same food. They are us."

Ion shook his head.

"You know how I love you, Ali. I wouldn't do this for anyone else but you. Still, I think you're wrong. You're endangering our mission for nothing. But I trust you enough to go along with your silly plan."

Codru nodded. "Me too. But let me tell you right now: it won't work. We're hundreds of miles from Moldova. This girl won't make it. She just can't. The Ottomans will catch her before dawn. Unless the wolves tear her apart, or she drowns in the Tunca. If you think that she's somehow going to walk to safety, think again."

Ali shakes her head, but there's nothing else she can do. She steps out the gate with Lena and the four guards, and prays for the best. She's got a bag to collect herbs and gave Lena one, too. Except that Lena's bag isn't empty. Ali loaded it with everything she could think about that could help. Water, honey, a dagger she stole yesterday, dried fruit. She even managed to draw a make-shift map for her to go north. But she knows it's unlikely.

"Are you ready?" she asks Lena.

"Yes."

"I'll keep them busy for as long as I can, but it won't be long. They'll come after you with archers and dogs, and I can't stop them."

"I understand. I'll do the best I can. Thank you, my friend."

"We can still go back, you know."

"No. I'll take my chances."

"Good luck."

Lena nods, and Ali heads east, taking the guards with her while Lena hides in the bushes. Ali walks away, pretending to pick a bunch of herbs she doesn't know and hoping that Lena will make it to where she's to meet the messenger taking her north. She stops breathing to listen, but hears nothing. She pretends to pick another herb, but the guard's head stops her.

"Where's the girl?"

"The girl?"

"Yes. The girl we left with. Where is she?"

Her heart racing, Ali looks around her like she's looking for Lena. But this is no good. They're already looking for her, much faster than she thought they would.

"She's gone to collect some special herbs," Ali says.

The guard frowns. "We go back now."

"But I haven't finished picking the herbs the validé sent me here for."

"We go back now," the guard says, and there's no question in his voice. He's done.

It's over, Ali thinks. Lena didn't have enough time to get away. But there's nothing she can do.

They head back. The guards circle, searching every path, checking under every bush. They look for Lena like dogs look for a rabbit, and there's nothing Ali can do to stop them.

"Did you do this?" the guard asks her.

"Do what?"

His face grim, he turns to his men.

"You two. Take him back to the validé. The rest of us will stay here to look for the girl. Tell the validé we won't return without her. Oh, after you drop him off, come back with the dogs."

Somewhere close, a wolf howls, singing his sorrow to the full moon, and Ali shivers.

CHAPTER 69
THE TRAP

Squeezed between a couple of low bushes, Lena watched the guards follow Ali down the path. She waited until she could hear them no more, then headed north towards the mountains, like Ali had told her to.

But going through the brush is no fun. The twisted bushes, the prickly trees, and the tall grasses with leaves as sharp as swords hold her back, scratching her arms and legs. Her pretty silk shoes made for the marble floors of the harem fare poorly against the sharp rocks and prickly branches that line the bottom of the forest.

But it's her one chance to freedom, and she'll take it. She struggles further and further until she glimpses the notch in the mountain that Ali told her to follow. The man that Ali said will show her the way to Moldova is supposed to be there, just an hour away.

Lena can't wait to go back. She misses them all — her mother, her father, and Ștefan. But what she misses the most is her freedom. Even now that she's running away, she's delighted to be free of walls and away from the never-ending rules of the harem. It's wonderful to be free, feel the wind in your face and have nobody telling you what to do, even for a moment.

Before long, everything hurts. But Lena pushes through, further and further from the path, the guards, and the castle. She switches the bag from one shoulder to the other, sips some water, and checks the map. Thank God for the full moon that gives her enough light to see Ali's scribbles. Keep north for at least an hour, the map says. It's not yet an hour, so she keeps north.

Just as she's about to change direction, the ground crumbles under her feet and she falls. Something sharp stabs her, and the excruciating pain takes her breath away. She crashes to the ground and lays there unmoving waiting to catch her breath.

When she finally looks around, she discovers that she's inside a hole, so deep she can't see outside. And a sharp pole is sticking up in the middle.

It's a trap. Not for her, of course. Who knew she was going to be there? It must have been set by one of the poachers who risk their lives to hunt on the sultan's domain. The punishment for that is death, but they're hungry enough to risk their lives for a deer.

Except they caught no deer. They caught her, and they wounded her badly.

Lena checks the damage. It's mostly scrapes and bruises other than the big gash where the stake ripped through her side. Fortunately, it didn't break through her ribcage. It hurts so bad that she can't lift her arm, but it won't kill her. Not yet.

But her hopes for escape are all over. She can barely stand, and she bleeds like a stuck pig. She rips off her shalwars and wraps them tight around her chest to cover the wound and stop the bleeding. When she did all she can do, she tries to figure out where she is.

But the trap is too deep.

She tries to climb out, but the dirt walls crumble under her hands and feet. The vertical pole in the middle is sleek and so smooth she couldn't climb it on a good day, even though she's a good climber. And this isn't a good day. She's trapped and hurt, and nobody knows where she is. Her only chance to survive is for the guards to find her. Even if she managed to get out of this trap, she can't walk all the way to Moldova. That was a stretch even when she was unharmed.

Now what?

Lena sighs. She hopes the guards will find her and take her back, but she did a good job of running away, so they may not find her while she's still alive. What can she do?

She opens the bag Ali gave her. She's got some water, a little food, a dagger, and the map. Should they find her, they'll know she ran away. She didn't need a map and a knife to pick plants. She should get rid of them, but she can't bring herself to get rid of the dagger. What if a wild animal falls in her trap? And the blade would allow her to take her own life rather than die from hunger and thirst. But the map is useless, since escape is no longer in the cards. She shreds the map and eats the pieces one by one. They're hard to swallow and bitter from the soot they make ink from, so she adds some honey to help them down.

She checks the dagger. It's sharp, slim and curved like a crescent. The narrow blade reflecting in the moonlight should make death easy. She'd have to place it above her left breast, between the ribs, and let herself fall forward on it. She's not strong enough to push it in all the way otherwise; the pain and the fear would stop her halfway. But if she falls into it, that should get the job done.

Oh well. If she dies, at least she won't have to return to the harem and get locked in. She'd never be given away like an unwanted kitten, and she'd never again have to do what she's told.

But then she'd never see another sunrise, or feel the wind, or laugh. She'd be dead.

She's still wavering as she hears steps. They're slow and cautious and heavy. God help her, she hopes it's the guards.

"I'm here! I'm here! Come get me out."

All noise stops. Lena shouts again to help them find her.

"I'm down in a trap in the ground!"

A shadow leans over the wall. Only one. And it's dark, ominous, and not human.

CHAPTER 70

HUNGRY BEAR

Lena's fingers tighten on the dagger that suddenly looks very small. She melts against the wall, wishing she'd kept her mouth shut, and holds her breath, hoping against hope that the darkness and the silence will drive the beast away.

But it's too late. He heard her shouts, and the smell of blood and honey draws him closer.

Profiled against the full moon's pallor is the head of the largest bear Lena has ever seen. He sniffs and snorts, making sure that's where the smell comes from, then starts circling the trap, looking for a way to get in. But there's no easy way. Even worse, there's no way out. If he leans in too far, he'll tumble in, and then it's both of them trapped in a hole four feet by four — one a giant bear, the other a scared, wounded girl.

But Lena has a dagger.

How do you even kill a bear? Because wounding him would do no good. It will just make him angrier, and there'll be no place for him to run. *I'd better scare him away now*, Lena thinks. She throws a clump of dirt at his head and shouts as loud as she can.

"Go away, you miserable beast! I'll kill you if you get any closer! Ugly, hairy, stinky monster!"

His head cocked in surprise, the bear stares down at her.

Lena yells even louder.

"Go away, you stupid lazy oaf! Find your own honey and trap your own food, you dirty piece of crap."

The bear lifts its head and turns away. Lena hopes she managed to scare him, but no. He's just turned to listen to some sound in the forest, but now he's back, getting ready to jump inside the trap.

"You won't be able to get out, you..."

An unearthly howl shatters the air, and the forest falls silent. Lena's heart races, and her mouth goes dry. What the heck was that? Just when she thought it couldn't get any worse. Was it the bear? No. He looks unsettled too, staring into the darkness of the forest.

The blood-curling howl splits the night again, and the bear cowers.

It's not him. Whatever it is, it's even worse.

Lifting his muzzle to the sky, the bear sniffs the air for the danger. He stands to its threatening full height wavering on clumsy feet and growls.

Another howl, this one close, then a black shadow leaps, throwing the bear off its feet. The bear screams a small, thin scream, odd for such a big animal, as they roll to the ground. For a moment, they teeter on the edge of the trap, ready to crumble into the snare, then the black shadow grips the earth with claws the size of Lena's dagger and drags the bear away, out of sight.

A low growl meets a terrible howl. Branches break, claws rip the ground, and the unseen fight showers Lena with clumps of dirt and leaves. A ferocious growl, then a scream, a growl again, then a whimper. The sound of branches breaking under rushed heavy steps, further and further away.

The fight is over. Slow, heavy steps, come closer.

The black shadow stares in. White fangs and amber eyes glow in the moonlight.

The ears are triangular and sharp instead of rounded. The head too. It's not the bear. It's a wolf. The biggest wolf that ever existed sits by the trap like a dog, looking in.

Like that's not bad enough, there's that smell. Lena can't put her finger on it, but it's not the feral scent of a wolf. It's something she knows well, and she struggles to remember.

The unblinking amber eyes stare at her. She stares back.

The wolf lays by the trap, its head on its paws, staring at her until Lena feels too weak to stand. She sits.

"Now what?" Lena asks.

The wolf doesn't blink.

"What are you waiting for?"

He doesn't answer. He keeps staring, and in a way, it's more unnerving than the bear. She knows exactly what the bear wanted: Food. And she was it. But this?

They sit like that forever, until the wolf pricks his ears and glances back to the forest. Moments later, he stands, and Lena hears voices. The guards are looking for her.

"Here! I'm here."

The wolf glances back, smiles at Lena, then disappears in the darkness.

The guards' heavy steps come closer and closer. Lena throws the dagger in the darkness of the forest, and she shouts. "I'm here. Come get me."

They do.

It takes them a while to lift her out and carry her back to the castle, since she can't walk on her own. By the time they drop her in front of the validé, she's exhausted and feverish.

The validé's eyes are ice-cold as they look at her. They peruse her bruised, bloody body, the make-shift bandage around her chest, the bag on her shoulder. She's not pleased.

Lena kneels next to Ali and struggles to bend and touch her forehead to the ground.

"What's this all about? What did you do?"

"I got lost, Your Highness. I went off the path to pick herbs, like Ali told me. I must have taken a wrong turn when I came back. Instead of heading back, I got myself deeper and deeper in the forest, then I fell into a trap."

The validé doesn't look convinced. "Let's see her bag."

A guard empties it at her feet. The water flask, the herbs she picked, the honey.

"Why honey?"

Lena can't think of a reason.

"To seal the plants, my lady," Ali answers, though nobody asked him. "You don't want the juices to run out. Dipping the stems in honey will keep all the power of the plants inside them."

The validé nods, but her eyes are on Lena. She looks through Lena like she's trying to read inside her soul, and Lena does her best to project all the joy she can muster.

"I'm so glad to be back, my lady. I thought I was going to die there, prey to the wild animals. I'm glad the guards found me."

The validé looks at the guards. "What do you say?"

The guard shrugs. "She was crying for help when we found her, my lady. She wasn't hiding. Otherwise, we would never have found her down there."

"OK. To bed, you two. But first, go have a bath, and Ali, you take care of her wound. I don't want a scar. We wouldn't want her to be ugly."

As they head towards the bath, Ali whispers: "Where's the map?"

Lena rubs her stomach.

Ali laughs. "Don't tell me that the dagger's there too."

Lena smiles, even though she's exhausted, and she failed. But she's alive. And she's got a friend.

As she falls asleep, she remembers the wolf.

He smelled like soap.

CHAPTER 71
A RISKY WAR
NICOPOLIS, BULGARIA, OCTOBER 1444

Like a fat silver snake slithering through the tall grasses, the Danube marks the border between the Ottoman Empire and Wallachia. And after riding south from Târgoviște for a week, Ștefan is mighty pleased to see it. They're finally getting to Nicopolis, where they'll join the rest of the Christian army.

Ștefan can't wait to see all these people he's heard so much about. Hunyadi, the White Knight of Christianity, Athleta Christi, as Pope Pius the Second called him. King Władysław the Third, of Hungary and Poland, who, at only twenty, carries the hopes of the whole Christianity on his shoulders; and Fružin, the last Tsär of Bulgaria's son. There's never been a more heroic gathering on a worthier mission.

Vlad Dracul pulls back the reins of his palfrey. "Time to stop. We'll camp here."

Ștefan bites his lips to swallow his disappointment. They're so close, just miles away from joining Hunyadi's army. And it's not even late in the day. But the voivode has spoken. The men dismount and start building their camp.

These are the strangest soldiers Ștefan has ever seen — though he hasn't seen many. With their scraggly beards, tall sheepskin hats, and leather vests instead of armor, they look more at home on the ground, gathering wood to build fires, making camp, and cooking in the large iron bowls hanging above the fire, than they are on their horses. And the horses feel the same. They're more used to pulling plows or carts than to having someone on their backs.

Ștefan told that to Mircea, and Mircea laughed. "Wait until you see them in battle."

"Let's go," Vlad says.

Mircea and Ștefan follow him with a handful of soldiers. They ride south towards the Danube, and Ștefan's excitement mounts again. Maybe he'll get to see the generals, after all.

Here, the Danube is a half-mile wide and slow as treacle. They dismount and leave two men to mind the horses, while the rest of them step into one of the long wooden boats waiting to cross.

The trip is silent. Vlad Dracul is deep in his thoughts, and, by the set of his mouth, they aren't happy ones. Mircea's quiet, too, and Ștefan wonders if he's having second thoughts about going to battle.

The boat lands at the southern shore, on Ottoman land. They step on the half-rotten wooden deck and walk towards the massive camp. The fields are ablaze with fires, too many to count. There've got to be thousands, all surrounded by men.

They head to the tallest tent but the guard stops them at the door. "Who are you?"

"Vlad Dracul of Wallachia with my son Mircea and my nephew Ștefan."

"Let them in," a gruff voice says.

The tent is more spacious than many houses. Taller too. The pole in the middle holds up the field of blue silk that surrounds Hunyadi's quarters. The hero himself sits at the table loaded with wine cups, bread and the little that's left of a whole chicken.

Ștefan's stomach growls, reminding him that he hasn't eaten since breaking fast this morning, but he's too excited to care, now that he's face to face with the great Hunyadi. Ștefan knows it's him by his famous mustache, which is curled up almost as wide as his shoulders.

The great man sets his cup on the table and stands to greet them. The richly dressed young man beside him stays put.

"Glad to see you here," Hunyadi says, handing a wine cup to Vlad Dracul and another to Mircea. "It took you a while."

Mircea blushes, but Vlad Dracul doesn't blink. "You're lucky to see us at all. If it wasn't for the young ones, I'd have stayed home."

"I'm not surprised. That's what I expected from you."

"As for you, I expected you'd have more common sense than to walk into this trap."

The young man sitting at the table intervenes.

"I persuaded him that it was time to show the infidels what we Christians can do. It's time to throw them out of Europe once and for good."

"King Władysław, I presume?" Vlad Dracul says.

The young man nods. With his gold-embroidered purple tunic and long blond tresses falling on his shoulders, he's handsome in a girlish kind of way. But he looks down his thin nose at them as if they smell bad, and Ștefan doesn't like him, even though he agrees with what he says.

Vlad looks at Hunyadi. "I thought you were smarter than that."

"Like you have room to talk."

Without being invited, Vlad laughs and sits in a tall chair. Mircea stands behind him, and Ștefan does the same. They face each other like two opposing parties.

The king drains his cup and slams it on the table. "We've had success after success, ever since we crossed the Danube. We took Vidin and Oryahovo. They fell to us like ripe plums. Nikopol is next, then Varna. I don't see what you, old-timers, are worried about."

What a jerk. Even if he's right, that's not the way to speak to Vlad Dracul and Hunyadi, two of the greatest heroes of our time. But he's the King of Hungary and Poland, so Hunyadi, as the voivode of Transylvania, is his vassal. *That's why*, Ștefan thinks. But that doesn't make him like the king any more.

"How many soldiers do you have?" Vlad Dracul asks.

"Sixteen thousand. And we're getting stronger every day. As we liberate the Ottoman territories, people pick up their weapons and join us everywhere. Bulgarians, Armenians, Croatians. More and more each day."

"Murad's going to have sixty thousand. And they aren't peasants who grab their ax and sickle to go to war. They're the best trained, best equipped, and most disciplined troops in the world."

"Murad resigned. He's somewhere in Anatolia, reading the Quran and guarding sheep. Mehmet is the sultan now. And he's only twelve and inexperienced."

"Really? And how experienced are you, may I ask? And what do you think Murad will do when he hears you've started a crusade? He'll come back faster than you can say Merry Christmas."

Władysław laughs.

"You obviously don't know. We blocked the Dardanelles. He can't come back from Anatolia, even if he wants to. He's stuck."

"You blocked the Dardanelles? How so?"

"With the Venetians and Genoese ships."

"So you haven't blocked the Dardanelles. They have. And they're a bunch of greedy bastards who hate each other. Murad will play them against each other and appeal to their greed. One or the other will let him through."

"They won't. The pope sent them. They are Christianity's soldiers, and they'd never break their vow, like I wouldn't. I vowed to the pope that I will lead the last crusade. We'll throw the Ottomans out of Europe and unlock Constantinople. And, God willing, we'll unify the Christian religions under the pope. Constantine promised that he'll convert to Catholicism. He, and the whole Byzantine Empire. There is no worthier goal."

Vlad's heavy eyes turn to Hunyadi.

"Now I get it. All but one thing. What did they promise you?"

Hunyadi shrugs and pours Vlad another cup of wine.

Vlad drains it and looks at the king.

"Your calculations are based on faith and hope. They're nice things, faith and hope, but they don't win wars. To win wars you need armies, equipment, and planning. Your army is barely a quarter of the Ottoman's. Your troops aren't either equipped nor trained like the janissaries are. The one thing you have going for you is this." He nods to Hunyadi. "You have the wisdom and the experience of the best general in the west. He's beaten me before, and he's likely to beat me again if he lives through this. Listen to him. I don't know if he can win this, I'm afraid he can't, but I know you won't. The one sure way to lose this battle is to go against his advice. Got that?"

Władysław's mouth narrows with spite as he glares at Vlad, but he doesn't answer.

Vlad turns to Mircea. "You still want to do this?"

His eyes bright, his cheeks flushed, Mircea nods. His heart burns with his thirst for glory.

Vlad sighs. All of a sudden, he looks old. His eyes meet Hunyadi's.

"You know this is a mistake. But you can't go back."

Hunyadi sips, his face inscrutable.

"Fortunately, I can. I leave you Mircea with four thousand men."

"But Father, you said six thousand."

"That was when I thought you people had a chance. I'll take the others home. I wish you luck. You'll need it."

He stands and nods to Hunyadi without even glancing at the king, then turns to leave.

"Vlad."

He stops.

"I'll do my best to take care of your son," Hunyadi says.

"And my men."

"And your men."

Vlad nods and leaves.

Mircea and Ștefan follow him, but Ștefan's heart is heavy. He didn't understand everything that happened, but his excitement vanished. He shivers, feeling that something terrible is about to happen.

CHAPTER 72

TWO BETRAYALS

EDIRNE

It's late. Edirne Palace is quiet but for the water whispering in the fountains, and the distant clatter of metal against metal as the armed guards walk by the door. It must be close to midnight when heavy steps wake up the sultan.

Mehmet grabs the dagger he keeps under his pillow. He's got his guards, but people's lives are cheap these days. Sultans' lives, too. His older brother died unexpectedly, and he'd be foolish to not be ready.

A knock, and the guard opens the door. Çandarlı Paşa steps in and falls to the ground, prostrating himself like never before.

Mehmet slips the dagger back under the pillow and sits up.

"Çandarlı Paşa. What a surprise. I hope you're here to tell me the name I asked for?"

"Yes, my sultan."

"Speak up."

"Our spy is a woman. Her name is Rózsa Fehér, Black Rose. She's the chambermaid of Erzsébet Szilágyi, John Hunyadi's wife."

"Really!"

"Yes. Rózsa has been with us for almost ten years. Her mistress trusts her, and tells her things she wouldn't share with anyone else."

"Why is she working for us?"

"She doesn't like Hunyadi. And she likes money."

"I see. Do you have proof?"

The vizier hands him a tattered parchment. "Hunyadi and Władysław met with Vlad Dracul in Nikopol. Vlad didn't join but he left his son Mircea and four thousand Wallachians. Their troops are heading to Varna."

"I see. That wasn't so hard, was it, Paşa?"

Çandarlı Paşa looks down.

"So what do you think we should do?"

"If only we could bring our Anatolian troops to Varna."

"Good idea. Let's do that."

"We can't."

"Why not?"

"The Venetian and the Genoese blocked the Dardanelles with their ships. We're completely cut off from Anatolia."

"Really? When?"

"A week ago."

"And why, pray tell, didn't you tell me sooner?"

"My sultan, you forbade me from talking to you until I tell you the name of my informer."

"So I did."

Mehmet thinks hard, but the only thing that comes to mind is that his plans to take Constantinople are thwarted. He's spent so many days and nights preparing, and, for now, that's out of the question. He must first address the threat from the west.

"What do you think Hunyadi's planning?"

"Their purpose is to occupy our territories south of the Danube and throw us out of Europe. That would unlock Constantinople from our grasp. And right now, between the blocked Dardanelles Strait and the Constantinople's grasp over Bosporus, our empire is effectively cut in two."

Mehmet sighs.

"How many troops do we have here?"

"Almost forty thousand. But, if you recall, my sultan, the janissaries haven't been paid, and they aren't happy. Our troops are in a bad place."

"Let's pay them then."

"We can't. Right now, we're strapped for cash."

"Why is that?"

"The truce that Sultan Murad signed with Hunyadi wasn't cheap. Add to that the many weeks of lavish ceremonies for your coronation, the low taxes, and the fact that neither the Serbs nor the Wallachians have paid their tribute this year. The treasury is empty."

"Well, then. Let's tell the janissaries we'll pay them next year."

"I'm afraid the promise won't be good enough, Your Highness. And there's one more problem."

"What?"

"The Karamanids are laying low right now, since Sultan Murad signed the peace treaty. But once they hear that we're at war with the crusaders and, with the Dardanelles closed, we're effectively cut off from Anatolia, they'll start making trouble."

Mehmet doesn't like this. No matter what he wants, he can't do. No matter what he tries, there's something to ruin it. Every direction he goes to, there's an obstacle. He's been sultan for only two months, and things are falling apart right and left. How the heck did Father do this?

"How did Father manage all this?"

"He was Sultan Murad. Twenty years in the saddle in battle after battle earned him the trust and love of the troops, the respect of his allies, and the fear of his enemies. You've only been sultan for two months."

"Still, how did he manage?"

"I don't know, my sultan. Somehow, he always figured out a way. That's why he's such a great general."

Mehmet sighs. There seems to be only one thing to do.

"Let's call him back."

Çandarlı Paşa's face lights up.

"Good idea, my sultan."

"Good. Çandarlı Paşa, before the night is over, send a messenger to Father and ask him to come back."

The light in the vizier's face vanishes.

"I'm sorry, my sultan..."

"What?"

"You'll have to do this yourself."

"What are you saying?"

"My sultan, I just returned from Anatolia. I went to ask your father to return. He refused."

Mehmet is crushed.

"You mean you went to see my father and asked him to return without speaking to me?"

The vizier prostrates so low that his forehead touches the carpet, but the answer still sucks.

"Yes, my sultan. You told me not to speak to you, no matter what, until I gave you the name of my informant. I couldn't do that. The one thing I could think about to save the empire was to call back your father."

He's technically correct, Çandarlı Paşa, but that doesn't do much for Mehmet. He feels betrayed, and he's so angry that he could kill the paşa on the spot. But he refrains. He'll do it someday. Not today.

He takes a deep breath. "What did Father say?"

"Your father told me that you are the sultan, and I should speak to you. That's why I came and gave you my informer's name. He also said that, after more than twenty years of war, he's earned his life of meditation and prayer. It's time for you to earn your title in battle."

Mehmet is baffled. Two betrayals in one, from the two people who are supposed to do anything to save the empire. The vizier, who betrayed him by going to his father behind his back. His father, who refused to come to help him save the realm in this time of utter need.

He has to figure out what to do, and he'd better do it soon. And, other than cutting Çandarlı Paşa's throat, he can't think of anything else he wants to do.

CHAPTER 73

SULTAN TO SULTAN

EDIRNE

This night has no end.

Mehmet twists and turns. He drinks fresh water. He paces. He has the eunuchs fan him as he lies in his lavender-scented bed. But nothing helps him rest. Endless thoughts about all the threats menacing the Ottoman Empire, his inability to handle them, and the grand vizier's betrayal torment him through the night. But the worst of all is his father's refusal to help. How could he do that?

Angry, muddled thoughts swirl through his mind, chasing each other. No matter what, he can't get his head in order. When the sky finally fades, he's glad that this night is over. He does his ablutions and his morning prayer, then sends for Radu.

The kid enters the room dwarfed by janissaries. He's pale and tired, and smaller than Mehmet remembers him, maybe because the question of his betrayal loomed so large in Mehmet's head. But he's as handsome as ever, with his silky blond hair, rose-petal skin and clear blue eyes, so wide that one can see the white all around them. He's scared, and Mehmet realizes that Radu doesn't know why he's here. He must be worried he's about to lose his head.

"Come sit with me."

The sultan takes his hand. "I'm glad you're back."

Radu's face shifts from terror to doubt, then delight. He smiles. "Me too."

Mehmet looks around at the janissaries, windows, and open doors. He remembers what Çandarlı Paşa told him: "These walls have ears." He can't have anyone hear what he's about to say. It's hard enough to tell Radu, who looks at Mehmet like he's God and won't judge him. He can't have the janissaries and the eunuchs listen in and tell others. He's been humiliated enough. He doesn't want the palace to know, and he surely doesn't need his enemies to know either.

"Let's go for a walk."

The janissaries follow them as they walk hand in hand along the corridors to the rose gardens that Radu loves. He loves listening to the fountains and writing poems about blooms, but today is not about that. Mehmet needs Radu as a soundboard to set his mind straight and decide what to do.

He signals the guards to stay far behind as they walk to a marble bench tucked under the grand old planetree, the most magnificent tree of the empire. Some say that's the tree that grew from Osman's breast, the founder of the Ottoman Empire. It may be just a legend, but Mehmet still loves the old tree with its generous shade, and the song of the wind through the leaves that have just started turning.

Mehmet tells Radu the story.

"Çandarlı Paşa went, without my permission, to call Father back. And Father said he isn't coming. I'm on my own."

"Not quite, my sultan. You have your janissaries and the vizier, the dignitaries, and the validé. And me."

"Thank you, Radu. Still, what would you do?"

"My sultan, you are wise and brave beyond your years. I'm not. But you're still so young. You've only been sultan for a couple of months. There's much to learn in the business of politics and war. I think you should call your father back, watch him, and learn from him."

"But he said he's not coming."

"He didn't. He sent away the vizier because he didn't want to interfere with you. You are the sultan now. If Sultan Murad came back without *you* asking him, it would look like he withdrew the trust he placed in you when he made you sultan. He must be expecting your call. He's fought for the empire his entire life. He wouldn't desert it now. And he wouldn't desert you."

"You think he'll come?"

"I have no doubt. But you have to make it clear that you need and want him back."

"How about the vizier?"

Radu shrugs. "He did what you told him to, my sultan. And what he thought was for the good of the country. He even gave you the name of his spy."

"That's true. Can you imagine that? This woman, their chambermaid for years, betraying them for money? It's unbelievable that somebody close to you could do something like that, and you wouldn't even know it."

"Yes. About my father."

"Yes."

"I thought he went to war against you even as I was here as a guarantee of his faith. I'm glad he didn't."

"Me too," Mehmet says, caressing Radu's long blond hair. "Me too. But I wish he didn't send your brother either."

That evening the sultan sits alone in his father's old study, remembering Radu's advice. His sharp quill squeaks and scratches the parchment, as his words flow onto the page.

Dear Father,

The Empire needs you. I need you.

If you're the sultan, please come back and lead your armies through this war.

If I am the sultan, I command you to come and lead my armies through this war.

Your loving son,

Mehmet

He rolls the parchment, seals it with red wax, and hands it to the messenger who'll take it to Anatolia. It shouldn't take more than a few days to get there and back. If Father decides to come back, it shouldn't take more than a week.

Mehmet is happy to get this worry off his chest. He's heading to bed when he remembers that the Dardanelles Strait is blocked, so Anatolia is effectively cut off from Rumelia. How could Father return with the troops, even if he wants to?

And, just like that, the lightness in his heart vanishes like it never was.

CHAPTER 74

A MUDDY MARCH

PODGORICA, BULGARIA, OCTOBER 1444

Just south of the Danube, in what used to be the country of Bulgaria but it's now part of Rumelia, the European half of the Ottoman Empire, the fall has passed its peak. The days are gray, the endless fields brown and bare, and the tree branches lost their leaves and clutch the sky like angry claws. Every day is shorter and every morning colder than the last. It's almost November as the crusaders march east towards the Black Sea.

They've been riding for weeks, and Ștefan's excitement has dwindled. This isn't the war he imagined. He was dreaming of fighting the infidels and covering himself with glory. He could almost see Hunyadi, resplendent in his white Milanese armor, bowing in front of him.

"We'd never be here without you, Ștefan. Thank you for saving my life. I wish I could reward you for everything you have done for Christianity and for me."

Ștefan would smile modestly. "Just knowing that I did my job is good enough, old boy. I'm happy to be of service."

Instead of that, there's been nothing but day after day of riding over muddy roads, through gloomy forests and empty villages. He's tired of being dirty and cold, sleeping on the bare ground, and eating half-cooked chickens stolen from somebody's yard. Weary of watching their men pillage village after village, stealing their food and raping the women. He has yet to forget how it felt to have a man push himself on him.

"We're stopping for the night," Mircea says. He's riding ahead of Ștefan, and he looks just as miserable as Ștefan feels. They may not talk much, but Ștefan knows that Mircea's ardor has faded too.

The men stop, dismount, and start building their camp. They lift tents, gather wood, build fires, and kill the sheep they took from the last village. They skin them, empty them and leave the tangled bowels on the ground for the crows and the dogs.

One of Władysław's men stops by Mircea. "The king wants you."

Mircea signals Ștefan to join him. They walk to the mud-splattered silk tent where the King and Hunyadi hold counsel every night. They step inside the thick silence and sip on the wine they've been offered, waiting for the king to talk.

Władysław empties his cup and slams it on the table. He looks at Mircea.

"We're doing good, aren't we? We should be there in less than a week."

Hunyadi's brow furrows. He speaks without looking at the king.

"We were supposed to be there by now. Every delay makes it more likely that Mehmet's going to come up with something."

"Come on, John. What can he come up with? He's stuck. You heard what the spies said. The Ottomans know we're coming, and they're fleeing Edirne in droves. Mehmet's janissaries revolted and burned down half of the city. Some Persian prophet predicted there'll be no war, and the crowds worship him. Mehmet himself invited him to the palace, but the grand vizier managed to catch him and burned him. The sultan and the grand vizier are at odds, and they butt heads at every step. I wouldn't be surprised if Mehmet himself decided to flee. Wouldn't that be something? We might walk into Varna, then sail into Constantinople unchallenged."

Hunyadi drains his cup and fills it again.

"I wish it was that easy. But it's not. Ever since Nikopol, each day has been harder than the last. Village after village became less happy to see us. The local resistance has grown. In the last three villages, not one man took up his weapons to join us."

The king pinches his lips like he smelled something nasty.

"That's your fault. I told you to keep your men in check. You shouldn't let them run loose and pillage. If you only hang a couple, the others would start to behave."

"The men need to eat. That's why they pillage. It's been weeks since we left home, and we're running out of everything, especially meat. And a leader can't hang his soldiers. Who would ever come to fight alongside you if they hear that you hang your own men?"

Władysław shrugs.

"Common, John! They're just peasants. It's not like they're high born! You'd only have to hang a few to set an example for the others. They should pay for the sheep instead of stealing them. And hunger is not a reason to rape the women and set the people's homes on fire."

"My men are tired, miserable, and angry. That pent-up rage has to go somewhere. And they've been away from their women for months."

Ștefan stares from one to the other. The two champions of Christianity don't seem to agree about much. He wonders what that means for the fights still to come, and he hopes the king is right, and there won't be any.

Mircea tries to break the tension.

"Where did you hear all that? Edirne revolting and burning, and Mehmet at odds with the vizier?"

"We have our own people at the castle who keep us updated on the sultan's moves," Hunyadi says, then turns back to the king.

"The peasants are the foundation of our country and our army. They deserve gratitude, love, and respect."

"Oh, please! Spare me the propaganda. There's nobody here but us. You know as well as I do, they're nothing but a filthy mob ready to go off at the slightest provocation. Or even without. Look at what they did to those villages. Are you going to curb them or not?"

Hunyadi's glare makes Ștefan tremble, but the king is made of tougher stuff. He smiles and says:

"Remember the Crown of Bulgaria? Still want it?"

When the boys head back to their quarters, Ștefan asks Mircea. "What do you think?"

Mircea shrugs. "That's not how I imagined greatness."

"Me neither."

"I hope they get their act together when we get to fight. If they keep butting heads, it will be a disaster."

"You think what they said about the sultan and Edirne is true?"

"Maybe. But don't forget it takes weeks for the news to reach us. Whatever was true then may not be true now. And I don't think Mehmet sits on his throne, shivering with fear that we're coming. I bet Murad isn't, either. Whatever they're doing won't do us any good."

"What can we do, then?"

Mircea shrugs. "Pray. And get there before it's too late."

CHAPTER 75
YOU'LL JOIN THE SULTAN
EDIRNE, OCTOBER 1444

Further south, in Edirne, the fall is about to turn into winter. The sun's still got power at noon, but in the early mornings, like now, it's cold enough to see your breath. The morning prayer's over, and Ali shivers as she carries in the food from the kitchens. It's a heavy tray loaded with fresh bread, hot morning soup, cheese, olives and grapes. She's relieved to set it in the middle of Hüma's carpet and steps back.

"Stay," Hüma says. She turns to Lena. "You too. Everybody else, out."

Ali's heart flutters. It's been a month since Lena's failed escape, and Hüma hasn't mentioned it since. Ali hoped she forgot.

"How's the wound?" Hüma asks, looking from one to the other.

"Good," Lena says.

"Let me see it."

Lena blushes but takes off her brown velvet kaftan and her white chemise. "Come here."

Hüma examines the wound, running her finger along it inch by inch. It healed well. Not much scarring left where the ugly, foot-long wound used to be. It's still pink, but it's fading, and you can barely see it unless Lena lifts her arm.

Hüma nods and glances at Ali. "Good job. Will it get better?"

"Yes, my lady. In another month or two, with the ointments I made for her, it will be just about gone."

"Good. Lena, I'm very pleased with you. All your teachers told me good things about you. They say you're proficient in the Ottoman language, you're working hard on learning the Quran, and you have a great attitude. They say that you're meek, helpful, and kind."

Ali's eyes widen. She happens to know that Lena isn't any of those things. Well, kind maybe. But meek? No way! But they both did their best to be good since the escape incident. Lena bit her tongue like never before, agreeing to the most unreasonable demands of her teachers. She sewed day and night without complaining, struggled to learn verse after verse from the Quran, and showed undue respect to her teachers. It now looks like it all paid off.

"That's why I have an extraordinary reward for you."

Lena's blue eyes light up with hope. *She's hoping that the validé will let her go*, Ali thinks. But that's nonsense. The validé can't let her go. As powerful as she is, the most powerful woman in the world, the validé is still locked in the harem. Even though she's Sultan Mehmet's mother and Sultan Murad's wife.

"You are to join the sultan tonight."

Lena stares at Huma with round eyes big as saucers. She doesn't get it.

"Sultan Mehmet doesn't yet have a harem. Not even a wife. I'm going to give you an extraordinary chance. I hope you deserve it, and you make him very happy. I wish you fertility and luck. Make me a grandson."

Lena's mouth falls agape. Ali elbows her.

Lena closes it, but she doesn't say what she should be saying. The validé thinks the girl is overwhelmed and overcome by gratitude, but Ali knows better.

"Your kindness is beyond belief, validé. She's too overwhelmed to answer, but this is an opportunity beyond her wildest dreams. She's beyond grateful."

Ali stares at Lena, urging her to speak.

"Oh, my lady, you are far too kind. I'm not worthy of such an honor. I'm just a poor Moldavian girl. I'm sure Sultan Mehmet can find much more suitable, better born, and more..."

"Sultan Mehmet will find nothing at all because Sultan Mehmet isn't looking. I am. As his mother, it's my job to make sure he's well taken care of. In every respect. And I think you're perfect."

"But, my validé, I'm..."

"Look at me."

The validé's eyes are mesmerizing. Two deep green fountains, contoured with dark kohl. They can frighten, charm, or subdue, but right now, they're warning Lena.

"I was an infidel's daughter. I was only thirteen when the sultan's men bought me for the harem. Sultan Murad had three wives and many other women. Still, one day I caught his eye, and I was lucky enough to please him and give him a son. He had other sons, but I only had this one. Still, by the grace of Allah, my son is the sultan of the Ottoman Empire, and I'm the validé. That may happen to you too if Allah thinks you're worthy. What you think doesn't matter. Go get ready."

Lena's cheeks catch fire. She bows, but doesn't leave.

She's got to get out of here before she gets in trouble, Ali thinks. She bows too, grabs Lena's hand, and heads to the door.

"Not you, Ali. You stay."

Hüma waits for Lena to be gone, then hands Ali a bag made of golden silk.

"I hope that's all you need."

Ali opens it. *The three raven tongues look fresh*, she thinks, though she's never seen a raven tongue before. The white cloth with rust-colored stains is dry, like it's been sitting for a while. And the long strand of hair, darker than the night, looks alive.

"Yes, my lady. That's it."

"When will I have the potion?"

"Remember what I asked you? You want it to work fast or slow?"

"She'll have to drink it every day, you said?"

"Yes, if you choose the slow one."

"How do I make her drink it?"

Ali remembers Smaranda's lesson.

"You need to find out what she wants."

"What do you mean?"

"What the most important thing for her? What does she covet? Why would she drink a bitter potion every day?"

"Oh, I already know that. She wants a son."

"Then it's easy. You just make her believe that drinking that potion will help her have a son."

Hüma smiles. "I'll take the slow potion. There's no big hurry since Sultan Murad is away."

"I'll have it ready in a week," Ali says, wondering what the sultan has to do with anything.

Then it dawns on her. The woman wants Sultan Murad's child, and Hüma's making sure she won't have it. She doesn't want her son to have brothers.

But who is it for? Both of Sultan Murad's wives, Halime Hatice Hatun and Mara Branković, have long dark hair. And none of them has children.

Who does Hüma Hatun want to kill?

CHAPTER 76

THE STINKY POTION

The Edirne Palace kitchens alone must be more spacious than the entire Kronstadt fortress, Ali thinks. The long gray buildings of room after room dedicated to feeding everyone in the palace, from the sultan to his women, eunuchs, and thousands of janissaries and servants string forever down the side of the back palace courtyard. And they're the palace's beating heart. Hundreds of trained cooks and their many helpers fuss over smoky fireplaces and scorching ovens, each doing what they do best. There are stew-makers smelling like mutton and pastry chefs white with flour and dairy-makers that turn fresh milk into yogurt and desert chefs whose hands are sticky with honey and so many others. Way too many for Ali to keep track.

Her tiny kitchen is attached to the soup section, and is no bigger than a cell. That's where the validé arranged for Ali to have her own private space that nobody visits uninvited. It's not much — just three steps in each direction, four brick walls with hooks and shelves where she hangs the plants she's drying, and a heavy black cauldron hanging over the fire, that bubbles and splutters, steaming a thick cloud of foul smells. The place reminds Ali of Smaranda's kitchen, but for Gigi, the crabby cat.

Ali's eyes tear as she stirs the thick dark potion with her long wooden spoon. She tries to keep away from the fumes, but she can't. The door is closed, so there's nowhere for the steam to go but swirl around again and again until she breathes it in.

She glances at the walls, wondering what else to throw in. Some mint? That should help the smell. And garlic. That's so pungent it will mask anything. And it helps with vampires.

She hasn't yet added the bloody cloth or the raven tongues, and just the thought of how those will round up the aroma makes her shudder. The smell is already so bad she's nauseous. Still, she stirs and stirs, wondering how Lena is doing.

She hopes the girl won't do anything foolish. Now, that Ali barely ever sees the boys, Lena's her only friend here. She may be headstrong and impulsive, but she's also honest, loyal, and caring, and Ali is glad to have her. Lena told her all about her parents and their flock of sheep up the mountain, and about her milk-brother Ștefan who's Alexandru the Good's grandson. That's why Ștefan's father, Bogdan, is one of the many contenders fighting for Moldova's throne.

Something stirs in Ali's mind. She's heard about Alexandru the Good before, but where?

From Mama Smaranda. She told Ali that Mother was one of the voivode's many daughters, which would make her Bogdan's sister. One of many.

But then... Ștefan must be Ali's cousin.

Out there, in Moldova, she must have a whole family she never met. Cousins and uncles and aunts. They wouldn't want anything to do with her — after all, Alexandru threw her mother out. Still, it's good to know you're not alone in the world.

She's so deep in her thoughts that she forgets to stir and burns the potion. The foul steam is gone, leaving behind the thick black smoke of charred herbs. Dang! She takes the cauldron away and opens the door to let out the smoke just as Radu gets ready to come in.

"Phew! What are you cooking? It smells disgusting!"

"I'm making a potion for Lena."

"Is she sick?"

"She has a wound that needs healing."

"I can't imagine how anything that reeks like that can heal." Radu steps in and looks around the kitchen. "Is this your place? I asked where I could find you, and they sent me here."

"Yes. The validé wants me to make some healing potions."

"How come you know how to make healing potions?"

"My grandmother was the village healer."

"Do they all smell so bad?"

"No. I forgot this one on the fire, and it burned."

"How do you get people to drink them? I wouldn't touch them with a ten-foot pole."

Radu examines the herbs and her utensils. He's about to check the basket where Ali keeps the raven tongues, the bloody cloth, and the hair when Ali steps in front of him. "You were looking for me?"

"Yes. First, I wanted to thank you. You were right. The sultan forgave me."

"I didn't do anything."

"You encouraged me and gave me hope. It turns out that my father didn't really join the crusaders, though he did allow my brother Mircea to. He and his four thousand men are heading to Varna with Hunyadi."

"How do you know?"

"Mehmet."

"How does he know?"

"Çandarlı Paşa finally relented and gave him the name of his spy at Hunyadi's court. It's apparently Hunyadi's wife's chambermaid. Can you believe that? Some people would do anything for money."

Ali's heart pumps in her chest. That's valuable information, if she can only figure out how to send it back. She's so preoccupied she almost doesn't hear Radu's words. "And second, I have a surprise for you."

Ali looks at his hands. They're empty.

"Stop by my place after the fourth prayer."

"I'll try."

"Don't be late."

'Thank you, my prince. Must get back to work now."

Radu doesn't realize that Ali's time is not her own. She's just a slave eunuch in training, subject to Hüma's orders, to the kapi agha's rules, and to the whims of the harem women. Unlike Radu, who's a hostage but also a prince, and he can do whatever he wants, whenever he wants.

Ali starts the potion all over again. She waits for the water to boil, then adds the herbs one by one. She picks the most bitter and foul-smelling she can put her hands on. She watches the steam rise and stirs carefully this time, thinking about how she can get hold of Ion or Codru to tell them the news. Mirko wants a bribe every time. One of these days, he'll check the food she sends and find the message. If he talks, that's the end of them.

She stops stirring the cauldron to write a message and hide it in her clothes, just in case she happens upon a way to deliver it.

The potion is finally ready. It's thick, dark brown, and it smells terrible. Ali stirs it once more, then takes the cauldron off the fire and sets it to the side to cool.

She opens the basket with the ingredients Hüma gave her. She picks the raven tongues and throws them in the fire. One by one, they sizzle and squirm, then turn black, releasing a smell of charred meat. Next, it's the cloth. Seconds later, is catches fire and merry flames consume its every inch. The dry blood burns last.

Ali picks up the foot-long strand of black hair, wondering who it belongs to. Hard to tell. She smells it. It smells of rose and jasmine, like all the women in the harem. It could be either of Sultan Murad's wives. Or one of the other women. But it's probably a wife. As validé, Hüma has power of life and death over the women. She could just send the eunuchs to kill them for any reason, she doesn't need to bother with Ali's potion.

Ali shrugs. She'll find out, one way or another. But for now, she drops the hair in the fire, and the long black strand writhes on the embers like it's in pain before vanishing in smoke.

CHAPTER 77
IN THE SULTAN'S BED

In the Edirne Palace's women's hammam, the steam is so thick you can hardly see. Playful rays of hazy light dart down from the round windows in the ceiling, and fat waterdrops condense on the white marble and drip in the cool pool one by one, like heartbeats. The water smells like rose and jasmine.

Lena lies face down on the marble bench, hoping they're almost done with her. Her skin burns from the scrubbing, and her body aches from the pitiless iron fingers that tried to shape her into a better version of herself. She's bathed every day ever since she came to Edirne, but she's never bathed like this.

The bath attendant flips her over. Fortunately, Lena's been here long enough to no longer care about being naked, even though she's grown curves since she left Moldova.

They scrub her stomach, her arms and her chest for the third time. They wash her hair twice with scented olive oil soap, then rinse her with hot water, then with cold until she's covered in goosebumps. They rub her with a soft white cloth to dry her. Thinking she's done, she sits up to leave, but half a dozen hands grab her and lay her back.

Time for hair removal. She lies there, wishing she'd never caught Hüma's eye, as they shave her with a sharpened clamshell, then pull out any errant hairs still left. Dehairing her every inch is a torture she didn't count on. When they're done, she tries to sit up again. But no. Now it's time for the skin-softening scented oils that make her more slippery than a wet fish. She curses softly, thinking that whatever will happen tonight in the sultan's bed can't be much worse.

She hasn't forgotten that day the posse caught her and they danced that crazy dance around her, ready to break her. She only escaped thanks to God and that old man who sunk his ax into the head of one of them to wake up the others. That memory still makes her shiver.

The bath attendant puts a soft blanket around her as they arrange her hair. They untangle it, brush it and braid it, pulling on it this way and that until Lena wonders if she's got any hair left.

They give her sandalwood sticks to chew on to clean her teeth and freshen her breath, then line her eyes with kohl. The attendants dress her in a butter-colored silk chemise that smells like lavender, a pair of sky-blue soft shalwars, and a gold-embroidered midnight-blue velvet kaftan, its large arm openings trimmed with fox. Thank God, she's ready.

Two eunuchs take her to the sultan's bedroom. The room is small and empty, but for a priceless prayer carpet and the large four-poster bed covered with red silk. They lay her in his bed and leave. Now all she has to do is wait.

Geveze, her old teacher, had told her what to do.

"When the sultan comes, stand and bow. Then remove your clothes, one by one, making sure he's watching."

Lena frowned. "So what do I do if he's not watching? You want me to shake him?"

The meek and mild Lena disappeared. Behaving didn't do her any good — look where it got her — so she went back to her unruly self.

Geveze sighed and shook her head. Thanks to her, the validé chose Lena. She hoped it wasn't a mistake. "He'll be watching. You slowly take off your kaftan, then your shalwars, then your chemise. Then lie next to him, look in his eyes, and pet him."

"Pet him? Like he's a cat?"

"Well, kind of like that. By this time, he should be taking his clothes off too. If he isn't, you can try to do that for him. But even better, caress him between his legs."

Lena's jaw dropped. "Between his legs?"

"Yes. Men like that. Even sultans. Just do it gently and wait."

"For what?"

"For him to react. Hopefully, by now, he should be up and ready, so you'd have nothing to do. Just let him do whatever he chooses to. And smile, whatever he does, even if you have a little pain. It will go away. Take a few deep breaths and relax. It will make it easier."

"Then what?"

"Then, when he's done, he'll fall asleep. If he tells you to leave, leave. The guards will take you back. If not, sleep there, and the guards will bring you back in the morning."

Lena lies in the sultan's bed, wishing she was back home in Moldavia. But she isn't. She'd better make the most of what she's got. She waits and waits. Then she has an idea: What if he hates her? He'll send her back and never want to see her again. Then she can stay in the validé's quarters and look for another chance to try to escape.

She smiles, satisfied with her idea, just as the door opens, and the sultan steps in.

They were right. He's young and handsome, with barely a dark shadow above his upper lip, red curls like his mother's and piercing green eyes who stare at her like he just found a snake in his bed.

"Who are you?"

"I'm Lena."

"What are you doing here?"

"Your mother sent me, my sultan."

"What for?"

Lens shrugs.

“What do you think? It wasn't my idea."

"Like I didn't have enough trouble already. The crusaders. The vizier. The janissaries. And now you?"

That's not the kind of reception Lena expected. She was worried about him abusing her, but that seems to be the farthest thing in his mind. He just glares at her like she's a nuisance.

Oh well. Since she’s started, she may as well go on with her plan to make him hate her and send her back. She gets out of bed and starts taking off her clothes. She drops her kaftan, then her shalwars, and checks that he's watching.

He is. Good. She takes off her chemise and stands stark naked in front of him. The next step is to cuddle him, but he's not cuddlable. He's still standing, fully clothed and wrapped in his leather armor, staring at her like she's got three ears.

"What are you doing?"

"Getting undressed."

"Why?"

"That's what they told me to do."

"What for?"

"To tempt you?"

Mehmet's mouth tightens in displeasure. Lena wonders what to do next.

“Then what?” he asks.

"I'm supposed to caress you like you were a cat."

“Are you kidding?”

“No. But you should have been horizontal by now."

"And if I'm not?"

"I don’t know. They never gave me a fallback plan. Can you lay down?"

The sultan laughs and lays down all dressed, kilij and dagger included.

"Now what?"

Lena shrugs and lies next to him. "Now, I caress you."

"Go ahead."

She tries to caress him, but it's not easy. Half of him is covered in his leather armor and tall boots. She does her best, stroking his arm, his legs, his hair. His hair is almost alive under her fingers, like a cat's fur is, sparkling in the dark.

"Now what?"

"If nothing happens, I'm supposed to caress you between your legs."

"Between my legs?"

"That's what they said."

He shrugs. “Go ahead.”

She caresses the silk-covered bump between his legs, thinking about her old cat. She’s a great mouser, Mitzi, but, like all cats, she only wanted to be touched when she chose to. But that was long ago. Lena hasn't seen Mitzi in years, and she wonders if she’s still alive.

"That’s not bad. Does that feel good to you?" Mehmet asks.

"Sure. I was thinking about my cat. I miss her."

"Would you like a new cat?"

Lena thinks, hard and fast.

"I'd much rather go back to Mitzi."

"What's next?"

"I think you're supposed to take over by now. And I should smile, comply, and never complain, even if it hurts. It's for my good and the good of the empire."

"And then?"

"Then, if you send me off, I should get out and have the guard take me back. If not, I'm supposed to sleep here, and they'll take me back tomorrow."

"Tell me about you, Lena."

Lena shrugs. "There isn't much. I'm a poor girl from Moldavia. My parents are sheepherders. I got caught by the Ottoman guards who brought me to the harem. Then your grandmother, Emine Validé, gave me to your mother. Your mother, in her wisdom, sent me to you."

"How long ago did you join the harem?"

"A year something? Maybe two?"

"If you had a choice — I'm not saying you do — but if you had a choice, what would you like to do?"

"I want to go home."

"Why?"

“There, I’m free. I can go wherever I want, do whatever I want, and live my life the way I chose to. It's not a rich life, but I have choices, and that's important to me. Here, nobody cares what I think, what I want, or what's going to happen to me."

"So you'd rather go home than be the next validé, the most important woman in the world?"

Lena nods. "I don't care about power. I care about freedom. The validé is not free."

Mehmet looks at her like he sees her. The person. Not the slave. Just her. He moves her hand away from his groin, but he doesn't let go of it.

"How about a deal?"

"A deal?"

"Yes. I don't need a girl. In between the crusade, the janissaries' revolts, and my family struggles, Allah knows there are few things I need less. But if I send you back, my mother will send me another girl before I can catch my breath. Then I'll have to deal with someone looking to become validé. I can't deal with that just now. I'll make you an offer."

Lena wonders how weird this all is. She's laying naked in the sultan's bed, and he hasn't touched her, but he's about to make her an offer.

"Yes, Sultan?"

"I'm not into girls. You are beautiful, but you're not my type, and I'm way too busy. But my mother doesn't care. If I send you back, she'll send another, then another, hoping to get a şehzade. How about you stick around for a while? You'll be my cover. As soon as I can, maybe a year or two, I'll let you go. I'll release you to go back home to Moldavia. In the meantime, I get a few months of a much-needed break."

Isn't that something? Lena thinks. What a plan! Truth be told, he's so handsome that she wouldn't mind going through the motions, but he's not interested. Oh well. As long as he lets her go...

"What am I supposed to do?"

"Sleep here. Pretend we had sex. Come back whenever I call you."

"Anything else?"

"I sure hope you don't snore."

Lena laughs. She puts on her chemise, then gets under the covers.

"I'd take that armor off if I were you."

CHAPTER 78

A FATED FEAST

EDIRNE OCT 1444

Edirne Palace zooms like a beehive in full swarm. Dozens of cooks dripping with sweat fuss around red-hot stoves, chopping, stirring, and baking. Hundreds of servants stumble under the weight of hefty coffers and baskets they load into carts. Janissaries and sipahis sharpen their kilijes and polish their helmets. The whole Edirne Palace is buzzing with some extraordinary excitement that everybody knows about. But Radu.

"What's going on?" he asks the young stable boy who's brushing his horse.

The boy shrugs. Nobody at the palace school knows either. He goes to Ali's kitchen, but Ali isn't there. He looks for Mehmet, but he's in a meeting with Çandarlı Paşa and other dignitaries.

Oh well. Radu gives up. He goes to take a bath, hoping it will soothe him, then starts to work on his Greek homework. But he finds no solace in today's assignment, a poem about bravery. He can't understand the Trojan War. Why would two princes kill each other over Helen, no matter how beautiful she was? He shakes his head and struggles through, and he's almost done when the messenger arrives The sultan wants him.

Radu drops the Greek assignment like it's hot and follows the man to Mehmet's quarters.

The sultan's private living room is ready for a feast. Blood red roses, their heads as big as cabbages, embalm the air with their heady perfume. The flickering flames of the thick candles reflect in the gilded Venetian mirrors. Heavy silver trays bend under their load of whole fried chickens, roasted lamb with garlic and lemons, dolma with spiced meat cooked with rice, soft cheeses, figs and dates, and unruly cataifs dripping with cream and honey.

Radu's mouth waters. "Wow! What are we celebrating?"

"We're celebrating my father, may Allah forever look upon him with favor. Sultan Murad is coming back to lead our army into war. Thanks for giving me good advice, my friend."

Mehmet fills two silver cups. He gives one to Radu and sips from the other.

Radu expects the usual sherbet, but it isn't. It's wine. In Wallachia, they served wine with every meal, even to kids, albeit cut with water, but here at the Ottoman court? Radu has never seen wine here. Not even for Mehmet's coronation. He thought that Allah was against pleasure-inducing drinks.

"This is good wine," Radu says.

Mehmet's eyes sparkle, and Radu wonders if he's on his second cup.

"I got it from Moldova. I didn't know their wine was so good. Otherwise, I'd have planned to invade them rather than Constantinople."

Radu laughs, hoping he's kidding. Now that the weight of the empire fell off his shoulders, Mehmet looks like a kid set free. He puts his arm around Radu's shoulders and leads him to the brocade pillows scattered on the floor. They drink, laugh and enjoy the heavenly food, their arms touching.

The sultan unsheathes his precious dagger to slice a chunk of roasted lamb and eats it delicately off its tip, as the custom dictates. Radu cuts a juicy slice of golden chicken with his own blade, he stabs it and bites little pieces. They rest their food on thick slices of crusty bread and wipe their hands on soft cotton cloths to sip on the wine the eunuchs rush to replenish.

"I'm leaving tomorrow," Mehmet says.

Radu's heart freezes. "Leaving? Where?"

"To war, of course. I'm going to meet Father and his army."

"But why? I thought Sultan Murad was leading the army."

"He is. But I'm the sultan. I have to be where my soldiers are. And I need to learn."

"When will you be back?"

Mehmet shrugs. "Whenever Allah wants me to. IF Allah wants me to."

Radu's heart sinks. He can't lose his best friend. His only friend.

"Can I come with you?"

“Oh, how I wish you could. But you're the enemy, remember? Your brother Mircea is one of the crusade's leaders. I know it's not your fault, but what will Father say? And the troops."

That may be true, but it’s hard to take. Radu sips on his wine, his heart in turmoil.

"So, you're leaving tomorrow?"

The sultan nods. "How do you feel about it?"

"I've never been so excited. I've studied battles since I was a child, but I've never been to a real one. Until now. I can't wait."

Mehmet’s eyes sparkle, and his cheeks flush with excitement. Radu wishes he could share his joy, but he can’t. He feels abandoned.

His best friend is leaving. The one person on earth who likes him just the way he is — a lame warrior, a lousy hunter, a poor hawker. He's not as good as Vlad at anything but for poetry, music, and Greek. But who cares about those? Nobody gives a hoot about poetry, music, and Greek. Especially not during a war.

“I'll miss you,” he whispers, taking another sip from his cup.

"I'll miss you, too."

Mehmet looks at him with loving eyes. His fingers touch Radu's face, trace his cheek, his chin, his lips. The fingers run down, soft as a feather, along his neck, then caress his hair. Mehmet breathes fast, like he's been running, and Radu wonders if he's feeling unwell.

Mehmet's lips touch Radu's ear and he whispers: "Come with me."

CHAPTER 79
THE ART OF PAIN
TOKAT, OCTOBER 1444

Sitting cross-legged in Tokat Castle's best room, Vlad watches Sevlet Paşa pour himself another cup of wine. He's already had quite a few. Vlad did too, but he stopped.

"I can't drink like you do, paşa. The wine goes straight to my head, and I fall asleep. My father's a good drinker," Vlad says, even though Vlad Dracul barely ever touches wine, "but he doesn't compare with you. In fact, I've never seen anyone who does. All this wine, and you're as sharp as if you've had nothing but water."

Vlad's lying, of course. The governor's eyes are heavy, and his tongue is thick and slow. But, emboldened by Vlad's praise, he empties the cup and pours another.

This has been their nightly routine for months now, ever since Vlad managed to endear himself to him and became a beloved guest. He's lonely, the governor. His family isn't here, since this is a fortress and a prison, not a place for women and children. They live in Amasya, hundreds of miles away, and he misses them, even though he goes to visit them every month.

"I've got nobody to talk to, here. The guards are just uneducated peasants. Not like you, prince. Here's to you." He lifts his cup to Vlad, then empties it and puts it on the table. Vlad fills it again.

"You've been the best thing that has happened to me since I came here. You appreciate my artistry and my work like nobody else does."

That much is true. Vlad is in awe of Sevlet Paşa's skill. He inhales his words and cherishes his lessons, and he's thrilled when the governor allows him to work on prisoners to extract information. And Vlad is an excellent student. So much so that these days the paşa mostly sits and watches, letting Vlad do the work. Like last night.

The guards brought the Hungarian messenger the sultan's troops had captured. The paşa sat and watched as Vlad secured him to the hooks and started asking questions. The man was stubborn at first, but Vlad got him talking without even cutting off his fingers.

"Where were you going?" Vlad asked.

The man shrugged.

Vlad smiled and grabbed the Pear of Anguish. He'd been partial to that tool ever since he'd seen it for the first time, but he'd never got to use it.

"Undress him."

The guards obeyed, and the man's clothes fell into a filthy pile on the floor.

"Secure him."

They shackled his feet to the hooks on the floor, four feet from each other, exposing the man's nether parts. Seeing him pale and shiver, Vlad felt a tickle between his legs.

He took the Pear of Anguish and dipped it in the bowl of sheep fat. He smiled at the paşa, and, like a good student, repeated his words one by one. "You don't want to use oil. Sure, it's easier, but we're not looking for easier. We're looking for the best. Oil is thin, and, once inside the body it gets warm and drips off, leaving you without lubrication when you need it most. Sheep fat is harder to spread, but it stays put even when it's warm, inside the subject, and continues to lubricate, making your work more efficient."

"Good job! You listen well!"

"I listen to every word you tell me, paşa. I've never met a man I'd rather emulate than you."

Vlad spread the fat over the pear with his finger, making sure the man could see it. Then he opened the pear all the way, until it looked like a blooming lotus.

"You know where this goes?"

The man shook his head.

"I'm about to show you. Do you remember where you were going?"

The man stayed quiet.

Vlad shrugged. He closed the pear back to its pear shape. He dipped his fingers in sheep fat, reached the man's back side, and greased it. The man shivered.

"You remember now?"

The man's maddened eyes looked from Vlad to the paşa and back. "Please," he said, "please."

"It's up to you, man. You only have to talk."

"Please!"

Vlad sighed like he was sorry to have to do that. His finger found the hole.

"Do I need to cut it open first?" he asked the paşa.

"Not for the pear. Only for the stake."

Vlad nods. With a slow, gentle move, he pushed the Pear of Anguish inside the man.

A terrible scream splintered the air, making the dungeon tremble. It echoed against the stone walls that reflected it again and again. The prisoners in the cells joined the chorus.

Vlad waited until the noise died down, then a little more.

He smiled at the man, wishing he could stroke the bulge in his own pants.

"Remember what I showed you? What happens next? How this opens?"

"To the Dardanelles," the man says.

Vlad is disappointed that the man caved so fast. But he's got time. This is just the beginning.

"Why?"

"Hunyadi sent me to talk to the Venetians and the Genoese."

"Venetians and Genoese? At the Dardanelles?"

"Yes."

"I don't believe you." Vlad reached for the screw that opened the pear."

"I swear! I swear! The Venetians and the Genovese are there, blocking the Strait with their ships! They're closing the Dardanelles to defend the crusader's advance to Varna, then Constantinople."

"Crusaders?"

"Yes. Hunyadi of Hungary and Władysław of Poland and Mircea of Wallachia. With almost twenty thousand men."

Vlad's jaw dropped. His brother? His brother advancing with the crusaders towards Constantinople? That's wonderful news. Also awful news. First, because Vlad isn't there to fight with them. Even worse: if that's true, the sultan is about to see to him being executed. They'll execute Radu too, but that hardly makes it any better.

"Why don't you start over. Where are the Christians?"

"I don't know where they are now. When I left them, they had just passed Nikopol heading to Varna."

"When was that?"

"Ten days ago."

"What are you supposed to tell the Venetian and the Genoese?"

"That there may be some delays, but the troops are coming and they should stay put. No matter what, keep the Strait to prevent Sultan Murad and his troops from returning from Anatolia."

Vlad returned to the governor.

"What do you think, paşa?"

"I think that's important enough that we should send messengers to the sultan right now. He needs to know."

The paşa looked at Vlad, and his eyes narrowed. *He's just remembered that I'm not one of his soldiers*, Vlad thinks. *Quite the opposite. I'm the brother of one of the crusaders and Sevlet Paşa's prisoner. I shouldn't be hearing this, let alone interrogate the prisoner.*

He's right.

"Let's go. That's enough for tonight," the paşa said.

Vlad twisted and turned that whole night, trying to decide what to do. But the answer's easy, really. He must escape.

CHAPTER 80

WILL YOU MISS ME?

EDIRNE OCT 1444

Back in the Edirne Palace, Mehmet and Radu walk hand-in-hand to the sultan's bedroom. Standing high in the corners, four thick white candles light the room, throwing deep shadows across the ceiling and dancing patterns on the marble floor. The room is bare, but for the bed, a chest, and the prayer carpet.

Of course, it is. Unlike Radu's bedroom, this is just one of the sultan's many rooms. Mehmet has study rooms and sitting rooms and audience rooms and a throne room, besides many others. The only thing the sultan does here is sleep. And pray.

Radu wonders why they came here. For prayer, maybe? He'd rather wait outside, since, unlike Mehmet, he's not a Muslim. He's Orthodox Christian, and he doesn't know how to pray to Allah. And he doesn't want to.

They sit side-by-side on the red-covered bed. Mehmet holds Radu's hand and sinks his eyes in his, and there's something there that Radu hasn't seen before. He doesn't know what it is, but it doesn't feel right. His blood warms his cheeks, and he looks away.

"Look at me."

Mehmet's voice is low and thick. *It must be the wine,* Radu thinks, struggling to hold his eyes.

"Are you going to miss me?"

"Of course," Radu says, though right now he's not so sure.

"How much are you going to miss me?"

Radu sighs, wishing he was elsewhere. This is worse than being with Vlad, who's always nasty. Mehmet isn't mean, but he's strange, and far too close for comfort. And there's something odd about him today. Maybe the stress of going to war? He's never been clingy before.

"A lot," Radu says, then walks into the other room to bring more wine. He hands Mehmet a cup and stands like he wants to study the prayer carpet, which is amazingly beautiful and very old, with spots worn out by the knees of many sultans.

"It's beautiful."

"You are beautiful. Come here and sit with me."

Radu can't say no. He sits as far from Mehmet as the bed will allow, but it's not far enough. Mehmet scoots closer and puts his arms around his shoulders, then starts playing with his hair. His cheeks are flushed, and he's breathing hard as he moves even closer to Radu, whose heart beats to jump out of his chest.

His eyes half-closed, Mehmet's lips touch Radu's.

Radu's heart stops. He explodes out of bed, and darts to the door, trying to pretend that nothing happened, but he's trapped. He wonders how to get out of here without hurting Mehmet's feelings. His guts tell him that something's really wrong, even though he doesn't know precisely what. But if he escapes, maybe Mehmet will sleep it off, and everything will be back to normal tomorrow.

"I have to go. I haven't finished my Greek homework for tomorrow."

"Don't worry about that. There's no school tomorrow. Come here."

Radu doesn't want to. Every fiber in his body tells him he shouldn't.

"I also have to feed my cat. I really need to go."

"Nonsense."

Mehmet walks to Radu. He embraces him, pulling him close. He's done it many times before, but never like this. His breath is fast and shallow like he's been running, and his heart beats frantically.

"I love you," Mehmet says. He lowers his mouth to Radu's and his hands slide down inside Radu's shalwars. Then Mehmet's tongue slips inside Radu's mouth, and Radu loses it.

His brain goes black. He forgets that this is Mehmet, his best friend. He forgets that he is the sultan. He forgets everything but this terrible assault over his body, which he can't take. He must escape.

He unsheathes his dagger and buries it in Mehmet.

The blood-curdling scream shakes the palace. Four janissaries rush in to kneel at Mehmet's side as he flounders in a pool of blood on the floor.

Radu takes off like an arrow, running faster than ever before. He cuts through the living room, jumping over the leftovers of their feast, out through the door, down the marble hallway that leads to the gardens. He hears the janissaries run after him, screaming. They shout at him to stop, and call for others to help catch him.

Radu doesn't stop. He flies through one empty room after another until he stumbles over somebody's leg. They meant to stop him, and he's about to fall, but he steadies himself and keeps running past another open space, through another corridor.

The janissaries behind him get closer and closer. "Catch him! Stop him! He attacked the sultan."

He runs and runs until he's on the last hallway before the gardens, where there are trees, bushes and places to hide. Just as he nears the end, he sees a silhouette cutting his retreat. But he can't go back, so he runs even faster.

It's Ali carrying a loaded tray. The eunuch sees him, and moves against the wall to let him pass. Radu's off into the garden when he hears the clatter of the tray hitting the floor and the janissaries swear, fumble and fall.

He heads towards the beautiful planetree, the tree from Osman's dream, the king of the trees in the sultan's garden. Radu climbs as fast as he can. Higher, higher, and higher. By the time a hundred janissaries light the gardens with their torches, he's out of sight in a tall forked branch.

He steadies himself and catches his breath. Now, that he has time to think, he wonders what the heck just happened. What went wrong with Mehmet? Has he lost his mind? He's always been like a loving older brother, and now this? Was he too drunk to know what he was doing? Radu has seen plenty of drunks doing stupid things, but never like this. It's like he's a woman, for God's sake! He's seen the drunk boyars in Târgoviște touching the servants like they shouldn't have, but those were women!

He wonders if he killed Mehmet. He never killed anyone yet, and he didn't have time to think, so he just stabbed wherever he could. Maybe he should have been more careful. He could have stabbed him in a leg, to avoid killing him. Or just the opposite, cut his throat and kill him, to help his father, his country and the crusaders. The Ottomans would kill him of course, but they will anyhow. He stabbed the sultan. What else are they going to do? Congratulate him?

And there's nowhere to run. He's inside the Edirne Castle, and there is no way out but through the gates, and they're all guarded by janissaries. And he has no help. Though Ali... He knows he didn't touch him. He was way past him when the tray fell. Did he drop it to slow the janissaries and give him time to escape? Either way, what can a little eunuch do? What can anybody do, for that matter? He's doomed. He may as well get down and let them get on with it. How long can he stay in this tree? He's thirsty already, and cold. And tired, but he's afraid to fall asleep. He'd fall off.

He finds a fork in the tree where he can sit on a branch and hug the trunk. He unties his belt and ties it around the trunk to hold him up if he falls asleep. Thankfully, he's so high up that the branches are slender, so the belt is long enough. Barely.

He cries himself to sleep.

He wakes up shivering. He's cold, but there's more. Something's moving in the branches, and Radu's heart starts pumping. Are there wild animals here? He stares, but he can't see much in the dark. Then he spots a pair of glowing eyes, and shudders. He'd fall if he wasn't tied to the trunk.

He fumbles to release the buckle and run as the glowing eyes get closer.

"Miaow!"

Radu laughs and cries as he hugs Sari.

CHAPTER 81

VLAD'S ESCAPE

Up in the tower of the feared Tokat Castle, Vlad's getting ready to escape. Sevlet Paşa is drunk as a skunk, and the guards left them long ago. Some went to relieve those who watch the prisoners, some went to sleep. There are a couple at the castle gates, but not many. There's no need, since here, at Tokat Castle, nobody wants in.

When the paşa's head falls on the table and his snoring rattles the stone walls, Vlad knows it's time. He takes off the paşa's kaftan and his turban and puts them on, then grabs his kilij and dagger. The kaftan's way too big, since Vlad is small and wiry while the paşa is a big man, but, in the dark, it will have to do.

He glances at the paşa. Should he kill him? It would be easy. The man is so drunk he wouldn't even know he died. But he remembers everything the paşa taught him, and decides to spare his life.

He heads to the gate, where the guards are chatting. They don't notice him until he's close. They must think he's the paşa, coming to inspect them so they stand straight, their arms to the side as Vlad gets close. By the time they realize their mistake, it's too late. The kilij whistles, and the head of the guard on the right falls to his feet before he has time to scream. The guard on the left gasps as the dagger slices his throat, then crumbles to the ground.

Vlad starts down the steep, dangerous steps towards the dungeons, then further down the mountain on the trail that's too steep for horses. That's why they keep the horses down in the meadows at the foot of the mountain, and they use mules to bring up the supplies.

The moonlight is scarce, and Vlad struggles to guess the precarious steps. He puts one careful foot ahead the other, wondering how much time he's got left. If he's lucky, nobody will notice anything until the changing of the guard, at the first prayer. That would give him almost six hours. If he's not lucky... Oh well. There's no point in worrying about that now.

The mighty Tokat Castle is nestled high inside Anatolia's mountains, hundreds of miles inside the Ottoman Empire's Asian half. And that's goddamn far from any place Vlad would like to be.

Varna would be best, since that's where crusaders are going to fight, but he'll even take the Dardanelles. Except that nobody offered them to him. Those hundreds of miles mean days and days of walking through this hostile land he doesn't know, with the Ottomans on his tail. That's no good.

He decides to head straight north to Ünye, a tiny fishing village on the Black Sea's southern shore. If he makes it there, he'll find a ship to take him to Varna one way or another. He can pay — he's got the paşa's purse — or stowaway for the crossing. His chances aren't great, but they're no worse than if he stayed here to wait for his execution.

Vlad takes the last step and he's down in the meadow now. Time to grab a horse. But they're guarded. And they have no saddle and no reins.

Darn. How about the caravanserai? The paşa said it's just half a mile away. They've got to have horses and tackle, since that's what they do. The inn is the exchange point for the travelers going to Amasya and Bursa, and it won't be guarded like Tokat Castle is.

Sure enough, the place is easy to find, since a torch lights the door to guide late travelers. Vlad grabs it and looks for the stables. He opens the door and stumbles upon something on the floor. It's a kid, about Radu's age, who sleeps in the hay to keep an eye on the horses.

The kid's eyes open wide as the dagger's blade slices his windpipe.

Vlad drops him back to the hay bed like he's still asleep. There's not much noise, but the horses still hear it. They smell the blood, and they don't like it. Nor do they like the torch, so they start whinnying and stomping in their stalls in protest. But Vlad doesn't care.

He chooses the black one with a white star on his forehead, thinking it's a good omen. He slips the torch in the iron ring on the wall and takes the horse out of his stall to saddle him. The horse rears and tries to bite, but Vlad hasn't grown up on a horse for nothing. He punches the horse in the nose.

The horse snorts indignantly, but submits to the saddle. He pulls back again as Vlad leads him out over the kid's body, but Vlad whips his rump, and seconds later they're outside. They walk slowly to let their eyes get used to the darkness, then Vlad jumps in the saddle and grips the reins. He's mounted and ready to go.

He looks at the sky. There are a million stars, but he's only looking for one. He finds the Big Dipper, the cart-like star formation, and follows the imaginary line at its end that leads to the North Star.

He'll head north to the sea. He's got less than five hours until they'll start looking for him, and about a hundred miles to go. Unless he gets lost. Lousy bets, but they're the best he's got.

He tightens his knees and pushes forward at a light canter, to make the horse last.

CHAPTER 82

I LOVE HIM

VARNA, NOVEMBER 1444

It's already November, and the wind whips the bare fields west of Varna like they've done them wrong. The days are short, cold and raw, with low hanging angry skies where ugly clouds chase each other. The light started fading to gray as Mehmet rides east with his army. He's about to see his father for the first time since Sultan Murad left for Anatolia, and he's not looking forward to it.

The last days before leaving Edirne were a mess, and Father must know it already, thanks to Çandarlı Paşa and his messengers. A lone rider moves faster than an army with its thousands of men on foot and its slow carts loaded with supplies. It took them ten days to get here, after he wasted the first three. And Father is sure to know why.

Mehmet shrugs and pushes on. He's the sultan, after all, isn't he? But he knows he's serving at the pleasure of his father. Murad has to only say one word, and Çandarlı Paşa, the janissaries, the whole Ottoman Empire, in fact, will welcome him back. In his three months of being sultan, Mehmet didn't do anything worth remembering.

Well, he actually did.

After Radu stabbed him, Mehmet spent the night moaning in pain while Akşemseddin, his doctor and tutor, attended to his wound.

Fortunately, the dagger only slashed the thick muscles of Mehmed's thigh. The pain was awful, but the injury wasn't much to worry about.

"You were fortunate," Akşemseddin said after cleaning the wound, pouring honey in it and covering it with a poultice of foul-smelling herbs. "One foot higher, and, if the knife sliced the large veins in your groin, you'd be dead already. If you were lucky, he'd only have cut off your family jewels, and the hope of ever having a son. Or fun, for that matter. One foot lower, and you'd never walk again. You should give thanks to Allah for watching over you."

Mehmet didn't want to give thanks to Allah. He couldn't imagine how he could explain to him what happened. He didn't think Allah would approve of what he wanted from Radu, even though the kid was just a hostage and an infidel.

"How long until I can ride?"

"Oh, you can ride tomorrow, no problem. But it's going to hurt."

Mehmet didn't ride the day after. Nor the day after that or the day after that.

Now he's about to meet his father, and he's not sure what to say.

Father's camp is everywhere, stretching as far as the eye can see. There are thousands of tents, fires, carts of supplies, and men. So many men. How many soldiers did Father gather? And how?

Mehmet dismounts in front of the tall sky-blue tent guarded by four janissaries and walks to the door. The guards cross their halberds to stop him.

Mehmet's blood rises to his head, and he wants to crush them. He's the sultan, how do they dare stop him? But they're protecting his father. So he takes a deep breath and swallows his pride.

"Father?"

"Let him in."

The guards move aside, and he steps inside the tent. It's austere, like most of his father's places. A cot. A prayer rug. A coffer covered in rolled parchments. A table covered with maps. And his father.

"Father."

Murad stands in front of him. He's smaller than Mehmet remembers, but his unsmiling face and fierce eyes are just as scary.

"Glad to see you, sultan. It took you a while."

Mehmet blushes. He knew it was coming, but that doesn't make it any easier.

"Sorry, Father. Things happened, and we started late."

"I heard."

Murad sits on the only pillow in the room, watching him, and Mehmet feels like a scolded child, even though his father hasn't said anything. Yet.

He takes a deep breath and squares his shoulders.

"So, what's going on? How did you get here?"

"We walked to the Dardanelles. Then we crossed and walked some more until we got here."

"How did you cross the Dardanelles? Çandarlı Paşa said the Venetians and the Genoese had blocked the straits."

"He was right. He usually is, by the way. In the future, it would behoove you to heed his advice. I know that doesn't come easy to you, but what makes a leader a great leader is listening to those who know better than they do. You'll be a better leader once you learn that."

Mehmet looks down, waiting for the rest. This is just the beginning.

"We paid them. Venetians and Genoese, like the rest of Christians, speak about their devotion to their God, but that's bullshit. Their God is gold. They'd do anything for it. So we paid. It wasn't cheap, mind you — a ducat per soldier — but I got them all through. And here we are. The blockade is still on, of course, since the crusaders don't know this. I bet the Genoese forgot to mention it."

"How many soldiers do you have?"

"Fifty thousand, give or take. We gathered more and more men as we headed north. I promised they'll get paid, of course. You'll have to see to that. We can't afford to break our promises. But with your ten thousand, we should be good. My last news is that they have less than twenty thousand, and many are undisciplined and poorly armed."

"We have three times more than they do! That should be a piece of cake!"

Murad looks at him with pity.

"It's more complicated than that, sultan. First, Hunyadi is a great general. Too good, really, I wouldn't mind if he somehow dropped dead before the fight. He's beaten me more than once, and I wouldn't be that surprised if he beats me again. He's rational, calculated, and fearless. Scary combination."

"Anything else?"

Mehmed knows he sounds like a sulky child, but he can't help himself. This war is not behaving like it should.

"Władysław, the newly elected King of Poland, is young and fearless. He's arrogant, undisciplined, and he's got a huge chip on his shoulder. Does that sound familiar to you? He's here to bring the Ottoman Empire back into Christianity, and he'll risk everything to cover himself with glory. He's unmanageable and unpredictable. He can win this battle for Hunyadi, or he can lose it. I don't know. Neither does Hunyadi, who's technically under his command, poor fellow, because Hungary is Poland's vassal. It's kind of like you are the sultan, but I'm leading the troops."

Mehmet looks down.

"And, finally Mircea. You know Mircea?"

"No."

"You should. Mircea is Vlad Dracul's eldest son. Seventeen or so, I think. He's just as hungry for glory as Władysław, but he doesn't have the same power. He's only got his four thousand wild Wallachians mounted on their mountain ponies. They aren't even soldiers, they're farmers and gamekeepers and blacksmiths. But they hate us more than all the others. They're mad we take their kids and grow them into janissaries. You'd think they'd be proud. You'd be mistaken. Mircea went to war so that his father could stay home. You know why?"

Mehmet shakes his head.

"Because of your friend Radu. And his brother. They're ours to kill if their father fails his oath. But you know that. So tell me what kept you home for so long."

Mehmed takes a deep breath, wishing he was anywhere else but here. "I got stabbed."

His father nods. He's not surprised. "How come?"

"Radu stabbed me in the thigh the night before we were supposed to head here."

"He's dead, then?"

Mehmet squirms. "He ran away."

"How far could he run? He was in the Edirne Castle. There, nobody goes in or out without our knowledge, not even a bird, let alone a kid."

"He ran to the gardens."

"And?"

"He climbed into the old planetree."

Sitting straight on his pillow, Murad stares at him without a word.

Mehmet paces, looking for a way to say it, but there's no way he can tell his father what he did to cause this.

Murad stares quietly at his son, waiting for him to sweat. And sweat he does.

"The janissaries found him, but he wouldn't come down."

"Then?"

"I... I asked him to come down, but he wouldn't. So I had them watch the tree."

"What for?"

Mehmet shrugged. "He was sure to come down at some point. He had no food and no water. How long could he stay there?"

'How long did he stay there?"

"He stayed there for three days."

"Then what?"

"Then, he came down."

"Why did you have to wait for him to come down?"

"What else could I do?"

"You could have the archers kill him from the ground. You could have the janissaries go after him and drag him down. You could cut the tree, or set it on fire, and get him down. More importantly, you didn't have to wait. You could let your men take care of him and come to Varna, as I asked you. Instead, you sat on your ass, waiting for that darn kid to get off a fucking tree. Are you insane? What the hell is this about?"

Mehmet looks down, wishing he was elsewhere, like most times he's with his father. He's never been his favorite son and he doesn't compare to Aladdin. But he is the sultan. Probably not for long. But today, Mehmet is sultan, by the choice of his father. Murad saddled him with this mess to be free to live a life of prayer and meditation in

Anatolia. He left him to deal with all this crap. So whether he likes it or not, he may as well hear the truth.

"I stayed there to save his life."

"What for? He deserved his death. Your men should have dropped his head on his father's doorstep. So what the hell are you doing?"

"I love him."

His father stares at him, and for the first time in Mehmet's life, he has nothing to say. He looks at his son like he's an alien.

"What?"

"I love Radu, and I will do whatever it takes to keep him alive. That's why I waited until he came down. I didn't want some glory-greedy soldier to cut his head off then send it to me expecting a governorship. I stayed there to protect him. I knew you could take care of yourself."

Mehmet takes a deep breath, now that he's got this off his chest. He's done it. He said it. To his father, of all people.

"What do you mean, you love him?"

The question surprises Mehmet, though it shouldn't. Love is not a thing in the Ottoman Empire. That's something they talk about in Western stories with damsels in distress and rescuing knights. Here, in the Ottoman Empire, it's all about producing heirs. And forging alliances.

Still, it is what it is, so he does his best to explain.

"Radu makes me feel complete. I am happier when he's around. Everything looks and smells better when he's in the same room. I..."

"You are out of your mind, and you're embarrassing me. Do you know the last time I slept with your mother?"

Mehmet blushes and shakes his head.

"The day I found out she was expecting you. How about Aladdin's mother?"

Mehmet shrugs.

"I never touched her after she became pregnant with Aladdin. Until after he died. Then, I took her back to my bed, hoping she would make me another son as worthy as him. You know why?"

"No."

"Because the life of a sultan is not about love. Not even about love for his children, let alone his women. The life of a sultan is about love for Allah and our duty to the empire. That's what makes us complete. We lay with our women to make sons, and once they do, we stop laying with them and look for another to make another son. Their job is to educate their sons to be the best they can be and hopefully become the next sultan. Love has nothing to do with it. The life of a sultan is about responsibility and duty. If you like a boy, take a boy. If you like a girl, take a girl. That's your fun, but be wise and be discrete. And that should never interfere with your duty to the empire. Never. Got that?"

Mehmet nods, his face on fire.

"Good. If something like this ever happens again, you are no longer sultan."

CHAPTER 83

NO RETREAT

NOVEMBER 9TH, VARNA

In the muddy fields west of Varna, the thousands of men hell-bent on saving Christianity are finally getting some time for themselves. All over the camp, warriors dressed in rag-tag uniforms clean and fix their equipment, see to their horses, or rest. It took them weeks to get here, and they're all exhausted, dirty, and losing their spark.

"It's time to remember what you're fighting for. This, God willing, will be the last crusade. This time we'll throw the Ottomans out of Europe, release their grip on Constantinople, and reunite the true God's Christian Churches under the triple crown of Pope Eugene the Fourth. God relies on you," Władysław tells his men, sitting in the saddle of his massive destrier.

Mircea, however, sits by their fires and laughs with his men. He drinks with them and talks to them about the things that matter: their kids, their crops, and how soon they can all go back home. Their faces light up when they see him, and Ștefan hopes that someday he'll be half as good a leader as Mircea is.

They are to rest here until the Venetian and Genoese ships arrive to pick them up to cross to Constantinople. And that's good, since they really need some rest before fighting Mehmet's army, which is much larger and better equipped. And they can use some time to plan and find common ground, since Hunyadi and Władysław don't seem to agree on anything.

A horse gallops by, covered in spumes. His rider whips him to go faster, and that's way too fast to ride through a crowded camp. He barely misses a couple of men carrying buckets of water, then stops by Hunyadi's tent. Two more riders follow. They all dismount and rush in.

Ștefan and Mircea glance at each other. Whatever's going on doesn't look good, so they head to Hunyadi's tent. The guards let them in, and Hunyadi signals them to sit without interrupting the messengers who speak all over each other.

"They're already deployed for battle..."

"Thousands and thousands of them. Maybe a hundred thousand."

"Maybe two hundred."

"Stop!" Hunyadi says. "Breathe."

Cardinal Cesarini, the Papal Legate, pours them wine. They gulp it down. King Władysław, sitting away from the others, glares at them with narrowed eyes.

"Did you actually count them, Captain Szilágyi?"

Szilágyi is Hunyadi's most trusted commander, and his brother-in-law. He's two decades older than the king, and he wears the scars of many battles. His glance says that much, but he doesn't bother to answer. He looks at Hunyadi instead.

"Close to a hundred thousand," he says. "Under Murad's tughra."

"Mehmet's, you mean," the king says.

Szilágyi throws him a dismissive side glance.

"I say what I mean and I mean what I say," Szilágyi says. "Murad's."

"He can't be here," Cesarini says. "Our ships closed the Dardanelles weeks ago."

Szilágyi shrugs. "I told you what I saw. They're only a couple of miles away, camped for the night. Feel free to go see yourselves."

"Thank you, Michael," Hunyadi says.

Szilágyi and his men leave, and the tension grows even thicker. The men think and drink without looking at each other until Hunyadi breaks the silence. His voice is heavy and tired.

"This isn't what we planned. We were going to rest for a few days, then board our ships and sail to Constantinople, where we were going to crush Mehmet, whose Anatolian army was stuck in Asia. Instead, we're here in Varna, exhausted and out of supplies; we don't even know where the ships are; and we have Murad with a hundred thousand Ottomans up our asses. This war has gone terribly wrong."

"If you believe your captain. But who knows what he really saw? Who? And how many?"

"Szilágyi is my best commander and I'd trust him with my life. If he says that he saw Murad with a hundred thousand Ottomans two miles from here, that's exactly what he saw. Go check if you don't believe him. I don't need to."

The king's mouth narrows into a thin line.

"What do we do now?" Cesarini asks.

"It's simple," Hunyadi says. "We either fight or we retreat. There is no other way."

"We can't fight like this. We aren't ready. Our men are exhausted and we're out of supplies. We need to retreat," Cesarini says.

"How and where?" Mircea asks.

Hunyadi unrolls a map and lays it on the table, affixing it with wine cups.

"We are here." He points to a dark green patch in the middle of the map. "This here, to our south, is Lake Varna, with its miles and miles of marshy shores. Here, to our east, is the Black Sea, where the Venetian ships should be. But they aren't. We don't know where they are, or when they'll get here. This brown patch to the north, is the Franga Plateau. It's a thousand feet high and covered by thick forest. We can't climb it. Less so with Murad up our ass. There's no way out but through Murad. He chose his spot well. I wonder how he knew we'd be here? He must have known it for a while, to get his ducks in a row like that."

"What are you saying?" Casarini asks.

"We don't have a choice. We fight. There is no retreat."

"Good. We didn't come all this way to retreat. God is on our side. We have the best men, and we're fighting for the glory of the Church," the king says.

Casarini shakes his head.

"What if we wait? The ships must come any day now. Maybe even tomorrow."

"We can wait. But Murad won't. If he knew enough to corner us here, he knows enough not to wait. IF the ships are coming. How did he come through the Dardanelles? Our ships may be history."

"He doesn't have a way to destroy our ships. He got through with one of his devilish tricks, but that doesn't mean he destroyed our ships. I say we use the wagenburgs. They should buy us a couple of days at least."

"What are the wagenburgs?" Ștefan asks, then blushes, embarrassed to show his ignorance in this meeting of important people, where he's barely tolerated.

Hunyadi doesn't seem to mind. "War carts. That's how the Hussites go to war. They tie a bunch of carts together, and use them as fortifications. The enemies have a hard time going through, while the defenders inflict severe casualties. You can move the carts and rotate them to your advantage. They're great, but we don't have enough of them. And that also means we leave Murad the advantage of choosing where and when to attack us."

"We don't know when, nor if the ships will arrive. How long can we hold him back?" Mircea asks.

"Not long. Especially since we're running out of supplies. Two or three days?"

The king has had it. "Let's go destroy Mehmed, Murad and the rest of the faithless bastards once and for all. God is with us."

Casarini shrugs, but Hunyadi has made up his mind. "To escape is impossible, to surrender is unthinkable. Let us fight with bravery and honor our arms."

"Spoken like a true man," the king says. "I'll be honored if you accept to lead our armies."

Hunyadi bows, and the meeting is over.

"What do you think?" Ștefan asks Mircea on their way to the tent.

"Father was right. Remember when he told them Murad wasn't going to get stuck in Anatolia? Weeks ago, he told them he was going to gather an army and meet them. He was right."

"He also told them they were going to lose."

"I know. I'm afraid he was right about that, too."

CHAPTER 84

BATTLE PLAN

VARNA

As a meager sun rises over Varna the morning of November 10th 1444, a hundred thousand men say their prayers. Some in Ottoman language, some in Polish, Hungarian or Romanian. Many think they're seeing their last sunrise, and most of them are right.

After a night with little sleep, Mehmet shuffles out of his tent watching the sky blush pink in the east, and he wonders if he'll ever go back to bed again. As a sultan, he knows that his chances of dying are small. But worse things have happened to sultans before. His glorious grandfather, Sultan Bayezid Ilderim, The Thunder, was taken prisoner in the battle of Ankara. Timur and his hordes of wild nomads locked him in a cage and paraded him for everyone to mock until Allah, in his kindness, took him away.

What happens if I die? Or I get caught?

Father would take back the reigns of the empire. No more meditation and prayer for him. He'd have to see to the business of the empire. He'd have another son. Mother would be devastated. She's unlikely to have another son, so her time as validé would be over. And Radu?

He can't imagine what will happen to Radu if he died. Sultan Murad would probably execute him, and that's terrible. *I'd better not die just yet,* he thinks, and heads to his father's tent.

"Good. I hoped you were up. How would you deploy the troops?"

"We outnumber them by two to one, maybe more. We should try to surround them."

"Deploy wide. I agree. We'll deploy all the way from the Franga Plateau to the lake. That way they can't escape, and they can't get behind us. Right here, it's almost six miles. So how would you deploy us?"

"You and I stay in the center on these two burial mounds. From here, we can see all the battlefield and react as needed."

"Agreed."

"The janissary archers should be up on the plateau. That gives them a great sight line and threatens the crusader's right flank."

"OK."

"The janissaries should be in the center. They will protect us and be able to go to whichever flank needs them."

"And?"

"Sipahis on each side. And the light cavalry on the left."

"Why left?"

"Because that's where we have the archers on the plateau. The cavalry will pretend to attack their right flank, then withdraw. They'll follow them and we'll annihilate them with the archers."

"Very good. That was the easy part. Now to the hard part. What will Hunyadi do?"

Mehmet has no idea.

"This is like chess. You need to think at least four moves ahead. What would you do if you were him?"

"He has fewer people. He should deploy on a narrower field. Like, here." Mehmet points to a point on the map where the field between the plateau and the lake narrows.

"Excellent. Then?"

"Maybe wait to see what we do? And respond to it?"

"Or? Where would you attack if you were him?"

"I wouldn't. I'd wait."

"Very good. That's exactly what he'd do if he had a choice. But he may not. The king is young, foolish and hard to control. Hunyadi will try to keep him in check. Let's hope that he can't. One more thing. What happens if we lose?"

"Lose?"

"It happened before."

Mehmet can't think about that. He can only think about victory.

"We need a fallback plan. We'll build a palisade and dig a trench in front of the janissaries, and we'll trap it with sharp stakes. If the heavy cavalry gets to it, that should take care of them. Or at least slow them down. They are fast and deadly, the heavy armored knights. And hard to kill, while they have a horse between their legs. But once they fall, they're as helpless as a turtle on its back. They're so heavy they can't get up.

"Behind the trench we'll have camels loaded with bags of silks and gold. If the enemy gets through, we'll have our men slash the bags, and spill the treasure. Those greedy knights won't resist the temptation, and they'll go for the loot. That should give us time to escape."

Mehmet wonders how his father got to be so wise. He hopes it will happen to him too someday, but doesn't hold his breath.

CHAPTER 85

THE BATTLE OF VARNA

NOVEMBER 10, 1444

A glorious morning rises over Varna. The sky is endlessly clear, a heartwarming sun smiles over the blue Varna Lake, the Black Sea, and the dark pines guarding the mountain slopes. And the armies.

Mounted on his horse, Ștefan watches the deployment of the troops. It's taken hours. The Ottomans are a wonder to behold. Like a well-practiced dance, they move in formation, stepping like one, on the beat of the heavy drums he can feel in his stomach.

The sultan's army is almost symmetrical: Cavalry on the left, cavalry on the right, and the famous janissaries in the middle. They're easy to recognize by their red uniforms and tall felt hats. Behind them, on an ancient burial mound is Murad himself, by the tughra that flutters in the wind. Standing ahead of the cavalry there's a row of irregulars armed with halberds, maces and bows.

"Who are those?" Ștefan asks.

Mircea glances at the Ottomans. He's mounted too, standing in front of his four thousand Wallachians, who are to be the reserve to be deployed wherever needed. To start, they'll stay behind, even though they're itching to fight.

"Those are the azabs. The sipahis and the janissaries are regulars. The army is their whole life, and they live to fight. The azabs are ordinary people that Murad only gathers when he goes to war. They're mostly here to do errands and harass the enemy. They'll be the first ones to go."

By now, the Ottomans are set in place, but the crusaders are still struggling. Szilágyi and his left flank are ready. They're Transylvanians and Hungarians, Hunyadi's most experienced men. The Czech, with their wagenburgs and bombards, are ready too. They wait behind the others to form the last line of defense. But Casarini, the bishops, and the whole right flank are still shuffling, looking for their spots.

King Władysław and his Polish knights form the crusaders' center. Sitting high up on their splendid coursers and clad head to toe in heavy armor, they're a sight to behold. Their glowing shields mirror the sun, and banners in every color of the rainbow dance above the forest of lances.

It takes forever, but Casarini and the bishops finally settle. The armies are ready.

A hundred thousand men face each other, half a mile apart, waiting for the signal to kill.

It's close to noon, and they're raring to go. King Władysław and his knights can hardly stay put. Hunyadi's heavy glare keeps them in place, for now. The Wallachians are stirring too, even though they're the reserve, so they'll be the last to go. The tension mounts as a hundred thousand hearts pound in a hundred thousand chests.

Suddenly, out of nowhere, a monstrous gale blows in from the sea. It's like God sneezed over them. Leaves soar like flocks of birds, grasses flatten, cattails bend, men waver. Things fly through the air that were never meant to fly. Tree trunks screech and fall.

The sudden blow hits the crusaders like a hammer. One after the other, the banners snap in two. The men cross themselves, gaping at their flags laying on the ground. Their honored standards, downed by a random gust of wind. This has to be a sign from God, they think, and cross themselves in fear. The only standard still standing is St. George's, Christianity's hero, he who defeated the dragon.

Ștefan shivers along with the others and wonders what's coming.

"What a wonderful omen!" Casarini says, and everyone stares at him like he's nuts. "Look at St. George, overcoming the dragon again. This is a sign that God is on our side."

Ștefan glances at Mircea. Mircea shrugs and opens his mouth to say something, but there's no more time. Murad's left flank explodes into action. The azabs burst forward into Casarini's flank like a storm, and the whole Ottoman army blasts into deafening noise. Horns blare, drums beat, cymbals crash, and warriors clank their swords against their shields, adding to the ruckus. But nothing is scarier than the roar blasting from thousands of throats: *"Allahu Akbar! Allahu Akbar! Allahu Akbar!"*

The crusaders are agape. They cross themselves and stick their heels in the ground, getting ready. All, but for Hunyadi's right flank.

The bishops can't resist an easy prey. They ignore Casarini's orders and take off to chase the azabs, who came forward to taunt them, then ran back. The bishops' mounted men crash through the irregulars and blast forward. Mehmed's light cavalry opens to let them through, then closes behind them before they understand what happened.

When they do, it's too late. There's no return. Murad's sipahis surround them and engage them in fierce battle. Sword meets sword, shields collide, lances cut through chain mail and flesh like they're nothing. It's a death-fest.

The crusaders' heavy armor protects them better, but the Ottomans are everywhere. Whenever one falls, two others take his place, and the fight turns to carnage. Seeing the debacle, Casarini flies forward to their rescue with the rest of Hunyadi's right flank.

Meantime, Szilágyi's Saxons on Hunyadi's left flank can't resist the provocation either. They break formation and burst forward, attacking Murad's right flank of Anatolian sipahis led by Beylerbey Karaca, Sultan Murad's brother-in-law. The Saxons cut thought the rows of azabs like a hot knife through butter. The irregulars' light weapons can't pierce the knights' heavy armor, and the huge coursers trample the azabs into the dirt. It's a free-for-all for the Saxons until the mounted sipahis surround them, cutting their retreat.

But even the sipahis' sharp kilijes struggle to break through the knights' armor. The Saxons pummel Murad's right flank with their double-edged heavy swords and long lances and inflict heavy casualties, while suffering only minor losses.

But the sipahis are countless. Hundreds of them rush to the Saxons whose retreat is about to be cut. Szilágyi rushes forward, bringing the rest of his men to their rescue.

Hunyadi watches both his flanks engaged in heavy battle. So do Ștefan and Mircea, who know that their turn is coming.

On the left, the Saxons fight for their life in the middle of the Ottoman right flank, with Szilágyi struggling to break through and free them.

On the right, the bishops are weakened, but Casarini managed to open a path for their retreat.

It's time for the Wallachians. Hunyadi nods left. Mircea lifts his sword. "*La luptă!* Let's fight!"

Four thousand Wallachians stand in the stirrups of their nimble mountain ponies. They lift their weapons above their tall sheepskin hats and shout as one: "*La luptă!*"

The earth shudders under the battering of sixteen thousand hooves flying towards the Ottoman right flank that's closing around Szilágyi. Mircea gallops forward, and Ștefan follows. One with his horse, Ștefan's flying high. His head is hot with the rush, his chest heaves with excitement, and he's invincible. He hears someone scream, and he's surprised to realize it's him, shouting words even he can't understand.

A cloud of arrows falls upon the sipahis like hail upon a wheat field, flattening them. The arrows are so many they hide the sun, as man after man releases his powerful bow.

They get close and switch from bows to maces, battle axes and swords. Iron clatters upon iron. Horses neigh, people shout, wounded scream. It's a cacophony of rage, hatred and pain. The Wallachians can't wait to pay back the Ottomans for their stolen children. Their boys, who are now the sultan's janissaries. Their girls, who are his wives. They take revenge for the women and children who are starving at home so that the yearly tribute can feed the sultan's army. Their wrath is stronger than the Ottoman's weapons, training and armor.

They're so enraged they don't care if they die, as long as they bring the Ottomans with them. Hate is a powerful weapon.

Ștefan raises his battle ax and sinks it into a sipahi's chest. The man screams and falls under his horse's hooves. Another one challenges Ștefan and lifts his kilij high above his head, ready to strike, but Ștefan's ax cuts through his shoulder, and the arm with the kilij falls to the ground. Astonished, the sipahi stares at the bleeding hole where his arm used to be while Ștefan moves on to the next. This one is wounded and unarmed. He begs for mercy, but there's no room for pity in Ștefan's heart. His ax splits the man's helmet, then his forehead, and the distance between the man's eyes grows as the ax drives them apart.

Five steps ahead, Mircea cuts through the sipahis like a peasant harvesting wheat. They leave behind a path of death and destruction, opening the way for Szilágyi and the Saxons to retire. They push forward, widening the path even further to make room for the wounded.

The Ottomans start to retreat. The Wallachians get ready to follow, but Mircea thunders:

"No! Don't chase them. It's a ploy."

The men give up the chase, but the Anatolian sipahis are on the run and Murad's whole right flank is crumbling.

Beylerbey Karaca tries to stop them. He waves his kilij and screams: "*Allahu Akbar!*" to encourage them, but they're already on the run.

To shame them into fighting, the brave Karaca roars another bloodcurdling battle cry and spurs his horse forward, charging into the crusaders. But a knight lifts his sword, and Karaca drops dead under his men's eyes. That's all the persuasion they needed. They run back, leaving bare the Ottoman right flank.

The Wallachians have suffered minor losses but made a major difference in the battle's fate. But it's not yet over. Hunyadi's right flank is about to collapse, and they need reinforcements.

Ștefan sighs. He's tired, but rest is for the winners and the dead. Since they're neither, they move on.

CHAPTER 86

LOVE AND DEATH POTIONS

EDIRNE, NOVEMBER 1444

While the battle of Varna is raging, the Edirne Palace feels deserted. Without Mehmet and his army, the palace has become the domain of women, children and eunuchs.

Ali wouldn't mind a little peace and quiet, but Hüma Hatun took care of that. The validé has been on fire since Mehmet left. Before that, in fact. Ever since the night Radu stabbed Mehmet and hid in the old planetree, Hüma has never looked happy.

At first, Ali thought she was worried about Mehmet's wound. How could she not? Even though Mehmet was in the care of Akşemseddin, the most famous doctor in the Ottoman Empire, the author of Maddat ul-Hayat, the Ottoman's medicine's most famous treatise, things can always go bad.

Akşemseddin thinks that disease can move from one person to another carried by bugs too small to see, but most people think he's off the mark. They won't tell him, of course, since he's Mehmet's mentor and a famous doctor, but who would believe there are things too small to see? Let alone that they can carry disease from one man to another?

Either way, Hüma has been like the sky in a storm: cloudy, unpredictable, and always ready to thunder. Even now.

She sits up in her bed as Lena brushes her long red hair with the utmost care, but she's not happy. Her cheeks are pale and her mouth tight, and she looks worried and old.

Ali feels sorry for her. "Are you worried about the sultan, my lady? I'm sure that Sultan Murad will take good care of him. He'll be back soon, just as strong and handsome as ever."

Hüma spares a smile but doesn't answer. There's something on her mind that won't quit, so she finally decides to let it out.

"Lena?"

"Yes, my lady."

"That night you spent with the sultan. What happened?"

Lena blushes and looks down.

"My lady?"

"You heard me. What happened?"

"Nothing happened, my lady. The eunuchs dropped me there and then the sultan came."

"And?"

"And we talked."

"And?"

"That's it."

"You didn't..."

"No."

"What did you talk about?"

"He told me that I was beautiful, but he was tired, and had a lot of things on his mind, with the war and the janissaries and other things. But he said he liked me and he'll call me back."

Hüma's face relaxed in the approximation of a smile.

"Good. I hoped he'd like you. Maybe we should get you trained in how to pleasure him. I'll take care of that. We have a few weeks before he comes back."

Lena's face drops, but Hüma is too excited to notice. She sends Lena away, then she turns to Ali. "Is my potion ready?"

"Almost, my lady. Just a couple more items and a few incantations, and it's ready to go."

"Can I use it on somebody else than the person it's made for?"

"It won't work. I have to make it specifically for that person if you want it to work."

"I see."

Hüma looks out the window where the gray November sky is deepening to black. She's thinking. Her eyes come back to Ali with a new resolve.

"Can you make love potions?"

"Of course."

What do you need for that? Hair and blood again?"

"Just blood from the person you want somebody to fall in love with. Then you give it to the other to drink. But you can make it stronger if you use blood from both."

Hüma nodded. "We don't have blood from both right now. How about you use Lena's blood for now. We'll make another when Mehmet is back."

"Yes, my lady."

Why would Hüma want Mehmet to fall in love with Lena? Unless...

"But, more urgently, I need another death potion."

"Who is this for, my lady?"

"It's for a boy."

CHAPTER 87

THE KING'S CHARGE

Mounted on his stallion on the burial mound overlooking the battle field in Varna, Mehmet is about to get whiplash from watching the three separate fights raging across the two-mile-wide battlefield.

The Ottoman left flank, with the Rumelian sipahis under Beylerbey Hadim Şehabeddin, looks good. They've surrounded Hunyadi's right flank and are about to crush it into nothing.

But the right flank is no more. Mehmet's heart ached as he watched Berlebey Karaca's heroic death.

"He was a good man, and a hero," Mehmet says, wondering what will happen to his aunt, Berlebey Karaca's wife. She'll probably get recycled, like most women of high birth do, should their husbands die. She's too valuable to rot in her stepson's harem. As the sultan's aunt, she could bring the Ottoman Empire a valuable alliance.

His father glares at him.

"He was a fool. His death was worse than useless, it was stupid. If he had a grain of common sense, he'd have retreated and regrouped his men, then got back into the fight. Now he's dead, and his men have all scattered. What good does that do?"

Mehmet's jaw falls. He hadn't thought about it that way. He only saw the man's bravery.

"Bravery without common sense is dangerous. It loses wars and armies. I'll take a sharp coward over a stupid hero any day," Murad says.

Now that the Ottoman right flank is gone, the crusader's left flank regroups to charge the Ottoman's left flank where the Rumelian sipahis are grouped under the Franga Plateau. King Władysław's shiny army follows them too. Overwhelmed by their enemies, the fierce Rumelians get forced into a hasty retreat. They break formation and struggle up the steep slope trying to escape the carnage.

The sun's halfway down, and the battle is at a standstill. Both armies are exhausted. They need to breathe and regroup. The flanks are mostly gone, but the centers, both Murad's janissaries and Hunyadi's knights, are still intact. The ravaged battlefield is a terrible sight, covered with the mutilated bodies of soldiers and horses, wrecked armor and weapons. The dying scream, the wounded pray, and the smell of the battle is something Mehmet will never forget. The stench of blood, sweat, and spilled bowels is so heavy that the fresh breeze from the sea can't touch it. Mehmet's stomach churns.

"Now what?" he asks.

"Now we wait."

"For what?"

"For someone to make a mistake."

"How do you know they'll make a mistake?"

"Anything they do will be a mistake. The only wise thing they can do is wait."

"For what?"

"For the Venetians to arrive. For us to get tired of waiting and leave. For their God to help them."

"And if they wait?"

"They won't."

"How do you know?"

"Władysław is young, arrogant and foolish. He'll force Hunyadi's hand, since he outranks him. He'd rather die than wait."

"But what if they wait?"

"If they wait, we lose. We already lost most of our sipahis. Our men are tired, hungry and thirsty, so we can't keep our position for too long. If they wait, we lose."

Mehmet stares at his father. He can't believe he speaks about losing like it's normal.

"But we still have the janissaries."

"And we'll keep them. Remember what happened to Bayezid Yıldırım? How Timur captured him and paraded him like a wild animal? That won't happen to us. We keep the janissaries."

Mehmet glances at the battlefield again. As terrible as it looks, he's burning to go and fight. He wants to get covered in glory. He can win this battle, if only..."

"Father..."

"No."

"But Father..."

"No. You called me back to lead the armies. I am back, leading the armies. NO."

Mehmet sighs, wondering if he should have left his father stay in Anatolia, when a bright ray of sun hits his eye.

The knights are back, hundreds of them.

Their armor mirroring the setting sun, their tall destriers dancing on their feet, their colorful plumes floating above their heads, they're the most beautiful sight Mehmet has ever seen.

"Father."

"I know. I told you."

They fall into formation behind King Władysław and lower their lances.

Władysław stares straight at Murad and lifts his sword above his head.

"For God and Poland," he shouts, then digs his spurs in his destrier's flanks, propelling him forward.

"For God and Poland," the others answer.

They start at a trot, break into a canter, then speed to a full gallop directed towards Murad and Mehmed who are waiting up on the mound.

The earth trembles under the pounding of the hooves, and a cloud of dust darkens the sun. The knights charge faster and faster, growing until they cover the horizon.

Mehmet's heart pounds. His throat too dry to speak, he touches his father's shoulder.

Murad shrugs.

"*Insha'Allah.*"

The knights are close enough for Mehmet to see their faces, and they all seem to be in a trance. Their wide eyes hold no reason or fear, just an all-consuming desire to kill. The horses' eyes bulge out, the men's faces shine with sweat, their swords rise high. They're steps away from trampling the janissaries.

With a blood-curdling scream, the first horse crashes in the hidden trap with sharpened stakes. The second follows. Then another. And another.

Mehmet's heart skips a beat. The anguish of the broken horses feels even more terrible than the wails of dying men.

The trench fills with corpses. The king's horse sees them in time, and jumps over the entangled bodies to land at the bottom of the burial mound. His long lance aims at Sultan Murad who's just steps away.

Mehmet stands frozen in place. He stares at King Władysław, whose blue eyes laugh with the joy of victory. A strand of golden hair flies out of his helm crowned with a shivering blue plume as he raises his lance for the kill.

Mehmet unsheathes his kilij to protect his father, but he's not a match for the king in full armor flying on his galloping horse like the god of revenge. Still, he spurs Rüzgar forward. But it's too late.

A janissary steps forward and stabs the destrier. The horse screams and rolls and crashes to the ground over his rider. The king tries to stand, but there's no more standing for either of them. Moving so fast it's hard to see, the janissary cuts off the king's head. His eyes are still open when the janissary picks it up, impales it on his own lance, and lifts it above the crowd for all to see.

King Władysław is king no more.

CHAPTER 88

ON THE LAM

AKKUŞ, NOVEMBER 1444

Hundreds of miles East of Varna, deep in the heart of Anatolia, the sky blushes to the east. There's nothing but mountains as far as the eye can see. Mountains ahead, mountains behind, covered by pine forests that smell like incense and drop soft needles under Vlad's tired feet.

He tries to think. It's been a while since he last passed a village. It should be full light in less than an hour, and he needs a place to hide for the day.

Walking the whole night kept him warm, but he wishes he didn't have to kill the horse. But he didn't have a choice. There was no place to hide him. A roaming lone horse would attract attention, and word of his escape must be out by now. They must have connected his escape with the horse's disappearance, and wherever they find the horse, they'll look for him.

He tried to steal another last night but couldn't find one. So he walked and walked through the night, but now he needs a place to rest for the day. But if he picks up the pace tonight, with God's help, by tomorrow morning he might be at the shore.

He's hungry, thirsty, and cold. Sure, he's got money, but you can't eat money. And he's afraid to show himself, in case someone recognizes him, so he keeps walking.

It's almost light when he falls upon a lonely hut. It's one of the humble shelters the shepherds use in summer. But now in November, it has to be empty. And, who knows? If he's lucky, he might even find something to eat.

The door is latched. He tries to open it, but can't, so he kicks it with his foot and crashes in.

He was right about the food. Right there, on the table, there's a chunk of bread, a piece of cheese, and two apples.

But he was wrong about the place being empty. Curled on the floor in the farthest corner, hugging his knees, there's a boy. About eight. He's so scared the white of his eyes shows all around as he stares at Vlad, but he doesn't say a word.

"What's your name? And what are you doing here?"

The kid stares.

Vlad tries again in Greek, then in Romanian. Still nothing. He grabs him by the shoulders and shakes him. The kid opens his mouth. There's a stump where his tongue should be.

Vlad lets him go.

He's heard about mutes. They are valuable, sometimes even more valuable than eunuchs. The deaf-mutes are the best, since they can't either hear nor share their master's secrets. Their eardrums get pierced and their tongues cut as young children. Some make it. Some don't. It's all in the cost of doing business for the slave traders, and the price goes up with the risk.

But what is this kid doing here, all alone, in an abandoned mountain hut? Unless it's not abandoned? Vlad takes another look at the kid. He's wearing shalwars, a chemise and a kaftan, just like everyone else, and he looks clean and cared for. What if somebody's coming for him?

Vlad shrugs. He grabs the bread and the cheese and starts eating. He eats an apple and fills his belly with cold water. He leaves the other apple and some bread and cheese for the kid, then curls up on the rough straw bed, covers himself with a filthy rug smelling like smoke and sheep, and falls asleep.

CHAPTER 89

SOPHIA

AKKUŞ, NOVEMBER 1444

Vlad wakes up feeling like someone's staring at him. He grabs his dagger and opens his eyes.

It's a girl. She's about his age, golden-haired and blue-eyed with long lashes.

"Who are you?"

"Vlad. You?"

"Sophia. What are you doing here?"

"Sleeping."

She laughs, and her laughter warms Vlad's heart. He lets go of the knife.

"How did you get here?"

"I walked. You?"

"Where are you going?"

"To Ünye."

"What for?"

"To find a ship to go home."

"Where's home?"

"Wallachia."

"That's far away."

"It is. What are you doing here?"

"I live here. Well, not here. Down in the village."

"So why are you here now?"

"To bring food for my brother." She points to the mute.

"So why is he here, then?"

Sophia blushes and looks down. "He ran away."

"From where?"

"From his master. My uncle sold him, but his new master beat him so he ran away and came home. But if my uncle finds him, he'll just take him back. So I hid him up here for now, while I figure out how to escape."

"Why should you escape?"

"He can't go alone. And my uncle is about to sell me too. He already has three customers, but he's holding them off hoping for more money. But I'll go soon."

To Vlad, that's mind boggling. How can you sell a child? A girl? But that's what Ottomans do. That makes him very angry.

"Why would your uncle sell you? Where's your father? Your mother?"

"Father died last year. Mother died when she had him." She points at her brother. "We belong to our uncle."

"Did he cut his tongue?"

"He had a barber do it. He said he spoke too much. And he's more valuable this way anyhow."

Vlad struggles with feelings he's never had before. He's feeling sorry for the kids. If there's one thing he hates, it's slavery.

"How are you going to escape?"

"I did some chores for the neighbors and earned a little money. I thought that if we made it to the shore, we may find a ship to take us to Varna. Or to Greece. I'll give them what I have, and I'll work for the rest. I'm a hard worker, and he'll help."

"What's his name?"

"Nikos."

Vlad can't believe when he hears himself saying:

"We'll wait for the night and we'll go north together."

Sophia's blue eyes light up. She hugs him, then goes to tell her brother.

I've got to be insane. Two runaways. A girl. And a mute kid. I should cut their throats and leave them here. It would be more merciful.

He sighs, turns on his side and goes back to sleep.

CHAPTER 90

KILL THE BOY

EDIRNE

Despite the lousy weather, the Edirne Palace is getting ready to party. The sharp November rain chills you to the bone, and the merciless wind whips the last leaves off the trees and cuts through your clothes, but who cares? Edirne has never been happier.

Sultan Murad's great victory in the battle of Varna was the battle of the century and filled every Ottoman heart with gratitude and pride. Thanks to the mercy of Allah and to Sultan Murad's wisdom, the true faith won again, this time for good. The army crushed the last crusade and, with it, the infidels' hopes. That's why the cooks sing, the eunuchs smile, and the women glow as they get ready to receive the heroes.

"He fought the King of Poland, and Hunyadi, and the papal troops, and the Polish and Hungarian knights, and the Venetian and the Genoese ships, and the Wallachians, and he won," Hüma says, as the hammam slaves massage perfumed oil into her skin to make it soft and dewy.

"He's a great general," Ali says, handing her a chilled lemon sorbet to sip on. "And when his time comes, Sultan Mehmet will be even greater."

Hüma sips on her drink.

"I hope so. Ali, I'm very pleased with you."

"I'm so glad, my lady. What did I do to please you?"

"Did you notice that Halime looks rather peaked these days?"

"No, my lady, I barely ever see her."

"Well, she does. Your potion has worked well."

Ali's heart skips a beat. So that's who the potion was for. Thankfully, the potion won't kill Halime. There's nothing there to kill her, just disgusting stuff to get her off her food and make Hüma happy for the time being. Sooner or later, she will demand results, but Ali isn't ready to kill anyone for her.

"I'm glad you are pleased, my lady."

"I got the hair and the blood for our next potion. I'll have the raven tongues tomorrow. This one should be fast though. I have no time to waste."

"Of course, my lady."

"Overnight, you said?"

"Yes, my lady. Once I gather all the other ingredients and make the potion."

Hüma nods, and Ali leaves with a big clump in her throat. Whoever Hüma is about to kill, Ali isn't into it. But there's only so long she can delay it. One way or another, she'll have to decide what to do. The easiest thing to do would be to just poison Hüma, but she's not so sure that's a good idea. If she does, what will happen to her? And to Lena?

She stops by to see Lena, who, now that she's the sultan's favorite, has her own room. She finds her sitting on her bed, learning her Quran.

"How is it going?"

"Awful. Quran lessons in the morning. Ottoman language lessons before third prayer. Pleasure giving lessons in the afternoon. Baths with epilation and exfoliation every evening. Can life get even more boring?"

"Sure it can. Just think about what would happen if Hüma abandons her plan to primp you for Mehmed. What would you do?"

"I don't know, but I can't wait to find out."

Ali laughs, and heads to her little kitchen to prepare the love potion for Hüma. She throws in sweet herbs that smell good. She has no idea what a love potion should contain — nor does she care — but she adds rosemary, mint, bay leaves and pine buds. There. It may not do much for love, but it will help their digestion and soften their cough. She adds honey and lemon and stirs, thinking. Should she get rid of Hüma, or should she weather this storm and see where it goes?

She's still stirring when Mirko opens the door. He has a message from Radu, who wants her to stop by and see him. She hasn't seen him since the night he stabbed the sultan. He's been confined ever since, and she wasn't assigned to bring in his meals, since Hüma needs her all the time for this or that.

She stops by the kitchens to grab a tray with grapes and quinces — an excuse for the janissary to let her in — and finds Radu talking to Sari, as usual.

He smiles and hugs her, but he's pale and peaked. It's like he shrank over the last few weeks.

"I'm so glad to see you, Ali. I missed you."

"Me too, my prince. Look what I brought you. How are you?"

He shrugs and signals her to sit. She crosses her legs and sits on a stuffed orange pillow. The room is small and cluttered, and Ali wonders how it must feel to be locked in it for weeks. No wonder he's pale.

"I'm OK." His clear blue eyes embrace her. "Thank you for coming to speak to me."

"Of course, my prince."

Radu stares at the guard pacing in front of the door and lowers his voice to a whisper.

"Ali, do you think the sultan is crazy?"

Ali's jaw drops. She, too, glances at the door.

"My prince, that may not be a wise question. But I think the sultan is sane."

Radu nods.

"I did too. Until that evening. That evening when I did what you know I did, he acted strange."

"We all act strange one time or another, my prince."

Radu nods. "I'm wondering if it was the wine."

"Very likely. He's probably not used to wine, and wine can make people go crazy. I'm sure he'd act very differently if he was sober."

"Thank you, Ali. I hoped you'd say that. That evening was scary."

Ali nods, and would like to hug him, but she can't. He's a prince, and she's just a eunuch.

"And now that he's returning, I don't even know what to be more afraid of: That he'll order me executed, or that he'll go back to doing what he did that night."

Ali itches to ask what Mehmet did, but she doesn't dare.

"He..." Radu glances at the door and lowers his voice even more. "He kissed me."

Ali sighs, wishing she could help. "You'll be all right, my prince. Everything will be OK."

"Thank you, Ali. I hope you're right. But just in case something happens to me, and we don't meet again, I would like you to have this."

He stands and grabs a piece of parchment and hands it to Ali. It's his Romanian poem.

In grădină către seară,
Lângă floarea de cicoare
E un roșu trandafir
Legănat de un zefir
In lumina care moare.

The evening falls over the garden.
By the chicory flower
Where a red rose sways in the breeze
In the dying light.

Ali thanks him with tears in her eyes. She knows how much that poem means to him.

"You'll be all right, my prince. And we'll soon meet again. You'll see."

Then she sees his bad haircut and the fresh wound on the back of his neck, and she's no longer sure.

CHAPTER 91

BACK

SILISTRA

Just south of the Danube, in Silistra, it's been another gloomy day. The sharp wind reaps the last dying leaves off the branches, a gray sky cries freezing tears for the dead, and the mud weighs the horses' hooves and the men's boots, sucking them in.

Ștefan hates mud, and the marshes of northern Bulgaria are nothing but mud. Even the patches of solid-looking ground turn out to be mud too, just more treacherous. The defeated crusaders have been crawling through the marshes for days, but they have yet to reach the Danube.

Not many are left. King Władysław's disastrous charge brought about not only his death, but also the death of every one of his Polish knights. Then Hunyadi spent many hours and precious men trying to recover his body, like anybody had a use for it. They all saw the king's head impaled on his lance, and knew that the battle was over. Lost was the handsome young Władysław, Poland's hope, with all his knights. Lost was Casarini, and his bishops. Lost were three quarters of their soldiers. And the few that were left didn't look happy to be alive.

Still, rain and mud notwithstanding, Ștefan is glad to be there with Mircea and their men. It's good to be alive, even though they're far from home, and there's lots of blame going around. Most of it falls on the dead, since they can't protest, but there's plenty left to share among the living.

Ștefan thought the Wallachians showed bravery when they rescued Hunyadi's left flank and helped destroy the sultan's sipahis. But others don't feel that way. Maybe because the Wallachians lost fewer people than most. Maybe because they're weary of Murad's men hunting them down and taking more men every time they get close. Maybe because they're tired and cold and hungry. Either way, there's no love lost between Mircea and Hunyadi.

They disagree on everything. When to start, where to stop, whose turn it is to keep lookout. Fortunately, here in Silistra, they'll cross the Danube into Wallachia, where Vlad Dracul is waiting with a small army that's larger than all their men put together.

Wallachia's voivode hugs Mircea and Ștefan, nods to Hunyadi and invites them to his tent. He pours wine. And, after days and days of drinking muddy water, this is the best wine Ștefan can remember.

"To the dead," Vlad Dracul says. "May the Good Lord forgive their sins, and have them rest in peace."

They each spill a few drops on the ground, as Orthodox tradition dictates, then drain their cups. He fills them again.

"To the living. May God forgive our sins and mistakes and give us better guidance next time."

They drain their cups again. Vlad looks at Hunyadi.

"What will you do next?"

Hunyadi shrugs.

"Start over. What else?"

"You had a pretty good peace treaty before the pope and that silly youth dragged you to war. Maybe Murad will agree to the treaty again. From what I've heard, his casualties were even worse than yours. He needs time to recover just as much as you do."

"It's not my decision to make. Now, that the king is dead, they'll have to choose another king. Ladislaus the Posthumous, the legal heir, is only five years old. Hard times are coming for Poland. And Hungary."

"Even more reason to make peace with Murad."

"Maybe. How about you?"

"I'll do my best to make peace with him. I hate paying the tribute and giving him devşirme, but I have no other choice."

"Sure you do. You're just about unscathed after all this, since your son made sure his men didn't get too close to the fight for fear of losing them."

Vlad Dracul's face darkens.

"What are you saying?"

"I'm saying that while we all lost most of our men, your Mircea brought his back. There's got to be a reason for that."

"There is. He's a good leader. He's not so stupid to get himself into battles he knows he can't win. Unlike your king, who lost his battle, his life, and most of your army. Whether you like it or not, Hunyadi, this has been the last crusade. And you lost it. Get used to it and move on. Now, get out of my land."

Hunyadi's eyes burn with hate as they shift from Vlad Dracul to Mircea.

"The apple doesn't fall far from the tree. No wonder your son is a..."

"You watch your mouth! You have three days to get off Wallachian land. Three. After that, I'll come after you and I'll crush you and whatever's left of your sorry army. I don't care if you go to Hungary, cross back into the Ottoman Empire or grow wings and fly to God. If on day four you're still on my land, you're history."

"I'll pay you back." Hunyadi heads to the door. "You'll be sorry you ever set eyes on me."

"I'm sorry already," Vlad says to his departing back.

He fills the cups again and turns to the boys. "You wish to hear the news?"

Mircea nods.

"Vlad escaped from Tokat. He's somewhere in Anatolia. I sent people to look for him, but they have nothing yet. I hope to find him and bring him back."

Mircea whistles, his eyes full of admiration for his younger brother.

"What a kid!"

Vlad Dracul nods.

"And Radu..."

"What did he do?"

"He stabbed the sultan."

CHAPTER 92

KILL THEM BOTH

EDIRNE

The Edirne Palace has never seen something like this. Not one, but two victorious sultans are coming home today: Mehmet, their golden boy, and their old favorite Murad. Scores of sweaty cooks work overtime, countless busy servants clean things already sparkling clean, and dozens of women take bath after bath to make themselves irresistible.

Just like the others, Ali runs around like a chicken with its head cut off, trying to deal with her many tasks: Hüma, the harem women, her lessons at the palace school. But no matter what, she needs to make time to see Ion and Codru. They need to get together to come up with a plan, so she called for a meeting. Now, when everyone's too busy to pay attention to them.

Because things went bad. These last few weeks, they've had no connection with Kronstadt. Whether it's the war, bad luck, or treason, the messengers that used to carry the news have disappeared, so they're on their own.

That's earth shattering. What are they here for? What can they do? Where should they go?

Ali is working on her potions, as usual, when Ion and Codru stop by her tiny kitchen. They're too new to go to war, but, like everyone else, they've heard about the great Ottoman victory, even though they don't know the details. Ali learned them from Hüma, so she fills them in.

"The King of Poland and Hungary is dead. Hunyadi's army has been decimated, and the voivode himself barely escaped with his life. The Christians have been crushed, and the crusade is over."

Codru and Ion stare at her, and the loss in their eyes is hard to watch.

"So then what are we doing here?" Codru asks.

Ion shrugs.

"Good question. Should we try to escape? All three? Or maybe just one, to reestablish the connection?"

"Should we wait?" Ali asks.

Codru frowns.

"For what?"

"To see what happens next."

"What difference does it make? We can't send the message anyway."

"We can't now, but that can change at any moment. When Hunyadi gets back from war, he'll surely send somebody over. And even if we can't send a message, we can still work on our mission," Ali says.

Codru sighs.

"Speaking about that. What exactly is our mission?"

"We came here to make the world a better place by undermining the Ottoman Empire and fighting for our country," Ali says.

"And how exactly will three kids like us undermine the empire?" Codru asks.

Ion shrugs. "All sort of ways. What if we kill the sultan?"

"Which one?" Ali asks.

"Good question," Codru says. "What if we kill them both?"

Ali stares at him like she's never seen him before. What happens if they kill them both?

"Now that's a thought. Sultan Murad has no other sons, and Sultan Mehmet has no children. The closest heir to the throne would be Orhan Çelebi, Sultan Murad's uncle. He's been a hostage in

Constantinople for years, and people say he's just a useless drunk," Ion says.

"That would mess up the Ottoman Empire but good," Ali says.

Ion nods.

"It's sure worth thinking about."

Ali watches them leave, wondering how the three of them could manage to kill both sultans and decapitate the empire. For now, nothing comes to mind, but there's no hurry. The one thing they have is time.

CHAPTER 93

PLEASE FORGIVE ME

Radu stands on the palace wall, looking down the empty road. He's waiting for the heroes to arrive, and the guard agreed to take him there, probably because he wanted to see them himself.

It's a gloomy November afternoon; the sky is low and gray, and a thin cold drizzle gives the wind extra sharpness. But nobody cares. The palace is warm with joy, laughter and cheering, and thousands of happy people await to cheer the triumphant army.

Not Radu. His heart is torn between fear, hate, and love for Mehmet, and he doesn't know which is stronger. One moment he can't wait to see him, the next moment he hopes he'll drop dead. But one way or another, he'll get to see him soon, and he's breathing so hard that he got dizzy with excitement.

A thunder of cheers erupts from thousands of chests as the first soldiers come into sight. They are the azabs, the sultan's irregulars, holding their halberds, sabers and the war scythes they call tirpans. They are always the first ones to fight.

Next come the janissaries, resplendent in their bright red uniforms and tall hats. They carry arches, kilijes and daggers, and they all walk as one. Finally, the sipahis mounted on their barded horses with their round shields glowing. In between them, the two sultans on their splendid mounts: Mehmet on his black stallion, Murad on his white. They ride shoulder to shoulder and foot to foot with their shiny armors mirroring the meager sun and their tughra banners flying proudly in the wind.

The cheers are deafening, as it's fit for a winning army. The whole country rejoices in this hard-fought victory. The Ottoman Empire is finally safe. The Christians have been crushed, and may never recover. This was the last crusade.

That worsens Radu's dilemma. His Wallachians fought in this fight, and many died. Mircea, his favorite brother, was there, and Radu wonders if he's still alive.

Then Mehmet. Radu hasn't talked to him since the night of the stabbing. Mehmet left the same morning Radu came down the tree. He put him on house arrest, and Radu was surprised that he didn't execute him on the spot. But he was in a hurry. He must plan to make an example of Radu and show everyone what the fate of someone daring to attack the sultan should be, but he was too busy. Now he's not.

The sultans reach the castle gate, which is taller than three people standing on top of each other, but not wide enough for both of them side-by-side. Mehmet looks at his father, and bows, letting him enter first. The applause is thunderous as Murad steps in followed by his son.

That's courteous, but that doesn't tell Radu who's the sultan, these days. Is it Mehmet or Murad? Not that it matters. There's no reason to believe that Murad would be more merciful than Mehmet. Whoever the sultan is, Radu is up the creek.

He sighs and returns to his room to tell Sari about the parade, but Sari is unimpressed. She'd rather have something to eat than all this talk. Still, she listens without interrupting, other than whipping her tail, which is one of the most endearing features of cats over humans.

His heart in turmoil, Radu curls in his bed, holding the cat. What will Mehmet do? How about Murad? What's in store for him?

The janissary at the door moves aside. Mehmet steps in, resplendent in his shiny armor. His green eyes shine as he looks at

Radu, and Radu doesn't know what to think. Is he angry? Is he happy? Is he here to kill him?

He drops the cat and bows to greet him.

"Radu."

"Your Highness."

"I'm back."

Radu nods. He couldn't help but notice.

"How are you?" Mehmet asks.

Radu thinks, then gives the most accurate answer he can fathom. "Alive."

Mehmet laughs, and steps towards him. Radu steps back.

"Listen, my friend. I wanted to say I'm sorry. I was drunk, and I was crazy. It won't happen again. You are my best friend. I'll do my best to make it up to you, if you forgive me."

Radu doesn't know what to say.

"Your brother is fine. Mircea was a hero in the battle. He fought hard and protected his men. He escaped, and so did his Wallachians. Your people are fierce fighters."

"Thank you, my sultan."

"Radu, I don't think you understand how important you are to me. You are my twin soul. I'm sorry for what happened, and I promise it won't happen again. Can we still be friends?"

Radu looks at Mehmet, his heart torn between love and fear. "My sultan..."

"Call me Mehmet."

"My... Mehmet."

"Yes."

"I'll try."

To find out what happened to Radu, Mehmet, and the others, read **Throne of Blood**, Book 2 in The Curse of The Dracula Brothers series. You may also enjoy its prequel novella, **Throne of Thorns**.

AFTERWORD

Thank you for reading Den of Spies. If you enjoyed it, **please take a minute to leave a review**, and tell a friend. That will help other readers like you discover this book, and I'd really appreciate it.

To find out what happened next, read **Throne of Blood**, Book 2 in The Curse Of The Dracula Brothers series. You may also enjoy **Throne of Thorns**, the prequel novella of the series.

RR Jones

ABOUT THIS BOOK

This book exists because of George R.R. Martin's Game of Thrones. Reading it made my itch to write my own GOT, set in my birthplace, Romania. Its history is just as tumultuous and breathtaking as RR Martin's later work.

But, since I wasn't ready to write an epic spanning countries, decades, and dozens of characters, I started writing what I knew: the ER. I wrote a medical thriller under the name of Rada Jones. That turned into a whole series that inspired another that features a charming cast of bomb dogs in the Afghan war.

Still, the urge to write my Romanian Game of Thrones gnawed at me until I wrote the first book, then the next and the next.

I put them aside for a couple of years to age. That works with meat, wine and cheese, so why not with books? When they felt ready, I let them fly into the world, and thus The Curse of the Dracula Brothers came to be.

Note: Radu, Vlad, Stefan, and Mehmet were real people that you can find in any history book of the era, and I did my best to respect the historical accuracy of events. The magical kids were not. Though who knows? They may be still roaming the Transylvanian forests, waiting for the right time to come out...

I hope you enjoyed Den of Spies, and can't wait to find out what happened to Vlad, Radu, and the magical kids. If so, read on!

About the Author

RR Jones was born in Transylvania, ten miles from Dracula's Castle. Growing up between communists and vampires taught her that humans are fickle, but you can always trust dogs and books. That's why she read every book she could get, including the phone book (too many characters, not enough action), and adopted every stray she found, from dogs to frogs.

After joining her American husband, she spent years studying medicine and working in the ER, but she still speaks like Dracula's cousin.

RR Jones, her husband, and their dog Guinness live in a tiny cabin in the Adirondack woods whenever they aren't traveling to faraway places. She spends her days writing, hiking, and day-dreaming about her imaginary friends.

facebook.com/RRJonesBooks
twitter.com/JonesRada
instagram.com/RadaJonesMD
bookbub.com/profile/rada-jones

www.ingramcontent.com/pod-product-compliance
Lightning Source LLC
LaVergne TN
LVHW091952020825
817740LV00002B/311
* 9 7 8 1 9 5 5 9 4 9 1 0 1 *